Euphoria

Based on a True Story

Ricardo de Leão

To laugh often, to win the affection of children, to earn the appreciation of honest critics and endure betrayal of false friends, to appreciate beauty, to find the best in others, to leave the world a bit better, whether by a healthy child, a garden patch…to know even one life has breathed easier because you have lived. This is to have succeeded!

Emerson

Introduction

My name is Sebastian Kosta, and I am a Senior Manager for one of the biggest consulting companies in the world called Accent. We have over 250,000 employees worldwide, and they are the smartest and brightest minds in business, period. In the simplest terms, my job description consists of being a "doctor" for Fortune 500 companies. Most firms or corporations, especially the blue chips, have major issues they cannot fix with their internal employees. So, they call us, the management consultants, at the standard rate of $300 - $700 per hour. Naturally, I don't end up keeping all the money. My company keeps the biggest piece of the pie, but I still walk away with a $250,000 salary and a substantial bonus which pretty much matches my salary. I am a successful executive with a Master's degree from the Wharton Business School.

Education was always very important in our family. It was my father's dream for each of his three children to obtain an MBA. He said, "son, if you get an MBA, I will give you a Rolex". I got my Rolex back in 2000. It wasn't just any Rolex, but a two-tone gold Submariner. That was my dream watch. Most people get that type of watch upon completion of their careers, successful completion at that. I, however, was lucky enough to get such a beautiful gift at the very beginning of mine.

By the time I turned 16, my family was already very prosperous, but that was not always the case. My father started out modestly, as a teller for a bank called Bradesco in São Paulo, Brazil. He worked at that position for twelve excruciating years while spending his nights and weekends studying for a Law Degree. His motto was, "hard work plus intense effort will lead to success in any field". Over the years, he was given an opportunity from the bank he worked for to become an expatriate and travel abroad. At the tender age of three, my family, which consisted of my parents and the three kids, me being the youngest with the older sister and brother, moved to New York City. The first, most important task faced by my family was the English language. We studied very hard to become proficient in the native tongue of our new home country. Eventually, English became my first language and Portuguese second. Later in life, Spanish would end up being my third.

For the first nine years, from when I was three to twelve-years-old, we followed my father from New York City to Paraguay, to Toronto, Canada to Singapore, and back to New York City. Finally, in 1984, we settled in Miami, Florida. I enjoyed the idea of traveling around the world and experiencing different cities and countries. I saw many beautiful places such as Bali, Indonesia where I was first introduced to surfing and witnessed the ultimate beauty of nature at its purest form. I also visited Japan where I rode the bullet train and saw the vastness of Mount Fuji with its majestic snow-covered peaks. In the summer of 1984, I visited Honolulu, Hawaii and fell in love with its fruits especially the exquisite yellow papaya. I was also fortunate enough to visit many countries in Europe such as Spain, France, Italy and England. My sister, on the other hand, wasn't that lucky. Because she was the oldest, she had to switch high schools three times. That meant constantly losing old friends and having to start from the beginning and forming new friendships. Since I was in the elementary school, I had no strong attachments and making friends was easy for me.

I am 32 years old, single and I have lived in Miami for over 20 years. As I've previously noted, my father worked very hard to make it to the top. After my family acquired considerable wealth, status and money became very important. My father became the President of a privately-owned Brazilian bank after retiring from Bradesco as a General Manager at the age of 55. My mother was a ten-million-dollar-a-year real estate broker. She was selling hi-rise condos to the rich and famous.

My parents lived in a very prestigious 4-bedroom high-rise in Miami, valued at over $4 million. They also owned many properties in the city, totaling over $10 million in worth. My parents always had nice cars such as BWM, Audi, Mercedes, Jaguar, Porsche, and most recently Maserati. They enjoyed dressing fashionably, buying only the latest high-end brands. Mom and Dad mostly preferred to socialize with the rich and successful people in the Brazilian circle of Miami. Among their prominent friends were the parents of one of the founders of Facebook. Eduardo Saverin was Mark Zuckerberg's roommate at Harvard, and he raised the primary capital for their startup. His father gave him the initial investment of $19,000, and he became the founding CFO of the company. Today Eduardo Saverin's current net worth is over $8 billion. Because of the close friendship between my and Eduardo's parents, my Mom and Dad were invited to Eduardo's wedding. When they came back to Miami, my parents enjoyed sharing all the highlights of that exquisite celebration. To summarize, my parents thought that the wedding of Eduardo was one of the most extravagant parties they had ever attended. My Mom and Dad see Eduardo's parents very often, and together they frequently go out and travel.

My Dad's example of working hard and never giving up, has inspired me to follow in his footsteps. I understood that money wouldn't buy happiness, but money guaranteed freedom and stability. And I resolved to become as successful as I possibly could and yes, to make a lot of money. By the age of 32, I already had a 2-bedroom condo in the Four Seasons Residences worth $1.8 million. I also had a vacation condo in Punta Pacifica, Panama, where I traveled to once a month to disconnect from the city life, reconnect with nature, and pursue my passion for surfing. I purchased the Trump Ocean Beach Club for $500,000 when I was 30 years old. Now, it is worth $750,000. But my most prized possession was my triple black Porsche 911 S Cabriolet. You see, ever since I was a young boy, I dreamed of becoming a race car driver. Unfortunately, my parents did not believe in such dreams. Rightly or wrongfully, they thought dreams were for kids. Adults, on the other hand, had to be realistic and ambitious. We had to work hard in reaching the highest levels of success in our careers.

I've always loved cars, especially the fast ones with stick shift transmissions. To me, the automatic transmission is too easy and boring. It's fine for city traffic and commutes. But stick shift, on the other hand, is for real driving, especially when it comes to a sports car. I drove my first stick shift car at the age of 15. It was a white 1984 Porsche 911 SC, and my friend Derrick, whose father gifted him such an expensive car at the young age of 16, was nice enough to allow me to take a very cute girl out to lunch in his Porsche. It was love at first sight. Not the girl, but the car. Later in life, everything I worked for, was to buy a brand new $100,000 Porsche. Which I ultimately did!

My love for women was as passionate and overpowering as the one I had for beautiful sports cars. I took pride in both understanding and seducing women. Sounds egoistic? Perhaps. But that's what I longed for as a young and successful man. Wherever I went, I met women from every nationality. In truth, I wanted to meet as many different ones as was humanly possible. I wanted to know them in every way – physically, mentally, spiritually, and emotionally. I loved to learn how women think and react to things. Everything about them was intriguing and attractive to me. I loved to get them to the point of emotional nakedness for physical one was fun but much easier, but emotional and spiritual openness were the ultimate goals I had when dealing with different women I've met throughout my life.

I was very particular in what I found attractive in a woman. If the room was filled with a hundred different women, and one would stand out and capture my attention, I would go for her with passion and conviction until that particular lady was mine. I did not discriminate; I found beauty in every woman. I had a very strong sex drive; that usually meant quantity over quality. The only problem with that approach – finding love was very hard. In the past, I was only interested in the physical connections and euphoric experiences. With that, I never seemed to find the "one" that matched all my needs and desires. I always wanted more and could never be satisfied. Being a successful man also made it more difficult to find a woman whose intentions were pure. The one who cared about Sebastian the man, not Sebastian, the power player. They all seemed to want the extravagant luxurious lifestyle I could provide rather than me as a person.

Another obstacle to a meaningful and serious romantic relationship was my career. My position of a consulting manager required constant traveling. I was moving from one place to another with what seemed to be the speed of light. That meant every week, from Monday to Thursday, I was on a plane traveling around the world. Sometimes it was New York, Mexico City, Panama, or Little Rock, Arkansas. It just depended on where the client was located. Over the past 8 years, I have been on approximately 700 flights and traveled over 5 million miles. The benefit of traveling that much was the travel rewards. I could pretty much fly anywhere and stay in hotels for free using my accumulated travel points. I also had the option to fly back home to Miami or have someone fly in to wherever I was working at for the weekend. The women I dated seemed to love the latter option. Who wouldn't want to travel on the weekends and stay for free at the best hotels while enjoying the best upscale restaurants and the nightlife? Who would refuse unlimited room service and spa services? It was a life of pure luxury and comfort...

Toronto

Chapter 1

It was 7 in the morning. I was sitting on the plane ready for take-off. I was leaving Miami and heading to Toronto where my new client called Hudd had its corporate headquarters in North America. That client was one of the largest providers of home and business security. Their biggest competitor was ADT. Hudd had 52 offices across the US and Canada. The company's revenues were approximately $4 billion dollars a year and they had over 40,000 employees. My job involved a three-month endeavor of shifting Hudd's current accounting operations from North America to Chennai, India. The first two months would be spent developing the current state environment from a system, process, and people point of view. And during the third, last month, I would have to be in India for the actual "go-live" implementation making sure everything ran smoothly. In industry terms, that was simply called business process outsourcing (BPO), and we were transferring 520 jobs to India. BPO was one of my companies, Accent's, primary services because it dramatically lowered the cost of doing business in companies and brought high profitability for the service providers like us. The primary goal was to lower operating costs specifically the cost of labor. A typical fully loaded accountant was approximately $49 per hour in the US. In comparison, in India, the same accountant would only cost $19 per hour. The trend of lowering operating costs started in the late 80s and has been going strongly ever since. Some BPO projects could last for years, with an average yearly profit of 50 million dollars or more for the company like Accent. We had many clients because it seemed that every major company wanted to move their non-core processes to places such as India, China, and Mexico.

Besides working, of course, I was looking forward to Toronto because that wouldn't be my first time in the city, and I was happy to be back. I was going to see one of the women from my past. Her name was Roberta Oliveira. She was a gorgeous and exotic Brazilian woman whom I'd met at one of the parties I hosted in Miami. I recalled meeting her for the first time. We were at the mansion's clubhouse located in Santa Pinta, a high-rise condo in Brickell. It was an old Spanish manor built in the 1920s which was completely restored to its original beauty. I rented it for the night for over 300 of my friends. My old high school friend, Mike McGrath, was in the city visiting from California. He served as a Marine and was allowed to take some time off from his military service. Mike was a major player in high school, and all the girls liked his boyish good looks.

That night, Mike and I met Roberta and her girlfriend Karla. They were from Brazil. Roberta had a beautiful dark-brown skin, the color of brown sugar, with chiseled facial features similar to those of Alicia Keys. It was an exotically intoxicating combination. Her body was perfect, just enough curves in the right places and a stomach to die for. She was so athletic, there was even a hint of a six-pack. She had a dark wavy hair with the beautiful highlights. She was a typical Amazonian woman from Brazil, and that night I lusted for her. She was the only woman I wanted at the party, and I resolved to make her mine.

I approached her at the party, and we talked for quite some time. My Portuguese was fluent but not perfect. I spoke with a little bit of an accent, and my vocabulary was no match for my English. She found my Portuguese accent to be cute; our attraction was mutual. I decided to take advantage of the connection between us and invited her to my limousine. From the party, we went to a VIP night club in South Beach called Privé; located inside the larger club called Amnesia. That Amnesia was a franchise of the original club Amnesia in Ibiza, Spain. I had been to Ibiza twice before.

Once at the club, we danced, laughed and started kissing immediately. I knew how to seduce her with my charm and sense of humor. I could sense she wanted more. She wanted me. My friend Mike was moving a little slower than I. He was more hesitant and didn't know how to approach or seduce a sophisticated and elegant woman. Since he left college and became a Marine, his playboy days in high school were a thing of the past. He had a girl he met in college and they were dating on and off for about 10 years. It was hard for him to be with another woman.

After we left Amnesia, we headed to my bachelor pad at the Four Seasons Residences in Brickell. Everything in my condo was tech savvy. As soon as I walked in, with one touch of the button, the lights dimmed, the window treatments were lowered, the perfect chill out lounge music turned on, the flat screen was also turned on to something eye catching like a sunset in Fiji, and the A/C temperature was lowered to make any woman want to cuddle. I believed technology was making our lives easier, thus, I always had the latest gadgets.

Once the mood at my place was set, I went to my room with Roberta and after many hours of seduction and foreplay, she finally gave in and we made passionate sex. Her best feature were her breasts. They were quite large and firm. They looked youthful. I always preferred natural breasts and hers were perfect. It was a wonderful night. We slept for a few hours and then she left. I never saw her again until now. Six years later. That was why I was so eager to see her and to be with her once again.

Another reason I was excited to visit Toronto was that's where I spent my early childhood. I lived in that city from the age of 6 to 10 years old. Ice hockey was my passion back then. Initially, I was terrible at it. I could barely skate. But eventually, with hard work and dedication, I became the best on my team. I became so good at hockey that I was playing on two leagues at the same time. One, was my regular team, and the other, was the All-Star team, with which we traveled to the tournaments all across Canada. Hockey was the sport I wanted to go professional with. I believed I could really do that. Unfortunately, soon after my admission to the All-Star team, my father took another position in Singapore, and my first question was, "Dad, do they play hockey in Singapore?" He replied, "no son, you are going to have to learn another sport".

All those memories made my return to Toronto very exciting. But I had a 4.5-hour flight ahead of me, and I needed to get some rest. I took out my Bose noise cancellation headphones and turned on what I called my "happy music". One time, on a business trip to Barbados, I discovered India Arie. As I was walking out of my hotel room with the TV still turned on, I heard this amazing soulful voice. In addition, the rhythm of the music and the bass were so hypnotizing that it made me pause and walk back. I listened to the whole song just to see who the artist was. The song was called "I Am Not My Hair" by India Arie. I felt an immediate connection between the song and my soul. I instantly turned my laptop on and purchased all Arie's albums. Approximately 30 minutes after liftoff, the soothing beats and lyrics of my "happy music" got me simultaneously relaxed and excited. I was instantly cheerful and optimistic about my future. India Arie became one of my favorite soul singers, and I very much appreciated her music.

I woke up about an hour into my flight to Toronto. I could not sleep anymore. I was too charged up about my trip. I was sitting in business class in the last row next to a blonde woman. She was in her mid-forties, absolutely gorgeous. I happened to notice that both of our seats wouldn't recline all the way back as they should've. They were pretty much stuck in the upright position. We were frustrated to have to sit in that position for the next three hours.

She looked at me and said, "since we are stuck here, sitting straight, would you let me buy you a beer? The next one is on you. What do you say?" I smiled and agreed; I was going to make the best of the trip. We ordered my favorite beer, Blue Moon Belgian White Wheat, and the stewardess even brought us some orange slices. The blonde had the right idea. I liked her way of thinking, "Turn a negative situation into a positive one." She was a pharmaceutical rep, and I knew from experience, part of the requirements for that job was to be beautiful, which she was, and to be very sociable, which she also was. We talked about our respective careers and our passions in life. We laughed quite a bit; so much so that the other passengers seemed jealous of how much fun we were having. Once the plane landed, I knew if I wanted to, we could've exchanged our phone numbers and perhaps pursue our new friendship further. Even though, she was indeed beautiful and interest-ing, I was satisfied with our flight encounter and didn't need more.

Chapter 2

Once the plane landed in Toronto's Pearson International Airport, it was a typical rush to be the first one out of the plane. Since I usually traveled in business class, I generally was right out the door first. The terminal was very modern and designed with glass and aluminum materials. There were lots of art works surrounding the terminal; I found them beautiful. I didn't have to wait long for my luggage. When I got to baggage claim, it was not too long before my two bags came out. The airport operation in Toronto was extremely efficient and since I was an expert in process reengineering, I always examined all the types of business operations, especially in airports. That particular airport was very well-organized, all the correct pointers were in place, and since English was the primary language, navigating through the airport was rather simple. For some reason, my awareness of the environment was always heightened at airports; perhaps for the security reasons after the tragedy of 9/11.

A soon as I gathered my belongings, I headed out to find my limo. When the doors from the baggage claim opened to the outside of the airport, I noticed a limousine driver holding a sign with my name, "Mr. Sebastian Kosta." I quickly approached him, shook hands and got into the car. It was a warm summer afternoon in Toronto. The driver put the luggage into the trunk, and we were off to my hotel. Once inside the car, he offered me a newspaper, magazines, and cold water. My job had many nice perks, a private limo with a driver was one of them. I typically did not talk too much to strangers; even if they worked for me. I was more to myself and only felt comfortable around friends I've known for many years. I tried to keep my life private, and I really didn't like small talk.

Forty-five minutes later we arrived at the W Hotel in Toronto. That was my favorite hotel chain. Wherever I had to travel to meet with the clients; Starwood was the preferred choice. I usually stayed at the W but at times, when not available, the Westin or the St. Regis were close seconds. Even though, I traveled a lot and mostly lived in hotels, I made sure that my condo back in Miami was as comfortable and luxurious as the W Hotel, if not better. And that was considering I rarely spent more than several days a week at home. I did not want these hotels to outshine my own bachelor pad, so I invested heavily to make it look impeccable and perfect in every way. Aside from all the technology I previously described, my place had a modern contemporary look. I had a natural taupe color leather sectional facing a pristine white leather sofa. There was a cowhide area rug imported from Brazil. The rug was made of small square pieces and the fur had a very soft touch. It was nice to walk barefoot to feel the contrast between the cowhide and a natural stone floor. The window treatments were all custom-tailored and motorized for simple open and close with one touch operation on my flat panel touch screen. My bedroom was straight out of an architectural digest magazine. The bed was built for a king. It had a high backboard with a combination of cherry wood and black leather. The two nightstands were made of the same cherry wood with a glass top. The lights could be turned on or off by simply touching the aluminum base. The base also had three dimmer settings which came in handy when I had female guests. The mattress was ordered directly from the W Luxury Collection. Sleep was important to me, and I needed the best. That's why I spent $10,000 on the mattress. In short, I valued tranquility and Zen in my living space and used only the best materials to decorate my entire condo.

Chapter 3

I arrived at the hotel right after 2 PM. I was not tired at all. It was too early to sleep, and I did not like taking naps. I decided I would go to the gym for an hour and then enjoy the pleasures of the Spa. I loved all the benefits of a five-star hotel. That's why I chose to live in the Four Seasons Residences in Miami.

I typically got a massage at least once a week. Sometimes twice, if I had the time. I've been physically active since the age of twelve and had a very athletic body. I was 5' 10' and weighed 205 pounds with about 10% body fat. In high school, I was a Roman Greco wrestler on the varsity team. At my strongest, I could bench press 415 pounds for one repetition. Those were four 45-pound plates on each side in addition to a 45-pound bar. I was exceptionally strong, and I worked very hard to develop that muscle definition, that was the reason why I really enjoyed a deep-tissue massage. It hurt like hell, but in some weird way, I liked the pain. Sometimes during my massage, I would feel so good I would actually fall asleep and start snoring. That was how I determined if the masseuse was very good. That was the standard I had for separating an average massage from the exceptional one.

Besides my strong physique, I was often told by women that I was very handsome. I wasn't the one to argue with the ladies. If they considered me attractive, I was all for it. It wasn't unusual for my friends or colleagues to point out that I had similar facial features with Patrick Swayze. In fact, when the movie "Ghost" came out, I was 16 years old, and I was in Brazil. It seemed everyone saw the resemblance between Swayze and me and had to let me know just how alike we looked. Later in life, my nickname became Swayze, and I would jokingly introduce myself to women as Patrick's younger brother. I always got a laugh or two out of that statement.

But back to Toronto. At seven in the evening, I was ready to dine. Since I didn't like sitting alone at the restaurant, I decided to order the room service. I chose a rib-eye steak, medium rare, and potatoes au gratin; my favorite. You could definitely describe me as a meat and potatoes type of guy. After enjoying my meal, I listened to some more of India Arie and had a glass of Merlot. That night, the glass turned into the whole bottle. Sometimes, I had difficulties sleeping, so I always traveled with Xanax which would help me relax and fall asleep. I often took Xanax for my naps before the big nights out. But that night, there was no need for Xanax since wine alone did the job. After finishing the bottle, I got in bed and watched the 11 o'clock news. I did not enjoy watching the news regularly. It was always filled with negative events. There was nothing positive in the news. Then or now. The truth was, I always fell asleep while watching the Tonight Show, and the show was always proceeded by the news. I watched Jay Leno's monologue and a portion of the first guest and then it was lights out.

Chapter 4

The next morning, I was up at 6 AM. It was Tuesday. My awakening in Toronto was followed by my usual morning routine. I was very methodical. At just about every hotel I stayed in, the configuration of the room was about the same. The king size bed faced the wall, to the front right, was a desk and near the entrance opposite the bathroom, was the closet. Due to the similar layout, I set my belongings in similar fashion independent of the hotel. I was particularly precise about organizing. Thus, all my shirts and pants were steam-pressed and neatly arranged in the closet by their colors. In the first drawer, I placed all my underwear and socks. The second drawer was for all my t-shirts and shorts for the gym. In the bathroom, all my toiletries were placed in the same area to the left of the sink. On the right side, there were my colognes. I always kept my iPhone charging at the same location, next to the desk. My laptop was on the desk. All my shoes were lined up on the floor of the closet, the black shoes to the left, and the brown, to the right. I was a bit of a clean freak. One might think I had an obsessive-compulsive disorder; I wouldn't call it that way. I might be the only person who wouldn't call my habit of organizing things an OCD. But I just loved for everything to be neat and in its place. My rationale for such behavior was, it saved me a lot of time since I didn't have to search for anything. It was an important part of my passion for being efficient.

At 6:30 AM, I was ready for breakfast. It typically consisted of an omelet with hash browns or eggs Benedict. Joining me for breakfast, was one of our firm's top partners. His name was Gary Duncan; he had a similar background as mine with an MBA from Stanford. He was a Managing Partner and had an incredible drive and laser-sharp focus. He was always on top of everything and never skipped a step. I have previously heard of his reputation for being a great managing partner and an all-around down-to-earth guy, a people's person. He's been with the company for just over 20 years. He started as an Analyst and worked his way up to the top.

Presently, he managed the Finance and Performance Management practice. With that, Gary coordinated over 2,000 people and had a P/L (profit/loss) of $600 million. He was one of the highest-paid partners. I estimated his salary to be in excess of $1.4 million per year. If his key performance indicators and metrics for his team were achieved, his bonus usually matched his salary. I wanted to get to know him and understand how he became so successful. I was always intrigued by success; from businesspeople to athletes such as basketball player Michael Jordan, tennis legend Roger Federer, soccer player Cristiano Ronaldo, race car driver Aryton Senna, and businessmen such as Steve Jobs and Bill Gates, and along with many other world-famous iconic people. What was their secret or recipe for success? How did they sustain high performance for extended periods of time? Were they simply the few special individuals touched by the hand of God at birth?

"Good morning, Sebastian. Nice to meet you. How are you?" Gary asked in his thunderous voice. Even though, it was our first meeting, he instantly made me feel like we knew each other forever.

"Good morning, Gary. Pleasure meeting you." I responded. "I had a great evening yesterday, and today, I am eager to learn more about this project. "You know Gary, I have never been to India. I heard it's a magical place where the people are nice and highly spiritual. I also heard that the native Indian people are very religious." I wanted to show I did my homework for the upcoming trip.

"Sebastian, are you religious?" Asked Gary.

I was taken aback a little. I could not believe how direct he was. Religion was like politics or sex. I preferred not to discuss it in business settings or with the people I barely knew.

"Well Gary, I believe in God 100%, but the word "God" has been misused over time, thus, I prefer to use the term Universe since it encompasses all the religions and faiths. I believe religion was created by men a few thousand years ago to bring order and justification to life. Why should Christianity be better than Judaism or Islam, or greater than Buddhism? I believe, religion is one of the problems in the world. We should rather focus on serving our faith and oneness with the Universe and being the good citizens on this small planet. Religion creates separation or individualistic philosophy with one faith considered better than the other. Unlike my parents, I don't go to church every Sunday. Rather, my home is my church and my body, is my temple. I meditate every day for my inner peace and joy." I sounded a little too passionate I thought.

Gary leaned back in his chair and said, 'Sebastian, you seem to have some interesting beliefs in life, especially in spirituality."

"Maybe. But that's what I think and feel." I replied sincerely.

"I believe we will have many opportunities to discuss these topics in more depth if you allow me?" Gary asked.

For some odd reason, I agreed with Gary. Not sure if it was my intense interest in the topic or because he was my boss. I hoped I would see Gary often over the next two months. But that prospect didn't look promising. In the month of May, I would be in Toronto to understand the current state of our deliverables and the existing gaps. The month of June, I would spend traveling to the Hudd's primary offices in Stamford, Connecticut; Chicago, Illinois and New York City. Therefore, I knew, I wouldn't have many opportunities to hang out with Gary before I was leaving for India in July. I, however, hoped that perhaps, I could meet him a few times in June.

By 7:30 AM, the limo was waiting for us. We were off to the client site. That's where Gary started explaining the project and my role within it.

"Sebastian, you know this is a very important project for us. If I am involved, it truly means this client has the potential of being our firm's top revenue generator in the US. We hope to have a long-term relationship with them. And while I am not going to be here every day, I will be getting constant updates from our other partners. I believe you are the key person in this project, and since I was visiting Toronto for the CEO summit, I figured we could have breakfast and share a limo ride to the office." Gary pointed out. "We will continue our conversations and see how you are faring. I will be here quite frequently in the month of June." He continued. "Therefore, let's put a memo on our calendars for drinks and some interesting conversations. Let's shoot for every Friday's at 8pm?" Gary suggested.

"Gary, that sounds great!" I replied. "I look forward to learning as much as possible from you."

After the initial personal exchange, Gary went straight to business.

"Our client, Hudd is a world leader in the security and fire protection services. They've been in business since 1818, almost 200 years, with $4 billion in annual sales and 48,000 employees. Hudd monitor's 781,000 alarm lines around the world and has more than 1,000,000 customer contracts." Gary said. "But Sebastian, this is only the tip of the iceberg." Mr. Duncan continued. "In 2003, they were purchased by the UTD (United Technology Developments Inc.), a large conglomerate, and now, they are a huge company we want to penetrate. If we do a good job with Hudd, then the doors will open for UTD." He summarized.

UTD companies are the leaders in aerospace, commercial and military aviation products (including helicopters and jet engines), in commercial building technologies (including climate control and elevator design), and in the design and production of the environmentally clean hydrogen fuel cells. They have been in business since 1853 and generated $31 billion in revenue. UTD was the 51st largest US Corporation and 141st in the World with over 4,000 locations in approximately 62 countries.

"As you can see Sebastian, we have a major opportunity here." Gary Duncan interrupted my thoughts about UTD. "Now, about your role in this project. You will be replacing Jim Leach. He had personal issue and was unable to do his job properly. Thus, he left the firm. You will have to pick up where he left off and hit the ground running. You will officially be the transition manager for the accounts receivable, credit, and collections. Remember, most of the work has been done. We were engaged in this venture for 16 months. You will be in charge of finalizing process documentation, process flows, standard desktop operating procedures, develop and deliver super and general user training, and oversea the "go-live" process in Chennai, India. This is a three-month project where we are simply lifting 520 seats from North America and relocating them to Chennai, India. Should be a piece of cake for someone of your caliber. I have you on my radar, Sebastian. If you can work at the next level successfully, you could possibly get promoted to partner in the near future. It's up to you." Gary finished his monologue.

After Dunlop's overview of the project-at-hand and its future potential during our ride, I started thinking how great of an opportunity was opening before me. There I was, sitting with one of our company's top executive partners and he was, for all purposes, telling me if I could get the job done, there was a good chance I could get promoted to Partner in the near future. I simply had to deliver and execute the project on time and under budget. I've been the manager in over 20 engagements for the past 8 years. That particular endeavor appeared to be the least complicated of all the projects I'd been working on in the past. Aside from that, I was thinking about my personal time. I was looking forward to having fun with Roberta and then exploring India.

It took us about 30 minutes to get to the client site from the hotel. It wasn't located in downtown Toronto, but rather in a suburb. It was in sync with a new trend of most North American companies building their satellite offices closer to where the employees lived. That minimized the commute and maximized their time at home with their families.

The site was located in new building, very modern, wrapped with borderless glass. Such design made it look very nice and elegant. It only had four stories and Hudd occupied levels three and four. As I entered the elevator, Gary mentioned I would be working on level 3 which he termed "the war room". I asked why he used that terminology.

"You will understand when you see it for yourself." He promised. I nodded. After showing my workplace, Gary would be heading up to the fourth floor occupied by the Hudd's top executives. Mostly, only partners were allowed on that floor.

As soon as the elevator door opened, I walked out into the atrium where I was met by the receptionist. Her name was Amy. She was an intern; straight out of the college and full of energy. She would be the person to welcome me to the team and show me around the office. First days at any job would typically make me anxious. I was entering the new environment with new people, different client situations, and many other variables. I was also aware that I only had two weeks to get very comfortable. After that period, the expectation of the client was that the newcomer would not only be fluent in their overall industry but well versed in their day-to-day business operations. My father always told me; my first most important goal was to simply find out where the bathroom was located. Following that practice, would make it easier to not get overwhelmed with all the details and stress related to the unfamiliar surroundings and the new people.

Therefore, I asked Amy, "before we get started with the tour of the office; could you please show me the restroom?"

"Of course, I can." Amy smiled. "Please follow me."

As we walked through the atrium and entered a long hallway which led to a huge work zone, I noticed four major open areas with desks in each one. Such floor plan offered no privacy to the employees but allowed open communication between everyone without having to get up and walk around. The aforementioned opened floor plan filled the entire work zone with noise. The whole environment seemed chaotic.

"I assume this is the so-called War Room?" I asked with a smile.

"Indeed." Amy confirmed. "This is where the magic happens. This is collectively where the top minds of our engagement team meet to conceptually design how this project is going to unfold ultimately leading to its successful execution."

I scanned the room, noticing men and women of all races and ethnicities working together completely engulfed by their laser-like focus on work. You could feel the intensity of these people since Accent always hired the same DNA. They had to be young, ambitious, and definitely

Type-A personalities. As always, I knew that I would make friends and also some enemies. Every project had similar group dynamics.

Amy showed where the bathroom was and goal number one was achieved. I used the bathroom and then washed my hands and face. I looked at myself in the mirror and said, "Okay, Sebastian, let's do this." I went back out where Amy was waiting.

"Sebastian, are you ready for your tour and the meeting with the team?" Amy inquired.

"Yes Amy, it will be my pleasure." I replied.

If someone performed an aerial image of the floor plan of the War Room; they'd see one large area, approximately 3,000 square feet. The tables were organized into four sections; the 4 major processes of the project. There were the General Ledger team, the Accounts Receivable team, Accounts Payable team, and the Information Technology team. I would be in charge of the Accounts Receivable team and my official title was the Accounts Receivable Transition Manager. Aside from the four process teamwork spaces, there was one section for the Senior Manager of the entire engagement. He was basically the floor manager and acted like a military drill sergeant using his watch as a tool to ensure the project was making progress as planned. There could be no delays.

"Sebastian, I want to introduce you to Premal Patal first." Amy suggested. "He is the team lead for the general ledger team. He will head up all the accounting as it relates to monthly financial reports, entering journal entries, reclasses, managing GL accounts, and working with the external auditors. Just like you, he is updating the current state processes and will later train the super users who came to Toronto from their homes in India. Once the super users (which are accounting supervisors in their respective areas) are trained, they will go back to Chennai, India and train the general users on the high-level processes and the standard desktop procedures to accomplish their jobs".

"It's a pleasure to meet you, Premal" I said. "I look forward to getting to know you better and working with you."

"The pleasure is all mine, Sebastian." Premal shook my hand.

"Where are you originally from?" I asked Premal.

"Originally, I was born in Mumbai, India, but I came to the United States early in life since my father was a professor, and we moved to Chicago. That's where I grew up, went to school, met my wife, and now, we have two small girls." Premal replied.

"Then, we have similar backgrounds since I was born in Brazil and later moved to America at the age of three." I pointed out. I also noticed that like me, Premal had no accent when speaking English. Besides that, I saw that half of his face was scarred by what seemed to be bad burns. His hands were also covered in scars. I wondered how he got those burns, but it would be the wrong time and place to ask. Just the thought of an excruciating pain Premal might have gone through, made me shiver inside. That guy would later become one of my best friends on the project.

"Well Premal, it was nice meeting you." I smiled. "I would like to meet you for coffee or drinks at some point, to get to know you better. If you don't mind?" I suggested.

Premal responded enthusiastically to my suggestion. He also mentioned that he looked forward to getting to know me better and assist wherever I needed help or advice.

After meeting Premal, Amy walked me across the room to the other table which was labeled accounts payable.

"Hi Amanda" said Amy. "I want to introduce you to our newest member Sebastian. He just flew in from Miami, and I am giving him the tour of the office and introducing him to the team leads. Do you have a minute?" She asked.

"Hi Sebastian, it is a pleasure to meet you but now is not the time for formal introductions." Amanda replied barely lifting her head. "I am in the middle of designing one of my process maps, so perhaps at the end of the day we can catch up? Sorry."

I looked at Amy with an odd expression and just hunched my shoulders up and down gesturing "okay then, whatever."

"I guess she is busy." I whispered to Amy rolling my eyes.

"Oh, don't worry about her." Amy smiled. "Amanda is one of our hardest workers and an overachiever. She hasn't been with the firm for too long, but she is moving up fast. Out of all the team leads, she is the only one who does not have a manager title. She is a senior consultant who works long hours since her goal, like yours, is the fast path to partner." Amy pronounced in a serious manner.

"It's important for you to know that Amanda has a strong personality and a very ambitious drive. She didn't come here to make friends. She is interested in doing her job only and exceeding the expectations of her clients and immediate supervisors." She continued.

"Thanks for the heads up." I uttered, feeling a bit taken aback.

"Since Amanda is busy right now, why don't we go over to the information technology table where you can meet Lee Choppard?" Amy quickly changed the topic. "Don't worry, Sebastian, Lee is super nice. I am sure you will get along." She said encouragingly after a bit awkward attempt at semi-introduction to Amanda.

As I walked over to the opposite side of the working area, I could really hear how loud the war room was. I couldn't image how anyone could talk on the phone or have any type of a meaningful business conversation that usually required concentration and at the very least, minimal noise.

"Sebastian, I want to introduce you to Lee." Amy's voice interrupted my thoughts.

"Hi Lee, my name is Sebastian Kosta, and I am the team lead for the accounts receivable team." I pronounced, extending my hand for a handshake.

Lee gave me a big smile and nodded her head. "Hello Sebastian, I welcome you to the team, and I welcome any questions you might have. I know that the travel and the first day can be a bit overwhelming. I would like to invite you tonight after work to a happy hour, at a local brewery, so that we can get to know each other better, and I can guide you over the dynamics of the team and how technology affects your area." Lee said enthusiastically. "As you can see, the war room is too chaotic, so we can meet after work at 6 PM and talk outside this place."

"That's a great idea! I look forward to meeting you and later your entire team to get an overview of my role in our project. Thank you for the invitation, Lee." I was truly happy to meet someone who was so welcoming and encouraging, especially after Amanda's cold-shouldered "welcoming".

"It would be my pleasure. Just stop by my workstation at 6, and we can ride together to Midtown. I know a good spot there." Lee waved signaling her need to return back to work.

"That's awesome!" Amy exclaimed encouragingly. "Look at you! You've already made a friend." She told me with a sincere smile. It was obvious, Amy was a positive woman and interested in making me feel comfortable and welcomed in this new business environment. "I told you, Lee was awesome."

"Okay, so now we have two more tables to go over." Amy made an immediate switch from an encouraging hostess to a business professional.

"The next one will be your team; the accounts receivable team. You will meet Jim Leach who is the person you will be replacing. He had a personal matter in his family and must leave the team. Today is Monday; therefore, take advantage of his time since he will only be here until Friday. You have a week to perform a knowledge transfer so that you can hit the ground running." She recommended. "I will also introduce you to your team of super users. You will have two months to train them on the accounts receivable processes covering the US and Canada. They need to know them well because they will be in charge of training all the general users when you go to India during your third month with us. As you can see, they are not fully acclimated to the weather here. It's summer in Toronto. But they still wear winter jackets." Amy continued explaining as we walked along.

"I can only assume it is extremely hot in India all year long for them to dress like this." I was thinking out loud.

As I walked towards the accounts receivable table, I could already notice my super users grouped together in ski jackets.

"First, let me introduce you to Jim Leach." I heard Amy's voice through my thoughts. "Jim came from our Atlanta office and has been with the company for 5 years. He is another manager in the Finance and Performance Management team just like you, Sebastian."

"It's a pleasure to meet you, Sebastian." Jim shook my hand.

"The pleasure is all mine." I replied while shaking Jim's hand.

"Scott, our Senior Manager, told me many good things about you, and apparently you are the perfect fit to replace me on this project. Unfortunately, I will be leaving the firm since my wife gave birth to twins, and she will need my help. Therefore, I can no longer commit to "the firm" with 100% travel and will have to work locally in Atlanta." Jim proclaimed with both happiness and sadness in his voice.

"But, don't worry Sebastian." He continued. "I've been working on this project for nine months and most of the deliverables are finished. You just need to meet with Scott and the steering committee to get a sign-off and perform a super user training. When you finish your introductions, come back to me and we will start reviewing my files and deliverables so you can get a good feel for where we are and where we need to be. It was a pleasure meeting you, Sebastian." Jim finished his monologue with a smile.

"Thank you, Jim. Will do." I replied.

"Well that went smoothly." said Amy. "You will be introduced to your super users after your next meeting with Scott McManus, the Senior Manager who has the overall day-to-day responsibility for the entire project. What you need to know about him is that he has a laser focus. You need to stay off his radar if not, he will micromanage you to death. Just make sure there are no surprises, and that your work product is on-time, and when they are presented, make sure a final version is provided. He absolutely despises going through the drafts and revisions. Work with the other team leads to help you present the final draft for his approval. You got it, Sebastian?" Amy asked knowing full well I got her.

Thus, I simply nodded in response. Afterwards, we continued with my introduction tour.

"Hello Scott, I have someone I want to introduce you to. I believe you have been expecting him. This is Sebastian Kosta." Amy made yet another introduction.

"Sebastian, this is Scott McManus our senior project leader," she said.

"Hi Sebastian, welcome to the team. I've heard a lot of positive things about you and your resume is top notch." Scott articulated energetically.

"Hi Scott, pleasure to meet you. I've heard great things about you as well." I replied.

"I have one question for you, Sebastian, are you a big swinging dick or not?" Scott asked with a smirk.

I immediately started laughing since one of my first jobs out of college was a Stockbroker at Morgan Stanley, and I read the book called "Liar's Poker" where the term "big swigging dick" was introduced to Wall Street. I continued to laugh out loud very strongly, and all of a sudden, Scott joined in my laughter. That was a good sign.

"My Wall Street days are behind me." I exclaimed amid laughter. "Back then, I was a big swinging dick, but now, I am a bit humbler. I would say that I am bit more of a rock star now." I suggested half seriously, half-jokingly.

Scott laughed even more profusely. "I am starting to like you, Sebastian. I believe, we got off on the right path and, even though, some people might regard me as an asshole; I am here to help you succeed." Scott became instantly serious. "You succeed; I succeed. The overall team succeeds. You got it?" He asked in a nonchalant manner.

I nodded.

"Work closely with Jim this week and try to absorb as much as possible. I know one week is tight but with your pedigree, I'm sure you can do it with no problem. I will meet with you this Friday afternoon to see how the transition went and what you learned. It was a pleasure to finally meet you face to face. Welcome to the team, Sebastian."

"Thank you, Scott." I replied with a smile. "The pleasure is all mine."

After Scott, it was the time to meet my team. The credit and collection and accounts receivable super user team. The first thing I noticed about the members of my team was, all five of the Indian nationals were wearing ski jackets in the middle of the summer in Toronto.

"So, are we all going skiing because I did not get the memo?" I asked jokingly trying to establish ease and friendly atmosphere with my new team from the get-go.

They apparently did not understand my sarcasm since no one laughed. So, I decided to introduce myself to them with a two-minute briefing of my experience and the overall objective of the AR/Collection Tower. My introduction did better than my attempt at a joke. The Indian nationals responded well to the account of my qualifications and our overall objectives. Afterwards, each one introduced themselves, and it was quite apparent that all of my team members were highly educated with accounting degrees from various Universities in India. Some even had masters' degrees. All in all, I was very impressed.

Our team lead was Shanti Rao and she was a CPA. She was very pleasant to speak with and showed much respect to me. She was also very kind. It was apparent by the way she spoke to me and the rest of the team members. You could tell she was a hard worker. Shanti would be my main point of contact with the super users. Vihaan Nair was our systems analyst. Vihaan would be tasked with systems integration from North America to India. Arjun Rangan was our business analyst. Arjun was the expert in business and financial modeling. Reyansh Venkatesan was our process engineer. He would make sure all the process flow charts were accurate, and then translated to desktop standard operating procedures. Our last team member was Rikki Banerjee; he was our accountant. Rikki would assist the overall team from accounts receivables and credit and collections from a process improvement point of view as it related to the accounting's best practices.

For the rest of the day, I worked at our team desk. I began with uploading of all the relevant files from Jim. The idea would be to review those files that night to get an overall understanding of the project and hit the ground running the next day, which would be Tuesday. My first week's goal was focusing only on the high-level files which discussed the scope of the overall project and the expectation of my deliverables for the AR Tower. Then, it was important to understand and make any necessary adjustments based on my current state evaluation.

For the next several hours, I focused on reading as many Power Point presentations and taking as much notes as possible. Usually, when I focused on my work, I entered a certain state of mind that rendered my surroundings mute and almost nonexistent. I concentrated on work, nothing else mattered. The constant chatter of the war room was no longer heard. My business experience included leading over 20 projects for several Fortune 100 corporations. Such an experience made me an expert in my field, and it was easy for me to quickly identify the current state environment of any company. Thus, I was able to communicate to our clients and partners from the position of knowledge and authority. As I was examining all the files and reports, I would periodically ask Jim for clarifications and confirmations of certain aspects of the project.

By the end of the day, Lee came over to my team desk and told me she was shutting down her laptop. She asked if I was ready to join her for a drink in Midtown. I was looking forward to our outing. I asked Jim if it was ok to stop for the day and return to our review tomorrow.

"Don't worry, Sebastian." Jim replied. "We have been working on this project for over 9 months, and most of the current state documents and process flows are complete. You simply need to develop the future state flows and SOPs and transfer the knowledge from the super users here in Toronto to the general users in India. This business process outsourcing is only a lift and shift. There is no transformation involved which makes it a lot easier. Enjoy your evening."

I was not overly optimistic about the project being easy because in all my years in consulting, I'd never had an easy project. Each project was different and presented its own complexities and challenges. That's why companies paid us the big bucks since they couldn't find solutions internally by relying on their own people.

Lee and I left the building and got into her rental car. She was a very young-looking woman. I guessed she couldn't be older than twenty-six. She had shoulder length brown hair. Even though, I was subconsciously trying to analyze Lee's appearance, I was aware that I had to keep my business relationships purely professional. Regardless of that, she wasn't necessarily my type. Thus, the aim of the outing was to get to know my colleague and hear the insights about our project. I was also interested to get Lee's opinion about the people I would work with and how I could better approach their personalities. Such information was essential for me to get up to speed quickly without stepping on anyone's toes. Lee seemed very nice and even though, I was about to learn all the aspects of the project, in detail, I was also eager to take a break form a long day at work and enjoy a relaxing drink.

We arrived at a place called Taurus, an English pub with the typical brass ornaments by the bar and plenty of mahogany wood. It was pretty dark inside.

"We are here. I hope you like it." Lee announced. "It's a nice local place which I discovered while walking in the area. It was love at first sight."

"Yes! Seems like a cool place." I agreed.

"So, Sebastian, what's your drink?"

"I prefer Johnnie Walker Black Label." I replied. "That is my father's favorite drink and I love thinking about my Dad. Even through the difficult times in my life, my father always stuck by my side. He is the smartest man I know, and I really look up to him." I said passionately.

Lee smiled and nodded. After that, she ordered a Cosmopolitan Martini. Our first toast was to our families back at home. The black label was on the rocks filled with ice all the way to the top just like my Dad would order. The heat of my hand would slowly melt the ice. The scotch tasted smooth and velvety with many spices adding excitement to the taste. I liked it, because it was pure and not filled with any sugar.

"So, Sebastian, what do you want to know about this project?" Lee asked after taking a small sip of her drink.

"Well, I would like to know the exact goal of this project, at a high level, and to understand various personalities of our team members? And lastly, what issues or matters, if any, I need to pay special attention to?" I got straight to the point.

"Seems like you are very methodical, Sebastian, and I will do my best to answer your questions". Lee noted and took another light sip of her martini.

"The project's objective, from a 30,000-foot perspective, Accent has been hired to perform a BPO project for our client Hudd. The area of focus is the finance and accounting departments all over the US and Canada. The goal is to transfer the seats of 520 North American employees to our delivery center in Chennai, India. This is not a reduction in staff but rather a reduction in payroll costs. You see, in North America the fully loaded cost per person is approximately $49 per hour. In Chennai, the same function can be performed at approximately $19. A classic labor arbitrage at its purest form. That is the power play here, and it will save millions for Hudd annually. Later on, the company can transform the function in Chennai and perform process improvement and continuous improvement. We will be saving money for many years."

"What will happen to those people whose jobs will be transitioned to India? I inquired after carefully considering Lee's reply.

"They will either transfer to another department or be given severance packages." Lee pointed out.

"What about the service levels?" I continued.

"We currently have general users in Chennai going through the accent neutralization training. We also have developed service levels agreement (SLAs) for the delivery center. This is basically a contract between Hudd and Accent on delivering services to the customer; be it an internal customer or external." Lee replied knowingly.

I smiled and assured Lee that the high-level objectives of the project were clear. After taking another sip of my drink, I took a deep breath and proceeded.

"So, now the hard part, Lee, tell me about the project team."

Lee smiled and nodded. "Sure, let's start with the general ledger team. The GL team is being led by Premal Patel. He is a bit older than you. He was born in Mumbai, India. He came to America as a young boy. He is married and has two small children. Since Premal is an Indian native, he might be able to help you with any language or cultural barriers during your "go-live" in Chennai. Premal is easy going and a fun guy to be around. If you like to go out drinking, he could be your drinking mate."

"I noticed, his hands and face had burns. Do you know what happened?" I asked.

"No, I do not." Lee's expression changed instantly. She appeared sad. "He has never opened up to us about what happened to him in the past."

"He must have suffered a lot." I wondered anxiously. "Is there anything I should worry about regarding his style of work?" I switched the topic.

"No, like I said, he is easy going and likes to get along with everyone. He is humble and hard working. I believe both of you will get along great, especially in India." Lee assured me.

"I hope that is the case." I echoed Lee's assurance.

After I heard about Premal, I wanted to learn everything I could about the Accounts Payable team leader, Amanda Perkins.

"So, tell me about Amanda?" I renewed my inquiries.

"Amanda is one of the fastest "up and coming" stars in our company. She finished her MBA from Harvard at the age of 22 and started as an analyst in our firm. She quickly was promoted to consultant and thereafter, became a senior consultant. She is very eager to learn all aspects of the business and wants to pursue a fast track path to partner. She is only 25 years old."

"Is this why she is the only team lead that does not have the manager title?" I asked.

"Yes, she is very ambitious, and everyone knows she wants to become a partner by the age of 30. Our leadership is giving her a chance to work at the next level. If she can be successful, perhaps she will be promoted to a managerial role once this project concludes." Lee relied affirmatively.

"Any concerns regarding Amanda?" I asked.

"Yes." Lee took a momentary pause. "Originally she was the accounts payable and collections team lead. The leadership team decided to give collection to the AR team, your track, and make it a more end-to-process. You should tread lightly and watch out for Amanda trying to interfere in your project since she used to lead it. She is highly competitive and will go toe-to-toe with you if needed. My advice is stay out of her way unless your process intersects with hers, and you need her input." Lee concluded.

"Thank you for giving me the heads up about Amanda. She sounds like a little pit bull." I pointed out.

After finishing my first round of whiskey, I felt relaxed, but my mind wasn't clouded, thus, I decided on going for another round.

"Lee, how are you doing with your martini?" I inquired.

"I'm pretty much finished. How about another round?" Lee offered as if reading my mind.

"Sure," I said. "I got a long night of work and an intense week ahead of me, so yes, definitely, another round."

"By the way, as managers, we all have expense accounts. Thus, business meetings which consisted of having alcohoic drinks, were covered." Lee noted with a smile.

The bartender served us our second round, and we continued with our conversation.

"Let us now discuss Scott, who oversees the Project Management Office, the PMO." Lee suggested. "Scott is an intense person. He is like a robot or a machine. He does not stop. Some people say he only gets 4 hours of sleep every night. He is a workaholic."

"Does he have a family back home?" I inquired.

"Yes, he has a wife and a small daughter. I believe she is 4 years old." Lee replied.

"Wow! How does he manage?" I wondered.

"Well, he believes in waking up every morning at 5am and jogging for 5 miles. He works at the office and at the hotel. He prepares his work at the hotel the morning before coming to work and also at night, after a full day at work. He does not watch television, and he only uses his phone for business, no social media browsing or things of that nature."

"But what about his family life?" I asked eagerly.

"He sees his family on the weekends and devotes his time to them. Sometimes, he flies them out to the project site if there are family friendly activities. As to work, especially the deliverables, he is very particular about not accepting the first drafts. He only wants the final drafts for the review by the PMO. Thus, Sebastian, make sure you turn in your final versions. Always! Or he might go ballistic." She finalized her overview of Scott.

"Thank you, Lee for providing me with the inside information regarding Scott and the other team leads. The only person left is you. Tell me about your Tower, Information Technology." I asked.

"Absolutely, Sebastian, I am in charge of building all the interfaces for all the systems we touch in dealing with the accounts receivable, accounts payable, credit, billing, collections, and the customer service. We are not changing anything, just the location. I have to know if any process change will affect the systems architecture and if it does, we devise an action plan and a road map. Remember, in Chennai, the general users will have to use the same systems with the same processes. It's simply a lift and shift versus transform and shift. It's much easier. I will also be involved in redirecting our 1-800 lines from North America to India. In India, the work hours will be shadowing the North American time zones. Once you get to India, you will be working the night shift. I believe your day will be start at 6 PM and end at 3 AM."

"Wow, I guess I have to adjust my body to be comfortable working the night shift." I exclaimed.

"Don't worry, Sebastian; you still have plenty of time. You do have to get your paperwork started with the Indian Consulate and all your necessary immunizations before heading to India. Entering that country has some of the most stringent prerequisites in the world, and I will assist by sending you an on-board document which outlines where to go to get your papers and immunization, hotels to stay, and an overall introduction to Chennai. The PMO office will take care of planning your flights and hotel stays."

It was almost 8 PM, and I still had a lot of work in preparation for a meeting with Jim in the morning. I thanked Lee for the drinks and her time. I took a taxi back to the W Hotel and spent the next few hours reviewing the materials which were provided to me.

At 10 PM, before heading to sleep, I decided to call my beautiful Brazilian friend Roberta, whom I haven't seen in many years. I just wanted to say hello and find out how she was doing. I also hoped, we could go out to dinner together. I decided to send her a text first.

"Roberta, it's Sebastian, your old friend from Miami. I am in Toronto, can you talk?"

It took almost ten minutes to get a response. "Hello, my dear friend, it's been a very long time since I heard from you. What brings you to my wonderful city?"

"Roberta, I am here for the next two months working on a consulting project and would love to see you. Can I call you now?"

"Sebastian, I can't talk right now." She texted back. "You won't believe it, but I recently got married, and my husband is here next to me. I don't think now is the right time. I will call you tomorrow during my lunch hour so we can catch up. Good night, Sebastian."

Oh my God, I could not believe it. All that time, I was thinking about her and the great time we had together back in Miami. She was so beautiful, and I really wanted to be with her again. I just could not believe she was married, but I still wanted to see her and just talk. She was one of those unforgettable women. I hoped I could get to meet her at least one more time, just to see her beautiful face.

As usual, I stayed up watching the local news and then, The Tonight Show with Jay Leno. I had one glass of Merlot just to unwind. As I drank, I kept on thinking about the night Roberta and I had at my party, in the Santa Pinta Mansion. I picked her out of 300 people, and then was lucky enough to spend the whole night with her. I could not believe I lost the opportunity to be with her here in Toronto. When it came to married women, I respected the relationship and would never want to interfere. But I was optimistic that perhaps, we could still meet for a few drinks or dinner. I went to bed hopeful that she would call me. I turned off the TV and slowly drifted off to sleep.

Chapter 5

I woke up the next morning at 5 AM and went straight to the hotel's gym. I ran for about 30 minutes, and then did 300 pushups and 300 sit-ups. That was my workout routine every morning; 5 days a week. After I worked up a good sweat, I passed by the hotel spa and purchased a strawberry, banana, and blueberry smoothie with whey protein. That was a great post-workout drink. My usual 45-minute workout did not only keep me in great shape while traveling but made me feel great and ready to take on the challenges of the day ahead.

I quickly went up to my room, took a shower, and got dressed. I could do everything in my sleep because I had the same routine. What I called unconscious knowing.

After getting dressed, I went to the lobby and requested a rental car. The concierge told me a mid-size car was available and would be brought to the front in approximately 15 minutes. That was enough time for me to order breakfast, pick up the rental and head to work.

My plan for that week would be diving heads down in reviewing all the files and covering the current state environment. I had two and a half days to examine all the materials before a 3 PM meeting with Scott that Friday to discuss what I would have learned to date. Talk about hitting the ground running. That was fine. I was used to the fast pace of management consulting. Plus, I would not have to perform any interviews or analysis since they already took place before, under Jim's supervision. I just needed to go over the work already created and determine if it was complete or any gaps existed.

We needed to have the three levels of process maps. Level, 1 being the highest level where we could see the whole process in a one-page Visio diagram. Level 2 was the same information but with more detail.

And level 3, was extremely detailed, down to the procedural level. The level 3 process maps were used to create our next set of deliverables; the desk top standard operating procedures (SOP).

What we had to keep in mind was the goal; to train the superusers in Toronto employing process flows and SOPs, in order for them to achieve expert levels with the accounts receivable, credit and collections operations. Once they were experts, they would fly back to Chennai, India to train the general users. Those users would be the AR/Collection clerks who would be performing the aforementioned functions on a daily basis after the "go-live".

The following few days were extremely busy. I was waking up at 5 AM and going to bed at 11 PM. I created a spreadsheet containing all the files to be reviewed and status bars for those files. That is where I kept my notes, and how I determined my progress. The idea was to examine my spreadsheet with Scott on Friday and to go over and discuss a visual diagram for the current state of the deliverables. I recreated a color coding for each file. Green meant the deliverables were completed, and no further work was necessary. Yellow meant the work was completed but needed revisions. And finally, red meant the file had to be redone due to the lack of information.

I reviewed over 40 files and deliverables during those two days, and determined all the deliverables for credit, collections, and accounts receivable were definitely in the red zone. I was stunned. There was a major problem because the work was incomplete.

When the original interviews of staff accountants and controllers took place, the developed process maps were incorrect, and many steps were missing in the process. I quickly determined that I would have to spend the first three weeks in June traveling to the shared service offices for Hudd in Chicago, Connecticut, and the New York City. The work would have to be performed rapidly. Therefore, interviews would have to be performed locally at each site, and after work, all the level 3 process flows would have to be completed at night. I would have to work hand-in-hand with my superusers in Toronto since they were tasked with creating the SOPs based on level 3 process flows. It would definitely be a major challenge to finish on-time, but as I mentioned before, that was not my first rodeo and every project had its challenges.

I created the Power Point for another deliverable. It was a work plan with a timeframe that captured all the necessary interviews and the estimated completion dates. I was basically starting over. What was done in 9 months would have to be redone within an extremely condensed time frame. The good news was; however, the future state deliverables would only be impacted from a system point of view, not from a process point of view. Again, that was a lift and shift operation where, for the most part, the processes would remain the same. Furthermore, my meeting with Lee Choppard would hopefully create more understanding of the system architecture and the impact on my process tower.

My two first days passed. I worked an 18-hour shift each day. Thankfully, the initial goal was achieved. I was prepared for my meeting with Scott the following day. My Excel was showing each reviewed file with the existing gaps. I was also prepared to discuss the work plan on how to close the gaps within a defined timeframe. All I needed was Scott's understanding and buy-in to move forward. By Thursday, I was ready for some much-needed rest.

After waking up early the next day, I wanted to get to the office as fast as possible to finish my preparation for the meeting with Scott. I quickly grabbed my breakfast bag-to-go, and by 7 AM, I was on my way. Since, traffic was light, I arrived at the office early, at approximately 7:30 AM. I thought I would be the first one there but, of course, Amanda beat me to it.

Apparently, she arrived at 7 AM every day while the majority of the team arrived by 8:30. I was always an easy-going person and preferred to get along with everyone, thus I approached Amanda and wished her a "happy Friday", She looked at me, said, "good morning" and returned to her starring at the laptop.

I figured she wasn't a morning person. I tried to preclude myself from thinking that she was just an unpleasant person. I, however, loved mornings. I loved waking up early and seeing the sun come up, listening to the melodies of the birds chirping louder and louder and feeling the breeze on my face as the sun warmed my skin. That was the time for nature's awakening, pristine and beautiful. Sadly, there was no beach in Toronto. The weather was perfect for a beautiful day by the shore.

I unpacked my bag, took out my PC, and began reviewing my two deliverables which were going to be the topic of the upcoming conversation with Scott. I made sure everything looked aesthetically correct, especially the color coding. I double checked for any misspellings since I was told Scott always wanted a finished product and not a draft. I went through the work products many times and at lunch, I decided to share a meal with Jim Leach, whom I was replacing.

"Hey, Jim." I said. "Since today is your last day, let me invite you to lunch?"

"Hey, Sebastian, that would be great!" Jim responded with a smile.

"If you want, we can do a working lunch, and you can practice presenting your findings to me as if I were Scott. Since I know Scott very well, I will give his exact feedback as if I was him." Jim suggested.

"Sounds like a plan, Jim. Thank you!" I was grateful for his desire to help me before meeting the all-powerful, no-mistakes-accepted, Scott.

We went down to the garage and got my rental car. At that moment, my phone rang. To my amazement, it was Roberta. I expected her call a few days ago, but I was still excited she called. I answered, and we spoke in Portuguese. I didn't want for Jim to understand us. Thus, I apologized and told him I had to take the call. He didn't mind.

"Boa tarde, querida? (Good afternoon, sweetheart?)" I said politely trying to contain my excitement since I was not alone in the car.

"I am doing great, Sebastian. I can't believe that after all these years you showed up in my hometown." Roberta noted.

"Yes, I am here working on a consulting project for about two months. I was really excited to come to Toronto for two reasons. First, to visit my old house where I lived from the ages of 6 to 10. And secondly, to see you, my Amazonian queen, and find out how you've been and what you were up to." I said in a serious tone being constantly aware of Jim's presence. "Damn working lunch!" I thought.

Roberta laughed at my flattery but also seemed excited to speak with me.

"Sebastian, we had a beautiful time then, and the memories are amazing, but I am married now." Said Roberta with what I hoped some sadness in her voice. "Let me be more specific." She continued. "I am happily married."

My initial excitement was instantly dashed. But I smiled to myself, imagining Roberta as a wife. The smile was rather painful.

"Perhaps I could still meet you for drinks and some catching up?" I asked hopefully. "Purely as friends!" I added immediately.

"That sounds like a plan, Sebastian. Why don't we meet for lunch? My husband would be suspicious if I went out by myself at night." Roberta replied.

"If you'd like, I can pick you up on Saturday. Where are you staying?" She asked casually.

"I am in downtown, at the W Hotel." I answered.

"Perfect, I will be there at noon. Beijos!" And without waiting for my reply, she hung up.

I hung up with a grin from ear to ear. Jim noticed my grin and asked if that was my girlfriend I was speaking to. I just explained that it was an old friend and continued smiling.

"What language were you speaking?" Jim was curious.

"We were speaking Portuguese. I am originally from Brazil but left at the age of 3."

"Wow, that language sounds really cool. I had no idea you were from there. I always thought you were an American since you don't have any accent whatsoever. I love Brazil especially their soccer team and Carnival… And the women, of course!" Jim started laughing mentioning, he missed his days of being single.

"Brazilian women are stunning." I agreed. "If you only saw my friend I was just speaking with." I continued. "She is truly one of the of the most beautiful women I've ever seen. But she is married now, and I must respect that."

We arrived at a local restaurant. The hostess seated us, and I looked at Jim while taking my PC out from its case.

"Are you ready?" Jim inquired.

"Yes, let's begin." I replied enthusiastically.

In the next 40 minutes, I performed a walk-through of my current state assessment. I highlighted the key points. I mentioned that the overall project was in the red, and that significant gaps existed. We then went through the solution areas and discussed the work plan to close those gaps. The overall discussion went very smoothly. I did all the required work and was fully prepared for Scott. Jim noticed the conviction and confidence in my voice while discussing the material. Indeed, I was ready to meet Scott.

"Sebastian, first of all I want to apologize. I see that you have done extensive work and have determined the project to be in the red. During the past 9 months, my wife and I had our second child. They are Irish twins born 12 months and five days apart. Our relationship has been tested due to my weekly travels. Because of that, I decided to change jobs and work locally in Atlanta, Georgia. I need to help my wife more, and I want to be there for my kids, to put them to sleep every night. This past year has been a very difficult one, and I believe you noticed that during the review of my current state deliverables. My head was not all there. Scott is aware of my personal issues, and he will not be surprised by your findings. You are ready, and I believe you will do fine.

We finished eating our lunch and then headed back to the office. While waiting for my 3 PM meeting, I focused on what I wanted to achieve with Scott. Number one objective would be building a trusted relationship. Number two, to walk him through the discovery process and methodology used to review the current state and gaps. Number three, to discuss solutions to close each gap and bring each process to a green status. Lastly, my fourth objective would be to gain buy-in. I needed Scott's support to proceed and contact each of the shared service centers, and schedule time with the controllers and their staff to conduct further interviews. All that needed to happen quickly in order to be ready for our "go-live" in Chennai, India.

It was almost 3 PM, so I decide to use the bathroom and wash my face. That was my usual routine before starting an important meeting. I walked across the war room and entered the board room. Scott was already there sitting at the head of the table. There was no one else in the room. He was on his cell phone discussing our project with one of the partners.

"Sebastian, please have a seat. I will finish this call in two minutes, and we will get started." He pointed to the chair.

I sat down, opened up my laptop, and took out my notepad in case I needed to write something down. Even though, I was confident in my analysis, I did not know Scott very well, and that made me a bit uncomfortable. He had a reputation for being tough and demanding. He had a laser focus. I needed to be on top of my game.

"Good afternoon, Sebastian." Scott ended his phone call and turned his face to me. "Sorry I kept you waiting but that was Gary Duncan on the phone, and he is the big boss around here. I have to take those calls."

"No worries, Scott. I know you have a busy schedule." I replied.

"So, tell me, Sebastian, is the AR tower in great shape and ready for the future state design or did we waste 9 months' time and effort working on the current state?" Scott immediately turned to business.

"Unfortunately, Scott, I believe it is the latter." I replied shaking my head over the situation. It wasn't easy or pleasant to announce that the company wasted a lot of time and money. But someone had to do it. And due to my job position, it had to be me.

"After careful and diligent analysis, it appears the AR tower has many gaps and the overall status is unfortunately in the red. But, I believe, with my experience and hard work, I can fix the problem in the next 3-4 weeks, and we can proceed as scheduled with our current "go-live" date." I summarized, trying to sound upbeat and hopeful.

There was little to no reaction from Scott. Just a simple nod of the head. He did not seem pleased rather the opposite; frustrated. I began to move closer so he could view my Excel sheet where I had the progress and gap analysis for each process.

Scott immediately said, "I only have 15 minutes of time with you before my next call. I don't want to focus on the poorly captured current state. If you say it is broken, we need to fix it. I want to hear your solution." He added.

I could hear frustration, even impatience in his tone.

"You know how difficult it can be to get on someone's schedule, therefore the next 2-3 weeks I would focus on two items. First, scheduling conference calls with each of the three controllers located in Chicago, New York City, and Connecticut. Those calls would be done in order to gather the data needed to complete level 1 and level 2 process maps. In order to obtain level 3, the most detailed, I will have to travel to each location in the first 3 weeks of June. The interviews would be performed during work hours, and then the flows will be designed at night in my hotel room. Once completed, I will send everything to my super user Shanti, our team lead, for her to develop the desktop standard operating procedure. Over the weekend, I would review all the deliverables for accuracy and completeness." I suggested my plan of action.

"Sebastian, your solution requires a lot of commitment from you and your team. Can you do it?" Scott inquired thoughtfully.

"Yes, sir. But there is one catch. Our level 3 deliverables will not be ready for our T-30 review. Only level 1 and 2 will be ready by then. Level 3 will be completed by the end of June. Approximately one week before our final T-5 review."

Scott took some time to think that through.

"You will have to nail the level 1 and 2 process maps and make sure they are perfect for our T-30 review. We will not be able to go back and start over again." He warned.

"I have been leading projects for our company for almost ten years. I have successfully managed over 20 projects during that time period. I have a track record of success, and I will devote all my efforts to making this project my priority and have it completed within our projected "go-live" date of July 11th." I tried to assure Scott.

"You are putting me in a difficult position. This cannot fail. In order for me to give the green light to proceed, I need for you to send me weekly status reports of your progress with the completed deliverables. If there are any errors or omissions, we will capture them sooner rather than later. Like you, I started my career in process improvement and I have done plenty of AR projects in the past. I will work with you to get this done."

"Yes sir." I nodded in agreement.

"Go ahead and start making your phone calls to their shared service centers." Scott encouraged.

"Thank you, Scott. I won't let you or the firm down." I stated.

"You better not, Sebastian, since your ass is on the line here." Scott replied with severity and seriousness in his voice. I had no doubt he meant it.

I took a deep breath, gathered my belongings, and went back to my workstation.

In total, I had to conduct six interviews over the phone in the next two weeks. I would have to work "day and night" to capture the data and create the process flows. Therefore, for the next few hours, I called the 3 controllers each in Chicago, Connecticut, and the New York City to introduce myself and explain our current situation. Ultimately, we needed to close the existing gaps. I spent about 20 minutes with each controller and finished our conversation by setting up several 1-hour calls: two next week, and the third, for the week after.

My day and week have finally finished. I was pretty exhausted, so I returned to the hotel and decided to check out the Spa. I felt like I needed a very good deep tissue massage, thus I purchase a 90-minute session. Halfway through the massage, I was pleasantly surprised to receive another phone call from Roberta. Normally, I would never in-terrupt my massage for any phone call, but Roberta was the exception. I told the masseuse to stop, and I sat up on the bed.

"Boa tarde, Roberta. How are you?" I asked excitedly.

"I am very happy that it is Friday. I had a busy week at work and am ready for a cocktail." She replied to my greeting.

Roberta was a manager for a very prestigious international choco-late manufacturer.

"I am assuming you will be spending happy hour with your husband?" I teased.

"Yes, Sebastian. He is the love of my life, and I enjoy spending all the time with him during the weekend since both our weeks are very busy." Roberta echoed my acidic tone.

"So, you won't even give your old friend a few hours to see you and catch up? Just for the good old times' sake? I continued.

"I told you before, we can meet for lunch. Tomorrow is Saturday, are you free at 1PM?" Roberta asked ignoring my tone.

"Of course, Roberta, I will clear out my schedule for you." I responded excitedly.

"Enough with the flattery, Sebastian. The lunch is simply to catch up as friends and nothing else."

"I know, I know. But it's hard not to flirt with you because I had no idea you were married and could only remember our past together. I will do my best to treat you like a friend. I promise." I knew I was lying. But I was ready to tell Roberta anything to make sure she didn't change her mind about meeting me for lunch.

"Write down my address." She said. "Let's meet at the lobby of my building at 12:30 PM."

"Ok Roberta. Looking forward to seeing you tomorrow." I was thrilled.

"Tchau, tchau."

I hung up the phone, apologized for the interruption and returned to enjoying the remainder of the massage. I even got to take a 15-minute nap because the masseuse was extraordinarily proficient at her work.

The rest of the evening I spent alone. Even though my job had its benefits, the downside was that it could get quite lonely. Most of the project team did their own thing for lunch and dinner. Almost all returned back to their homes on the weekends to spend time with their families. I, on the other hand, would not be able to visit my hometown in Miami, due to the project time constraints, but would have to spend many weekends in Toronto, without seeing friends or family.

I was hoping to spend those weekends with Roberta. As it turned out, that would not be the case. Since I did not have a girlfriend back home, my nights and weekends would be mostly in solitude. Even though I liked my crazy lifestyle back home in Miami, that made my job here tougher by not having a girlfriend. I had little to no support system. I tended to briefly speak with my parents about once or twice a week just to let them know how I was doing. But, in actuality, I really did not have anyone that I could just speak to openly about the intricacies of my job and the difficult times. Most of my coworkers were married with children. They would speak with their wives every night. I missed that closeness.

The next morning, instead of going to the hotel gym, I decided to go for a longer run around St. James Park. It was one of the nicest parks in the city with a gazebo and water fountain. It made running a bit challenging since the park had a few hills. At times, my legs would burn, and I could feel the buildup of lactic acid fatiguing my muscles. After about one-hour jogging, my lungs were tired, and I decided to sit on a bench. It was early, approximately 8 AM. I liked getting up early especially on the weekends. Sometimes, I would get up as early as 5 AM and watch the sun come up. Over time, I became a morning person. There was something special in the early morning. At least for me. I enjoyed its magical stillness as if in a state of anticipation for nature's awakening to the sunrise. I enjoyed the moment when I would hear the world around me, coming alive. That particular time of the day would inspire me and push my creativity to the new unknown levels.

I went back to the hotel and had my usual eggs Benedict with hash browns and a large glass of freshly squeezed orange juice. I loved fresh orange juice because when I was a young boy, I would visit my extended family in Brazil, and they always served the best breakfast with hand-squeezed orange juice and the freshest bread from the local bakery. The smell of the fresh bread and home-brewed coffee would wake me up immediately. The rest of the morning, I spent in my room catching up with an old book and listening to music. Even though, there would be no intimacy with Roberta, I was just happy to see her. I was looking forward to catching up and seeing her after so many years.

I took a shower and got ready for lunch. Since, I was unsure of where we were going, I decided to wear a blue sports blazer, a white button-down shirt, and jeans. I always preferred to be overdressed for any occasion. Once in my car, I entered Roberta's address into the GPS. My ride would last for 23 minutes. Enough time to think and listen to my favorite Coldplay mix.

The time went by quickly, and I arrived at my destination in less than the initial calculation. There were two towers; the North and the South Tower. She was not clear in which one she lived but simply mentioned the lobby. I decided to stand in between the two towers; which were approximately 100 feet across each other and had a large awning connecting the two buildings. I waited for about 10 minutes, and then suddenly, she appeared, but she was not alone. Perhaps, that was a friend; a single friend I hoped. I became a bit nervous and excited at the same time.

Roberta looked the same. She was tall and dark: she had curly hair with light brown and blonde highlights. As she walked towards me, she gave out a beautiful glowing smile. Her friend was a bit shorter and younger. She also had dark tanned skin but was a bit lighter than Roberta. Her hair was long, chestnut-brown and silky smooth. She had more of a petite figure. It was crazy that in an instant, I wasn't sorry about Roberta being unavailable. I was smitten by the woman next to her. I was hoping she was actually a friend that would be coming to join us for lunch and not a next-door neighbor. Otherwise, I'd have to make up an excuse to Roberta, and drop the lunch with her in order to introduce myself to her friend or whomever that beauty was.

"Boa tarde, Sebastian, how are you?" Roberta greeted me with a stunning smile revealing her perfect pearly white teeth. It's been a while, but you haven't changed a bit. Still the handsome devil."

"Hi Roberta! Great to see you as well!" I replied excitedly. "You know how much I used to love it when you flirted with me?" I continued. "Is this woman one of your neighbors in the building?"

"This is not my neighbor, louco! This beautiful girl is my younger sister." Roberta laughed.

"Wow! Nice to meet you, younger sister. I see beauty runs in the family." I beamed while looking at Roberta's sibling.

"Since you are in my city and you are not too familiar with it, I thought it might be nice to bring my sister to lunch and she can show you around the area." Roberta suggested.

"What is your name?" I asked Roberta's sister as she kept on dazzling me with her smile.

"Renata." She replied sweetly.

"Pleasure to meet you, Renata. Sebastian." I shook her elegant hand with long fingers.

"Likewise, Sebastian." Said Renata.

"I am thrilled you will be joining us for lunch." I noted with the same beaming smile.

"As you know Sebastian, I am a happily married woman now, but Renata is younger and unattached, thus, she can show you around since she knows all the cool new places in Toronto. Just remember…" Roberta leaned to me and whispered, "This is my sister, my baby. I expect respect and chivalry towards her."

"Have no doubts, Roberta. As you know, that's how I treat all women." I noted in a serious tone.

I went ahead and gave both Roberta and Renata kisses on the cheeks. Such a greeting was commonplace in Brazil. Believe it or not, some places in Brazil even kissed three times on the cheeks.

"It is my pleasure to meet you, Renata." I repeated excitedly. "I look forward to going wherever you decide to take me. I am sure it will be an adventure."

"Let's go, guys." Said Roberta. "Let's take my car."

"Today, we are going to a Brazilian restaurant called Copacabana. I am sure you missed our traditional food."

"We do have a couple of places in Miami, but I rarely go. It's always nice to get a taste of Brazil. I miss those times, during my early childhood, with my aunts, uncles, and cousins." I noted. "So, every time I have a Brazilian food, it brings back those good memories of my culture and my family. These days, I rarely go back to Brazil and almost never get to see them."

On the way to the restaurant, the two sisters sat in the front, while I was chilling in the back seat. During the ride, I mostly conversed with Roberta while Renata listened to us with a smile.

"Querida Roberta, are you married for real?" I asked knowing that indeed Roberta was married for real.

"Yes, Sebastian." She answered seriously.

"So, who is the lucky guy?" I proceeded with the questioning.

"He is Canadian, and I met him on match.com." Roberta replied nonchalantly.

"What?" I was stunned. "You married some guy from the internet? I knew you were a bit crazy but an online dating website! Call me traditional, but I like the old method of serendipity. Do you remember how we met?"

"I believe, we met at your party at the Mansion, in Miami." Roberta answered with a semi-smile.

"Yes Roberta, we met purely by chance that night." I exclaimed. "The moment I laid my eyes on you, I knew I had to meet and get to know you better."

Through the rear-view mirror, I saw Roberta's beautiful smile. I knew she was recalling that night, as was I.

"I will never forget that night, Roberta."

"Neither will I." She nodded thoughtfully.

Renata, who was silent the whole time, suddenly turned to her sister and asked if we hooked up that night.

"You never told me about Sebastian in that way, Roberta." She sounded like a child who wasn't in on a secret.

"We kissed very passionately and danced all night together." Roberta smiled. "It seemed as though the stars were aligned, and it was only the two of us that night." Roberta's face looked dreamy. "Everyone around us was just a blur."

"Sounds like a fairy tale." Renata said excitedly.

I was listening to the beautiful sisters discussing our short affair with Roberta, and just smiled feeling both sad over it being over so fast and happy about being the main topic of their exchange.

"So, tell me, Roberta, how, did this match.com get you the man of your dreams?" I asked after some silence.

"It was quite simple, Sebastian. I am older now, and I can't spend every weekend at the clubs. With Match, I selected all the qualities I was looking for in the man and then, all of a sudden, I got a list of the potential suitors." Roberta started explaining. "I went through their profiles, and if I liked what I read, and I was physically attracted, I used Skype to make sure the profile matched the face." She continued. "You know there are a lot of liars and posers on the internet and some can be quite creepy, so, I reviewed my husband's profile and we had similar backgrounds and similar values. To top it off, he was very handsome." Roberta's face lit up. It was obvious she loved her man. "We Skyped a few times and then decided to meet at a public place. You see, his parents immigrated from Brazil. Not only did we speak Portuguese to each other, but also we had similar tastes in just about everything. I used to think opposites attract but through my experiences, especially in dating, the more similar someone is to you, the better the chances you have in being with that person forever." Roberta concluded her brief story.

"Well Roberta, I am very happy that you found someone who makes you happy. At the end of the day, that is what really matters." I noted while realizing that I was genuinely happy for Roberta.

By then, we have reached our destination and all the three of us got out of the car and Roberta went to ask the hostess for a table. Renata did not say much during our drive to the restaurant. She would simply display a gorgeous smile or laugh but overall, she didn't really speak.

"Renata, are you the quiet one in the family?" I asked after we sat down.

"Yes, I am a bit of an introvert. I adapt to the company. So, if I am with a very outgoing person, I become outgoing. If not, I simply keep to myself. I basically react to other people's energy." She responded.

"So, tell me Sebastian, are you an introvert or an extrovert?" She asked.

"Well, I guess I'm an extrovert, if not, we are not going to have any fun, right?" I attempted at a joke.

"No, seriously, Sebastian." Renata pressed on.

"Seriously speaking, I am the perfect mix between an introvert and extrovert. Like you, it depends on the environment I am in and the people I am with." I responded seriously. "I like spending time by myself either reading a book or at the beach. But when I am with my friends and have a few drinks, my alter ego comes out and I can be quite charming and humorous."

For the first time, Renata laughed at my sarcasm.

"Sebastian, I am sure you are familiar with Rodizo style eating from Brazil?" Asked Roberta.

"Yes." I nodded.

The Rodizio style restaurants offered approximately 13 different cuts of steak. They were displayed on the large skewers and the waiters came to the table offering the meats. The patrons were given the red or green cards. Green meant "keep serving" and red signaled to stop. There were also salad bars with many different styles of vegetables, sides and hot dishes.

"Pace yourself, Sebastian." Roberta laughed.

"I'm sure you both will have to carry me out of this place since I absolutely love meat." I chimed in catching Roberta's laughter.

For the next hour, we ate like kings and drank a few Caipirinhas; made with a type of rum called Cachaca. It's the spirit derived from sugarcane alcohol. It tasted like a very sweet lemonade, but very strong. I typically had only one or two drinks. Most of the conversation was between Roberta and me. Renata simply listened; always with a glowing smile. Once I had two drinks, I felt a bit tipsy, and started focusing my attention mostly on Renata. I knew I had to be the outgoing one, so she could break out of her shell and talk more.

"Renatinha, do you also look for men on the internet?" I asked teasingly while winking at Roberta.

"No." Renata replied seriously. "I am more of a traditionalist like you; I believe in things happening for a reason. I think the right man will come at the right time. If it is meant to be then it will last and a relationship will flourish but, you have to put yourself out there. If I were to stay at home waiting for the man of my dreams, it would either have to be the mailman or the handyman."

All three of us laughed out loud.

"How is your friend Mike the Marine?" Roberta changed the topic.

"Well, it is very rarely I get to talk with Mike. Now that he is flying helicopters over Afghanistan; he is pretty much off the map. He might call me every few years to see how I am doing and what our friends from High School are up to. He basically has two lives; as a helicopter pilot and his private life in San Francisco with his wife and kids. Next time I hear from him, I will mention you said hello." I replied.

The waiter brought the check, and I immediately reached for it. Roberta was about to object, but I insisted. "Thank you, but this one is on me."

The sisters thanked me, and we headed back to their complex.

During our ride from the restaurant, I started sensing the effects of the alcohol. I felt very relaxed and I was in a great mood. We did not talk too much on the way back, but I could not stop admiring how beautiful they both were. I began to drift off and started imagining if it was possible to be intimate with Renata, Roberta's younger sister. I haven't seen Roberta in over six years, and now she was married. Renata was the only consolation to my otherwise disappointing discovery about Roberta being deeply in love with her husband.

Renata was 28 years old; four years younger than me and six years younger than Roberta. Would I have a shot to accomplish the challenging feat of sleeping with both sisters? Does Renata know I slept with her sister? In the past, I slept with women who were friends with each other, but never sisters.

We arrived at their apartment building. I was unsure if this would be the last time I saw them. As I was about to say goodbye, Renata suddenly asked me if I would like to go out tomorrow on a boat.

"Are you interested, Sebastian?"

Roberta jumped in and mentioned she would not be able to join us but that I should go.

"Sebastian, go with my sister. You need to meet people here in Toronto, to make your trip fun and exciting. Remember, tomorrow is Sunday, and you need to have fun. I call Sundays, my fun days. So, go with my sister but remember to always respect her." Roberta said with an encouraging smile.

Inside, I felt like I was a little kid in a candy store. I always liked a challenge, and that was a big one. But out of respect for Renata, I would only seduce her if I noticed an interest coming from her first. I would never want to take advantage of her. She must choose to be with me. It had to be mutual.

"It will be my pleasure to go out boating with you and your friends, tomorrow." I replied gratefully.

"Great!" Exclaimed Renata. "I will pick you up at your hotel tomorrow at 10 AM. Does that work for you, Sebastian?"

I nodded "yes" and grinned from ear to ear. I couldn't believe I was going to spend the entire day with Renata. That would allow me to focus solely on her. I have always thought that in life things didn't just happen, every event and occurrence had its reasons. I was thrilled.

I gave them both kisses on their cheeks and proceeded to my rental car. I stood by my car and watched them enter the building. When I got in and closed the door, I let out a huge yell. Perhaps I was a bit immature, but I got fired up and could not contain my emotions. I turned on the radio and happily headed back to the hotel. Our first meeting was a complete success, and I was eager to see where that journey would take me. Not knowing the unknown made life so exciting. I was hoping and looking forward to the two adventurous months in Toronto.

My first goal in the project was to complete the deliverables and be prepared for the Advisory Board Review on T-30 days and T-5 days before "go-live". My second goal was to seduce Renata and have a romantic summer fling. Who knew? Maybe I could even bring her to India with me. I knew I was getting too ahead of myself, but I just couldn't stop dreaming about Renata. Only time would tell.

For the rest of the day, I focused on my work deliverables and went over my calendar to plan the conference calls for the next two weeks.

After lunch with the two sisters, I was so excited that the work felt light and easy, even my studying was a breeze. I got a BA in finance for my undergrad and an MBA in International Business. Thus, for me, the North American accounting practices were easy to learn and understand. I spent the rest of the day preparing for the next week and at night, I decided to watch a movie in my room and order in. Sometimes, it was nice just to be by myself. I enjoyed the night feeling eagerly optimistic for the next day.

PART 2

Renata

Chapter 1

The following day, I woke up and had an extra hard workout. I did my usual run in the park and once the 30 minutes were up, I decided to do HIITS (high-intensity interval training). The idea was to run as fast as possible for 5 minutes and then walk briskly for 1 minute, then repeating the entire routine for a total of 30 minutes. That helped increase my stamina and build a lean muscle mass. It was the training performed by the best track and field sprinters; especially those competing in short distance runs such as 100, 200, and 400-meter sprints.

Once I finished my cardio, I went to our building gym and performed my usual 300 sit-ups and 300 push-ups. For me, that was the best full body training when I was not at home. When at home, I would simply do a cross fit class for 45 minutes, 3 days a week. I always worked on my abdominals, my weakest spot. While it was lean and toned, the six pack I craved was barely noticeable. There was little I could do to improve that without liposuction. I've already started looking for a doctor in Miami who could suck out the last remaining fat, so the appearance I always wanted would be achieved. I just needed to find some down time for the recovery.

I finished my workout at 9:30 AM. Afterwards, I needed to take a quick shower and meet Renata at the lobby. Since everything in my room was well organized, I was able to get ready quickly. I took a cold shower to give me that extra burst of energy and felt mentally and physically strong. I went downstairs and waited for Renata. At exactly 10 AM, she showed up in her powder blue Mini Cooper convertible. She pulled up, gave me her gorgeous smile and said, "Bom dia, Seba (jump in)!"

I did not hesitate and jumped over the door.

"See, just as you ordered." I pronounced with a huge smile.

We exchanged kisses and were off. We had about 20 minutes to get to the yacht club, so we simply enjoyed the ride. There was no need for much talk. Renata drove and drank her coffee while I enjoyed the music and the ride. It was quite breezy in her convertible, but I loved to feel the wind in my face. It made me enjoy the moment and feel alive. After we pulled up into the parking lot, Renata turned to me and smiled.

"Sebastian, we have arrived. Could you please get some bags out of the trunk?"

"Of course." I replied enthusiastically.

As I walked up to the trunk and opened it, I discovered several bags filled with the Brazilian appetizers called salgadiñhos which could be translated into English as the salty appetizer trays. The most popular appetizers were pão de quejo, empadas, coxinhas, and esfirras. I was so excited to see all the goodies that I couldn't help myself and reached for one.

"They taste amazing." I exclaimed. "Wow, Renata, I am impressed with the food."

"Wait until you get on the boat where my good friend Luca will offer you just about any drink you desire." She said excitedly.

After we finished gathering all the food, we went to the dock. There, I saw a beautiful 40-foot Sea Ray Sundancer.

"Wow, so which one of your friends owns this beauty?" I asked while admiring a stunning white boat gently rocking on the dark blue water.

"That would be Luca." Renata replied. "He is a wonderful person and a great friend. He has helped me a lot in Toronto; it's hard only having my sister here."

We walked across the bridge connecting the boat to the boat slip, and Luca helped me get on the boat.

"And whom might this young man be?" Asked Luca.

Renata responded, "this is Sebastian, an old friend of Roberta's. He will be staying in Toronto for the next two months. I wanted to show Sebastian around and, of course, for him to meet you."

"Welcome onboard, Sebastian." Said Luca with a welcoming smile.

He gave me a very firm handshake which made me question his friendship with Renata. He was not young. I would say, early 60s. He had a beer belly and a long salt and pepper hair. I feared, perhaps he was her "sugar daddy", since in Miami this type of relationship was all over the place. I decided to simply be a guest on the boat and let things play out on their own. If he truly was her boyfriend, I would soon find out and our adventure would be over.

We pushed off and Luca took control of the boat. We slowly left the yacht club at pretty much idle speed. I took off all the ropes and stored them in their locations.

"Hey Luca, is there anything else I can help you with?"

"Yes, Sebastian, please untie the buoys and place them inside the containers. When you're done, come up here so we can actually talk and get to know each other." Luca replied in a relaxed manner. It was apparent he could tend to his boat with his eyes closed.

I placed the buoys in their bins and then walked up to the captain's chair. "So, Sebastian, what brings you to Toronto?" Luca asked without ceremonies.

"Well, the main reason I am here is for business. I work for one of the biggest management consulting companies in the world and we are involved in a business process outsourcing project. We are transferring the jobs from North America to India." I answered while studying Luca attentively.

"That's very interesting." Luca noted as if speaking to himself. "How long have you been in consulting?"

"Ever since I finished my MBA; so about 8 years."

"I have also noticed you are good with languages. You know Portuguese?" He asked with a smile.

"Yes, I'm fluent in English, Portuguese, and Spanish. You see, I was born in Brazil and all my family is from there so, it's pretty much my first language." I explained.

"And how did you learn Spanish?" Luca continued his friendly interrogations.

"Before starting my MBA, I decided to live abroad, in Spain. I was there for 6 months in a Spanish immersion program. I studied during the week in Madrid and would explore the outside cities on the weekends. In total, I went to 13 cities in Spain. It was a wonderful trip, and I formed some great friendships which I still maintain today."

"Well, Sebastian, it seems like you have a wonderful background and have lived a lot at your young age." Luca appeared very impressed.

"Yes, thank you. The motto I follow, is to live each day as if it was your last and to learn every day as if you would live forever." I replied with pride.

"What about Roberta? How did you meet her?" He went on.

"We had common friends in Miami where every weekend we would end up at the same nightclubs. I never really met her until she came to one of my parties. We connected that night and have kept in touch ever since."

"What about you, Luca? How did you meet these two beautiful sisters?" I finally flipped the conversation and questioned Luca.

"I was recently divorced and wanted to get out more and make new friends. I always went to the Eaton Center to shop and one day, I decided to stop by the Copenhagen store to buy some chocolates. That is where I met Roberta. She was the store manager. She was always very nice to me, and I invited her to my art gallery where I had new artists displaying their works. Art is what we have in common. From there, I met her sister and I am like their older uncle. When the group goes out, I join them. I feel like I am a young man again when I am around them. Well, not as young as you but overall we have fun and we make each other happy." Luca beamed when speaking about the sisters.

While Luca and I were chatting, Renata took off her flower dress and appeared in a sexy swimsuit. Her stunning body was in full display. She wore a Brazilian bikini in bright white. It was a beautiful contrast with her dark tanned skin. She ran up to the deck and asked about the drinks.

Luca hugged her around the waist and announced the bar was officially open. Their friendship seemed odd to me. Something in my gut told me, perhaps there was more to their relationship. I went to the back of the boat, took off my shirt and sat down. I simply wanted some solitude and time to observe the two of them together to maybe get a better understanding of their dynamics. Maybe my intuition could tell me more. I did not want to drink too much, so I had an ice-cold beer.

As I sipped my beer, I watched Luca driving the boat and Renata standing by his side. I must admit that I was a bit disappointed, maybe even frustrated, but I resolved to not let it bother me and just enjoy the day. I've never been on a boat in Toronto. Most of the time, the weather was cold. I could not imagine making the investment for a boat where you might only use it for 3 months out of the year. It was the end of May and surprisingly the weather was very nice. It was a bit cool in the shade but great in the sun. I decided to move up to the front of the boat where I could lay down and get some sun. In spite of the weird intimacy between Renata and Luca that bothered me a lot, I was still glad to be there enjoying myself. I could've been at the hotel, by myself. I closed my eyes and soaked in the sun. It warmed my face and even with my eyes closed, I could hear the seagulls flying by and the sound of the waves splashing on the side of the yacht.

"Seba…Seba…" I heard her soft sexy whisper through my daydream. I opened my eyes and the first thing I saw was those beautiful honey colored eyes, a stunning smile, and rosy cheeks. It was Renata.

"Are you enjoying the sun?" She inquired.

"Indeed, I was enjoying it so much, I passed out. But then I saw an angel and she said my name." I added flirtatiously. "Renata, how are you so beautiful?"

"Thank you, Sebastian. Thank you for your sweet compliment. I guess I could thank my parents and their genes. I have native Brazilian blood from the Amazon and a mixture of some Portuguese from Europe."

"You are so exotic." I continued. "I'm not trying to flatter you, but I always say it when I see true beauty. Yours is rare."

"Thank you, Seba. You are very kind."

"So, I have a question." I proceeded. Finally, Renata paid attention to me instead of hanging around Luca. And I was going to ask every question I had.

"What kind of relationship do you really have with Luca?" I asked directly. "I saw how he holds you and touches you. Is he your boyfriend? I finished realizing I was a bit scared of the truth. "If he is your boyfriend, I would understand."

"No," Renata answered plainly. "He is not my boyfriend. He is simply my friend; a very good friend. He has always been there for me during the difficult times. I've known Luca for many years, and not only has he helped me, but I have helped him after his divorce. You see, Luca was very outgoing in his 20s and 30s, but then he got married in his early 40s and missed living life. Life for him became a routine. I was able to introduce him to a younger crowd and since he has a young soul, he enjoys it. We are only friends, Seba." Renata finished her long explanation, and silence ensued between us.

"By the way, why do you care if I am single or not?" She spoke out after a long pause.

I didn't say anything back but just smiled. Now I knew her status. That made me feel better. Mind you, I didn't know why I even cared or what exactly was on my mind regarding Renata. After our conversation, I went from being dreamy and concerned to wide awake and reinvigorated.

For the rest of the afternoon, we cruised around Lake Ontario and enjoyed our day. In my mind, I was already satisfied with Renata's position and did not want to pursue her in front of Luca. Perhaps, there was history there which she didn't want to disclose. Out of respect for Luca, his boat was not the place for me to be selfish for my own needs or desires. I simply wanted to take the time off from the project and enjoy a few hours in the sun. As I've mentioned before, after speaking with Renata, I hoped I had a chance to get closer to her. I found it tantalizing that she was curious about my questioning. To me, it was like planting a seed in her mind. After that, I just needed to proceed with caution and further develop our friendship.

At six o'clock in the evening we returned to the yacht club. Luca perfectly docked the boat at his slip, and we gathered our belongings and headed to the parking lot. I thanked him for welcoming me to his boat and for being a great host. I looked forward to the possibility of cruising once again. In Miami, boating was a weekend thing all year long. While personally I wasn't keen on the idea of owning a boat, I was grateful to my friends who had them and always invited me to join for the fun outings, great parties and relaxing sails. With all that, I always kept in mind their expressions about the two best days of owning the boat, which were the day one bought it and the day it was sold. Owning a yacht required a lot of work, time and money. That is why I looked forward to the next time boating with Luca.

"Thank you for your hospitality, Luca. I have to say I absolutely love your boat." I shook Luca's hand.

"My pleasure, Sebastian, anytime you want to go for a cruise let me know. Friends of Roberta's and Renata's are my friends, and they are always welcomed on my boat." Luca replied with his toothy smile.

We packed back into Renata's car. And I jumped into it instead of just getting in regularly.

"Hey, do you think you are some type of a superhero? This is not a bat mobile!" Renata teased me.

I replied with a laughter.

Chapter 2

As we drove back to my hotel, I remained silent simply enjoying the sunset and the warm breeze in my face. I thought about our conversation on the boat. It was short. But I managed to ask some pointed questions, and I was pleased with Renata's replies. At that point, I believed I had a chance with her. I just needed the right time and place to start making my moves. I was unsure of when this would occur, but I was hoping sometime in the near future.

"Renatinha, what a great day I had with you." I finally broke our lingering silence. "I never imagined I would be cruising in an incredible yacht with you on Lake Ontario. I love when the unexpected happens. I really enjoyed getting to know you better. So, when is our next date?" I asked in a nonchalant manner.

"Date, what do you mean date?" Renata nodded her head to me.

"Well, I feel that we are just getting to know each other, and I would love to get to know you even better and also have some fun in this city."

"Do you like dancing?" Inquired Renata.

"Yes, after a few drinks I am an expert at dancing samba, meringue, and salsa." I stated laughingly. "You see, back in Miami I had a few classes, so I know my place on the dance floor."

"Oh really, I would like to see this dancer." Renata rolled her eyes jokingly. "I know you have a busy week so why don't we plan for Friday? I will take you to a salsa club called Santos. They play all types of Latin music, and I think you will like it. Let's not call it a date but an outing." She suggested.

We pulled up to the entrance of my hotel. I gave Renata a big smile and said, "I look forward to our date on Friday."

She laughed and said, "make sure you bring your dancing shoes. I have high expectations."

I jumped out of the convertible and grabbed my belongings and walked to the driver's side where she was sitting. I leaned over and gave her a kiss on both sides of her cheeks.

"Thank you for an incredible day. Have a good night." I whispered into her ear.

"See you soon, Sebastian." Renata replied appearing completely unfazed by my closeness.

I returned to my room feeling optimistic about what I termed a potential "summer romance". I knew that a serious relationship could not happen since she lived in Toronto and I lived in Miami. I also did not believe in long distance relationships. I simply would take it day-by-day and see what would happen. I felt excited about the adventure and the summer was just starting.

I spent the remainder of Sunday evening locked in my hotel room. I ordered room service and prepared for the upcoming work week. The goal of the week was to develop level 1 high-level design of the accounts receivable process in three different Hudd locations. By the end of the week, I needed to send a draft to Scott, the program manager, for review as we agreed, along with a weekly status report. If the designs were complete and accurate, I would then send it to Shanti, my team lead, to create the new standard operating procedure. I focused on the questions for my interviews to be held that week. I worked until about midnight and decided to call it a night. Since I was still a bit excited about the time spent with Renata and our upcoming "date", I decided to take a Xanax to relax my mind and fall asleep as quickly as possible.

Chapter 3

For the following five days, I focused on work only. I was heads down at the office and then later, at the hotel. I needed to accomplish my task and have a successful project. My promotion to partner depended on this project, and I was relentless in pursuing my goals. I proceeded to contact the controllers and set up conference calls to get a high-level understanding of their accounts receivable process.

I dedicated Tuesday and Thursday to those calls. They went very smoothly, and my questioning allowed me to create Visio diagrams of the process. By the end of the week, I created a draft for each of the three different locations in the US. I felt confident in my deliverables, but they would be in draft format until I obtained a sign-off from Scott. On Friday, I sent the drafts of all three level 1 Visio diagrams to Scott along with a status report of my accomplishments for the week and my plans for the next week. I ultimately expected for the next week's drafts to be approved and finalized. I would then schedule a second meeting with all the three controllers to perform a deeper dive and draft level 2 Visio diagrams. Those two deliverables would conclude the team's expectations for the month of May.

In the meantime, my team from India would be working on their related sections on the standard operating procedures for the general users once we "go-live" in India. I felt great about the week's progress and was ready to turn my attention to Renata.

When Friday rolled in, I was looking forward to reaching out to Renata and making some plans for the evening. At our last meeting on the boat on Lake Ontario, I was able to get her phone number. Thus, I decided to call her. After I was finished with lunch, I had a few spare minutes. I dialed her number; the phone rang but there was no answer.

I did not want to leave a message so, I hung up. I figured I would try again, after work.

I left work rather early, at 5 PM. I wanted to go back to the hotel and get a massage. I called the hotel concierge and reserved a 6 PM appointment with the masseuse. I requested a woman masseuse and wanted her to perform a deep tissue massage for 1 hour. Upon arriving at the W, I went straight to my room to take a quick shower and change into my robe for the massage. I slipped into the flip flops and headed down to the Spa.

At the Spa, I was greeted by the hostess who in turn introduced me to Jessica, my masseuse. We walked into the private room and she told me to take off my robe and wrap myself in a towel. Jessica stepped out for a few minutes to allow me to change and get situated on the table. About 5 minutes later, she knocked on the door and came back inside. I was already laying down comfortably on my stomach, ready to relax. She started by rubbing some eucalyptus oil on my calves and began placing pressure with her strong thumbs and fingers.

"Mr. Kosta, please tell me if I am applying too much force. I want to make sure this is pleasurable and not painful." She pronounced quietly in a professional manner.

"The pressure is good for now, but once you work on my back, I would like more pressure." I whispered, hoping that was the end of talking and I could slip into the relaxing semi-sleep.

In my mind, deep tissue massages were performed well only if a moderate degree of pain was felt. I did not like for them to simply rub oil on my body. My muscles needed to release the lactic acid from my morning workouts. She continued to work up my legs and until her hands were rubbing the area between my outer upper thighs and buttocks. It really felt amazing and I had a sense of peace. My mind was clear except for one thing; Renata. I wanted to see her so badly tonight. I was also looking for a fun Friday evening. By then, the masseuse moved up to my back and she started using her elbows for a deep stimulation. Admittedly, that was a bit painful, but I enjoyed it, nevertheless. After working on my arms, hands, and fingers she proceeded to work on my neck and head. At that point, I began dosing off.

"Mr. Kosta, could you please turn over on your back?" I heard her voice.

We were about halfway done when I heard my phone ring. I knew it wasn't' really allowed to leave the phone on loud when getting a massage, but I apologized to Jessica, explaining that I was expecting an important phone call. She nodded and stepped away as I answered the phone.

"Hello, this is Sebastian Kosta."

"Hello Mr. Sebastian, this is Renata. I noticed that I had a missed call from you." She said.

"It is so nice to hear from you, Renata. I called you earlier so we may plan for our date tonight." I stated in a relaxed tone, even though I was thrilled she called.

"You make me laugh when you call it a date. We are just friends, Sebastian. I want to take you out so that you can see the city and meet new people."

"But you are the one I want to see the most." I replied sincerely, while signaling to Jessica she could continue. "I am in the middle of a massage. And you are so important, I answered the phone. See?" I teased.

"How nice, I wish one day I could have the same luxuries as you." Renata murmured dreamily.

"Whenever you want one, just let me know." I offered. "We can even have a couple's massage."

"That would be nice." She replied in a manner that left me guessing whether she was being polite or would really think that it would be nice to get a couple's massage with me.

"So, here is the deal, Sebastian. I can pick you up at your hotel at 9 PM, and I will make reservations for dinner at Santos at 10. We will probably get there early, but we can sit at the bar and have a drink or two before being seated. The place gets fun and loud only around 1 AM. That's when you better have your dancing shoes on since you've mentioned you were a great dancer." Renata managed to plan out our entire evening in a few sentences. I found it very sexy.

"Wow, the expectations are high. I will not disappoint." I laughed.

"I hate promises, Sebastian. People never live up to their promises." She retorted.

"You are one tough cookie. Okay, I won't promise anything, but you will have the time of your life with me."

We both laughed out loud. I hung up the phone, apologized to Jessica again, and enjoyed the remaining 20 minutes of the massage.

Since it was only 7 PM, I decided to further enjoy the Spa and spent about 20 minutes in the steam room. That was a good way to clear my lungs, nostrils, and improve my skin's appearance. Since our date was confirmed, I felt a sense of a bliss. I could simply enjoy my time alone. I thoroughly loved meditation and I practiced it every day. Breathing was important, in fact, I considered it the most important aspect of meditation.

I cleared my mind of everything and just listened to the steam being released into the air and felt the sweat beading off my nose. I had a towel which I used to rub the dead skin off my face. I wanted to make sure I was looking the best for our special night together. I finished by taking a cold shower to close all my pores. The cold shower was also the best way to feel instantly alive. I put my robe on and headed back to my room to get ready for Renata's arrival.

Chapter 4

At 9 PM, I descended into the lobby. I decided to dress in black for the evening. I was wearing one of my finest black shirts from Facconable and matching pants. The belt was from Hermes; with a silver buckle and in black leather. The belt alone cost me over $600. To add a relaxing touch to my look, I slipped into shiny, black, double-sided buckled wingtips by Ferragamo. I left my shirt open around the chest area for a more casual appearance. The last detail was a black Hugo Boss blazer. I was going all out, ready for Renata, ready for the new possibilities and dressed to impress.

When exiting the lobby, I immediately noticed Renata's convertible Mini Cooper. As soon as she saw me, she waived. I simply gave her a big smile and approached her car. In my usual fashion, I jumped in and immediately gave her two soft kisses on each cheek but this time, a little closer to her lips. I took a quick glance at her, noting how stunning she looked in a sexy yellow cocktail dress. Yellow complemented perfectly with her dark brown skin, which looked even more exquisite since Renata applied bronze shimmer all over her legs and arms. She literally sparkled. Her face appeared absolutely radiant and flawless. She was sun kissed and glowing.

"Wow, Renatinha, you look amazing." I exclaimed admiringly. "I love your dress, and your skin looks radiant. Did you skip out on work today and went to the lake shore?"

"Thank you, Sebastian." Renata smiled. "I actually did go to work. But right after, I went to catch some sun."

"No wonder, you are glowing. You didn't do all this to impress me, did you?" I asked flirtatiously.

"Of course, not." Renata rolled her eyes. "I am a traditional girly girl who always gets dressed up no matter the occasion. What about you, Sebastian? You have the "men in black" look tonight. I must say you look very handsome. I love your belt."

"Thank you, Renatinha." I replied feeling completely happy.

We left the hotel, heading to Santos. It was only a 15-minute drive to the night club. As soon as we arrived, Renata valeted her car and approached the door man who controlled the velvet ropes. She said we had a reservation but since we arrived earlier, she asked if we could sit by the bar until our table was ready. The gentleman was kind enough to open the velvet ropes and allow us inside. As we walked in, I saw a huge bar sprawling along several walls of the restaurant. We followed the host through the sitting area until we reached our place by the bar. Since it was Friday, it was rather busy, and the bartenders were working franticly. I quickly got the attention of one of the two bartenders and ordered our first round. I started off with a Grey Goose vodka tonic and Renata asked for a cosmopolitan martini. As was my habit in Miami, I also asked the bartender for two shots of Jägermeister. I loved to start my outings with Jäger, no reason why. I just did. It gave me extra energy and a nice start for a hopefully fun night ahead.

I looked at Renata and gave her a frozen shot glass.

"Cheers to a great night!" I toasted.

"Cheers!" She echoed me.

It only took a few seconds and the glasses were empty. For the next half an hour, we sipped our drinks and talked about our past and the things we had in common. We both loved to travel and live each day as if it were our last. She liked working out and sports in general. The conversation was very natural and we both felt comfortable. In fact, we were so engulfed in our talk, the noise of the place and its commotion seemed to disappear. For the time, we were completely alone, just talking and sharing our life's' experiences. Our return to reality happened only when the bartender gently interrupted us by informing our table was ready.

By 10 PM, the place was getting packed. As we walked to our table, I noticed that the restaurant was filled with young Latin beauties. It almost felt like I was attending a Miss Latin America contest. Normally, that would be a distraction for me but since Renata was so beautiful, the other women paled in comparison. She was by far, the most exotic and attractive woman in the nightclub.

I walked around the table and pulled her seat back and waited for her to sit down. After I took my place across from her, we resumed our interesting conversation. We talked and laughed, and the chemistry between us was unmistakable. I always believed, one of the secrets to a woman's heart was through laughter.

"Do you like Toronto, Sebastian?" Renata asked.

"I believe, I've mentioned before that I lived in Toronto in my childhood, from the age of 6 to 10. I loved Toronto then, I love it even more now." I looked intently at Renata.

"What do you like about the city?" She inquired holding my gaze.

"I was fanatical about hockey. By the time I was 10 years old, I was playing simultaneously on two teams and traveled around the country as a member of an all-star team. I really believe if I had stayed here, I would have become a professional hockey player."

"That is so exciting!" Renata exclaimed. "I bet a part of you wonders if that dream would have come true if you and your family had decided to stay here."

"Yes, absolutely. That always crosses my mind." I noted dreamily.

"Renata, tomorrow is Saturday, and my day is open, no plans for now." I instantly changed the topic. "I was thinking about doing two things. First, visit my old house in York Mills; where I lived for almost 4 years. And secondly, I would like to visit, for my second time, Niagra Falls. To make the trip even more exciting, I plan to rent a motorcycle. Would you like to join me tomorrow?" I asked hopefully.

"Oh my God, I am scared of motorcycles but the thought of cruising to the Niagara Falls sounds very exciting." Renata beamed. "Okay, Sebastian, you're on. Sounds like an adventure."

"Yes, this way we can visit my past together and you can get to know me even better. I think it will be lots of fun." I was absolutely thrilled.

The food arrived and it looked amazing. Toronto was famous for its seafood and lobsters since it was relatively close to the northeastern coast. I ordered a 4-pound lobster which came with a huge tail and claws. As soon as it was served, I asked the waiter to take it back to the kitchen and remove the shell. Since that was our first date, I did not want to make a mess. Renata ordered a petite filet mignon. She liked it medium rare just like me. We continued our conversation for the next hour and enjoyed the food. I felt great because no matter how the evening ended, she'd already committed for a second date. Everything was going according to plan.

By midnight, after a delicious dinner, hours-long conversations and energy-boosting shots of espresso, we were ready to check out the night club section. The club was roped off and it was located to the left side of the bar near the back of the restaurant. A large crowd was forming to get inside. I walked up to the VIP security guy and requested the best table with a bottle of Veuve Clicquot. He smiled at me and during our hand-shake, I passed a hundred- dollar bill to expedite the process. I knew my way around the clubs, and I wanted to treat Renata like a princess. We were instantly let through the velvet ropes and the VIP waitress took us to the table in front of the stage. She mentioned our bottle of champagne would be arriving shortly.

At our table, I took off my blazer and set it aside on the lounge and started immersing into the vibe of the music. We were among the first several couples inside the club and, besides that, I knew the night clubs would start getting fun and pumping somewhere around 2 AM. Since the music was loud, our conversation was reduced, and we focused more on small talk and body language communication. I was an expert at analyz-ing body language, especially that of females. I could easily tell if the woman was interested or not.

In our case, Renata had a constant glowing smile and as we moved to the rhythm of the music, I could see her playing with her long and silky dark hair. It was always a good signal to me when a woman played with her hair. It was a sign of a flirtatious attempt to have my attention focused exclusively on her. That was working, and I was zeroed in on her. I hoped and wished that night we would become more than just friends.

Since the dance floor was empty and one of my favorite songs from Enrique Iglesias, "Bailamos" just started to play, I quickly grabbed Renata's hand and took her to the dance floor.

"Baila conmigo, Renatinha?" I invited her repeating the words of the song.

"Claro que sim." She joined in.

The night has officially started, and I knew how to dance well so I did my best to impress. I wanted to get close but not too close. My hands were touching her body forcefully. I was not shy, especially in the clubs, and I took advantage of the fact that we were the only ones on the dance floor. Both men and women watched us dancing to the beats of flamenco.

I learned that beautiful dance while living in Spain for a few months learning the language and the culture. Apparently, I was not the only one who liked flamenco. During the dance, I would let go of Renata fantasizing she was a bull that I wanted to strike down and take control of. As she moved passed me, I would scream out "Ole!" We had a great time; all smiles and laughter.

I was proud of myself. I was proud of how I set up the night, how everything was coming along. I felt like an architect, overseeing a construction of the beautiful cathedral, whose results were exceeding, even his own expectations. We danced for hours and when the last song ended, I gave Renata another kiss on the cheek, this time inching even closer to her luscious lips. We finally decided to take a short break.

By the time we returned to our table, the dance floor was getting filled with people, and the Latin music continued to pump out loudly. Our waitress has already placed the champagne bottle in the ice bucket standing proudly on top of our table. I waved to Renata, inviting her to sit near me and not across. I wanted to make sure she was close to me. At that point, my hands were in constant physical contact with hers. I paid attention to not do anything she would be opposed to, but so far, she was submitting to me.

I reached towards the ice bucket, grabbed the bottle, and twisted the muselet exactly six times counter-clockwise and the wire cage came off the cork. Then I squeezed the cork, and it almost popped out immediately. The champagne overflowed and gently splashed by Renata's shoes. She was beaming with energy and excitement.

"Sebastian, don't waste the champagne." She giggled.

"Don't worry; we can always buy another one." I winked at her.

"You're crazy, Sebastian."

"Yes, crazy for you." I whispered while looking intently at Renata.

Suddenly, Renata moved closer and gave me a kiss… on a cheek. Before I could think of wishing she kissed my lips, she said, "I am going to the bathroom to freshen up. I will be right back, don't go anywhere." And off she went, while I stared desirously at her gorgeous body flowing across the club.

I took that time to reflect. I could not believe I was so far from home; in another country and in a nightclub, I had never been to before. I was with the most beautiful woman in the club, hell... in the entire city of Toronto. I desired her so badly, as bad as I wanted her older sister only a short time ago. Of course, until I met Renata and shifted my attention to her. The challenge I created for myself could be possibly resolved very soon. That didn't look so difficult anymore. But I caught myself realizing that bedding her was not what I really wanted, I started liking Renata, really liking her. She was charming, elegant, sexy and smart. I made her laugh and she made me laugh. At the end of the day, happiness was what it was all about. And I felt happy with Renata by my side.

"I'm back." I heard her voice amid my thoughts. "Did you miss me?"

"Immensely." I replied honestly.

"So, let's make a toast to our first date?" I murmured in her ear. "Do you now agree this is our first date?"

"Sebastian, you are too much." Renata rolled her eyes. "But, to be honest, I am having a lot of fun with you, so why not? Let's call it our first date." She said looking straight into my eyes. I loved how fearless and open she was. An Amazon…

We picked up the champagne flutes, toasted and took our first cold sips of the bubbly. Its chilled taste was a bit dry and not too sweet. It was just perfect; just like our evening. After enjoying the champagne, we decided to remain seated at our table and just listen to the music. The club was full to capacity. It got pretty crowded. The music switched from Latin Pop to Salsa. I was excited. I loved Salsa.

It was past 2 AM, and I decided to show Renata how it was really done Salsa-style. I looked at her, and it seemed she was thinking the same thing. After cool champagne and some rest, we were ready to go. I grabbed Renata's hand and gestured towards the dance floor with my head.

"Let's go!" I said.

She nodded and we elbowed our way through the crowd. They started playing the song called Azucar Negra, Black Sugar, by the infamous Cuban singer Celia Cruz. It was very popular in Miami and was being played in all the best Latin clubs. I began moving to the rhythm of the music while wrapping my right arm around Renata's waist; pulling her close to me. With my left arm, I guided her around the floor. We did spins and drops. I was even able to do a few lifts in the air. It appeared we were dancing so well, the people around us moved to the sides letting us take over the dance floor. They started clapping and cheering. I led, and Renata perfectly followed along. She had a natural Brazilian rhythm and definitely knew how to dance. I moved with flare and confidence. Our dance was so intense and in-rhythm, we were so into it, so passionate about it, that I felt the sweat on my forehead, and I even noticed Renata's back started gleaming. I found it incredible hot and sexy. When the song ended, I leaned her down, almost touching the floor, and raised her back up mid-way. We froze basking in the crowd's applauses. I looked at Renata and I knew my moment had come. I slowly gave her a kiss, first on the left cheek and then on her right cheek and then, with passion, I finally mastered enough bravery to move closer to her succulent rose-colored lips and passionately cover them with mine.

It seemed the world stopped at that moment. We were locked in our kiss, in the same position I had her at the end of the song, half-bent on my arm. After several seconds, I lifted Renata with fervent intensity and gave her another kiss before she could even recover from the first one.

When I released her, she took a deep breath and uttered, "Ai meu, Deus (oh my, God)!"

We returned to our table hand-in-hand and sat down. I poured another glass of champagne, and we let the drinks cool us down. We still didn't catch our collective breaths. Thus, we decided to rest and watch others dance.

"Renatinha, do you want to get out of here?" I whispered in her ear.

"Why? Where are we going?" She asked with a flirty smile.

"We have a long and adventurous day ahead of us tomorrow, and I want to make sure you get your beauty rest." I noted authoritatively.

"So, you want to leave?" Renata sounded disappointed.

"Yes, we still have to drive back, I don't want to risk it since we both have been drinking. I promise, you will enjoy tomorrow even more than our time here today."

"You are raising the bar, Sebastian." She said while staring straight into my eyes. "I like that." She got up demonstrating her readiness to follow my advice.

Once we got into Renata's car, we lowered the top, and drove back to my hotel. I was happy with the wind blowing in my face as I was silently relaxing and reflecting on our great night together. I knew I was in control of the situation, the wild lioness was semi-tamed, and if I wanted to, I could go further and invite her up to my room. I quickly considered the opportunity, but I didn't want to rush, I didn't want to do what most other men would. Actually, I wanted for her to lust for me. I've already realized, I did not want for this to be a one-night stand. Instead, I didn't mind developing our rising affection into a summer romance when we both enjoyed being in each other's presence but for only for a few months. After my work project finished, I would have to head back to Miami, then we would determine our future. I was open to anything.

When we arrived at the hotel, I turned to Renata.

"Thank you for an incredible evening." I whispered to her. "I enjoyed your company very much."

"Thank you, Sebastian." She murmured in reply.

"Can I get a "good night" kiss?" I inquired in a hushed tone.

"Sebastian, you know you don't have to ask." She echoed.

I leaned over, grabbed the back of her neck and pulled her close to me. Our lips locked passionately. The kiss continued for quite some time, one of my hands touched her thigh and things started to get hot. I forcefully willed myself to stop and took a deep breath.

"Renata, I have to go before this goes any further." I breathed out fighting my powerful desire to take her right there. "We need to get up in a few hours, I think it's best I leave."

Renata's smiling face was radiant. I could see that she was ready for me and I wanted to be with her. I wanted for her to wait until her instinctual, almost primal cravings would get the best of her, and she would not be able to resist any further. I gave her a few more kisses and said I would call once I woke up. I headed upstairs to my room, and before I knew it, I passed out.

Chapter 5

I was awakened at 9 AM, by the loudly annoying sounds of the alarm I set the night before. I thought five hours of good sleep would be sufficient. As soon as I opened my eyes, I reached over to the nightstand and picked up my cell phone. I wanted to be Renata's personal wake up call. The phone rang three times, and then I heard her sleepy voice.

"Good morning, my dear. This is your official wake up call." I said playfully.

I heard her yawn, then she cleared her throat. "Good morning Sebastian. What time is it?"

"It is 9 am, and it's time for round two." I continued in the same manner.

"Oh my god, are you crazy waking me up this early on a Saturday?" She pretended to complain.

"I'm going to get ready and then, I will go to the local dealer to rent a motorcycle." I said. "That will give you enough time to take a shower, get ready, and have breakfast. Take your time. I should be at your place around 11 AM. I will call you once again so that you can meet me downstairs." My voice suffered no objections.

"Okay, Sebastian, that should give me enough time." She still sounded sleepy. "But let's keep off the drinks today. I woke up with a headache." Renata moaned.

"Take a few painkillers and leave the rest up to me. Riding the motorcycle will make you forget of any pains you might have. You will love it." I assured her.

"Sounds good. I will wait for your call."

That morning, rather than performing my regular routine of running and then calisthenics, I decided to just do 200 pushups and 200 sit ups. That was enough to get my blood pumping, and I would still have enough time to eat and rent the motorcycle.

As soon as I finished my short workout, I took a shower, and got dressed in blue jeans, a white t-shirt, and a black leather motorcycle jacket I always traveled with. I headed down to the lobby and asked the concierge where I could rent an Italian motorcycle. I wanted either a Ducati, MV Agusta, or an Aprila. He told me that Toronto only had a Ducati dealership, and it rented the motorcycles by the day. He gave me their address, and I was on my way. The place was about 20 minutes away. Thus, I got into my rental car and entered the address in the GPS.

I arrived at the dealership and felt like I got to heaven. Back in Miami, I owned 3 motorcycles in the past. All three were Italian naked bikes. They were called naked because they had nothing covering the engine and their frames were exposed. Their seating positions were also more upright like that of a bicycle stance, which increased the comfort.

I knew my way around the dealership, and I wanted to look for the perfect bike for the upcoming ride. A salesman greeted me by saying, "Hello my friend. My name is Doug. Are you looking to buy a new bike?"

I said, "no, I am looking to rent a bike for today."

"I suggest, you rent for only half a day since it is almost 11 AM." Doug proposed. "Today is Saturday so we close at 8 PM. What kind of a bike are you looking for?"

"I want a Ducati Monster 1200R red with white stripping." I replied while looking around.

"Well, we do have a Monster 1200R, but only in black with red stripping." He replied searching for the bike with his eyes.

"That will be fine." I nodded.

"With insurance and half a day use, the cost is $550." Doug stated.

"That works for me. Can we expedite the paperwork and anything else needed, so I can get out of here in the next 20 minutes?" I asked impatiently.

"Yes, sir. Just give me your driver's license, insurance and the credit card." Within exactly 20 minutes I left the dealership.

The bike was amazing. I accelerated hard; feeling all of its 150-horsepower pulling back off the handlebars. I smiled; I knew today would be a fun day. Ducati's have always been known for their immediate power and sound. The V-twin engine had plenty of torque and no one could mistake the deep loud growl of a Ducati Monster. Any tiredness I might have felt from last night's partying was immediately washed away by the intense rush of adrenaline. I pulled into the street and before riding, I sent a text to Renata informing her I was on my way and should be there at 11:30 AM. She quickly responded, she would be ready and waiting downstairs.

I arrived at her condo and took off the black helmet; matching the bike and my leather jacket. I saw her waiting for me by the lobby. She was stunning as always.

"How's my angel doing?" I asked flirtatiously. My voice sounded like we spent the whole last night making passionate love to each other. "Did you get enough rest?"

"No, not really, I feel pretty tired." She responded grudgingly while hiding half of her face behind huge sunglasses.

"Well, you look great." I decided to encourage her. She indeed looked amazing. She was wearing tight red designer jeans with lace ups in the front and a small black shirt showing off her midsection. Her hair was pulled back in a ponytail. I reached for the second helmet and gently placed it on her head. I then fixed the two straps in the locked position. Since she was petite, the helmet looked rather large on her head, but she still looked cute. I gave her a kiss and she got on, behind me.

"Sebastian, where do I hold on?" She asked anxiously. It was obvious riding a motorcycle wasn't something she was used to.

"Well, you can either hold on below the seat or place your arms around me. Whichever you feel more comfortable with."

She shrugged, and then went ahead to place her arms around my waist.

"Hold tight." I screamed while turning the bike on.

We were off with the same thrust and acceleration I used when riding out of the dealership. Renata let out a big yell.

"Wow!!! Oh my God, Sebastian, the rush is amazing." That was the Renata I expected, fearless and adventurous. "I like it when you go fast. Keep going." She yelled in my ear.

She was a thrill seeker, just like me. I loved the adrenaline rush sports such as skydiving, bungee jumping, and hand gliding. I've done all of those before, but my true passion was driving sports cars or motorcycles.

We would have to ride for about an hour and half to reach Niagara Falls. I planned to arrive and check out the falls and then have lunch somewhere we could still see the massive power of the water falling over the cliffs. At the end of the day, we would head back to Toronto and visit my old neighborhood in York Mills.

The next 90 minutes were purely magical. The roads were mostly straight with a few curves here and there. Whenever I did encounter the curves, I powered through, and Renata held me even tighter. Riding a bike always created a more intimate environment. In order for her to feel safe, she would have to hold on to me with all her might. Also, right under her, was this awesome, powerful Italian engine that would hopefully make her feel excited. Its vibration should've been a source of pleasure for her. At least that was my fantasy. I could not see her, since she was behind me, but I could hear the sound of her voice which consisted of pure excitement. We did not talk too much; it would be difficult with the helmets on, but whenever we did stop at a light, I would turn to the right, hold on to her leg, and open my visor to speak.

The conversations were brief, usually just a statement or two on how we both felt at the present moment. Once we were getting close to Niagra Falls, there was a high overpass ahead of us. I accelerated to about 90 miles per hour on the way up. As soon as we reached the top, I let go of the throttle and just cruised down. As the engine's noise died down, the silence became more prevalent. As we were gliding down, we saw Niagra Falls for the first time. It was a splendid sight. We were able to observe the power of nature at its finest. The mist was all around us, and we could smell the water as we approached the Falls.

I decided to drive around the streets surrounding the Falls in order to see all its glorious angles. We also looked for a place to have lunch. It was 1 PM in the afternoon, and we were hungry. After a few laps, we found a wonderful restaurant on a cliff facing the main waterfall. I assumed the restaurant was the place most tourists stopped to eat at. Since we were in the beginning of the summer, there were lots of people walking the streets and enjoying the outdoor restaurants. We entered the place and asked for a table outside. The hostess informed us the wait was approximately one hour. Even though we were really hungry, we had no other choice and decided to walk around and take pictures while waiting. We took several pictures individually, together, and a few selfies. Normally, I wasn't too interested in taking pictures, but then, I thought taking pictures of that particular day would be important since it was something that I would not want to forget.

By 2 PM in the afternoon, our stomachs were growling. We headed back to the restaurant and asked the hostess about our table. We were starving. She informed us that we were next.

"Perfect timing!" Renata exclaimed excitedly.

We were seated at the outside patio and the view was spectacular. We could hear the sound of the water falling. The powerful impact of the waterfall created a mist all around the venue, which made it look magical. It wasn't a high-end restaurant, so we decided to be simple and order two sandwiches. I picked a crab cake sandwich, and she had a tuna salad croissant sandwich.

"Renatinha, did you enjoy last night with me?" I asked after taking several bites of the sandwich and calming my stomach.

"Oh my God, yes, Sebastian. It was an amazing night. I haven't had that much fun in a long time. I don't think I've ever danced so much. My legs are still sore." She replied with a smile.

"I feel the same way. When I am away from home, working, I never get to go out dancing. But last night was special. The way you danced with me; following each and every move and ending it with an amazing kiss. Your kiss took my breath away." I murmured while gazing into Renata's eyes.

I reached over the table and gave her another kiss. She didn't object.

"I must say, Sebastian, you are a charmer." She noted. "It seems, you always know all the right things to say at the right time. Not only are you a natural at dancing but also an amazing kisser. Can I have another kiss?" I was thrilled. The fortress has officially fallen.

I paid the bill and we walked out holding hands. We left the bike parked by the restaurant and decided to walk to the edge of the waterfall and take some more pictures. We became so playful with each other like two children. As we walked towards the Falls, we often stopped for passionate kisses. We had a great time with silly happy smiles planted across our faces. After about 20 minutes, we decided to venture down the Falls. There was a path which took us very close to the falling water. We knew that without protective raincoats we would get completely wet, but we did not care. We enjoyed the moment and wanted to experience our time together in the best way possible. It took about half an hour to walk down where the path led to a bridge. The bridge was surrounded by visitors in yellow raincoats. We weren't concerned about getting wet, we knew we would dry up quickly on the way home.

Renata and I took a few more pictures and put the camera away in my motorcycle jacket. After reaching the furthest point of the bridge, we noted how strong the impact of the falling water was. We heard it falling hard down below and we were surrounded by its cool mist. The moment we were experiencing seemed surreal. I could have not planned that any better. It definitely exceeded my expectations, and I was sure she felt the same.

After many passionate kisses, we decide to start heading back up the trail towards the restaurant. Once we arrived, it was almost 4 PM. Even though we would love to stay longer by the Falls, we still had several stops to make. I was especially looking forward to visiting my early childhood neighborhood before returning the bike by 8 in the evening.

We mounted the bike, strapped our helmets on, and headed back to Toronto. Once again, we encountered the same overpass but that time, I did something different; more exciting. I accelerated up the overpass, just like I did before, but as we started our decent, I let go of the throttle and told Renata to trust me. I let the motorcycle cruise down the overpass by slowly letting go of the handlebars. I stretched out my arms backwards and a few seconds later Renata let go of my waist and then grabbed my arms. We were gliding down the overpass without holding onto anything at all. We remained in this position for about ten seconds. A few cars passed by, and the people in them stared at us. They probably thought we were crazy.

I was always a bit of a daredevil and things like that seemed natural to me. It felt great knowing I had her full confidence. I grabbed the bike and pulled the throttle forcefully. Our remaining ride was incredible. We relied on communication by touch. We felt synchronized, and I was looking forward to sharing my childhood memories with her.

After about an hour or so, we arrived at York Mills. It was a quiet residential neighborhood. The houses were simple and affordable. I recalled it having lots of trees. There was also a local park, where I used to ride my bike down the creek enjoying getting lost in nature.

My old address was two twenty-five Banbury Street. I didn't remember how to get there. I was too young when we lived at that address. But I looked it up in the morning and knew exactly where to go. We pulled up to the house, turned off the bike, and took off our helmets.

"Is that it?" Renata asked while stretching her gorgeous body.

"Yep, this is the house I lived in from 6 to 10 years old. I must say, it looks exactly how I remembered it. It had the address posted above the garage in cursive writing, and the tulips I helped plant with my mom were still there. It felt as if the time didn't pass at all. I stood and stared at the house imagining how the new families filled it with the new sounds, smells and memories. Renata remained close by, but she didn't speak. She understood I needed some quiet time. After taking a few pictures, I decided it was time to go. There was a car parked outside, and I didn't want to make the residents of the house feel uncomfortable.

We slowly cruised down the street and saw another house where both my brother's and my friends lived. They loved playing street hockey.

"Hockey was our sport." I suddenly said, even though Renata and

I were silent. "It was the sport I believed I could go professional with." I continued while Renata just listened to me.

We turned around and made a left turn on York Mills road. We cruised for about 5 minutes and suddenly, I hit the brakes. I saw my old hockey rink. It was called York Mills Arena. I used to come here every day after school to practice. At the end of each training, my mother would pick me up and give me a Mars chocolate bar. I shared my memories with Renata.

"That's amazing, Sebastian." She said. "You still remember those days with your mom, and you were so young."

"Yes." I nodded. "Those days are unforgettable."

We were pressed for time; thus, we didn't go into the rink. We took some more pictures and then headed back to the Ducati dealership.

The sunset was slowly setting in; by the time we arrived at the dealership it was 7:45 PM, and we were tired, excited and filled with the incredible memories from our adventure. I turned in the bike, and we finalized the paperwork. We got inside my rental car and drove towards the city center.

"Renatinha, are you starting to get hungry?" I asked.

"All the excitement has definitely sparked my appetite." She replied.

"How about we go back to the W hotel, where I am staying, and have some dinner? Perhaps a few glasses of wine too; in celebration of a great day." I suggested excitedly.

"That sounds like a good way to end the night." Renata noted.

"Great, there is this highly rated sushi restaurant, and I would love to take you there. Do you like sushi?"

"Yes, I love sushi." Renata answered with a huge smile.

We arrived at the hotel at around 9 PM. By now, all the people working there knew me well. Therefore, they attended to us like we were royalty. From the valet opening the doors of the car to the two doormen welcoming us back. As always, W's attention to the clients and patrons was at its best. Plus, I was always a good tipper. We walked directly to the sushi restaurant, and I asked for a table for two. It was not busy, so they immediately led us to the corner booth. We sat right next to each other; our hips almost touching.

"Do you like raw fish?" I asked Renata.

"You mean sashimi?"

I nodded without replying.

"Yes. Salmon sashimi is one of my favorites." She said.

"Then, let's get a boat." I suggested. "We can order salmon, tuna, and white fish for the sashimi and then two rolls. I usually start with a tuna tataki as an appetizer. We can start with that if you don't mind?"

"You are a sushi expert. That all sounds great and I can't wait to eat. I am starving." Renata was impatient. I loved how open she was. I loved her raw character.

"So, tell me, are you feeling better than in the morning?" I asked knowing the answer.

"Yes, it's amazing." Renata exclaimed. "As soon as I hopped on the bike and we started cruising, I completely forgot how sick I was feeling when I woke up this morning."

"Yes!" I nodded. "That's because of the adrenaline."

"I think so. I was so scared and at the same time, excited about the experience. I completely forgot how I initially felt."

The waiter brought a bottle of a fine California cabernet wine called Rodney Strong. He poured the glass for me to taste and as usual, it was velvety smooth with notes of wild berries and a hint of vanilla. We toasted to an incredible weekend and to more exciting times ahead. I moved closer to Renata and began kissing her passionately. We got so caught up in the moment, we completely forgot where we were. We didn't care if people were staring at us. I wanted to be with her, and my intentions were clear. She did not hold back. She started rubbing my leg with her foot. Our emotions were raw, and the feeling was intensely mutual.

As soon as the tuna tataki arrived, we grabbed our chop sticks and began devouring our appetizer. I wanted to have some fun, so I started feeding Renata. Sometimes the food would hit her lips but not get in her mouth immediately. Our fooling around was exciting, I wanted to tease her. I continued to feed Renata when the rolls were brought in, but they were so big, she struggled to open her mouth so wide.

"I know you can take it." I teased her. "Open your mouth wide. Now swallow it. In order to get a full taste of a roll, you have to eat it whole. It's an insult to Japanese culture to eat sushi in pieces.

Even though she was petite, she managed to swallow each piece like a champ.

After dinner and a few glasses of wine, we decide to skip dessert and headed up to my room. I grabbed her by the hand, and we walked through the lobby towards the elevator bay. I always preferred to stay on high floors in hotels, so we went up to the 44th floor, where my room was located.

As soon as we walked in, I threw Renata on the bed. I then took off my shirt and slowly approached her. I've spent days thinking about that moment, and I knew the time had come. As we kissed, I started to caress her hair. Her long, silky hair was beautiful. For the next few minutes, we danced in bed. I slowly took off her shirt and removed her pants. She had matching black lace bra and panties. I lusted to be with her. I could not resist her, I wanted all of her for myself. I moved Renata on top of me as I continued kissing her passionately. My tongue intertwined with hers; our tongues were dancing with each other. With one flick of my fingers; I took off her bra. I pulled her closer so her nipples could be in my mouth. I teased her more by slightly biting the tip.

"Sebastian, you are driving me crazy." She breathed out loud.

Once I heard that, I turned her over to her back. I kissed Renata some more before reaching down and grabbing the sides of her panties. I then forcefully ripped and pulled them off. She was now completely naked. I stood up admiring her beauty. The light was still on. I never liked having sex in the dark. I wanted to see what I was doing. I wanted to see her face in full ecstasy.

"Oh my God, Sebastian. You ruined my panties." Renata whispered deliriously.

"Don't worry. I will buy you another pair." I replied in a low voice.

I couldn't care less about the panties or anything else in the world for that matter.

I took off my jeans and boxer shorts. I slipped back into the bed with her. I intended to make our first night together the one she would never forget. I let my hands do the talking. With my left hand, I grabbed her left breast and my right hand touched her pleasure zone. She was completely wet. I could feel her desire for me. I rubbed her intensely until her breathing got faster and louder. I wanted to bring her close to an orgasm. When I knew she was almost there, I backed off.

"What are you doing? Why are you stopping?" She moaned panicky.

"Relax; we have all night ahead." I whispered. "Trust me like you trusted me on the motorcycle today."

"Okay, Sebastian."

We couldn't keep off of each other. After a long day of riding and sightseeing, we should've been tired, but we weren't. After kissing her endlessly on the lips, I wanted to explore all of her. I started moving down, from her lips to her neck, tracing her skin with my tongue. First, her breasts and then, working my way down to her stomach. I always thought, a woman's stomach, was one of the sexiest parts of her body. After making her laugh, because of the sensitivity around that area, I buried my head between her legs. She moaned loudly. As I fondled her with my tongue, she once again started approaching orgasm, and I continued for a few more minutes and then stopped abruptly.

"Oh my God, Sebastian. You are killing me." She could not handle being teased anymore, she had to have a resolution. She grabbed me by the head and pulled me up to her face.

"You are driving me crazy. Fuck me, Sebastian." She whispered.

Those were the words I was waiting for. She was ready. I was ready. I turned her over on her knees. I got behind her and inserted my manhood. I felt like we were riding the bike again but this time we were riding each other. I grabbed her long black hair and pulled it backwards. I thrusted forcefully riding her wildly. After some time in that position, she wanted to be in control. She moved in perfect rhythm and rode me like a horse. When she wasn't moaning; she was smiling. I gave her a few taps on her bum. Just like we did it on the dance floor, we kept with our rhythm and pace. With each upcoming moment, we were getting closer to the point of ecstasy.

I turned her over once again, this time to the missionary position. I was on top of her and was ready to finish. We were making love for what felt like half an hour and we were both ready for the final moment. My pelvis was hitting against hers. I was deep inside of her. The motion got faster and after a few minutes, she started to moan heavily while breathing sporadically. She sounded as if she just finished a 5-minute sprint. Her sweaty body was shaking forcefully. Even though, my hair was rather short, she pulled on it. Her eyes rolled upwards. When I saw that, I knew it was time for my release. I moved downward and hugged her tightly continuing feeling her legs tremble.

After it was all over, we lied next to each other unable to move or speak. We were both starring at the ceiling in amazement. I could not believe how great the last two days were and how much fun we had with the culmination of tonight's euphoric sex. My business trip to Toronto turned into much more than I expected. I was blessed with a great job, which involved traveling, meeting new people and promised remarkably exciting adventures. After some time of immobility, I was ready to get up. I went straight to the shower.

What seemed impossible became possible. The "sex with Renata" challenge was solved, but I started feeling that it turned into more than that. I was starting to really like her. I honestly felt she could eventually become my girlfriend. The only problem was the distance between us. Perhaps, she could come with me to India for a month. I was excited to be with her and wanted to share more experiences together. I finished taking the shower and returned to the bedroom. I was naked except for a towel wrapped around my waist.

"Wow, Sebastian. You really must be working out a lot. You are in amazing shape." Renata murmured admiringly.

"You know how Miami is. Everyone works out like crazy. It's almost a standard for everyone to look their best." I replied.

"So, Sebastian, I have a question for you."

After hearing her mention a question, my antennas quickly turned on, and I prepared for some sort of curve ball.

"Back in the day, when you met my sister, did you sleep with her?" Renata asked point blank.

"Sleep with your sister?" I played stupid.

"Yes. Did you?" She insisted.

"No, of course not." I lied. "We were just friends. She knew my friends and I knew hers."

Renata smiled. "Come on, Sebastian, you can tell me the truth."

"I already told you, I did not sleep with your sister." I was a bad liar, and I was sure she could tell by the look on my face.

"I will keep asking you because I believe there was something there. At least in the past." Renata waived her finger.

I laughed and then told her that we only had one night together, kissing. Thankfully, we decided to leave the conversation there. She got dressed and gave me her ripped panties. "You owe me a pair."

I gave her a kiss and she left.

Chapter 6

I woke up the next morning feeling invigorated. It was Sunday. I went through my normal routine of working out, eating breakfast, and getting a mid-morning massage. When I came back to the room, I checked my cell phone and noticed, I had a missed call. I thought it was Renata, but actually it was my friend Laura, from Miami. She was a girl I've met through my circle of friends. Mostly, the friends who liked going out clubbing in South Beach. She was a beautiful, tall brunette and quite young. She was 24 years old and originally from Brazil. Laura had a large group of Brazilian girlfriends. They were my friends as well. We had a lot of fun together. The girls knew the owners of the best clubs and got tables and bottles for free just for being attractive.

I dialed my voicemail and heard, "querido, Seba, how are you? This is Laura and it's been some time since we've seen each other. I remember the last time we met, you mentioned about the so called "party of the year" which was happing next weekend. My girlfriend and I would love to go with you. I believe you said it was this Saturday. Can you please call me so we can make plans to go together?"

The last couple of times I ran into Laura, I spoke about the so called "best party of the year." I did not know she was interested, but I explained, that wasn't a regular party. The party was organized and hosted by a very well-known plastic surgeon in Miami who liked to have galas where drugs were in abundance. It was mostly for swingers and single, young women. I decided I would call Laura back and give her more details to make sure she was still willing to go given the circumstance.

I dialed Laura's number, the phone rang a couple of times and then, she answered.

"Hello Laurinha, this is Seba returning your call. Sorry I missed you, but I was finishing my morning workout." I said.

"Hi Seba, how are you?" Laura sounded excited to hear me. "I am doing great. Are you in Miami?"

"No, I am in Toronto, working on a project for a couple of months."

"Oh." She appeared confused. "Are you going to be in Miami this weekend? I am dying to go to this party, and I wanted to know if I could come with you and bring my friend Ana?"

"Yes, Laura, I will be flying in on Thursday night. But you remember what I told you about that party?"

"Yes." She uttered with excitement in her voice.

"It's a swingers' party, mostly couples and single girls. It can get really crazy. I'm worried you won't feel comfortable in that type of surroundings…" I cautiously suggested.

"I already spoke to my friend Ana, who is beautiful, and I told her it was a wild party." Laura assured me.

"So, you are down?" I wasn't going to play Laura's parent. I warned her; I told her the truth. The rest was up to her.

"Yes, we both are."

"What about drugs, have you tried ecstasy?" I proceeded.

"No, I haven't. But I have many friends who have, and they said the experience was amazing." She giggled.

"Okay, so let's meet at my apartment next Saturday; you and Ana. You have to wear a costume. So please, wear something very exciting and sexy. Come early, around 9 PM. We can have a drink, and I will explain more about taking ecstasy." I instructed.

"Do you still live at the Four Seasons, in Brickell?" Laura inquired.

"Yes, I still do. Get ready girl, you are going to have the best time of your life. See you next week."

"Take care Seba. Bye."

Just talking about the party to Laura got my heart racing. It was held once a year, and it was ultra-exclusive, because it was attended by the prominent businessmen, doctors, attorneys, and the entrepreneurs. The invitation had to be received directly from the owner of the house.

He would then provide me with a random number. I replied by confirming I was attending with two women. Upon arrival at the velvet ropes, at the doctor's house, I would only provide my number and last name.

The drugs were abundant at the party; mostly cocaine and ecstasy. I tried cocaine a couple of times but noticed, I was allergic. At the time, I was experimenting with ecstasy. The first time I tried it, was on a trip to Ibiza, Spain. It was one of the most amazing drugs, because it made me feel extremely euphoric, carefree and full of confidence. The drug made anyone be what they wanted to be. That freedom made it possible to pick up the most beautiful women in the club. It felt like the brain was running at its optimal mode. Until ecstasy, I've never felt so alive, in the moment, confident, and extremely content.

I was told that back in the 1950s-60s, it was an experimental drug for the introverted psychiatric patients suffering from depression. They would take the pill and show tremendous signs of improvement. With ecstasy, I could walk up and convince any woman to be with me that night. It, kind of, made me feel super- human. My connectedness with music, especially dance music, was incredible. I felt like an instrument, like a vessel for the sound. My awareness levels increased dramatically. I could feel like I sensed everyone around me. I wanted to touch those who were the closest to me. I became very touchy feely and full of love. Have I also mentioned it dramatically increased my sexual libido? I was excited for the party and the night with Laura and Ana. The rest of the afternoon, as hard as it was to focus, I worked on my deliverables for the week ahead.

The next day, at work, I took the elevator up to the 3rd floor and said hello to Amy, the receptionist, and continued on to the war room. The first person I saw, was Premal. We shook hands and greeted each other. I looked over to where Amanda was working and as always, she had her head down, busy and determined. I approached Lee's team table and said hello and wished her a good morning and day.

"Hey Sebastian, can we meet this afternoon to discuss the system integration architecture for your account receivable processes?" She asked. "I know you will be conducting Level 2 designs this week, and

I want to make sure you capture how your process works from an IT perspective."

"Sure, Lee. How about we meet after lunch?" I suggested.

"That works for me." She replied with a smile.

I sat down with my account receivable super users. It was obvious, I made them very busy last week by asking to update the standard operating procedures based on my level 1 designs.

"Good morning, Shanti, how was your weekend?" I greeted Shanti.

"It was very nice. We went sightseeing in Toronto and did a little shopping. And how was yours, Sebastian?"

"Let's just say it was good but as usual, it was too short. How is the work going?" I became instantly serious.

"It's going very well. With your high-level designs, I was able to create a template for the standard operating procedures. That way, whenever you give us further details, I can simply add those to the existing template." Shanti answered.

"Does your outline match my processes?"

"Yes, they all do. What we are missing is just the content. In the next couple of weeks, when you finish the level 2 and 3 maps, we will be able to enter the missing information. As the team lead, I have assigned the sub-processes to all of our team members. Therefore, the completion of the document will run in parallel to your interviews and should be updated rather quickly."

"Thank you for the update, Shanti. Keep up the good work." I encouraged my team member.

After checking on everyone, I got back to my desk. I opened my laptop and started preparing for that week's conference calls, to develop level 2 process maps. I reviewed the current state processes and noted that our company had an elaborate database for best practices for each finance process. For the next few hours, I was working on designing an outline for my interview questions. Just like during the previous week, I would call Hudd's counterparts in Chicago, Connecticut, and New York. The only difference was, last week I called the controllers, but that time, I would be reaching out to the accounts receivable supervisors or the team leads. The objective was to contact the lower level teams for the updates on the details of how they process accounts receivables. The level 3 difference was, it went to the procedural detail of how to perform each task. Most of the level 3 specs would be used for the standard operating procedures. My calls would be scheduled for one hour on Tuesday, Wednesday, and Thursday. On Thursday afternoon, I planned to go to the airport straight from work. I was flying back to Miami.

I was heads down working, when I felt a tap on my shoulder,

"Sebastian, can I talk to you for 5 minutes right now?"

It was Scott, the Senior Manager, who was responsible for the delivery of the project.

"Of course, Scott." I replied. "Follow me."

I stood up and walked across the room. As typical, the place was very noisy since it was one big room for all the teams to work in. As I walked over to Scott's area, I quickly noticed Amanda glancing at me, in her usual cold manner.

I sat down with my notepad and pen ready for taking notes.

"You won't need to take any notes." Scott said. "I just wanted to inform you that I read your status report from this past Friday. I am pleased with your progress. I believe, so far you are on track. But it will get harder in a few weeks when you will have to travel to three different states to capture the level 3 flows. Are your super users ready?" He inquired worriedly.

"Yes, they have built the template for the document structure and will be adding content in real time as we go." I was calm and self-assured.

"Just a few items that need your attention, which are coming up fast. First, you need to visit the Indian Consulate here in Toronto to get all the necessary documents and medical requirements to obtain your visa to enter India. I believe, it takes 30 days to process, so please take care of it next week. Amy can assist you with their website and instructions in moving forward. Several of us have already gone through the process, so Amy knows how to help you. Secondly, you need to start preparing for your T-30 day "go-live" meeting which will be held next month with our Senior Leadership Team and the leadership from our client counterparts. It is crucial that all the T's are crossed. Please, make sure what you deliver is accurate and it gives us an overall picture of where the AR tower stands." Scott was speaking quickly, and his demeanor was very serious. "We hope all your critical path items are green. A similar meeting will be held at T-5 days to "go-live" to make absolutely sure we can flip the switch and take over the operations from a service delivery point of view. Both of these meetings are critical, and we need to nail them. If you feel, at any point in time, you have an area which is yellow or red, please let me know in advance, so I can inform the Senior Leadership. Thank you for your time, Sebastian. You can now go back to your team desk. Remember, if you win, we all win." Scott shook my hand and walked away.

I took a deep breath, feeling the pressure building up. After several moments, I walked back to my workstation. Immediately, I added the two meeting dates to my calendar and noted, I would have to figure out the exact items I needed to review for each meeting. I would add those items to my weekly report for Scott. It was getting close to lunch time and as planned, I wanted to spend that time with Premal. I wanted to get to know him better since we would be going to India and work the night shifts together.

I turned my seat around 180 degrees. "Hey, Premal! What do you say about grabbing a quick bite to eat?" I suggested loudly since the noise of the room made it impossible to speak normally.

"Sounds like a plan." He gave me thumbs up. "I just need 5 more minutes to finish up, and I will meet you at the elevator lobby."

I decided to go to the men's room and afterwards, if time permitted, to clean up my workstation. I went to the elevators and checked my phone. I noticed a text message from Renata. It read, "how's it going, bonitão?" That meant, how's it going, good looking. "Querida (how are you)? I am at work. I miss you. Do you miss me?"

"Yes, our night together was amazing. I want to see you again." I wrote back.

"I don't know, Sebastian, this week, I'm all tied up at work." Renata replied in her text.

"How about I tie you up to my bed?" I suggested.

"Lol. You are too much. Let's do this; I will try to see you one of these nights. You won't know when; it will be a surprise."

"Okay, beijos. Big kiss." I ended the messaging and put my phone away.

Our back and forth left me smiling. At that moment, I saw Premal walking toward me across the lobby.

"Nice smile. Looks like you are one happy camper, my friend." He noted.

"Yes, let's just say I am having fun here in Toronto."

"Sounds like you met a girl." He guessed.

"A true gentleman never talks about private affairs." I blurted out.

"I got it. Ready to go?" He asked.

"Yeah, let's go to the deli downstairs and get a sandwich?" I proposed.

"Works for me. Today is Monday, and I am sure we both have a lot on our plate, no time for long lunches."

"I agree." I nodded.

We went inside the deli, ordered our sandwiches and sat down.

"So, tell me, Premal, where are you from?" I started.

"I was originally born in Mumbai, India, but my family immigrated to the US when I was 6 years old."

"That's really interesting because I'm also from an immigrant family. We are from São Paulo, Brazil. I came here when I was only 3 years old. Have you completed your formal education here in the States?" I asked.

"Yes." Premal answered. "I did all my schooling here. As you can hear, I do not have an Indian accent."

"That's true." I agreed. "Do you still speak your native language?"

"Yes, I do."

"Then you're the guy I want to hang out with in India." I teased.

Premal responded with a laughter.

"So, tell me about your Tower?" I continued.

"I am responsible for general ledger. That means all the monthly reports related to accounting. Therefore, the journal entries and reclasses needed on a monthly basis. I make sure the company's books remain clean and are an accurate reflection of the financials on a daily and monthly basis."

"I assume you have an accounting background?" I inquired with interest.

"Yes, I did my undergraduate in accounting and then got my law degree." Premal nodded.

"Wow, you are an attorney." I exclaimed admiringly.

"Yes, I practiced for a couple of years, but then, I got bored with the job. What I like about consulting, most projects are 3-6 months long, so everything stays fresh and never gets old." Premal noted correctly.

"Are you married?" I asked.

"Yes, I have a wonderful wife and two girls at home. What about you, Sebastian?"

"No way, I am definitely single. Living in Miami, makes it rather hard to have a serious relationship, and I might as well forget about getting married at all." I laughed.

"You don't want to get married?" Premal was sincerely shocked.

"I did when I was in my 20s, but as I got older, I found it harder and harder to find true love. Most of the women in Miami just want your money or the lifestyle. To find someone with true intentions and who has not lost their innocence, is almost like a pipe dream. It's a vicious cycle in Miami, the men get burned, so they only want to sleep around, and the women also have been burned, so they are always looking for the bigger and better deal. I just have fun, and if one day, I meet the right one, then I will know. When you see so many bad examples, it's easier to separate the gold from the garbage."

"That's a good point, Sebastian. I have never looked at it that way." Premal sounded relieved after my explanation. He might have initially thought I was a degenerate player.

We enjoyed the 30 minutes of time we spent together and then headed back up to the war room.

At our office's entrance, I saw Amy and immediately asked her to send me the welcome package for the consultants, which included the preparation for flying to India.

"No problem, Sebastian, I will instantly send you the package via email. If you have any questions, feel free to ask me." As always, Amy was helpful and sweet.

"I will. Thank you, Amy." I replied warmly.

I softly taped Premal on the shoulder. "It was nice having lunch together. Let's see if we can hang out in India."

"Absolutely." Premal exclaimed enthusiastically.

I walked back into the war room and headed directly to Lee's workstation.

"Hi Lee, are you ready to discuss the IT system architecture for the AR Tower?" I asked.

"Yes, Sebastian. Why don't you grab a seat and we'll get started?"

"As you know, accounts receivable is about managing the payments which are due to Hudd." Lee started as soon as I sat by her desk. "The service was performed and billed to the customer. The customer has 30 days from the invoice date to make the payment on time. Once it is past due 30 days, a demand notice goes out. Additional demand letters are mailed at 60 and 90-days intervals. After 90 days, those past due accounts are turned over to our collection's agency. It is critical to have the accurate management reports and also the capability to track the demand letters which were mailed. If the collection's agency fails to collect, then those amounts are considered bad debts."

"What is the accounting system used by Hudd?" I interjected.

"They currently use Great Plains." Lee pointed out.

"What are some of the other systems involved?" I continued.

"They use Hewlett Packard (HP) for scanning and indexing documents. Aventail is the system used to gain access from the delivery center to Hudd's firewall. Activity Based Management by ACK is used to track work activities performed by the account receivables' clerks. It's a form of performance measurement for implementing continuous improvement. They will be also using an e-fax rather than the traditional fax machine. All of those systems will have to be tested and approved before the T-5 'go-live' meeting." Lee knew her stuff. I liked it.

"What about the phone calls coming into the delivery center from the US customers?"

"Each tower has been assigned to modify their current voice and fax flows from North America to India. It will have to be seamless for the customer; as if nothing has changed. But from a system point of view everything will have to be rerouted." Lee finalized her break-down.

"Thanks, Lee. Great explanation concerning the overall system architecture." I stated.

"One of my deliverables, is to build the detailed system architecture for each of the towers. I will start to develop a draft and would like to have further meetings to validate your work." She suggested.

"That will be fine, Lee. I am always available." I got up and shook Lee's hand.

For the following two days, I was very busy at work and did not focus on anything else. On Wednesday, I left work at around 6 PM, and drove back to the hotel. Once I walked into the lobby, I received a text from Renata.

"Hi, love your business casual attire." The text read.

I paused and glanced around the lobby and the bar.

"You are getting warmer." She texted again.

I walked toward the bar and there she was. Renata was wearing a grey trench coat with high heels.

"Renatinha, what are you doing here?" I exclaimed.

"Well, you have not called me since the weekend, so I decided to surprise you." She sounded semi-disappointed and semi-resolute. She gestured at the bartender asking for the tab.

"I'm sorry. I was very busy at work, darling." I tried explaining myself.

"Come on Sebastian, let's go up to your room." She didn't seem interested in my excuses.

We quickly entered the elevator. Its three walls were covered in mirrors.

"So, what's up with the coat? It's not raining outside and it's quite hot." I asked slyly. "Did you forget it's summer right now in Toronto?"

"Do you like my heels, Seba?" She murmured seductively. Before I could even answer, Renata opened her trench coat.

"Because that's all I am wearing." She grinned.

As soon as she revealed herself, I was in awe of her beautifully naked body. All I saw, were her white bikini tan lines. I immediately grabbed and kissed her passionately. I was a bit concerned since the elevator doors could open at any time. And as on cue, the elevator stopped, and we hustled to separate from each other and wrap up her coat. An elderly couple walked in and looked suspiciously at us.

"Excuse me, are you going up?" The lady asked in a strict voice.

"Yes, we are going up." I replied simultaneously trying not to burst out laughing.

"Oh sorry, we actually need to go down to the lobby." The older gentleman said apologetically.

They walked out of the elevator and as soon as it closed, we started laughing. We got out at the top floor. I was so turned on, I had difficulty walking. Renata knew that, so, she grabbed my package through my pants and playfully dragged me to my room.

"Now, that's a total surprise." I uttered.

"I told you to expect a surprise this week, didn't I?" She asked friskily.

"Yes, you did." I nodded feeling blood pulsating in my crotch. I didn't want to talk at all, but I played along. "So, why the coat and the high heels?" I asked, my lips touching her ear.

"Well, my panties are expensive, and I didn't want you destroying another pair." She replied breathing hard.

"Good point."

We embraced and fell on the bed, kissing passionately. That was another night I would never forget. Even though, I had a rule about not taking any woman seriously; Renata was the exception. Not only was she beautiful and exotic; she was full of life, had a glimmering spark in her eyes, and was always smiling. I felt as if we were compatible and perhaps, we could have a relationship; at least for the summer. I woke up in the middle of the night, and noticed, I was alone in bed. I did not hear Renata leaving the room but apparently, she had an issue with spending the night outside of her home. She did leave me a message on the bathroom mirror. In red lipstick, she wrote, "you're an amazing guy, love Renata."

Chapter 7

The next morning, I woke up full of excitement about Renata's surprise visit. Besides that, I was thrilled about flying back home to Miami. It would be the first time since I came to Toronto to work on my new project. My mind instantly shifted from Toronto to the crazy weekend ahead with Laura and her friend Ana. I packed my bags, enjoyed a quick breakfast and headed to work. I was there for half a day only, and then I went directly to the airport, dropping my rental car off along the way.

My flight was scheduled for 4 PM. Once I boarded the plane, I decided to get into my happy mood and turned on some India Arie. As soon as the plane took off, I fell asleep for the duration of the flight. We arrived at Miami just after 8 PM. I was so used to the airport routine, from getting off the plane to picking up my luggage, I could literally do it in my sleep.

Normally, I left my Porsche parked in the airport parking garage, but since I was out of town for 3 weeks, I left my baby at home. I flagged down a taxi and headed to Brickell where my apartment at the Four Seasons was located. It took about 20 minutes to arrive there. As soon as the taxi pulled up to the valet, they opened the door and Stevan, the valet manager, exclaimed,

"Welcome back, Mr. Kosta! Did you have a good flight?"

"Yes, thank you, Stevan." I was so happy to be back in Miami.

"Let me help you with your bags." He offered. "Your apartment is 52A correct?"

"Yes, thanks, Stevan." I responded and placed a good tip in his hand.

I was pretty exhausted, but once I entered my apartment, I was glad to be home. I missed my panoramic views from the 52nd floor. The view at my apartment was comparable to the one I observed when landing on the tarmac at the airport, about an hour ago. The windows of the living room and bedroom were from the floor to the ceiling; 9ft tall. Usually, when I arrived at home after any flight, I would make a double apple flavored hookah, sit down on my couch and listen to chill out music from the famous Café del Mar in Ibiza, Spain. It was very tranquil, and it enriched my soul. Also, breathing through the hookah relaxed me tremendously. That was my form of meditation.

The bathroom shower could fit 6 adults, and it was made out of black volcanic slate tile. The main shower head was on the ceiling and it felt like a heavy rain shower was falling down. Then, I installed three jets on each side of the shower stall to massage the body. I designed the entire apartment to be better than any hotel room I'd previously stayed in. If not, it would not be special enough for my taste.

I grabbed my bags and unpacked them. Since I was very organized, I quickly placed the dirty clothes in the washer and then folded everything back in its right place. The setup of my home surroundings was almost identical to the hotels I stayed in; therefore, I could do everything with my eyes closed.

We had a restaurant in the lobby of the building called Edge Steak and Bar. I phoned and ordered a filet mignon with mashed potatoes. While I was waiting for the food, I decided to call Laura to plan for the weekend.

"Hello, Laurinha, how are you, sweetheart?" I said once Laura answered. "I've just arrived back at my place and wanted to discuss the party on Saturday."

"Hi, Sebastian. Welcome back to Miami." Laura replied. "What about the party?"

"As you know, it's regarded, in Miami, as the best party of the year. It's very exclusive and almost impossible to get in. But once you are in, you will be exposed to the lifestyle of the rich and famous." I noted excitedly. "It truly is a rock star environment, where anything goes. I'm not big on drugs, and I don't think you are either, but I am warning you, there will be a lot around you." I continued. "You see, in Miami, the rich people such as lawyers, doctors, and the big executives love the hedonistic lifestyle."

"What do you mean by 'anything goes'?" Laura asked suspiciously after listening to me without any interruptions.

"The men, that are officially invited, can only bring women. Therefore, with the excess mixture of beauty and drugs, people openly display their lust for each other. There are lots of couples who choose to swing with their partners." I paused. Laura's silence was deafening.

"Don't worry, you will be with me, and I know the owner very well." I hurriedly attempted to calm her. "You will have the best time of your life. Try to get to my place by 9 PM. We will have a few drinks, smoke a hookah, and then head out to the party. We should be there by 11 PM. Remember, it is extremely important for you and Ana to wear something super sexy. I want for the three of us to make an amazing impression once we arrive." I concluded.

"Don't worry, Seba, I have already spoken with Ana, and we have an idea which I think will knock you off your feet." Laura assured me.

"Take care, love." I smiled.

"Beijos."

The dinner arrived, and the filet was cooked perfectly, medium rare. I enjoyed eating by myself and then went back to work for a few hours.

The next day, on Friday, I was planning to continue focusing on work since I had to finish developing the level 2 process flows and then, send them to Shanti and Scott for review. I also had to send my weekly report to Scott to demonstrate my team's progress for the week. After watching the late local news and the Tonight Show, I fell asleep quickly.

When I woke up on Saturday, I felt so good I almost jumped out of the bed. I think, it was because I did not go out on Thursday and Friday nights. Thus, I was completely refreshed. I took a good shower and had breakfast. Once a month, I would choose a nice location and run half a marathon, approximately 13 miles. It was my endurance training day. As I've previously mentioned, I liked a good challenge and a little bit of pain. I was also excited, because that night was the big party with Laura and Ana. I was feeling extra motivated. Not only did I want to look my best, but even more, to feel my best.

The party had the potential of being an unforgettable one. Even though, I started liking Renata very much, I was still officially single. In my world, my wife was my company and my kids were my toys. Therefore, I had three children; my 911, and two motorcycles. That morning, I took my MV Agusta Brutale 900R to calculate a 6.5-mile length of open road for a run.

I went downstairs to the garage, and there were my 3 babies, all covered up. I took off the cover of the Brutale and placed it inside the front trunk of the Porsche. I was ready to go. The idea was to first drive to Key Biscayne and start measuring the distance from the Sea Aquarium. Once there, I would drive toward Coconut Grove until I hit the 6.5-mile marker on my bike's odometer. Since the bike had over 150 horsepower engine and it was a beautiful morning, I completed the trip fast. The rush made me concentrate on every acceleration, braking, and cornering. It forced me to focus all my attention on that moment. I could not think of anything else but the bike and the street. Every time, I rode my bike, I developed tunnel vision. It felt great, because I had no worries on my mind, just me and the bike. As I drove by, people turned heads. I had a racing exhaust which enhanced the sounds of the motorcycle to another level.

When I arrived at the park, I began to stretch and loosen up my muscles. I did a few sprints for further relaxation. Then I began my planned journey from the Coconut Grove public park to the Sea Aquarium. It was not an easy run because for the most part the road was flat. At around 3 miles, there was a very large bridge, the Rickenbacker Causeway, connecting the mainland of Miami to Key Biscayne.

The hardest part was the uphill run to the top of the bridge. I would have to face that challenge on the way to the Sea Aquarium and also, on the way back. Even though, it was physically painful at times, for me, it was more of a mind game. I was raised by my father to never quit. So, I marched on all the way just past mile 6. At the Sea Aquarium, I turned around and told myself, I was already halfway. There was no quitting here even if I wanted to, since I purposely did not bring a cell phone or the money for a taxi. All I had were my keys to the motorcycle. I had to make it to the park in Coconut Grove.

I took off my shirt and wrapped it around my waist. I always believed when things got tough, those individuals who faced the challenges or fears head on and fought with grit and determination, would ultimately succeed in whatever obstacle faced in life. I was born and raised that way. I pushed and pushed up the bridge then down the bridge. I was running for over an hour, and I was past the halfway mark. I continued to monitor my legs, knees, and feet for any possible injuries. I actually felt great, my body was in top physical shape, and anyway, that was not my first time.

At 2 hours and 13 minutes, I arrived back at the park. I was drenched in sweat and scorched by the sun. I walked around for a few minutes to normalize my breathing along with a final stretch to avoid any cramping. Then, I got on my bike and accelerated so hard that the front wheel came off the ground. Mission accomplished. Now it was time to relax and enjoy a massage and then sit by the pool and have lunch.

While at the pool, I called the valet and asked them to detail my Porsche for the evening ahead. I was informed, my car would be ready by 6 PM. There was a restaurant by the pool called Bahia Mar. There, I ordered a club sandwich and an ice-cold Blue Moon. Once the beer arrived, I literally drank the whole thing in a matter of seconds.

"I'll take another round, please." I told the waiter.

At around 3 PM, I decided to go back to my apartment, to chill out to some music by Jack Johnson and smoke a hookah. I hated all forms of smoking, but I recently discovered hookahs and since the smoke was filtered through the water and the tobacco was flavored, it made smoking them very pleasurable. In my house, smoking hookah became a ritual for me and my friends on the weekends.

The hookah relaxed me so much, I decided to take a power nap in preparation for the party. I slept for about two hours and woke up at 7 PM. By then, it was time to get ready. I took a shower and picked out my clothing. I wanted to 'dress to impress' for the grand party. I chose a navy-blue suit by Brioni, a white Facconable dress shirt, and a black leather Gucci belt. I decided against the tie. That would make me too dressy. The 'tie look' was better for a formal event, and I didn't want to appear too formal, rather European chic. I had a collection of watches, and tonight, was a special night, so I decided to wear my two-tone Rolex Submariner. I finished the look by leaving a 5 o'clock shadow on my face and styling my hair with a bit of wax.

By 8 PM, I was ready to go. As always, my housekeeper polished the apartment. It was sparkling clean with a seductive aroma gently floating in the air. I wanted for Laura and Ana to walk in and have an amazing first impression. It was equally important, they felt comfortable and secure with me. Since I had about an hour to kill, I decide to make a drink. My father's favorite drink was Johnny Walker Black Label. I became so accustomed to seeing him drink Black Label that it became my favorite drink as well. As usual, I filled the glass with ice all the way to the top and then poured two fingers of Scotch. Then, I went to sit outside on the balcony with my drink.

I left the balcony door open, so I could hear my favorite band, Coldplay. Usually, when I was alone, I would turn on Coldplay because their music allowed me to go deep into my inner self. Each song was special and one of a kind. I don't even know how many times I listened to their albums, but it was almost daily. They were a form of inspiration for me. Their music touched my soul.

At around 9 PM, I received a call from my building's concierge.

"Good evening, Mr. Kosta." He announced politely. "I have two young ladies who would like to come up to your unit."

"Good evening. That will be fine, please let them in. Thank you." I replied in an even tone.

All of a sudden, I got excited to see Laura and Ana, especially how they were dressed. In Miami, image was everything and many people knew me, so I wanted to impress those attending the party, particularly the host. I quickly dimmed the lights, opened the shades completely and turned my entertainment system on. I usually liked to start the night with cocktails while listening to lounge or chill out music. Then, after a few drinks, switch it up to house or dance music.

In 2005, I was among those few lucky people, at least from those I knew, who could afford a high definition flat screen TV. The innovation was just catching on and gaining popularity. Later, it became more affordable. I was also an early adopter of Apple TV. With that device, I could watch all the music videos for free using YouTube. That was the first type of streaming service ever made, and it was fantastic. Initially, it was slow and did not work well at all times requiring some patience. Overtime, however, as the internet download speeds increased, the images became perfect.

I heard the doorbell amid my thoughts about my obsession with the latest gadgets. My two girlfriends have arrived. I had a smile on my face even before I saw them. I was dying to find out how they were dressed. And once I did open the door for them, my jaw dropped. They were wearing black dominatrix outfits with thigh-high boots that went up way past their knees. In addition, they were dressed in knee-length matching black faux leather coats. To top their looks off, they wore black shiny latex bras and panties with fish net stockings underneath. To add mystery to their looks, they wore masks on their faces and held whips in their hands. They looked like sexy twins from the wildest fantasy.

"Oh my god, you both look amazing." I exhaled. "This look exceeds all of my craziest expectations."

Not only did they dress amazingly for the party, but they were incredibly gorgeous with or without the costumes. I met Ana a few times at the clubs but never really got to know her. She was prettier than Laura if that was even possible. At only 21 years old, she had the most gorgeous face with maturely seductive eyes. She could definitely be a Victoria Secret angel. With the heels on, they were about 2 inches taller than me; about 6 feet tall.

"Welcome, ladies!" I stepped aside letting the girls come into my apartment. "Tonight, this place is yours. If you need to crash here, don't worry, you can. I want you to feel comfortable. Please, let me take your coats off, so we can relax on the couch. The bar is officially open, what would you like to drink?"

"What are you drinking?" Ana smiled.

"I am drinking Scotch, but I have a full bar. What's your favorite drink?" I mimicked Ana's flirtatious tone.

"Well, when I party, I drink Grey Goose Vodka with Red Bull."

"Oh, I see!" I laughed. "You are not planning on sleeping tonight."

"Well, if this party is as good as you say it is, I want to stay up all night and then watch the sunrise."

"What about you, Laura?" I turned to my friend.

"I will have the same as Ana."

I approached the bar area and made the drinks for the girls.

"Here you go, ladies." I handed the chilled glasses. "To an amazing and unforgettable night." I suggested.

"Cheers to that!" Laura loved my toast.

"Party time!" Exclaimed Ana.

"Have you ladies ever tried hookah?" I inquired. "Some places call it shisha".

"No, what is it?" Ana asked.

"It's an old form of pipe smoking which comes from the Middle East, places like India, Turkey, and other Arab nations. It is very popular after dinner". I explained.

"Does it get you high?" Ana continued her queries.

"No, it makes you very relaxed and a little light-headed at first. I like to do it when my friends come over for a pre-party. Each person smokes for a couple of minutes and then passes it around."

"Ok, then! Let's try it!" Laura said excitedly.

I got up and walked over to the kitchen. I opened a double apple flavored tobacco and prepared the hookah head. I then covered it with the aluminum foil and using a toothpick poked several holes on top. I poured some water into the glass vase, for filtration, and then lit the charcoal. I placed the ready shisha on top of the coffee table, by the couch.

"Let me go first, I will light the charcoal and get it working." I offered.

After breathing in and out deeply for a few minutes, a lot of white smoke started coming out of my mouth. It tasted clean because the water filtered the smoke and the apple aroma filled the apartment with a fresh fruity scent of an apple orchard.

"Okay, who wants to go first?" I inquired.

Laura raised her hand, "I do!"

I passed the hookah to Laura and told her to breathe in deeply. Being a novice, Laura enthusiastically inhaled and when she exhaled, the smoke billowed out of her mouth in huge clouds. It was cute and funny. She looked like a sexy dragon. After about 3 minutes, she announced that she felt relaxed and light-headed. She loved it. Ana quickly took her turn and also enjoyed her first experience.

Once all of us got the hookah buzz and were lazily sipping our second round of drinks, I brought up the subject of doing ecstasy.

"For the past six months, I have been experimenting with ecstasy and I have to be honest, it makes the nightlife, especially the club scene so much better. Have you ever tried it?" I asked.

Laura nodded yes, and Ana mentioned she'd never tried ecstasy but was curious.

"So, what happens when you are on ecstasy?" Ana inquired.

"What I always do is test the pill to make sure it's 100% MDMA. If not, I simply throw it away. It's not worth the risk to put something in your body when you don't know the origin. Let me show you."

I went into my bedroom and got the ecstasy pills. I kept them in my nightstand's drawer along with the tester kit. I put everything on the coffee table and then opened the test kit and scrapped off some dust from the pill. After about one minute, the paper changed the color to blue. That meant it was 100% MDMA.

"See this is the real deal, so don't worry." I waved the paper in the air. "All the effects of this ecstasy will be natural, and I will guide you through those." I assured Ana.

"What are the effects?" Ana was part curious, part concerned.

"First, you take half a pill and wait for 30 to 40 minutes. "I began. "You will instantly feel warmth spreading all over your body. Next, you will start getting a real kick out of the dance or electronic music. I must tell you, it's divine. The beats and the sound will be coursing through your veins, you'll want to dance."

Ana listened attentively. She looked like a schoolgirl in a dominatrix outfit. It seemed I was explaining math before the big exam.

"You will have an incredible increase in energy, and you will become very compassionate to people around you, even strangers. In fact, you'll want to touch them." I continued. "You will also gain unreal self-confidence, you will feel like the queen of the world, nearly superhuman. When you take the second half at the actual party, the total effect will kick in, and you will feel euphoric. I call that state, north of happiness. You will feel free, the gravity will not exist, every touch and sound will be raw and powerful. And I will be with you girls all the time. So, just relax and enjoy." I finalized my explanation.

"Sounds amazing, Seba." Ana whispered dreamily. "But what are the side effects?"

"The first thing you'll notice, your jaw moving by itself, so I recommend you suck on a lollypop or chew gum. If not, you could hurt yourself by chipping a tooth or biting your tongue. Also, your jaw might be sore the next day. Just remember to drink lots of water. Absolutely no alcohol after we leave my place. If you feel like the effect is diminishing, drink a red bull, and it will last a bit longer."

Ana and Laura exchanged mysterious glances with each other and nodded to me.

For the next half an hour we chilled on the couch and chatted about trivial things.

"Ladies, it is 9 PM, are you ready to get this party started?" I finally pronounced after checking my watch.

Their faces lit up. They nodded in unison like they were twins.

"Alright then, let's do this. Let's take half a pill now. I will tell you when to take the other half." I said while reaching for the bag.

I gave half a pill of ecstasy to each.

"See you on the other side." I grinned as the three of us placed their respective halves in our mouths.

I've discovered through my experimentation, ecstasy changed one's perception of reality. It almost felt like entering a new state of consciousness. The overall effect lasted for about 4 to 6 hours.

"Here is some water. If at any time, you don't feel well, let me know." With that we went downstairs to the garage.

My black Porsche was waiting for us. I let the girls in and then got behind the wheel. I immediately lowered the convertible top for the girls to enjoy the ride even more. We drove out of the garage and headed in the direction of Star Island, the home of the rich and famous. It was a private island located on the MacArthur Causeway, right before the bridge heading over to South Beach. It only took us about 15 minutes to arrive there.

Once we arrived, there was a stream of cars waiting to cross the bridge. There were two security stations. The first check point was at the entrance of Star Island. The second, would be at the Mansion where the party was held.

The party of such magnitude and wealth couldn't be happening without every luxury available, including valet parking. I tipped the valet attendant $50 and asked to park my car upfront, so I could leave whenever I wanted.

We approached the red velvet ropes, and the door man immediately came forward.

"Good evening, sir." He said ceremoniously. "Do you have a number and your last name, please?"

I gave him my favorite number, which was 3, and my last name, Kosta.

"Perfect, sir. I do have you on the list with the two women accompanying you." He looked at the girls and smiled.

"Yes, the beautiful ladies right next to me." By then, I noticed Ana was feeling the ecstasy. She was constantly touching me. And while I was talking to the doorman, Ana was dancing to the sound of the music coming from the mansion. As we were led into the house, I marveled at the crowd forming by the entrance. Some people were the lucky guests while others tried to talk their ways into the party of the year. Thankfully, we didn't have to do that.

As we walked past the velvet ropes, there was a professional photographer ready to take pictures of each guest. The party was sponsored by Bacardi, therefore the backdrop for the photo shoot, had the logo of the famous Bacardi bat. The whole thing gave the vibe of a red carpet event. Most of those in attendance were the crème de la creme of Miami. Those definitely were the A-listers.

After the photography session, it was time to be greeted by the host. His name was Dr. Charles. He was a very successful plastic surgeon whose specialty was breast enhancements. He graduated from the University of Miami and did very well for himself. After twenty years of practice, he had a huge client base and his name was well-known throughout the community. He was also known to have the wildest parties in Miami where anything went, especially the swinging and the drugs.

I met Charlie and his wife Melanie many years ago through common friends. Charlie was in his mid-forties, and his wife was in her early thirties. Melanie was the first to greet us. She walked across the hall with a huge smile and said.

"Hi Seba, how are you my dear? Give me a kiss."

For some odd reason, even with her husband next to me, she kissed me on the lips. Another oddity, she was topless. Her husband's work was staring in our faces. She had the perfect breasts, and it was really hard to focus on our conversation when her tits were right before my eyes.

"So, tell me, who are your beautiful girls?" She asked while measuring up Laura and Ana.

"My close friends. Laura and Ana. Best Brazilian export." I smiled proudly.

"Why is it that Brazil has the most beautiful women?" Melanie grinned. "They are both so gorgeous, and I love their dominatrix outfits. Very appropriate for tonight's party and the best outfits I've seen so far."

I guessed Laura started feeling the effects of the ecstasy. She raised her hand with a whip and snapped it with force and conviction. She quickly kissed Melanie and Charlie and moved passed them stating she wanted to go inside the mansion, so she could hear the music better.

Once we finished greeting the owners of the house, I quickly grabbed both Laura and Ana and pulled them aside.

"How are you feeling?" I whispered.

Ana felt really good and was ready to dance. Laura echoed the sentiment.

"Okay, then let's get some water, and we'll take the second half of the pill." I suggested.

We went to the bar and asked the bartender for three bottles of water. The bartender nodded and smirked. He knew the club scene, and he definitely figured we were rolling ecstasy that night. He gave us our water and wished us fun. I told the girls that apparently, they've already gone through the so called "wall". I could see their eyes were dilated, they were fidgeting their hands and feet, and they were very touchy feely.

"Let's go ahead and take the other half of the pill. Now you will feel the full effect of ecstasy, so let's stick together and party hard."

As we walked around the grand mansion, we could see it was executed in traditional Spanish architecture style. The party was mainly held in the living room and the outside terrace, where the pool was located. The view was incredible. It spread over the water overlooking the entire skyline of Miami. There was a private dock with a beautiful yacht right past the pool. The mansion was easily worth around $25 million dollars. The dance floor was the whole living room and the outside patio. There were four bar areas and a huge topless mermaid ice luge sculpture, where anyone could get shots.

I invited Laura and Ana to come with me. We walked up to the sculpture to drink the ice-cold alcohol that was traveling through an ice path within the sculpture.

"Ladies, what would you like?" Asked the bartender.

They gave me confused looks. They were rolling. I told the bartender to mix Grey Goose with a little bit of Red Bull. Then each of us took turns kneeling down and placed our mouths on the bottom of the ice sculpture. Then the bartender mixed the shot and poured it down the luge.

"Oh my God. It's so cold, but it tastes amazing." Ana exclaimed.

Then it was my turn. My favorite shot was Jägermeister, especially ice-cold. It went down real smooth.

By midnight, the party was packed. There must have been around three hundred people. We were rolling hard and kept flowing with the music. Occasionally, I would run into some friends, and we spent time talking, but my main focus was on Ana and Laura. I noticed they were moving their jaws forcefully, so I gave each some gum to chew on.

"Have some gum. It won't be that obvious you are rolling." I told them. "Also, wear your glasses, so no one sees your eyes."

Ecstasy gave a feeling of intense euphoria making one's eyes wide open. Therefore, it was good to chill out with some sunglasses on. We obviously were not the only ones rolling. Many others were chewing gum or sucking on lollypops and wearing sunglasses.

Ana came up to me and spoke loudly because of the music, "I feel amazing, but my heart is beating fast."

"Yes, that is a normal side effect. It just means you are rolling very hard. Just don't drink anymore Red Bull for now." I instructed her.

We went outside by the pool and started to dance like we were in a night club. I loved the music, thus I decided to check out the DJ. When I looked at him, I was stunned. On the second-floor balcony was DJ Tiesto himself. Apparently, he was in town that weekend for a performance at one of Miami Beach's famous night clubs and so it happened, he knew Charlie well. I saw Tiesto before when I went to Ibiza in 2003 at a club called Amnesia.

"Laura, Ana, look up at the balcony." I pointed up shouting over the music.

"Who is that?" Asked Laura.

"It's Tiesto." I replied triumphantly as if I was the one, he came to spin for.

"Are you kidding me?" Laura was shocked. "I can't even imagine how much the owner is paying for him to play here."

"I'm sure it's a fortune. So, are you girls having fun?" I grinned.

"Oh my God, I feel amazing." Ana replied while moving her body to the rhythm of the beat. "I have never felt so good."

"I just feel like dancing until the sun comes up." Laura added. "I have so much energy, and I have never felt the music so intensely. It's as if the music is inside of me."

I nodded happily. I was having the best time, and I loved that my girls shared the sentiment.

As we moved to the middle of the dance floor, which was packed with people, I could see that almost everyone was on some kind of drug. I observed them touching each other and kissing, while some were dancing very erotically. Many of the women present were models, so the party was filled with beautiful people. The DJ started to mix the music to get the crowd jumping up and down. I was losing my breath, but I never felt so alive. I was in the moment, and all my senses were aroused. My vision was sharper; I could see every tiny detail around me. I didn't only see but felt everyone and everything. It was intoxicating and empowering. My sense of smell was heightened; I could smell everything around me, perfumes and colognes, alcohol, including the natural jasmine scent coming from the plants in the garden, around the pool. My sense of touch was also intensified. I wanted to touch and talk openly to just about anyone.

At that moment, I had no insecurities. I just wanted to connect with everyone. My energetic and positive conversations were fully reciprocated. I quickly made friends with complete strangers. My confidence level was through the roof. Anything I wanted, could be mine tonight. In a moment, I noticed that besides me, Laura and Ana were experiencing the same euphoric sensations. The three of us were in the zone. We did not have to speak to each other but simply unite with the music and look at each other, and we knew what each one of us was thinking or feeling.

I grabbed Laura and kissed her. It was an intensely passionate French kiss. Ana appeared to feel left out and said she also wanted a kiss. I switched over and started kissing Ana. We acted like we were alone, but we were surrounded by a huge crowd of people. As I was kissing Ana, Laura pulled me away and announced that she felt left out. I switched again. The beats of the electronic music kept us dancing, and the ecstasy made us act like hedonistic animals.

I didn't want to make anyone feel left out, thus, I pulled both girls to myself, and we had a three-way kiss. I was kissing them, and they were kissing each other. I felt like I was in heaven. Many around us stopped and started staring. I was sure they were on drugs, but even they couldn't believe what we were doing in the middle of the dance floor. After our intense public make out session, I was thirsty, so I told the girls to have fun while I would get some water.

I walked towards the sea dock where the bar was located and waited in line. By 2 AM, our party reached its full capacity. The music was blasting, and the laser light show was spectacular. A few people started calling out to others to join them in seeing something. I was curious, so I went there as well. After walking a bit further, I noticed a man holding an alligator on the rope and on the right-hand side, there was also a tiger on a leash. I couldn't believe what I was seeing. I decided to go back to the dance floor and bring Laura and Ana to see those beautiful majestic creatures.

On my way to the dance floor, I noticed a circle of people around something. As I approached, I noticed Ana in the middle of the circle with a blonde girl on her knees. The blonde girl had lifted Ana's dress and pulled down her panties. To my utter shock, the blonde girl was licking Ana's pussy. I was stunned. I had no idea Ana, who was only 21 years old, was interested in women. Not to mention being a complete exhibitionist. Or maybe it was my ecstasy and pep talk that drove my girls to the edge of the limitless self-expression and zero fucks given. As for Laura, I did not know where she was.

I left Ana to enjoy herself and walked inside the mansion where in the living room, I found Laura sitting on the couch. I sat down next to her.

"Are you okay?" I asked.

"Yes, but the ecstasy is hitting me hard. I needed to sit down." She mumbled in reply.

"Here, I brought you water. Drink a lot." I encouraged.

We sat there for about 10 minutes until she felt better, and then we walked back by the pool.

"Is that Ana???" Laura asked with shocking notes in her voice.

"Yes, apparently it is." I nodded.

They were still by the pool and people were watching Ana being pleasured by another woman. Ana was moaning and staring up at the sky.

I felt someone grab my shoulder, I looked away from Ana and saw Charlie, the host.

"Looks like your girl is having fun. You never disappoint me with the women you know, Seba." He looked very pleased. "You are always with beautiful women. I am really glad you brought particularly these two. I think they attract more attention than the tiger."

I was glad Charlie was happy. But the blonde who was eating Ana out wasn't with me, and Laura stood next to me. But that didn't matter at that point. I was taking all the credit Charlie was willing to give.

Usually, summers in Miami were very hot and humid. That one wasn't an exception. Thus, we decided to go back inside the mansion and hang out in the living room with the A/Cs on full blast. It was about 3 AM, when I noticed that some people left the party, probably hitting the clubs on South Beach. Laura and I decided to stay, because that party was held only once a year. Ana was meeting new people and enjoying herself.

Laura and I were relaxing on the couch listening to Tiesto. After a long silence between us, she suddenly said she was feeling another wave of high coming. Before I could even reply, she asked me to kiss her. I did. The sparks between us started instantly flying. We began hungrily touching each other. Her hand grabbed mine pushing it down between her legs. I was feeling her. She was very hot and wet. I moved her panties to the side and started playing with her. She grabbed my head forcefully and moaned.

Suddenly, I felt someone licking my fingers. When I looked down, I saw a hot blonde interchanging between licking Laura and my fingers. I didn't feel comfortable with that scene in the living room, so I stopped what I was doing and asked Laura if we could get out of there. She immediately agreed.

"Why don't we get Ana and go back to my place?" I suggested.

We got up and went towards the pool to find Ana. She was sitting on a lounge chair with the same blonde girl and a man, who was probably the blonde's boyfriend or husband.

"Hey, Seba, have you met my new friends? Ana's face lit up when she saw us. "This is Romina and her husband Rafa. Romina, Rafa, meet my friends, Seba and Laura."

After we exchanged greetings, Rafa complimented me on Ana and Laura, stating how beautiful they were.

"We were wondering if you wanted to go back to our place and party?" Romina proposed.

Ana got instantly excited. It was obvious she was down. Luckily, Laura, who was the older wiser friend convinced her not to go. I've done many things sexually but never swung with another couple. Laura grabbed Ana's hand and whispered, "We are leaving. We are going back to Seba's place."

Ana smiled and nodded in agreement.

We walked back into the mansion. What we saw inside resembled a hedonistic orgy place. Most women were topless, and most men were all over them. It was almost 4 AM, and the things were intensifying. People were either about to swing or got mixed up in an orgy. I've seen enough. It was time to head back home. I said goodbye to both Charlie and Melanie and thanked them for the fun evening. They tried to keep us from leaving and stay for the after- party, but we politely declined.

"We are having our own after-party." I thought.

We walked out of the door, jumped into my convertible and drove off. There was a lot of police on the roads, so I had to be careful. Even though, we did not drink much alcohol, we were still under the influence.

The top was down, and we listened to Tiesto on the way back to my apartment. The streets were empty, and we just enjoyed the breeze in our faces. All of us still felt the effects of the ecstasy. We were chewing gum, and our eyes were wide open.

"How are we going to pass out?" Ana wondered.

"We are not." I said. "We are going to watch the sunrise and have a glass of wine."

"Sounds like a plan. I don't want for this night to end." She grinned.

"The night is not over." I assured Ana. And Laura nodded with a smile.

We took the highway back to Brickell and then pulled up to the Four Seasons. I left the car with the valet, and we went up to my apartment.

The moment we walked in, I pressed a few buttons on the touch-screen, and the dance music came on. The girls got on top of my couch and started jumping up and down to the music. Must've been the ecstasy kicking in again. I let them play, and I went to the bath-room. I had a feeling the night was going to get crazy, so I decided to take 100 mg of Viagra. The ecstasy was great, especially for women because it made them feel euphoric and they got sexually aroused. For men, things worked differently. The heartbeat was so fast and intense, it was hard to get an erection. The widely known solution to that was Viagra. Typically, it took about 30 minutes to kick in. So, I went to the kitchen and made a hookah for us to relax and calm down. I changed the music to Café del Mar for a chill out session.

I made my usual hookah with double apple tobacco and placed some ice cubes in the water, so it would be cold filtered. I inhaled first to get the hookah lit and for the smoke to come out strong. Ana was sitting to my left and Laura to the right. We started by playing a game, of checking if we could pass the smoke around. First, I took a few strong puffs and then kissed Ana simultaneously blowing the smoke into her mouth. She immediately started coughing and laughing. I told them I wanted to pass the smoke from my mouth to Ana's and from Ana's to Laura's. We tried again. That time, the smoke went into Ana's mouth and then she pressed her lips against Laura's and breathed out the smoke. Laura was able to inhale it but failed to exhale.

We kept trying until it finally worked. I passed the smoke to Ana's mouth, and then Ana passed the smoke to Laura's mouth, and then Laura finally exhaled all the smoke.

For the next hour, we continued with games such as Truth and Dare, Twister, and many others. We had lots of fun. The Viagra has taken effect completely, and I went to the bathroom once again. I quickly changed into a white robe with nothing underneath. I then returned to the living room and invited the girls to join me in the shower. They laughed and asked me to give them a preview of what they were getting. I agreed and opened up my robe. Their eyes opened wide when they saw how hard and ready, I was. I sat on the couch between them, and we started kissing each other. Then Laura grabbed my package and started playing with it.

"Okay, before we go too far here, let's undress and take a shower." I exhaled.

The girls did not hesitate and quickly took off their clothes. They stood before me completely naked. I had to take a minute to admire their beauty. Both were absolutely gorgeous: tall, slender and tanned. Laura had bigger breasts, but Ana's were very perky. I knew what was about to take place, and I couldn't wait any longer.

We walked into my large shower and once there, we began kissing. The water was falling on us and the jets were hitting in all the right places. First, I wanted to wash them. So, I took the soap and started slowly caressing their bodies in turns, admiring every curve. I lathered Laura, and Ana washed my back. She massaged my shoulders all the way down to my butt and then my legs. After we were clean, we focused on our erogenous zones. The touching was very intense, and everyone was feeling great, both mentally and physically. Before things got over-heated, I suggested getting out of the shower and proceed to my bedroom.

Once there, the girls told me to lie down on my back. Afterwards, Laura mounted me and sat on my face facing my feet, while Ana kneeled down between my legs at the end of the bed. At about the same time, the three of us started performing oral sex on each other. Both girls focused on my manhood, and I focused on licking Laura's pussy. We could still feel some effects of the ecstasy, but by then it was very mild. The feeling of them sucking and licking me was incredible. As you can imagine, I ended up having sex with both of them. That was one of the best sexual experiences of my life, the night I would remember forever.

Feeling exhausted and ready to pass out, we managed to come out to the balcony and watch the sunrise while enjoying chilled white wine. We could hear the birds chirping and Mother Nature awakening. We've shared the unforgettable experience indented forever in our memories. After about half an hour, we were done. Sleep was a must. I suggested to the girls to take one pill of Xanax which would help them sleep better. The three of us took the pills and then passed out.

Chapter 8

I opened my eyes and looked at the time, to my horror it was 2 PM. I jumped out of bed, because I needed to get ready for my flight back to Toronto at 6 PM. I woke the girls up and called for two taxis. I took a quick shower and ordered some food to-go for us from room service. In about 20 minutes, I was all dressed up and ready to leave.

When the bell boy appeared with our breakfast/lunch, I thanked him and asked to charge it to my account.

"Ladies, I had an amazing night, and I thank you for that." I said while handing each girl their sandwiches. "I have to go back to Toronto tonight, but let's make sure we keep in touch. Cool party, right?" I grinned.

"It was the night I will never forget." Ana said dreamily.

"Seba, that will be our little secret. Ok?" She asked worriedly.

"Of course. I am the man of my word." I assured her.

The three of us left the apartment and headed to the lobby. The taxis were already waiting outside. One for the girls to go home, and one for me, to the airport. I figured, I should be there by 4 PM, about two hours before my flight. International flights usually required to arrive three hours before the departure, but I knew that two hours was fine as well. On the other hand, unlike my usual light travel, that time, I had lots of luggage, and that made me feel anxious. I was leaving Miami in May and wouldn't be back until the end of June. From Toronto, I needed to fly to Montreal to overview the collection agency for Hudd. Then, I would spend approximately three weeks between Chicago, Stanford, Connecticut, and then New York City. There, I was meeting with the accounting clerks and performing a deep dive to review the level 3 processes and understand every detail essential for the creation of the level 3 process maps.

The upcoming month was going to be intense with lots of traveling. And I was excited about that. The only issue that made me feel terrible, was my inability to spend quality time with Renata. However, I was going to dedicate the upcoming weekend to her. I wanted to make her feel very special.

While I was waiting for my flight, I called the American Express concierge to set up a weekend for us in Montreal. I was intent on making it unforgettable for her. The truth was, I liked Renata very much. Furthermore, I enjoyed spending time with her. I was even contemplating inviting her to India but was not sure if she would be up for the adventure. I was certain India was beautiful, but we weren't going to New Delhi or some other exciting destination. Chennai did not have much tourism or shopping, but I was going to make a final decision based on the next few weeks with her.

Thankfully, there were no delays, and the plane departed on time, at 6 PM. It was going to be a long night for me since I was arriving to Toronto around 11 PM, and then I needed to rent a car and drive to the hotel. I would be lucky to be in bed by midnight. The upcoming week would be intense with a blistering pace. I required all the rest I could get.

Once our flight took off, I put Cafe del Mar music on and dosed off. I slept through the entire time and was awakened by the sound of the captain's voice.

"Ladies and gentlemen, prepare for landing." I could not believe how quickly the time flew by. Once again, I was in Toronto, far from home, after one of the most magical weekends of my life. As soon as we landed, I headed to baggage claim and waited for my luggage. Toronto's airport was top notch, and every process was measured and made as efficient as possible. I grabbed my bags and headed to the rental car desk. True to my prior calculations, I arrived at the hotel at 11:45 PM, even 15 minutes earlier. By midnight, I was in bed.

Chapter 9

The next morning, I was not going directly to the Hudd corporate office, but to the Indian Consulate to complete all the necessary paperwork as well as my prescreening interview. The Consulate was about 30 minutes away from the hotel, and I figured it would be a good time to call our Senior Project Manager, Scott McManus and check in. The phone rang a couple of times and he answered.

"This is Scott, can I help you?"

"Hi, Scott, this is Sebastian. I arrived late last night. I wanted to take 5 minutes to give you an update." I suggested.

"Sure, Sebastian, go ahead." Scott sounded pleased.

"As you are aware, my team and I completed the level 2 process flows, and we are ready for the design of the level 3 process flows and standard operating procedures. Right now, I'm on my way to the Indian Consulate for my prescreening and will head to the office afterward."

"Just so you know, Sebastian, the Indian Consulate has a lot of requirements for business travelers. When you finish your appointment at the consulate, make sure to immediately schedule all the vaccinations that are required and those that are optional. There's a whole bunch of them. It's kind of scary that you need to take all of those precautions, but better safe than sorry." He paused. "Also, if you ask for an expedited visa, you should be able to pick it up in 3 days."

"Thanks for the heads up, Scott." I replied. "The next 3 weeks are critical for my deliverables. I will make sure to keep you up to date as my progress develops. This Friday, I will spend the day at Hudd's Collection Agency office in Montreal, to shadow the process. The following week, I will be in Chicago, and after that, in Connecticut, and lastly, the third week in June, in New York City. All my flights and hotels have been booked, and the meetings have been scheduled. I just have to reconfirm with each office controller this week and prepare for my interviews."

"Sounds like you have your hands full. Stay focused on the mission, and I know you can get it done. Just remember, next Friday, June 10th, is your T-30 meeting where our top partner Gary Dunlop will be physically present. He will be here to review if you are on track for the 'go live'." Scott reminded me.

"Yes, Scott. I have it on my calendar." I nodded.

"Okay, good luck at the consulate, and I will see you later in the office."

In preparation for my visit to the Indian consulate, I already had a check list which included the following: my US passport, two copies of the visa application form, 2 passport sized photos, one Accent invite letter, and a cover letter. During my initial screening, I would have to leave all those documents at the consulate and then pick them up in three business days with the expedited service. The visa fee would have to be in cash or bank cashier's check. Once completed, I would have to go to a medical clinic to get vaccinated in my preparation for the flight to India. My travel packet had a list, which included the recommended vaccinations which were the following: hepatitis A, malaria, tetanus, typhoid, and MMR. As for the optional vaccinations, those were meningococcal, hepatitis B, and polio.

I was a bit concerned over such an amount of precautions, to say the least. I've traveled all over the world throughout my entire life, but I'd never had to deal with such stringent vaccination requirements. The whole thing was unnerving.

After about 30-minute drive, I arrived at the Indian Consulate. I had all my paperwork ready and once there, I took a number and sat down to wait for my turn. While waiting, I started reflecting on the threesome I had that weekend. After many interesting experiences with women in the past, a threesome was something I've never done before. I couldn't deny how great it felt. With the added effect of the ecstasy, I didn't think I'd ever felt so good. Over time, experimenting with ecstasy, I learned how to control my mind and body allowing me complete awareness of the environment I was in. It felt like a chess game, and I was the champion. Life appeared so much easier, so carefree. Almost like a computer game, where possession of a joystick guaranteed full control.

My day dreaming was cut short when my number was called. I got up and approached the clerk.

"Hello, I believe you called my number. 32?" I asked.

The clerk looked at me. "Yes. That's right. Please follow the officer." He suggested and pointed to the man standing next to the door into the room next door.

I walked in. There was a small table with the two chairs facing each other.

"Sir." The officer said. "Could you please have a seat and prepare all the required documents for your visa application?"

"Absolutely." I responded readily and took out my US passport, the two passport sized photos, my companies official invite letter, a cover letter and the cashier's check.

He took some time reviewing all the documents and then asked when I was planning to fly to Chennai, India. I told him, if everything went according to plan, I would be departing Toronto on July 8th.

"Sir, is your trip for business or for pleasure?" He inquired.

"Well, hopefully both." I could not contain myself and started laughing.

The Indian officer was not amused.

"Sorry officer, I was just kidding. Here is the letter from the company detailing my business trip." I instantly changed to a formal tone.

"For how long you will be staying in Chennai?"

"I will be there for one month. I am expected to depart on August 5th." I replied. "That is assuming everything goes as expected." I added.

He took his time looking over all of my papers and then placed them into a manila envelope.

"Thank you for your visit today." He finally said. "Because you've applied for the expedited process, your visa will be ready for pick up in 3 business days. I would suggest you come back this Thursday, preferably in the morning, to pick up your passport with the new visa."

I nodded gratefully and extended the cashier's check to him. After that, I was out the door. The process was actually easier than I expected. For some reason, when around government officials, regardless in or of what country, I always felt a bit anxious. Anyway, I got into my car and headed back to work. I still had to go for my medical clearance at some point that week and get all the vaccinations. But that wasn't going to happen that day. As it was, my morning was pretty much shot, and I still had a lot of work to do in preparation for my trips in June.

I needed to get back to work as soon as possible to meet with my team to discuss the areas where we needed to gain further knowledge from the client and obtain detailed interviews. It was already 11 AM. I was anxious. I called Shanti, my team lead, and told her that I would be arriving at the office around noon. I asked for her to order lunch for everyone; I wanted the whole team discussing our next steps while eating together.

Once I finished with Shanti, I decided to call Renata, just to say hello. I actually missed her. Even though, I had a wild weekend in Miami, I was thinking about Renata. I didn't feel guilty over my weekend escapades; Renata and I were not officially dating at that point. I was still a single guy.

The phone started to ring. After the third ring, she finally picked up.

"Hello, Seba?" Her voice sounded like I'd disappeared two years ago and now called out of nowhere.

"Yes, Renata it's me." I said cheerfully. "I just wanted to call and let you know I was back in Toronto."

"Great. So, how was your weekend in Miami?" She asked pretending to sound casual.

"I would have to say it was a classic weekend. We went to a party on a private island, and they had DJ Tiesto playing. It was absolutely amazing. You know how the summers are in Miami. The parties are insane, and the clubs are legendary. You should come to visit, Renata." I suggested.

"It's funny you've mentioned Miami, Seba." She laughed. "I am leaving next weekend to Miami with my sister. We will be there for the whole month.

"No way!!!" I exclaimed. "Then for sure you can visit my place, and we can go out."

"Sure." She responded.

"Ok, Renatinha. I've just arrived at my office. This is a crazy week for me. Actually, a crazy month, but I want to see you. I have a surprise for you, but I have to tell you in person." I pronounced.

"Then expect another surprise visit from me, Seba." She promised. "Just like last time. I can stop by at any moment."

"Awesome, I can't wait to see you." I grinned.

While finishing up my phone call to Renata, I arrived at our offices and immediately went up to the war room. There, it was business as usual with all the phones ringing, and everyone talking simultaneously. I walked up to our team table and greeted everyone.

"Did you get lunch for everyone?" I turned to Shanti.

"Yes, Sebastian. I've already ordered meals for our entire staff and advised them regarding the subject of the meeting." She replied.

"Ok, let's get started." I took my seat and looked around the table noting that all my super users were present.

"Vihaan, have you met with Lee Choppard and reviewed the technical architecture of all the systems they are currently using?" I addressed the man who was my systems engineer.

"Yes, Sebastian. We have reconfirmed the user licenses. The number of seats will be the same in Chennai as in North America. With the level 3 process maps we can go further and reconfigure the system design as needed. That does not take long. I assume about 3 days of programing and then another two days of testing so about a week."

"Great, Vihaan, keep me up to date with your progress." I encouraged him. "Do you need for me to collect anything in particular on my trips coming up in the month of June?"

"Just find out what financial systems are used in each location and what instance they are using. I will also need to know the touchpoint and when passwords are needed." He replied.

"Sounds good." I nodded to Vihaan. "Arjun, you're up." I continued. "Since you are my business analyst, I want you to redesign our project plan. You need to obtain updates from me daily and then, at the end of the week, a final version must be given to me. I will share the project plan with Scott, so he is aware of our progress and where we are headed next."

"Shanti." I turned to my assistant. "Please keep the notes of all of our meetings."

"Yes, Sebastian." She nodded.

"Reyansh, since you are the process engineer, I want for you to be in constant communication with me for the next three weeks. I am going to create templates for the interviews, but you will need to use them to convert them to process flows. You do understand the standard format Accent uses for the process maps, correct?" I addressed Reyansh.

"Yes, sir. I am familiar with those. I've done many process maps in my previous engagements."

"Remember, if you don't understand any of my notes or inputs you need to reach out to me immediately." I looked straight at him. "We are in a tight time frame, people. What was done in 9 months needs to be completed in 3 weeks. There is no room for mistakes or any delays. Therefore, I have an open communication policy. My door is always open. I don't care about the time or the method. Call me, email me, or text me. Don't hesitate to reach out with a problem or an issue. Just no surprises, please." I finalized my statement. That time, I was looking around the table at each of my team members.

We ate our lunches and for the rest of the day, we were saturated with our tasks. I spent most of the afternoon planning for next week. I called all three of the controllers and confirmed the times. I also searched our best practices database and found excellent templates for accounts receivables. By the end of the day, I changed my focus from accounts receivable to collections. I reached out to my last team member, Rikki, who was an accountant.

"Rikki, tell me please, how does the collection process work at a high level?"

"Sure thing, Sebastian. At most companies, a lockbox is set up at a bank and all the payments and payment stubs are received at the centralized location. The bank then applies the cash to the correct account. Sometimes, we are missing the payment stub, so research needs to be performed to determine which account must be credited. From a system point of view, we use crystal reports to generate delinquent reports where we can see the accounts that have yet to pay us. Typically, the accounts are classified in days, therefore, 30, 60, and 90 days. After 90 days, you have to see what the company's policy is. Most turnover the account to an outside agency at the 90 days plus mark. You will have to gain understanding of what types of calls are placed, and which letters are sent."

"Finally, if collection is not successful, does the agency report it to the credit bureau?" I asked Rikki after listening to his lengthy but very important insight.

"This is the general process, but I am sure, Sebastian, you will learn a lot more on Friday when you are physically present at the Hudd collection agency. They decided to keep collections internally, so the complete process will be there for you to capture." Rikki advised.

My weekly schedules were designed for Monday and Thursday travels. Thus, I would spend only half of my time at the office on those days. On Monday, I was going to the client site, and on Thursday, I was flying back to Miami. For the month of June, however, I would fly from the client cities to Toronto rather than Miami. It didn't sound like a lot of fun, but for me, the pressure was on to deliver, and I knew I was on Scott's radar to execute on time and under budget.

I recalled the meeting I had with one of our top partners, Gary Dunlop, who said if I could perform at the next level and be successful in our engagement, I could be considered for partner. Becoming partner, would guarantee my career growth, and I would never have to worry about money again. I would have many options in the business world, and I could ask and get anything I wanted. At that time, those included, a big house, fast cars, beautiful women and traveling the world. I wanted a limitless life of excess and fun. That was my vision, and I had to have it. I was prepared to do anything to achieve my dream, including working long nights and weekends, mostly in isolation. Even though, I had many friends in Miami, I was all alone while working and traveling for work.

For the next few days, I concentrated on preparing for my interviews for account receivables as well as my visit to Montreal to learn more about Hudd's collection process. By Wednesday evening, around 8pm, I was exhausted. I had a long and tough day at work, and I needed a break. I decided to stay in my hotel room and enjoy a bottle of cabernet. I was in full relax mode when someone knocked on the door. A bit irritated about the disturbance, I got up to open it. But there stood gorgeous Renata, and my irritations instantly turned into excitement.

"Oh my God, Renatinha. What a wonderful surprise to see you." I said stepping aside and letting her come in. "I missed you so much." I whispered while pulling her close and giving her a tight hug.

"Hi Seba, I am also very happy to see you. You got me very intrigued when you mentioned you had a surprise for me, so I just had to visit you. Where is my surprise?" She sounded like a little girl who was searching for a gift on Christmas Day.

"Whoa, slow down, Renata." I laughed. "Surprise is like a fine bottle of wine. Just like the one I am drinking." I pointed to the bottle of cabernet on the coffee table. "You need to sip it slowly and enjoy all the tastes and aromas. If you drink it too fast, you won't enjoy it fully." I continued as she followed me to my bedroom. She was silent.

"I will tell you, but you will have to wait. Let me get dressed, and I will take you to dinner at this really nice French restaurant across the street from the hotel."

"You know, Seba, I hate that you are trying to keep secrets from me, but I guess I don't have an option." She finally said.

"No, you don't." I teased her.

I changed and we headed down to the lobby. As usual, I was warmly greeted by the hotel staff. The weather was so beautiful, we decided to walk to the restaurant. There was a warm breeze, the sky was clear, and we could see all the stars above us. However, what made us stop and look up in fascination, was a perfectly visible and intensely bright full moon. We walked happily, hand in hand. It felt great to have Renata by my side, and I was sure, she felt the same. We connected, both physically and mentally. If she lived in Miami, I would've definitely made her my girlfriend. That thought alone was strange for me, but I was falling for her. We didn't have to talk much since we could feel the magic between us. As if the time stopped, and we were fully enjoying the moment. We weren't thinking about tomorrow, rather focusing on now.

We arrived at the restaurant. Since I knew a little bit of French, I wanted to impress Renata. I asked the hostess, in French, for a table for two away from the bar but next to the window. Renata smiled and looked at me with fascination in her eyes. It was a big deal coming from her.

As we approached our table, the hostess pulled back Renata's chair. I politely stopped her.

"Please allow me to take care of the young lady."

"Of course, sir." The hostess nodded and stepped aside as I helped Renata with her seat.

"Enjoy your dinner." The hostess said walking away.

"Thank you." Renata and I responded in unison.

The restaurant has been owned by a small French family since the early 80s. The ambiance of the restaurant was amazing. It felt like we teleported back in time to Paris. It was rich in décor and filled with lounge music. The atmosphere was laid back, and I didn't want for the night to move too quickly, so I ordered two glasses of wine.

"So, tell me Seba, what is this secret you are keeping from me?" Renata said while we waited for our wine. "I am dying to know."

"Ok. I will tell you, Renata." I smiled. "But first, I have to point out that I don't believe in coincidences. I met your sister for a reason."

"Ok…" Renata appeared confused.

"Meeting your sister was fun. But the most important outcome of that meeting was, it led me to you. I've known many women in my lifetime, but I can tell, you are special. You are not like the rest of them. You have this inner glow, soft, comforting energy about you. I feel like I am at home with you, peaceful and cozy."

At that point, after I paused to gauge her reaction, Renata appeared radiant and excited. Her smile and her eyes sparkled. Her entire focus was on me and my words.

"Tomorrow, at 6 PM, we are taking a short flight to Montreal. I have already made all the arrangements for the two of us including flights, hotels, and even some fun events to attend." I announced.

"Oh my God, Seba. Are you serious?" She breathed out in complete amazement. "Have you really?"

"With you, definitely. I do have to work on Friday, but for half a day only. That way, you can sleep in and enjoy the morning at the spa. When I get back, I am all yours for the rest of the weekend."

"Sounds like so much fun. I can't wait to go." Renata exclaimed beaming with joy.

"Well, you just have to sleep on it since we are leaving tomorrow."

"You're an amazing guy, Seba."

"I know, I am." I grinned. "I aim to please."

After our romantic dinner, we headed back to the hotel. Rather than just holding hands, Renata grabbed my right arm and held me tight.

"So, Renata, tell me about your dreams. What do you want in life?" I inquired.

"Oh, I don't know. I don't need a lot. I just want a guy like you that makes me happy."

"That's it? Just me?" I teased her.

"Well, I have always dreamt of having a happy family with kids, a comfy house and growing old together. I've never really fantasized about being rich, just happy."

"Yes, money does not bring you happiness." I agreed. "But it helps. This weekend, however, I want to spoil you. It makes me happy seeing your beautiful smile."

We approached the hotel.

"Do you want to come up?" I asked casually.

"Absolutely." Renata grinned.

Once in my room, I told her I didn't have much music since I only had an iPod with the ear buds, but the W Hotel had a radio and a CD player which had a cool music collection. I turned it on to enhance the mood. The song was instrumental and seemed like the sounds were coming from heaven. It put us in a relaxing mood. We fell on the bed and started kissing passionately. It was a dance between our tongues and lips. We were so intense, that we bit each other several times. Hers lips were beautifully plump and soft. Just our kissing alone got me instantly aroused. I knew, that was going to be another special night. Truly special, because we had feelings for each other. It wasn't just sex anymore.

Thus, we didn't have sex. We made love. It was unreal for me. I've never made love before, I only had sex. What is the difference you might ask? Love is something more than just having sex. It's the connection between two human beings on multiple levels. There is a tremendous depth. It felt like the stars aligned, and only the two of us existed on the planet. We were both connected and lost in that vast universe. It was pure "nirvana." The fruit of the Gods. The unforgettable experience and moments of intimacy. I didn't remember for how long we were making love, but it was a long while. I didn't remember falling asleep as well. But we woke up in each other's arms.

Chapter 10

The next day, we were leaving to Montreal. Before that, I still needed to work for half a day and finish preparation for my visit to Hudd's collection agency. Renata and I left the hotel in the morning and went our separate ways. Unfortunately, the romance had to pause, because we had to go to work. Renata went to the mall where she was the manager for the Swiss chocolate store called Copenhagen, and I went to the war room.

Even though I went to work, I could not stop thinking about last night. Renata had struck a chord in me. I was unaware I had such profound feelings for her. I wanted to be with her. With her I was at peace. I counted the minutes to lunch time. I was planning on working until 1 PM, and then pick up my princess. Those few hours went by very slowly, and all we could do was to text each other.

"Renata, are you busy?" I wrote.

"Not really. The mall only starts to get busy in the afternoon and guess what? I won't be here right." She replied.

"No, sweetheart, you're coming with me."

"So, you are all mine this weekend?"

"Yes, all yours." She texted.

"I have a lot planned for us. It will be a very special weekend."

"You know, Seba, I am getting used to us. I don't want for this summer to end." She said.

"Don't think about the future. Stay in the present with me." I tried distracting her from overthinking too far ahead.

"Ok, Seba, but I am starting to have feelings for you." She texted.

"You know, Renatinha, I feel the same way."

"Do you?"

"Yes, it's an unbelievable feeling, and I want to hold on to it for as long as possible." I replied. "Listen, I am not feeling productive today and it's almost noon. How about I come and get you now? Even though it's only been a few hours, I miss you." I couldn't wait any longer.

"You do, Seba?" She asked in the text.

"Yes! I am going to leave now and get some lunch for us, so we can eat in the car. Then we can stop at your place and pick up your clothes before going to my hotel. From there, we can head straight to the airport." I planned everything out, of course.

"Ok, Seba. I will wait for you here at the mall." She responded.

It was amazing. As soon as I left work, the time just kicked in and started moving much quicker once again. I picked Renata up at the mall, and we shared a light lunch, right in my car. We stopped at her place. Thank God Roberta, her sister, was not there, so we grabbed some clothes and zipped up her bag. We did the same at my hotel, and we were off to the airport.

By 2:30 PM, we had about an hour until boarding.

"So, this is your life, Seba?" Renata asked while we were waiting at our gate. "Going from the airport to the airport, crossing paths with complete strangers wherever you go. I can see how lonely you must feel, going to all those places. So, for how long have you been a consultant?"

"I am going on ten years." I replied.

"And in those ten years, you have not had a serious girlfriend?" Renata inquired.

"Define a serious girlfriend?" I smiled.

"Well, I believe it is someone you love and are committed to and have at least 6 months of history together."

"In those terms, I have not had a girlfriend in the past ten years." I answered thoughtfully.

"But knowing the way you are, you had many lovers." Renata stated.

"You may say I've explored women in all the places I'd been to. It is the only way to keep it exciting and not feel lonely. The difference is, with those women it was typically a one-night stand type of experience. I don't feel that way with you. You make me happy all the time. I feel an incredible positive energy when I am around you. I know that with you anything is possible. Any dream I have can be realized with you by my side…" I said honestly looking straight in Renata's eyes.

We were interrupted by the announcement coming from the loud-speakers. "All passengers departing to Montreal, your flight is now boarding. All travelers in first or business class may now board the plane."

"That's us." I got up. We picked our carryon bags and joined the line. One of the perks of traveling a lot was always getting upgrades to business class. That allowed me skipping the long lines and sitting up front on the plane. We also had the advantage of unlimited alcohol.

As soon as we took our seats, I asked the stewardess for two glasses of champagne. I liked to travel in style and today, I was with the most beautiful woman I've had the pleasure of meeting. Her chiseled features, button nose, and a contagious smile always made me happy. She was joyful. Full of positive energy and her spirit was young and still innocent. If she only lived in Miami!!! I shook off my sentimental disposition resolving to stay focused and enjoy the present. It would be silly and useless to overthink stuff.

"Cheers! To an amazing weekend." I toasted with Renata as the plane's engines went on full throttle. The torque of the engines could be felt throughout the cabin, and we simply placed our heads back and held our hands together. In less than a minute, we were ascending.

It was going to be a short flight from Toronto to Montreal, about an hour and ten minutes in total. It was nice to be up in the sky. I always used flying time to dream of a future that encompassed all my needs and desires. Being there with Renata was extra special. I hoped that finally, I had someone to share my experiences with and explore new places together. Peeking at the silhouette of her face made me realize just how lucky I was. They say, one of the biggest mistakes a person can make is to become successful and rich and not have anyone to share it with. I had plans for us in Montreal, and I was grateful to have such an amazing person to share those plans with. During the flight, we continued getting to know each other. We talked about our past lives, and how we were raised. All in all, we had similar backgrounds and wanted the same thing – Love.

We were so caught up in our conversation, we didn't even notice how fast the flight passed until the Captain announced the upcoming landing.

"Ladies and gentlemen, we are beginning our descent to Montreal. Please fasten your seatbelts, close your trays and bring your seats back forward to the landing position. We will be landing shortly."

"Oh my God, Seba. I am so excited to get to see the city." Renata exclaimed appearing as joyful as a little girl on her birthday.

"Yes, Renata, me too. It's called the Paris of North America. It is intricately unique and old fashioned. I think, we will have fun here." I smiled.

"Tell me, please tell me, what are we going to do?" She asked while holding my hand during the landing.

"Sorry, Renatina, some things are better kept unknown." I teased. "That way, your excitement will be boundless."

"Fine, but I feel like a little kid who is ready to open her Christmas gifts." She echoed my earlier sentiment.

"I believe, once we are done with this weekend, you will feel as if it was one of your best gifts. Remember, I aim to please you at all levels." I promised.

We walked off the plane and since most international airports were labeled in the same manner, we quickly found our way to baggage claim. We grabbed our bags and flagged down a taxi. Unfortunately, there wasn't a W Hotel in Montreal, but I was able to book a room at the even more prestigious St. Regis. It was not a modern chic hotel like the W, but more elegant and richer in décor. It was the type of hotel that felt expensive. As usual, everything was covered by my travel points. The rest would be at my expense. I wanted to make this weekend unforgettable for Renata. A memory she would keep for a lifetime.

We arrived at the St. Regis a little past 6 PM. The St. Regis Montreal was not as large as the one in the US, rather a boutique hotel. The building occupied a corner street in downtown Montreal. There was no grand entrance. But, once inside, it felt like an old palace in France. The floor and the ceiling beams were covered in expensively rich wood. The crown moldings were beautifully hand carved. Not only did the interior design appear straight out of an *Architectural Digest* magazine, but it was obvious the hotel was properly and perfectly maintained.

Once we entered the lobby, we were welcomed by the concierge who met us with champagne.

"Sir, madame, welcome to the St. Regis. We hope your stay with us will be splendid. Please remember not only I, but our entire staff, is here to serve you. If you need my assistance in setting up the reservations for any local restaurants or exciting excursions, please allow me to be of service." He pronounced ceremoniously.

"Thank you very much. I have planned this weekend myself. But I will surely contact you if we need anything." I replied politely.

"Yes, sir. Please do."

Then, the two bell boys came and asked for my last name. After proper verification, they picked up our luggage and left to take it to our suite. We took the elevator up to the 15th floor, which brought us straight to our private lobby. The floor had only one suite, and it was all ours for the weekend. We walked through the white wooden double doors into the large foyer masked entirely in black marble. Our apartment was immense and ultra-luxurious. Renata immediately started exploring it. Her sincere fascination gave me even more pleasure.

She went to the left, and I walked to the right. It was a 2-bedroom suite with a living room and full kitchen. About 1,200 square feet in total.

"Can you believe this place? It is unreal!" Renata exclaimed.

"I'm happy you like it." I smiled.

"Seba, this is over the top. Even with your high standards."

"Yes, wait until you see the master bath. Let me show you."

I took her hand and lead Renata past the living room and the kitchen to the far end, towards the master bedroom. Even though, the hotel was built and designed in traditional style, the rooms were contemporary and up to date. They had all the latest technologies: a 65" HDTV hidden in the ottoman, right in front of the bed. It would rise up at a touch of the remote. The bed itself was made out of mahogany wood and had 4 large posts.

"Come see the master bathroom." I invited Renata.

And as soon as she walked in, her mouth dropped. The place alone was almost the same size as the master bedroom. It had two vanity mirrors with a 20" HDTV built-in behind them. An oversized white marble shower stall was encased in glass with an overhead rain feature. Right in the middle of the master bathroom, was a jacuzzi that in size was similar to a pool. As I walked around it, I turned it on. There were 22 jets in total, and its floor produced miniature air bubbles. It was so big; one could actually swim from one side to the other.

"So, are you down for this?" I asked with a grin.

"Are you kidding me? Absolutely! I can't wait." Renata giggled.

"It's a no clothes establishment." I joked.

"Not even swimming suits?" She played along.

"Nope." I replied in authoritative manner.

"Do you want me to take off my clothes right now?" She teased.

"I think a little dessert before dinner will work just fine." I whispered as I approached Renata embracing her in a passionate kiss. While we continued kissing, I was slowly undressing her until she stood in the middle of the opulent bathroom in her red bra and red satin panties.

"I want you to take them off, Seba." She breathed out.

I nodded and while kissing, I opened her bra with one hand revealing her supple and perky breasts. I kneeled before her and kissed her belly button. In one swift motion, I pulled down her thong. Then, it was her turn. She took off my dress shirt and slacks.

"What about now? Can we go in like this?" Asked Renata.

"I am not the one to break the rules." I laughed in reply heading towards the exit to bring us champagne. Renata appeared confused watching me walk away.

"I thought you got cold feet, Seba." She said when I returned with a bottle and flutes.

"With you??? Never!!!" I leaned and kissed her.

While I was gone, Renata got into the jacuzzi filled with bubbly water. I poured champagne for us and joined her there. We were on the opposite sides looking intently at each other. After taking a few sips of the champagne, I placed my flute on a special table and rested my head on my raised arms. I then stretched my legs all the way until my toes were touching Renata's.

"Why are you so far away?" She murmured.

"Because I just want to take some time appreciating your beauty." I replied in whisper.

As I answered, I reached for my champagne glass and swam closer to Renata. Once my lips were touching her wet cheek, I suggested a toast.

"To enjoying every moment together."

Renata smiled and we clinked our flutes.

We left our glasses on the side of the jacuzzi and started touching each other. With the water's slow movement, our contact resembled a dance in the water. It was a slow dance but full of passionate energy. Every touch was magnified, and our primal urge begged to be satisfied. I turned Renata around, so her back was pressed against my chest.

"Open your legs." I asked. My lips behind her ear.

After she obliged, I positioned her right in front of one of the jets, with the pressure of the water aimed directly at her pleasure zone. While Renata enjoyed being stimulated by the jet, I caressed her breasts and kissed the back of her neck. Within a few minutes, Renata was breathing hard and moaning in ecstasy. I knew she was ready; thus, I thrusted my manhood inside of her.

As we made love, we moved rhythmically around the jacuzzi. We continued our dance until I could no longer control myself. I simply held Renata tight as we were simultaneously reaching orgasm.

After recuperating, Renata looked at me and whispered, "what an amazing start to the weekend. Thank you, Sebastian."

"It is my pleasure." I replied. "Let me help you out of the tub. I will bring you a robe."

We dried off and moved straight to bed. We had a long day of working and traveling, so we decided to get some room service and call it a night.

Chapter 11

The next morning, when Renata opened her eyes and stretched, I was already dressed and ready for work. Still sleepy, she sniffed and smiled. The air was filled with a delicious aroma of coffee mixed with breakfast goodies.

"Seba, what time is it?" She murmured while sitting up and stretching again.

"Good morning, sweetheart. Did you sleep well?"

"Yes, I slept like an angel."

"I also slept very well." I echoed. "Listen, it's 7 AM, and I have to run to my client site this morning, but I won't be long. I ordered some coffee and breakfast for you, so enjoy."

I proceeded to pick up the tray and brought it to the bed, placing it right before Renata whose face was filled with delight and joy. I then picked a beautiful ripe strawberry from one of the plates and moved it across Renata's lips.

"Here, taste it. Delicious, right?" She bit into the berry lustily while looking at me with a seductive expression in her almond-colored eyes.

"I will be back at the hotel around 3 PM. In the meantime, go shopping and buy yourself some outfits. Here is my credit card. There is no limit on this card. Impress me, darling. You will need at least 3 outfits. One for tonight. Pick out a colorful dress that is fun and flirtatious. For tomorrow, I want you to buy a hot red dress, and for Sunday, pick out a white outfit that highlights the contrast of your beautiful brown sun-kissed skin tone. For both Saturday and Sunday, the outfits should be sexy but comfortable. You can contact the concierge, when you are ready, and they will have a limousine ready for you to drive to Eaton Mall. It's the best place to shop in Montreal."

"Oh my God, Seba. Is that a challenge?" Renata grinned. I could feel excitement radiating from her. You planned this all out for us."

"No." I whispered into her hair. "I planned it out for you." Renata gasped before my lips covered hers, and I could taste sex and strawberries in her mouth.

When I arrived at the client site, I walked up to the reception and asked for John Nagy. John was the Director of the collection agency for Hudd, the man in charge. In a few minutes, I was approached by John himself. We exchanged warm greetings. It was our first face-to-face meeting, but we did speak over the phone prior to that.

"Hello, John. How are you?" I asked while shaking his hand.

"I'm doing well, Sebastian. Thank you." He replied. "How was your puddle jump? Pretty short flight from Toronto? Huh?"

"Yes, thank God. I don't like traveling anywhere for longer than 6 hours. I start feeling restless."

"Well then…" John laughed. "Your flight to India will be interesting. A challenge to say the least."

"Don't remind me." I shook my head. "Twenty-two hours on a plane is way too much for my taste. But hey! It's the job. Someone has to do it."

"Better you then me." John stated.

We walked over to John's office.

"So, John, I will be here until 3 PM. I would like to shadow your agents by 30, 60, and 90 days past due on account receivables. I want to understand the process, the systems used, and the types of personalities involved." I went straight to business.

"I must warn you, Sebastian. Lots of personalities in this office! Take advantage of the time here to learn how they interact with each customer. When your collecting the money, it's a fine balance between being respectful and courteous and firm and direct. If not, you will never recover the company's money."

I nodded in agreement.

"Are you ready to get started, Sebastian?" John asked.

"Yes, who is my first victim?" I looked around.

"That will be our lovely Victoria. Let me invite her to meet you." John picked up his phone and dialed her extension. He then asked Victoria to come into his office.

"Sebastian, she will be joining us shortly."

Victoria appeared ten minutes later. She would be the first collection agent I was going to shadow.

"Victoria, please meet Sebastian from Accent. He is a consultant who is helping our company move our financial operations from North America to India." John made the introduction. We shook hands. "Please sit with him and discuss your work duties." He asked.

"Sebastian, the best way to learn is to participate. You will get your own headset to listen to the three agents as they are working." John continued. "When you're done with Victoria, she will introduce you to the next agent and will go forward until your analysis is complete. Circle back with me at the end of the day, so we can discuss next steps."

"Sounds great, John." I replied. "I really appreciate the hospitality."

After John left, I joined Victoria at her workstation. We took our seats, and I put the headset on.

"Have you ever been to a collection agency?" Victoria inquired.

"No, I have not. This is the first one that I get to visit in person."

"Let's do it then. And welcome, Sebastian." Victoria smiled and dialed the first contact.

For the next hour, I listened to sweet Victoria charm her way through the discussions with her customers. She was originally from southern Georgia, and as nice as any person could be. The phone calls were friendly and pleasant. She reminded the customers that their payments for the home security services were past due. Most customers thanked her for the reminder and promised they would be mailing in their checks. In between those talks, she would turn her headphones off and explain things to me. Like for example, only 50% of the customers who promised to pay would actually do so. It would be up to the next agent then to try and collect at the 60 days mark. Overall, it was an interesting experience but as the day moved forward, I couldn't stop thinking about Renata. She was probably shopping and having the best time of her life, and I wanted to be with her.

I was delighted when the session finished at approximately 11 AM, because I could finally take a break and call my girl.

"Renatinha. Querida. Como você esta?" I asked when I heard her accented, "Alô", on the other side.

"Hello, my angel. I am doing wonderful. I am having a lot of fun here at the mall. Since I got here quite early, the only place open was the manicure and pedicure salon, so I did both. I am off to look for my dress for tonight. You said it should be fun and full of color correct?" She sounded excited.

"Yes" I replied delighted by her enthusiasm.

"Are we going to an art function?" Renata tried to guess.

"I pledge the 5th, my dear. It's a surprise."

"I can't win with you." She playfully changed her tone to that of a little girl.

"Nope." I laughed. "You can't. By the way, if you get hungry, there is a restaurant called Le Petit Maison which has unbelievable crêpes. They are super thin and crispy. The last time I visited Montreal, I ordered the chicken cordon bleu. It was amazing. If you have room for dessert, you can choose the dulce de leche crêpe with vanilla ice cream. Trust me, they are delicious. I wish I could be there with you. I will call you later." I made a kissing sound.

"Please call me, Seba. I miss you a lot." She moaned.

"I miss you too, my love" I responded before pressing "End" and returning to my work.

I refocused and went back to Victoria's workstation.

"Victoria, can you please introduce me to your 60-day agent?"

"Certainly, let me walk you over to Jacob's desk." Victoria got up from her seat.

It was a large open space similar to the war room, but even larger, and the cubicles were taller with a bit more privacy. It wasn't as noisy as well. We approached Jacob's desk as he was finishing a conversation with one of the customers. He was nice but demanding. He even offered to take a credit card over the phone.

"Hi, my name is Jacob. It's a pleasure to meet you." He said after Victoria caught his attention.

"Hi Jacob, my name is Sebastian from Accent Management Consulting." We shook hands.

"Yes, John Nagy already came by my desk and gave me a heads up about you stopping by."

"Great, gentlemen. Sebastian, I will leave you to shadow Jacob. If you have any follow up questions, you know where to find me." Victoria said before walking away.

"Please take a seat and here are your headphones." Jacob said.

By then, I already knew the drill, and we immediately got to work. Jacob was younger than I or Victoria, and I found out he was single and straight out of college. He mentioned that for every successful collection, he would get a bonus. He was driven by money, which was normal. He was very determined to collect and did whatever was necessary to get the customer receivable to zero. He was not as pleasant as Victoria. But persistent and straight to the point. If he figured the customer was not ready to pay immediately, he would back off. Then make detailed notes in the customer relationship management software preparing the next agent for a call back.

After approximately an hour, I believed I heard enough. I understood the process well.

"Thank you, Jacob, for allowing me to shadow you here today. I have one more agent which I need to meet, and I believe you know who that person is."

"Your welcome, Sebastian. Let me introduce you to Samantha. She handles everything that is 90-days past due."

"Samantha has a tougher job. But her commission structure is greater, so I guess it must be worth her while. Let me just warn you, she is a tough cookie. She is a single mom and does not take bullshit for an answer. I guess our personalities define our job roles, but you will soon see, she is not as nice as most of us." Jacob warned.

We walked over to the back side of the office. There seemed to be a lot more privacy where Samantha was sitting. She was a very pretty African Canadian. When we came up, Samantha was on the phone, she pointed at the chair inviting me to sit down and placed her finger over her mouth; suggesting for me to be quiet. Definitely a tough cookie.

As I listened, I could tell the tone of the conversation was different compared to the other two agents. Her conversations were in toe with the customer discussions rapidly increasing in pitch and volume. She seemed to have little to no restraint. She wanted to earn her commission. It was obvious by her voice and motivation. She would not accept no for an answer. She even discussed terminating customers' accounts and sending them to fair credit reporting agency which would negatively impact their credit. As soon as she finished her killer call, I took a deep breath.

"How are you, Samantha. Pleasure to meet you." I said with a semi-smile.

"Another fucking day in paradise. Right?" Her humor made me laugh.

"Glad that you are so happy on a Friday." I teased.

"Damn right I am. Not only is it Friday, but it's payday. So why are you here? To evaluate my job. Get rid of me?" She looked at me ready to fight.

"Well, that would not be my function. I am only here to learn your job, understand the touchpoint, and the systems involved." I continued in a calm demeanor.

"So, you're the fucker who is taking my job to India, right?" She was seriously confrontational.

"Listen, that is an internal discussion you need to have with your employer. I don't make employee decisions. I am unsure of what they are planning for you and therefore, I recommend you speak with your supervisor." I suggested.

"Yeah, they told me some hotshot consultant would be here today. I guess that is you. You better not take my job from me. I have bills to pay and mouths to feed." She stated angrily.

At that point, I determined my learning process was complete. I decided to finish taking my notes and head to John Nagy's office.

"Thank you, Samantha for your time. I wish you the best." I said calmly.

"You damn right, asshole. I'll be seeing you." Samantha roared through her teeth.

Without replying to Samantha's last words, I got up and walked away. I approached John's office and knocked on his open door. He was with his secretary.

"Sebastian, are you all done?" He beamed at me.

"Yes, let's just say you have some interesting personalities here."

"Oh yes, we do." John nodded in agreement. "We have analytics to support each of our decisions, and we believe the position requires personalities that progressively get tougher." He explained.

"So, John, this brings me to an interesting conversation I had with Samantha."

"Oh!!! She is a tough one." John exclaimed.

"Yes, she is, but have you communicated with your employees regarding their statuses once this project is completed?" I inquired.

"That is an HR area, and I believe they have identified those who would be transferred to new positions and others who would be laid off."

"If you don't mind me asking, John, what is going to happen to you?"

"Oh, I will be fine. They are not keeping me. I will be laid off." John stated calmly.

"Wow, really?" I was shocked by his mellow disposition.

"Yes, they gave me a very nice severance package which included one full year of pay." He continued. "Like I said before, I am fine with the move. It's what is best for the company."

"So, what's next for you?" I asked.

"I am not sure yet. Perhaps, I will follow one of my childhood dreams. You know, do something I really have a passion for. I have a creative side, which was dormant for many years. I just need to water it, and I am sure something will grow. A new beginning." John replied thoughtfully and hopefully.

"I wish you all the best, John. Thank you for all the hospitality. I studied the process many times before, but it's different when you get to experience it in person. Thank you once again. I will walk myself out." I got up and shook John's hand.

When I left the site, it was 2 PM. I knew Renata was still shopping at the mall. I thought I might join and give her some ideas. I decided to call her.

"Renatinha, I'm out!" I announced happily.

"Are you, babe?" She mimicked my joyful tone. I probably sounded like I was out of jail instead of finishing my workday.

"Yes, and I am on my way to you. How are you doing with your shopping?"

"Not good. I bought only one dress. I feel overwhelmed. I need your help, Seba." She begged.

"I will be there in about 20 minutes." I laughed. "I think this is going to be lots of fun."

"If you ask me, it's a bit stressful, because I don't know where we are going and what we are doing."

"Relax, sweetheart. I will be there soon."

The taxi dropped me off at Eaton Mall, and we decided to meet at the food court. As soon as I arrived, there she was, sitting in the middle of the crowd, looking absolutely lost. In my eyes, the image of her, so innocent and confused, froze in time. She was a beautiful gem stuck in one place with all the people around her moving fast. I decided to sneak in and surprise her. I carefully reached around Renata's head and covered her eyes with my hands.

"Guess who?" I whispered softly kissing her neck.

"My babes. You're here!" Renata screamed out with such happiness and relief like she was in the snake pit and not at the upscale mall. "It's been a mission trying to shop all by myself. I had no idea what stores to go to and what clothes to pick out." She uttered hopelessly. That made her even cuter and sexier at the same time. I loved how sincere she was.

"Don't worry, my dear. Everything will work out fine. It always does, right?"

She exhaled a sigh of relief. "I'm so glad you're here. I don't think I could do that by myself."

"Ok, please give me my credit card back and follow me." I playfully commanded. "Let's go to the new section of the mall, where all the upscale boutiques are located. This mall was recently renovated, and it became very glamourous. Many celebrities come here to shop and today, you are the famous girl. The one everyone wants to meet and imitate." I teased her lovingly.

By then, Renata purchased a white dress only, for Sunday's event. We still needed to get one for the evening and the other one for the next day's outings.

"Tell me, Renatinha, which dress do you want to buy now, the colorful one or the red one?" I inquired while leading my girl through the new upscale section.

"Well, I am anxious to find something for tonight, and now that you're here, I am dying for your opinion."

"Ok, let's walk into Versace first. In this store, everything is bright and colorful. I am sure we can find something here." I suggested.

We walked into the store, and after about 5 minutes of browsing through the aisles by ourselves, we were approached by an elegant tall blonde.

"Good afternoon, can I assist you in finding something in particular?" She asked in upscale English with a dry German accent.

"Hi. Yes, please. Could you help this beautiful woman next to me? She needs a gorgeous and colorful outfit." I responded to the German blonde.

"Of, course! With pleasure. I'm Nora by the way." She introduced herself. "But before we get started, may I offer you some refreshments, wine or champagne?"

"Pleasure to meet you, Nora. Sebastian. And this is Renata. We would love champagne, thank you." I said looking at Renata, who nodded in agreement.

"I will be right back. In the meantime, please continue to browse."

We walked around the store checking out different outfits, shoes and accessories. Everything was sexy, bright and gorgeous. It was Versace! And Versace always remained true to its nature of freedom, sex appeal, and celebration. Renata looked like a kid at the candy store. She sparkled with joy and fascination. We were having lots of fun together. The mood was light and playful.

When Nora returned with our champagne, she left again and minutes later, she wheeled in a rack with six or seven dresses on it.

"I picked these while observing you." She stated. "You are beautiful and exotic. Where are you from?"

"I am from Brazil." Renata beamed.

"No wonder. I've always thought Brazilians were one the most beautiful women in the world."

"Thank you." Renata responded. I just smiled enjoying watching her surrounded by luxury and admiration.

In the meantime, Nora picked the two dresses from the rack, held them in her hands, and showed them to us. The styles of the outfits were sexy and wild.

"What do you think? Do you like any of them?" She asked.

Before Renata could even respond, I got up, approached the rack, looked at the remaining ones hanging and those held by Nora.

"Not exactly." I summarized. "Maybe something less wild and a bit more elegant? Renata is stunning, and I want the dress that would highlight and not overpower her beauty or make it too much. Do you know what I mean?"

"Certainly!" Nora nodded. "I believe I know exactly what you are looking for. I feel your vibe. Trust me, I've been doing this for many years."

She went through the store and quickly picked out several outfits. Without speaking to us, she hung them on the rack and stepped away looking over each one. I knew the one I liked, but I decided to see which one Nora was going to suggest. She reached for my secret pick. It was an obvious match for Renata, it screamed her name. It was a two-piece outfit. The bottom was a flared mini skirt to highlight Renata's perfect long legs. The top was a simple halter with a nice cut at the cleavage and mid-rift length to show off Renata's flawless stomach. The set was a beautiful yellow with the flares in various bright colors. It was a perfect outfit for Renata's dark olive skin tone and gorgeous body.

"Renatinha, why don't you try this on?" I suggested. I could see she loved the outfit. She was very excited.

When Nora set up the fitting room for Renata, she nearly ran there. It was obvious she couldn't wait to try it on. She emerged five minutes later and twirled around showing herself from every angle.

"Wow, you look amazing." Nora exclaimed. "The yellow looks great on your skin."

I looked at her, and she did look great, she would've looked great in anything, but something wasn't right.

"Seba?" Renata looked at me. "You don't like it?"

"You are gorgeous, babe. Anything you wear looks great, but I think it's too much, too much color, too overwhelming. Your beauty is too prevalent to add such bright colors to it. Let's try the same but in white, maybe?" I turned to Nora. "Do you have it in white?"

"Actually, this outfit comes in two colors; yellow and white." Nora pointed out.

"Perfect, let's try the white one." I proposed. Renata, being the sweet non-confrontation girl that she was, agreed and returned to the fitting room.

She came out several minutes later looking happy and excited.

"I prefer this one. Do you like it, Seba?" She inquired hopefully.

"I love the white on you. This is perfect." I was floored actually. Renata looked like an Amazonian queen. I turned to Nora. "We will take this one."

When we paid and walked out of the store, Renata wrapped her arms around me and planted a huge kiss on my lips.

"Thank you, babes. I really love the dress, and I am so happy that you are here helping me. I was lost without you." She whispered.

"You will never be lost when you are with me." I replied with a smile.

We walked through the mall, holding hands, and enjoying each other's company. We had one more dress to find; the red one for an outdoor event. After window shopping through the top designer brands, we approached the Prada store. There, in the window display, we saw a mannequin dressed in a light grey piece. Renata and I agreed, the same dress in red would be perfect for her. We entered the store. Before I could even address the salesperson at Prada, my phone started ringing. I looked at the number. It was work. I had to answer.

"Hello, this is Sebastian Kosta."

"Hello, Mr. Kosta. This is Gary Duncan. Do you have a few minutes?" Asked the voice on the other side.

"Absolutely. Hold on one second." I replied and muted the call.

"Babes go inside the store. If they have the dress you want, then pay for it with my card. I have to take this call, but I will be right back." I told Renata.

Renata nodded and entered the store.

"How's it going, Gary. Are you in Toronto?" I returned to the call.

"Actually, that is the reason I'm calling." Gary stated. "I will be in Toronto exactly one week from today. Next Friday, we are having our T-30 review for all our end-to-end processes. First, I wanted to know if your tower, the AR tower, will be ready by then?"

"I won't have the level 3 detail design by then, but the rest of our work deliverables will be ready. Our overall project manager, Scott McManus, is aware of my planning, and he has been kept up to date about our progress. At T-5 everything will be completed." I assured Gary.

"It needs to be, Sebastian. We are counting on you for the success of this project. I would like to meet with you next Friday, at 8 PM. I have a few additional items I would like to discuss with you. Are you available?"

"Sure. At the W?" I asked.

"Yes, we'll have a few drinks and discuss some items. Remember,

Sebastian, if you can knock it out of the park on this engagement, there will be high probability we will consider you for partner." Gary told me.

"Thank you so much, sir. I won't let you or the firm down." I said.

"I will see you next week, Sebastian."

I hung up the phone and took a deep breath. I knew the next two months would be critical for my future at the firm. It was time to make my moves.

I walked into the store looking for Renata. I found her at the check-out. Prada had the same exact dress in red, and Renata loved it.

"I'm all done. Mission accomplished." She beamed at me.

"Great, let me help you with your bags. We can go out to the main entrance and catch a taxi back to the hotel." I told her.

"One second, Mister." Renata waved her little finger before my face. "Now that I have all the three dresses, where are we going tonight?"

"Follow me." I said. As we walked out of the mall, I pointed up at a huge billboard advertising Coldplay's live concert.

"Tonight, I am taking you there!" I announced excitedly.

"Are you kidding me???" Renata was shocked. "We are going to Coldplay?" She double-checked.

"Yep. We are. They are my favorite band, and the stars must have aligned because we are here with them."

"Oh my God. I can't wait to go." Renata clapped her hands.

"Soon, my love. In a few hours we'll be there. Let's go back to the hotel and relax a little bit and get ready."

"It's going to be a fun night." She was so excited.

We arrived back at the hotel feeling happy and full of energy. Renata was so overwhelmed, she took her shoes off, climbed on the bed and started jumping. I connected my iPod to the speaker/CD player, and we turned on some Coldplay to get ourselves ready for the concert in the evening.

It was about 4:30 PM, and I just wanted to relax in bed with Renata by my side while listening to Coldplay songs. Since I knew most of the lyrics, I sang out loud to Clocks, Yellow, and The Scientist. The Scientist was an interesting song, because it talked about a loving relationship which would not pass the test of time. I was thinking that song could be applied to our relationships as well. We faced a long-distance test, and our summer romance was doomed to end at some point. It seemed strange but while being with Renata, I already missed her.

We rolled around in bed, singing and kissing. Knowing that eventually our relationship would end, gave me a sense of urgency and a must to enjoy what we had to the fullest.

At around 6 PM, Renata decided to take a shower, but she did not want to be alone, not even for a second. She asked if I would join her. I agreed but asked her to behave because we had the time for shower only. We still needed to get dressed and eat dinner. If that didn't work out, we could always eat at the concert. After the shower, I spread the towel across our bed and laid flat on my stomach.

"Renata!" I called out. "Could you please come here and give me a back massage?"

She didn't answer, but within seconds, I heard her approach. She then started slowly rubbing my back.

"Do you want for me to put some lotion on?" She asked.

"Yes, that would be nice." I murmured in reply.

She squirted some lotion into her hands and applied it on my skin.

"Could you try to do it stronger?" I suggested. "I like the massages that give me a little bit of pleasurable and pain. You can't have one without the other."

Renata tried but she wasn't strong enough physically for the pressure I expected from a message. Alas, she wasn't a pro. I was asking for too much.

"Sebastian, I don't think I am strong enough to do this." She complained as if she heard my thoughts. "Can I just enjoy rubbing your naked body?"

"Of course, my dear." I laughed into the pillow.

"I can definitely feel you work out a lot." Renata complimented me. "I can see every muscle on your back. Let me investigate further down."

She rubbed my lower back until she reached my butt.

"Oh my God, it is so firm and hard. You must do lots of squats." She exclaimed excitedly.

"Actually, it's from sprinting." I replied and quickly turned her over. She ended up on her back under me.

"Seniorita, our fun is just beginning. Even though, I enjoyed you rubbing my butt, let's get ready for tonight." I whispered into her lips following my words with a kiss.

I was ready in minutes. Literally. I put on my comfortable jeans and a white baseball shirt with the words Coldplay on it. That, of course, was no comparison to my little diva. She took almost two hours to get dressed and ready. I was going nuts from her running around the suite or standing before the mirror for what seemed like hours. I wanted to get going to my second Coldplay concert. The first one was in Miami, in 2003.

"Babes, are you ready?" I finally lost patience. "It's almost 8 PM, and the warmup bands should be starting to perform."

"Yes, I've just finished with my makeup. I'll be right out." Renata called out.

A minute later, she appeared, looking so stunning, she took my breath away.

"You look stunning." I stated. "I know that I am going to watch Coldplay with the most beautiful girl on and off the stage."

She beamed in response.

"Let's head out. I already called a taxi to take us to the venue." I started walking towards the door holding Renata's hand.

"What about the limo from the hotel?" She asked.

"The venue is located at the Air Canada Center which is relatively close to the hotel. Also, whenever there are concerts or sports events, the hotel reserves the right to choose who gets to use the limousine since there are a lot of VIPs staying at the hotel for those events. We'll be fine. Trust me. I take taxis all the time in my line of work. Tonight, you will be my VIP, and I will make sure all your needs are met." I assured Renata.

"I am so excited, Sebastian." She exclaimed. "You really know how to make a girl feel special."

Once in the lobby, we asked for a taxi to the Air Canada Center.

"Are you attending the Coldplay concert, sir?" The valet attendant inquired.

"Yes, we are." I answered excitedly.

"It should be a splendid night. I am sure, a young couple like yourselves will enjoy it. Let me flag down a taxi."

In a few minutes, we were on our way to the event.

"How long will it take to get to the Arena?" I asked the taxi driver as we started moving.

"Well, I would say from the hotel to the arena it's about a 5-minute drive with no traffic. But tonight, its Coldplay, so you can add another 20 minutes to the ride."

We weren't in a hurry. We had plenty of time. Plus, I was not planning on making Renata walk the streets in her high heels. We sat back and enjoyed the ride. I was excited and yet, calm and relaxed. Something about being with her just felt right.

The famous hockey arena was filled with excited crowds. We got out of the taxi, and I grabbed Renata's hand.

"So many people around. Stay close. I don't want to lose you." I told her.

We walked over to the nearest entrance, to the east side of the building. At that point, we could hear the bands playing, filling the air with great music and electric excitement. We were impatient for the concert to begin. We both knew we were about to experience something amazing.

I started following Coldplay in 2001. Since their inception, Coldplay released three very successful albums. Even being an up and coming young band, they struck a chord in my soul. For me, every song created a euphoric state of happiness and peace. For some reason, Renata made me feel the same way. I pulled her close and gave her a big kiss.

"What was that for?" She smiled after catching her breath.

"I don't know. I am just really happy. Happy to be here with you." I exclaimed.

"I think I am falling for you, Sebastian." She whispered in my ear.

"I still can't believe you planned this special weekend. When I look around, all I see are thousands of moving people, but you are the only one standing still before me. I really do care about you, Sebastian."

Her words made me deliriously happy, but I said nothing, just kissed her hand.

"Our seats are located in the 100th section which is directly above the stage. It's the first section in the arena where we can sit and enjoy the show."

"You mean to tell me you didn't get the ground floor center stage seats?" Renata teased me. "I kind of expected that from you, Seba."

"Yes, it was my original plan, but remember the trip was planned in the last minute. By the time I purchased the tickets, the ground floor was sold out. At least here you can choose to stand up and dance or take a break and sit down." I explained.

"First of all, I was kidding, Seba. I was just teasing you about the seats. Second, sit down??? I'm definitely not planning to sit. Are you getting old on me?"

"Never!" I laughed.

After we found our seats, we looked around. The arena was packed with people of all ages. I would say that most of the audience was in their 20s and 30s. Since we arrived later, the last warmup band was playing. Coldplay was next, starting around 9 PM. We still had some time before the main event.

"Renatinha, do you want a beer? We have about 20 minutes before Coldplay starts." I asked.

"Sure, but I like my beer very cold. How we say in Brazil, 'stupidly cold'." She replied while dancing to the music of the warmup band.

"At your service. I'll be right back."

I ran up to the concession booth and purchased two ice cold beers, and since I was already there, I bought two concert t-shirts to memorialize the event. I was back at our seats in ten minutes. I gave Renata her beer.

"Taste it. Is it cold enough?" I teased her.

"Oh yes, it's perfect."

"And this shirt is for you, to take back to Toronto. Look, on the back it has today's date. This way you can remember me and our special weekend together."

Renata wrapped her arms around my neck and gave me a kiss.

"Why is it I don't meet guys like you in Toronto?" She was happy, but her voice was sad.

"Well, technically you did meet me in Toronto." I played a smart-ass to cheer her up.

"You know what I mean." She insisted.

"Yes, I would say the same about you and the girls in Miami." I echoed her sentiment.

"Let's just pretend this night is forever, and there are no goodbyes." Renata stated looking straight in my eyes.

I nodded in agreement, even though, I knew that most likely, we would both have to go back to our separate cities and lives.

Our sad moment was broken when the lights went out, and the music stopped. The warmup was over, and it was time for Coldplay. First, the bass guitar started playing a melody from the song Square One. Then, the band came out, and the crowd erupted in roaring applause. We stood up holding our beers.

"We better finish it before we wear it." I told Renata pointing to our beer bottles.

Before she could reply, Chris Martin came out dancing in front of the stage. We could see him very well since we were dead center. But still, a little too far away to notice the details. Thus, we had to focus simultaneously on the big screens and the stage.

For the next 15 minutes, we did nothing but danced and jumped up and down. We did not have to talk to each other. The third song was called Yellow. It was one of my favorites. It had a slow and steady beat and was very romantic. I loved that song so much, that I knew all the lyrics by heart, and I sang the whole song to Renata. From the flashes of the pyrotechnics, I could see the beautiful silhouette of her glowing face and her mesmerizing smile. I was a lucky man to be with her. What started as a personal challenge, ended up being the woman I deeply cared for.

"Look at the stars, look at how they shine for you." I sang for her as we kissed in between songs. It felt like we gravitated towards each other as if we knew one another from a previous lifetime.

After non-stop dancing and singing, we decided to take a break for the next few songs. We sat down to enjoy the moment. We didn't talk much, it was too loud, and we really didn't need to talk; we just held hands. The music that surrounded us, made us feel warm and happy. We were about halfway through the concert, and my favorite song "The Scientist" started to play. It commenced with a slow piano melody. That song was different from the rest. It stood out. It discussed finding love, and then having to lose it. In summary, that was possibly our, Renata's and my, theme song. I knew the song by heart, so I sang it to Renata while she was dancing.

"Renata, it's a shame that it appears our future will not allow us to be together. We live different lives in separate cities." I suddenly yelled out.

"Don't talk about the future, Seba. You're going to ruin the moment." She responded. Her facial expression instantly changing from elated to sad.

"It just seems so strange that I have always liked this song but couldn't relate to it. Now I know, it's about you." I continued.

Once the light came back on, I could see tears in her eyes. I was angry with myself for ruining the happy vibe. But I couldn't help feeling that way and thinking about the future.

All my life I was looking for the right girl, only to find her in another country. Renata was that girl. I found her. She was beautiful. We had similar personalities and views on life. Who said opposites attract? We both loved life, we both knew how to appreciate things we had, and we both looked for that special someone to share that inner passion for living, joy, fun, and adventure. I knew we had the same values. In short, we were a good match. The only problem was the distance. In addition, the distance was going to widen even further, dramatically further, since I was soon departing for India. The nagging painful feeling of inevitable goodbye was torturing me from inside. The more I was with Renata, the sadder I felt about being without her. As much as I tried to just enjoy the moment with her, I couldn't shake off the ache in my heart, and the inner clock that was ticking away the time before we would be apart.

After an hour and a half, the concert was coming to an end. The lights turned off, and the ensuing silence was broken by the screaming fans. Then after about a minute or so, the lights came back on, and the last song, Fix You started. It was beautiful and one of my favorites, about trying to find love. In all my travels to far off places, I met plenty of women, but never a soul that would look me in the eye and love me back from the inside out. I knew Renata was fighting the same sadness in her heart.

As soon as the song ended, the band thanked the fans and bid farewell. The magical concert was over. Even though, it was an amazing experience, we felt a little sad. But I was an eternal optimist, upset with myself for souring our great evening. To make up for that, I took Renata's hand in mine, kissed her and whispered to her that we should just trust in fate and whatever was meant to be would be. She smiled at me.

"Now, let's get out of here and have some fun." I grinned back at my girl.

As we maneuvered our way out of the arena, the crowds were dense, and people were singing Coldplay songs. I navigated through the crowd holding Renata's hand tightly.

"Don't worry." I told her. "I am not going to lose you."

When we finally walked out onto the street, we discovered it was raining. We looked around, and it seemed everyone was involved in a "get a taxi" war. Some taxi drivers were not even interested in picking anyone up. They apparently didn't want to get their interiors wet. I didn't think it made sense for us to spend an hour trying to hail one. Thus, I looked at Renata and asked, "how about a nice stroll through the rain?"

"What, you want to walk back to the hotel?" She asked in disbelief.

"Yes, it will be fun. Come on. Let's be adventurous and have some fun." I pulled her hand and started running. The rain was pouring hard;

we had no umbrellas or raincoats. Just me, in my casual clothes, and poor Renata in her beautiful new dress. Mid-run, she asked me to stop. When we did, Renata carefully took off her heals. She looked miserable.

"You are crazy, Sebastian, but I guess there is no other way." She said.

"Nope. When was the last time you ran in the rain?" I asked laughingly.

"A very long time. I must have been in my teenage years."

As we ran, our clothes were getting drenched, and our faces were all wet. Even though the rain got us, it did not damper our spirits. Even soaking wet, Renata was still beautiful. She was a natural beauty. She did not need makeup or a fancy dress. What I liked the most, was her spirit. She was full of joy. The problems and complexities of the world we lived in, did not seem to have tarnished her at all. She was youthful, happy, and full of life.

We reached the hotel in about 20 minutes. It was 11:30 PM, and we were dying to take our wet clothes off. We went up to our room, and I asked Renata if she wanted to join me in the jacuzzi. She appeared speechless when I asked the question. She was about to ask me the same thing.

"Sebastian, we are definitely thinking the same." She giggled.

We immediately took off our clothes and jumped in. I had a cold bottle of champagne ready upon our return. We toasted for an amazing start to the weekend; Renata could not wait to hear what was next.

"So, I have to give it to you, our first night was truly magical. I had no idea that Coldplay was so good." She said.

"Yes, I think they are going to be the next U2 or the Rolling Stones. They have all the talent to continue writing great music and performing. I hope to see as many of their concerts as possible in the years to come."

"Seba, how do you plan on competing with our first date here in Montreal?" Renata teased me.

"You said the right word, "competing". We are going to an event tomorrow where it's all about competition." I replied looking straight at her.

"Where are we going?" She insisted.

"Well, I don't want to spoil the surprise, but we are going to take a drive somewhere. For you to get to know me better, the weekend consists of sharing my passions with you. Tonight, you experienced my passion for music with my favorite band. Tomorrow, you will discover another piece of me. Trust me. It will be fun." I explained.

"I still don't know why the red dress." She wondered out loud.

"Enjoy your champagne, and tomorrow will be another day." I smiled at her.

"Thank you, Seba, for planning this whole weekend out for me." Renata whispered.

"Like I told you before, I always aim to please."

After some time in the jacuzzi, we decided to take a shower. We lathered each other up while enjoying every touch and the intimate closeness we shared. Washing led to kissing and touching. After drying off, we slipped under the covers in our enormous and comfortable bed. Only then we realized how tired we both were. However, before ending the night, I wanted to do one more thing for Renata. And since the night was about my passion for music, I took my iPod, connected the headphones and placed them over her ears.

"I want you to listen attentively to this song. It has a direct connection to my soul and hopefully, to yours as well." I whispered to her.

I turned the iPod on and raised the volume. The artist was one of my favorite soul singers whom I discovered on a business trip to Barbados. Her name was India Arie, and the song was called "Brown Skin". It was about Renata and her gorgeous complexion. I dimmed the lights and let her listen. I didn't hear the song because Renata had the headphones on, but I knew it by heart and could see the song on Renata's face. She was smiling, she loved it. I knew she would. It was all about Renata. It was her weekend, her night of being the queen she was in my eyes. I wanted her to experience heaven on earth with me.

After many intense kisses and soft touches all over her body, I spread her legs and entered her. She was wet and very warm inside. I could tell she was excited to be with me. As she listened to the song, I was busy doing my best to please her. I did not want to orgasm before her. After many positions and intense thrusting, I felt ready, but she was not. Since our sexual relationship was relatively new, I was still learning what worked for her. I rolled over placing Renata on top of me. That way, she could control the rhythm. I held on to her perfect perky breasts. She moaned with pleasure. I grabbed one of her hands and placed her other hand on her pussy; right on her clit. She knew herself better than I did, so I let her concentrate and manipulate herself while she rode me. Within seconds, her legs buckled and squeezed my torso. It was time. She was ready, and so was I. We kept accelerating the movements until we froze. Renata fell awkwardly backwards and started shaking and moaning loudly. I, however, could not finish in that position, so I covered Renata with my body; missionary style. It was a perfect switch, and we orgasmed at approximately the same time. She was tired, but her face displayed pure ecstasy.

"Amazing." Renata breathed out.

"What's amazing?" I asked trying to normalize my breathing.

"You are." She whispered. Her eyes were closed, she was semi-asleep.

"Good night, my princess. Get your beauty rest, for tomorrow is another exciting day."

I kissed her forehead. We fell asleep in each other's arms.

Chapter 12

The next morning, we were awakened by the loud ringing of the phone.

"Good morning, Mr. Kosta. This is your wake-up call. It is 7 AM, Sir." Announced the voice on the other side.

"Thank you very much." I replied sleepily.

"Sir, I also wanted to let you know, your special reservation will be arriving at 8 AM and will be waiting for you upfront." He continued.

"Oh yes. Thanks once again. We should be ready for her by 10 AM." I replied.

Renata turned over and looked at me. "What do you mean you will be ready for her?"

"Good morning, baby." I laughed. "Don't worry. I am all yours. Soon, you will see. Why don't you start by taking a shower and getting ready?" I kissed her hand.

"You're not going to join me?" Renata asked.

"I would love to, but I have to work out. I always have to exercise. This is the time I use to charge my body and soul to prepare for the day ahead." I explained. "I won't be long. The workout should only take an hour. I asked for breakfast to be served up here. So, when I get back, we can eat together. Let's just plan to be out the door by 10 AM, ok baby?"

"Seba, you all about the surprises." Renata looked at me adoringly.

"Indeed, baby. Because that's what makes life magical. I will see you soon."

I went for a jog around the city, to experience it firsthand. I always thought it was better to experience new places on foot rather than on those double-decker buses. That way, I could stop anywhere I wanted and take the time to admire everything any city had to offer. It was also a good opportunity to get out and reflect on my time with Renata. I was contemplating on bringing her to India. Part of me was assured it would be a lot of fun. An adventure. But at the same time, I wasn't going to a touristy destination. There was no shopping district or much of anything there. For the most part, she would be trapped at the hotel. I decided I would not take her along; that would be too selfish of me. One month abroad, in a 3rd world country, was not the place for Renata, especially since I would be working the night shifts and sleeping during the day.

After about 30 minutes of running and thinking without actually seeing anything around me, I was back at the hotel. I wasn't satisfied with my distracting run, so I decided to hit the gym. For the hotel of that magnitude, their gym was too understated, but it had all the necessary equipment to break a sweat. Since I always followed my routines and rituals to the ninth, I performed 300 push-ups and 300 sit-ups. I kept my workouts simple and effective. That way, I could do them anywhere.

As I got off the elevator on my way to the room, I crossed paths with the lady who was about to bring our breakfast. I asked her, if it was fine to take over her duties and bring the breakfast cart in myself. She smiled and let me take the cart.

When I approached our room, I rang the doorbell. I heard Renata's voice.

"I am coming, please give me a second." Once she opened the door, she saw me.

"At your service, my lady. Your breakfast is here." I said ceremoniously.

"Seba, you don't stop to amaze me." She stated and wrapped her arms around my shoulders planting a kiss on my lips.

"Your welcome." I laughed. "I am going to take a quick shower but go ahead and start eating."

I jumped in and took a quick cold shower to instantly calm my body after the exercise. It was a good way to stop sweating. Once I got out, I noticed that Renata lost her plush white robe and was only wearing her bra and panties. As I towel dried my face, standing by the bathroom door, I took the time to admire her exotic beauty. I considered myself very lucky to have her there with me. I dropped the towel and approached her gently kissing her bare olive shoulder.

"Cover up before I lose control, and we will either be late for the surprise or skip the breakfast." I whispered into her neck. She giggled and placed a piece of aromatic freshly baked croissant into her mouth.

"I need to get dressed." She noted and got up from the bed.

"Let me know if you need help with the red dress." I said while slowly sipping the coffee.

"Actually, let me hurry up and put it on." Renata disappeared. While I was finishing up her croissant, she returned.

"Can you zip up the back?" Renata asked and turned around before me.

"Of course." I smiled. The red looked stunning against her flawless back. After I pulled the zipper up, she turned back around.

"How do I look?" She twirled.

"Very hot." I exclaimed. I couldn't get enough of her.

I got dressed in minutes, and we headed down to the lobby. When we stepped out into the front of the hotel, I saw a stunning brand-new red convertible Ferrari. At first, Renata didn't think it was for us. But then, the valet attendant opened the passenger door and invited her to get in.

"Sebastian, are you kidding me?" She was astonished.

"Well, you didn't like the taxi yesterday, so I decided to upgrade." I grinned. "Are you ready for her?"

"Oh my God! You are crazy, Seba!" Renata started laughing.

"Yes, crazy for you." I replied before getting behind the wheel.

Once inside the car, Renata turned to me.

"So, the red dress was supposed to match the car?" She asked.

"Well, yes, but not exactly. Remember how I told you about the competition?" I asked.

"Mmm, not really."

"Anyway. Today is the qualifying session for the pole position for the Grand Prix of Canada. Click it baby, we are going for a ride." I grinned.

I turned the car on, and the engine roared with gusto. I loved the sound of the red beast. As soon as I tipped the gas, the car instantly accelerated, and we headed to the Isle of Notre Dame. As I pressed the paddle shifter to change up through the gears, we could hear the melodies of the Ferrari's engine. For me, that was like listening to the best orchestra. I loved the adrenaline rush and driving that particular car with Renata by my side, gave me butterflies in my stomach. It was a beautiful day and we enjoyed the open top convertible.

Renata looked amazing in her sexy but elegant red dress and over-sized black Gucci sunglasses.

"Have you been to a car race before?" I inquired without taking my eyes off the road.

"Never." Renata replied.

"Well, unfortunately we will not be able to see the race today since the actual race is tomorrow. I already have plans for us tomorrow. But we will see the competition for pole position. Some say it's even more exciting." I explained.

"Really? How so?" Renata smiled.

"Because it's man versus machine. That is done to check who gets the fastest one lap around the Gilles Deneuve Circuit."

"Seba, can I ask you a question?" She asked after some time spent listening to the roar of the engine.

"Go ahead."

"Why are you so into cars and motorcycles? I know you have a Porsche back home, and our motorcycle ride to Niagra Falls was amazing. And now this Ferrari. You seem to be obsessed with these toys."

"Well…" I laughed. "When the man is a boy, he loves small toys, as he grows up the toys get bigger and more expensive. But here's the real expla-nation, as a young boy, I dreamt of being a race car driver. Unfortunately, my parents did not like my dream and did not have the funds to sponsor me. Therefore, I took that internal drive to compete and used it to race to the top of my career in business. If I could not be a race car driver, I would have enough money to buy the cars and perhaps race on the weekends as a hobby." I concluded.

"So that's what you do? You race on the weekends?" Renata continued.

"Yes. Back at home, I typically go racing at Homestead once a month, in my Porsche. My local dealership sponsors those events for the owners of Ferraris and Porsches."

"Do you dream about having this car one day?" Renata placed her hand over mine.

"A Ferrari? Yes. Of course. I learned how to drive a stick shift in a Porsche. And don't get me wrong, I love my car, and it was always my dream to have a Porsche. But the next step, is a brand-new red Ferrari."

"So, in some ways, you can say your dreams have come true." Renata suggested.

"Most." I specified. "Once I make it to partner at my firm, then I will be able to trade-in my Porsche for a Ferrari. Then all my dreams would have come true. But I am sure, there will be new dreams after those." I laughed knowing that once I make it to partner and get a Ferrari, I would want something else, bigger and pricier.

"Wow, Seba. It must be exciting." Renata's voice was filled with open admiration.

After about a 30-minute ride, we arrived at the racetrack. It was a narrow island connected to the mainland by an overpass. As we drove over, we could see all the 18-wheeler trucks inside the paddock of the track. Since my company, Accent, was a sponsor, we had a hospitality suite where we could relax and have lunch and a few drinks. I had no idea whom I might see or meet at our suite, since my secretary made all the reservations for me.

"This place is really beautiful." Renata exclaimed. "It looks like we are on the coast of France."

"Have you ever been to the French Riviera?" I inquired.

"No. Just saw it on picutures in popular magazines." Renata responded.

"One day." I laughed and took her hand. "This place is indeed beautiful. I've never been to this location, to see the Formula 1 race. Let's go to the hospitality suite first, get a few bottles of water and then we'll take our seats?" Renata nodded and walked out of the car. I could not believe how good she looked in the short red dress. It was perfect for the event and the season.

We walked towards the entrance of the paddock line, and the crowd opened up before us, thinking we were VIPs. I was not sure whether the Ferrari or Renata made them think that. As we entered, a boy in a Ferrari hat approached me and asked for my signature.

"I'm sorry, kid, but I believe you have me mistaken for someone else." I smiled.

"Sir, you must be famous if you have a Ferrari and a girl that looks like that." He said with a fascination in his demeanor.

Both Renata and I laughed. I signed the boy's hat to make him happy.

When we approached the hospitality suite, I presented my credentials. As we walked in, the woman working there gave us our paddock tickets which offered us an unlimited entrance anywhere on the premises. It was the best way to see the racers, their teams and the race cars. In addition to the tickets, we were given two pit passes. Those allowed us to get up close and personal with the teams. I had a friend who raced in the Indy Car series, who knew Juan Pablo Montoya. We would join the McLaren Mercedes team during the pit stops, to understand their strategy and execution. We left the suite and headed for a stroll to look at all the cool cars.

"Here, water for you, in case you get hot." I handed a bottle to Renata. She gave me an appreciative look and smiled.

"Let's walk up and down the paddock. We have about an hour until the pole position starts." I suggested.

"So, Seba, we are not watching the race today?" She inquired.

"No. This is only the qualifying for tomorrow's race."

"And why are we not coming back tomorrow for the Grand Prix?" Renata persisted.

"Well, since our flight from Toronto, I told you, I wanted to make you feel special. I wanted for us to share this weekend filled with many different things, without repeating anything. Tomorrow, we will have something else to focus on; key word "focus". I also wanted to show you what I was about through the events I planned. Everything we do, consists of my passions. I think it is very important for the couple to enjoy one another's hobbies and interests. With me, life never gets old or boring. I love adventure and I hope the adventures you experience with me will ring a happy bell in your memory every time you think of me."

Renata listened to me very carefully. She didn't respond when I finished talking. But I could see, she understood what I was trying to say. Thus, I took her hand, and we strolled up and down the paddock.

About half an hour into our walk, we caught the roar of the engines. They sounded like the motorcycle engines but loader and throatier. They kept revving them up and down.

"What's going on?" Renata asked.

"I believe they are warming up their engines." I replied. "I think qualify will start soon, but I am starving." I pronounced pulling Renata back towards the suite.

It was 12:30 PM, and I wanted to get a quick lunch at our hospitality suite. Upon entering the suite, I caught a whiff of the food, and my mouth started watering. There was a buffet style lunch with hot plates and all types of delicious salads. We helped ourselves and sat down. Once seated and eating, I looked around the suite. I didn't see anyone from the Toronto office. I guessed most of the people there were from the Montreal division. We didn't mingle at all. We were short on time. The plan was to have a quick lunch and head over to our seats, to enjoy the race for pole position.

"Seba, tell me how pole position works?" Renata asked me. "If I am going to watch this event, I want to at least understand how it works."

"You are right, baby." I smiled. "You see, in Formula 1, winning the pole position is almost like winning the final race on Sunday. Most of the winners of pole position go on to win the races. That is, of course, if their cars don't break down or get into accidents. They also get points for winning, and I am sure a lot of money. Now, the basics. Two attempts are given to race one lap as fast as possible. Each driver tries this alone on the track. Whoever gets the fastest lap in two attempts will be the pole position winner. The order of the start will also be determined by each driver's time in qualifying. The closer they are to the pole position, the better the race result should be, minus any race incidents." I concluded.

"I think, I got it." Renata said. She appeared to be speaking to herself more than to me. "So, each driver has two tries to go as fast as possible to win the first-place spot?"

"Yes, that is correct. You see. I believe the qualifier is as or even more exciting than the race itself. In Formula 1, there isn't much passing after the first lap. Also, it's very important for you to know that watching this live is completely different than on TV. Here, we only get to see a straight-a-way or a curve. While on TV, we can watch the whole racetrack. But unlike on TV, here, you get a chance to see the cars and the drivers, to experience the excitement and feel the live roars of the engines."

"How exciting, Seba!" Renata exclaimed and clapped her hands. "I can't wait to see this."

"You won't have to wait for too long because it's starting shortly." I got up and offered my hand to Renata. "Let's go babes, let's see that!"

We hurried to the Wall of Champions and took our seats.

"Wow, these are really nice seats." Renata noted.

"Yes, they are perfect. We are right by the final curve going into the final straightaway before the finish line." I explained. "We will be able to see the cars pass the finish line, and simultaneously check the final standings board for who finishes first."

"Seba, I don't know how you pulled off planning this weekend after working so much during the week." Renata said admiringly.

"Well, I did my best, but I have to the give credit to my secretary. I just told her what I wanted, and she did everything else."

For the next two hours, we watched the qualifying for the Canadian Grand Prix. It was a lot of fun to see the fastest cars in the world fly by us at blistering speeds. Every time a driver obtained a pole position, Renata got excited and jumped up and down. She did not know much about the sport, but she easily caught on the fever of the competition.

After the event, we decided to change scenery from the Wall of Champions and visit the McLaren Mercedes pit crew and Juan Pablo Montoya. The pits were close by; after a 10-minute walk, we were there.

"How are you guys doing?" We were warmly welcomed. "Welcome to the team. Here, you will be able to see the pit strategy in full execution. Later on, JP will come in for his pit stops. He is already in the car awaiting his turn. I believe he is next." Said the Chief Crew Strategist.

We looked over the monitors and saw JP was indeed next in line. That would be his first attempt at claiming the pole position.

"Seba, tell me how you know Montoya?" Renata inquired.

"Well, I don't actually know him. But I know several race car drivers from the IndyCar series that live in Miami. On occasion, we enjoy riding motorcycles on weekends. I heard Montoya is a natural at the sport. Gifted from an early age. He's done very well in Formula 1. He is also a major celebrity not only in his home country of Colombia but all over the world." I noted. "The rumor has it, before Montoya jumps in the car, he is in one of the trailers having sex with a local fan. Then he straps on his helmet and goes at it."

"Really, Seba?" Renata laughed. "That sounds like something you would do."

"You're hilarious." I replied laughingly.

Suddenly, we heard the tires burn out, and Montoya was off. As soon as he left the pits, we lost the sight of his car. From that point, we had to depend on the screens inside the pits. One showed live TV broadcast, and we could see the car moving around the track. The other, the sector times and if Montoya was ahead or behind those times. In a mere 1 minute and 15 seconds, he was back in the pits. He was unable to capture the pole position. Montoya was currently in 5th place. Later that afternoon, Montoya tried the second run but was unable to surpass his time.

We decided to head back to our seats to watch the rest of the qualifying. After almost two hours, we were tired of moving our heads back and forth watching the race cars pass by. In the end, the winner of the pole position was Jenson Button from Great Britain. My favorite driver Michael Schumacher, from Germany, classified in second place. The third-place winner was a young Spaniard Fernando Alonso.

"So, I have a question for you?" Renata spoke out after a long silence.

"Go ahead, shoot." I turned my face to her.

"You mentioned, in your early childhood you wanted to be a race car driver?"

"Yes, I did." I nodded.

"Do you think you could be here today if given the opportunity?"

"That's a tough question to answer, but I believe if you're passionate about something and you are willing to bust your ass doing the hard work, then yes, I do think it is possible." I explained. "But, like I've mentioned before, my family did not have the financial means to sponsor me, and you need millions to get to Formula 1. Now, I just enjoy my passion for racing on the weekends with my Porsche and my motorcycles. I feel the most alive when my adrenaline is pumping fast, and I am truly in the present moment. My mind does not wander to the past or to the future."

As we spoke, we made it back to the car, and I opened the top. It was almost 4 PM, and I wanted to drive back to the hotel. I had a CD, which I purchased at the Coldplay's concert the night before. We listened to it as we enjoyed the sounds of the Ferrari engine in the background.

"Thank you, Seba." Renata murmured.

"For what?" I asked without taking my eyes off the road.

"For everything. The hotel, the dresses, Coldplay, the race today. No guy has ever done that for me." She explained.

"I am an all or nothing type of a guy. When I met you, I knew there was something special about you." I took a quick glance at Renata. "What's the point of having money if you can't share it with someone you like?" I inquired.

Renata's face was illuminated by the sun, and I noticed a few tears streaming down her cheeks. I reached and gently wiped the tears from her face.

"'Why are you tearing up?" I whispered.

"Those are happy tears." She replied and smiled. I reached for Renata's hand and kissed her fingers as we continued driving. We didn't talk for the rest of the ride, but we knew our hearts were filled with joy…and love.

When we arrived at the hotel, we were greeted by the night valet team. They opened Renata's door first and then mine.

"Did you enjoy the Ferrari, sir?" The valet attendant asked me.

"Too much I must admit. I need to get one of those toys one day."

"Enjoy the rest of your evening, sir." He said.

"Thank you." I nodded and extended my hand with a generous tip for the team.

At the lobby, we were welcomed by the concierge.

"Did you enjoy the races today, madam." He asked Renata.

"Oh yes, very much." She smiled and whispered; her lips by my ear. "Seba, how did he know we were at the race?"

"He is the one who reserved the Ferrari for us." I whispered back.

"Oh, ok. Now I get it."

We wished a good night to the concierge and entered the elevator that took us up to our private lobby entrance into our hotel room.

"Hungry?" I asked Renata as we walked into the suite.

Renata didn't reply. Instead, she stretched on the bed.

"I think right now I just want to lay down for a while. Come here and join me." She invited.

I walked to the bed and sat down.

"Come on. Lay down next to me." She insisted.

There we were again, laying at the foot of the bed and staring at the ceiling.

"You know, Seba, I typically wait for a guy to say it first." Renata broke the silence in her gentle voice.

"Say what first?" I asked.

"You know, that special word. The "L" word."

I kind of figured out where Renata was going from the start, but I wanted to hear that from her. I smiled and turned my head to Renata.

"I know that we've only known each other for a month, but, Seba, I am falling in love with you." She whispered timidly.

"You know, I was thinking about this very moment during our ride from the race." I echoed her tranquil demeanor. "I mean, here I am, with the most amazing girl, doing the things I am most passionate about. You don't criticize or question me; you go with the flow. I was always very scared of commitment. It's a big word for me. It means that I am committed to you no matter what. And even though I do feel the same towards you, I believe I lack the necessary commitment because we live in separate countries. If you lived in Miami, it would be a totally different story." I said bitterly.

"Let's say I moved to Miami. Would you love me then?" She asked tears glistening in her gorgeous eyes.

"Are you kidding???" I exclaimed, sitting up instantly. "I don't need for you to move to Miami to love you. I am already in love with you. I just don't know where this relationship is going to end up due to the distance separating us."

"Let's just pretend that somehow and someday I will be with you in Miami." Renata continued. "Let's not let our distance hurt our weekend together, and the time we still have before you travel to India."

"I think you are right." I agreed. "As much as I try living in the moment, I struggle to remain in it and tend to overthink sometimes."

We agreed that our conversation was getting too deep. Instead, we decided to get ready for a nice dinner.

"What type of food are you in the mood for tonight?" I inquired while stretching comfortably on the bed.

"Since we are in the heart of this amazing city, why don't we go for a walk, visit local restaurants, and check out their menus. Let's be spontaneous and live in your moment?" Renata teased me.

"I like that idea, Renata. But don't say "your" moment. Our moment." I smiled and we kissed.

We walked out of the hotel and stopped.

"To the left or to the right?" Renata asked.

"I always choose the right." I replied staring adoringly at her as she nodded without any objections, as always.

We walked hand-in-hand, enjoying Montreal's beautiful streets, modern buildings in downtown, and the historical architecture of the Old Port. Montreal was always foodie's paradise, and it was easy to walk into random places and discover the best meals ever. We found several streets in the Old Port part of the city that were closed for car traffic and open only for pedestrians. There, people walked leisurely, enjoyed fine dining or great shopping, and historical sights.

"Since you are heading far away to India, I want to give you something that will both protect and remind you of me." Renata said pulling me into some store she spotted as we strolled around the Old Port.

That particular store sold different types of bracelets. There was one that immediately caught Renata's eye. It was beaded and made from sandalwood. She picked the bracelet up and smelled it.

"Wow, Sebastian! You have to smell this. The aroma is incredible." She placed the bracelet right under my nose. "Like something from the far east, earthy and mystical."

At that very moment, the store's owner appeared from the door in the back. She greeted us, and then noticed Renata holding the sandalwood bracelet.

"Are you interested in the mala beads?" She asked.

"Yes, we are." Renata nodded.

"This one is from China. They are handmade by the Tibetan monks exiled together with the Dalai Lama. They live in India now. There are exactly 108 beads in this particular bracelet."

"Why 108?" I inquired.

"It's for mantra. There are three short phrases which you will repeat 108 times. Such as "I am brave, I am wise, I am strong." Each time you rub the bead with your two fingertips, say the mantra, and move on to the next one." The owner explained. "The mala beads are used to quiet the mind. In times of crisis, just hold the mala beads in your hand and repeat the mantra until you feel calm and centered."

"Sebastian, I want to buy this bracelet. It will protect you in India. You've never been there, and I'm worried about you." Renata told me and turned to the store owner. "How much is it?"

"Those are authentic Tibetan mala beads. The bracelet costs $50, but I will sell it to you for $40."

Renata smiled and reached into her wallet. She extracted the money and gave it to the old woman. The owner placed the bracelet into a blue velvet pouch and gave it to Renata.

"When you get on the plane on your way to India, please wear this bracelet." She said in the most ceremonious manner, like she was knighting me.

"Babes, are you serious?" I asked with a chuckle.

"Yes, I am very serious about this. If I believe it will protect you, then you have to wear it." She was adamant.

"Okay, fine I will wear it." I gave up but was unable to stop laughing, mostly, because Renata was so solemn about the whole thing.

After the bracelet thing, we continued to explore the Old Port. We finally stopped near Mondavie, a traditional French restaurant. It boasted excellent local cuisine and a cozy ambiance. Perfect for the two of us.

We were at the midpoint of our weekend getaway. Even though, we were inseparable since we arrived in Montreal, we couldn't get enough of each other. There was a gravitational pull between us. And it was stronger than anything I'd ever experienced before.

We sat down at the table for two and asked for a bottle of Cabernet. I quickly glanced over the menu, ordering a plate of manchego cheese and Prosciutto di Parma. When we were served with our wine and appetizer, I raised my glass.

"To the unforgettable moments together. Love you, babes." I toasted.

Renata smiled and after our first sips we leaned towards each other and kissed. That kiss was unforgettable. I could taste vanilla from the wine on Renata's luscious lips.

"You know, Seba. Everything feels like a dream. Please, tell me I don't have to wake up. These past couple of days have been magical for me, and I will never forget them." She said dreamily.

"Well, this hasn't ended yet. We are continuing; and tomorrow there is one more special event." I replied.

"Can you tell me about it? Or I have to wait until tomorrow?"

"I think we had enough surprises for one day. Plus, by now you know me pretty well. You can trust me with good planning?" I laughed.

"Is tomorrow's event one more of your passions?" Renata wouldn't give up.

"Yes."

"Can you at least tell me why I need to wear the white dress?" She persisted.

"The reason for the white dress is it's the final championship at the Rodgers Cup. It's a tennis match between two incredible athletes; Andre Agassi and Rafael Nadal. I thought white would be perfect for the occasion."

"Oh my God, I love tennis. I grew up playing tennis back in Brazil." Renata clapped her hands in excitement.

"Really??? I had no idea." I echoed her tone. "Then you will definitely enjoy the match. Do you know about the players?"

"I know Agassi but haven't heard about Nadal." She noted honestly.

"I can understand that. He is young. But for sure the next upcoming super star. He is only 19 years old but has already conquered the clay at the French Open. I think you will enjoy tomorrow. It won't be as crazy as our other dates though."

While we chatted, we enjoyed our dinner and desert. We finished the bottle of wine and had a great conversation about life in general. We had such a good time getting to know each other that we didn't notice how the evening and darkness took over the sunshine. It was getting late. I suggested for us to return to the hotel. The next day was going to be long and eventful. Right after the tennis tournament, we were heading straight to the airport. We enjoyed our last stroll through the beautiful streets of Montreal. Even though, I cherished every moment spent with Renata, I knew that once on the plane back to Toronto, my focus would switch back to the project and its completion.

I was selling a fairy tale life to Renata knowing full well that in order to turn our everyday into the past weekend filled with luxury and extravagance, I would have to get that promotion to partner in the firm. That's if I would end up with Renata. That, as well, wasn't a guarantee.

When we were at the hotel, at our suite, we couldn't resist each other, even though we were exhausted. The only difference was, our love making was much more passionate and urgent. It was our last night in the paradise. Furthermore, our souls were connected, and we were in love. That was new for me since I'd never loved a woman before. I was with many women, but no one could compare to Renata. She was not only beautiful, she was unique. The thought of that being our last night in Montreal was very unpleasant, but I took ahold of myself. Since we agreed to only focus on the moment, I pushed away the anxiety of the possibly of not having Renata in my future.

Chapter 13

The next morning, I woke up before Renata. I was an early riser. No matter where I was, I was typically up at sunrise. I took advantage of my early awakening and ordered room service. That way, Renata could be awakened by the smell of the hot coffee and fresh pastry. The men's Championship was at 2 PM, thus, we had plenty of time to get to Rodgers Arena.

After finishing a glass of freshly squeezed orange juice, I decided to focus on myself while Renata was still asleep. Even though, the weekend was all about pampering, impressing, and making her happy, I decided to spend some time alone concentrating on my physical and emotional health. That way, my soul would feel alive, and I'd be ready for the day ahead.

I put on my jogging shoes and wrote a note for Renata, just in case she woke up before I returned. I left it on the pillow next to my sleeping beauty. It read, "Went for a jog. Enjoy the breakfast. Be back soon. Love, Seba."

As I exited from the hotel, I set the timer for 30 minutes. I planned to be back within an hour. While jogging, I liked to think about my life and how grateful for and proud I was of everything I'd achieved. Some people thought of me as egocentric but in life, I had to make me the number one priority. If I wasn't in good health, I couldn't take care of myself or others. I considered it a mistake that too many people were fully focused on everyone and everything but themselves. From an early age, I knew that if I took care of myself and did well, then I could easily care for others. I used my free time to read a lot and acquire new skills such as photography, dancing, and writing. I kept a journal of ideas and goals. In fitness, I set a goal of running a marathon.

I've done half marathons a couple of times but never the whole thing. Professionally, I wanted to make partner within a year or so. Proudly and thankfully, I was on track for both of my professional and fitness goals. My train of thought was interrupted by the alarm of the timer. I headed back to the hotel.

It was 8 AM. I turned around and followed the same path I initially took across downtown Montreal. The only difference was, I wanted to beat my own time, so I increased the pace. Renata was my inspiration. There was a chance that she'd already woke up and read my note. I did not want to leave her alone for too long. I planned for the room service to arrive at 8:30 AM. I wanted to be back by then.

The running got tougher, and I could feel my lungs expanding and contracting as I was drenched in sweat. I was looking forward to a cold shower to tone my body and awaken the senses. There was nothing like a runner's high; it was hard to achieve but amazing to experience. I loved the adrenaline rush. Whether I was hang-gliding in Rio de Janeiro, Brazil, bungee jumping in Acapulco, Mexico, or sky diving in Panama City, Panama, I craved the rush. It was unbelievable.

I arrived at the hotel at 8:28 AM, 2 minutes ahead. I was happy, I was able to beat my own time. I waved to the two employees as I jogged by the front desk and then jumped into the elevator. When the elevator stopped at our private foyer, I noticed the door leading into the suite was open.

Renata was awakened by the room service I ordered. As I walked in, the staff was there setting up breakfast for two at the sofa lounge. I greeted them and went straight to our bedroom.

"Good morning, sweetheart!" I smiled to Renata who looked completely disoriented, still semi-asleep.

"Hello, Seba. Already up?" She mumbled.

"You know I have this internal clock set to sunrise. I woke up, had nothing to do, so I decided to go for a jog." I replied.

"I think you are kind of addicted to working out. Even on vacation you do your pushups and sit ups. You are like a machine." Renata teased.

"Well, I believe if I take care of myself then I can attend to you better both during the day and night."

"Funny, Seba. You do entertain me, that is for sure." Renata stretched and got off the bed.

"Listen, go ahead and start eating. Don't wait for me." I suggested. "I am all sweaty and dying to take a cold shower."

The butler finished setting up the table and left the room, and while Renata enjoyed her coffee and croissant, I went to the shower. First, I turned my iPod on to some chill electronic music and connected it to a Bose docking station. That music reminded me of my times in Ibiza when I enjoyed watching the sunset over the water in some chic lounge. It felt like a massage for my soul. I first shaved and then jumped in the shower. I turned the cold water on. Immediately, I felt the chill cooling down my head and body after the excruciating run. I must have burned around 1,000 calories in one hour. My body was on edge. Now, it was time to refresh and recover to have an amazing day with Renata.

"Renatinha, do you want to join me in the shower?" I yelled out trying to scream over the music. "The water is nice and cold."

Moments later, Renata walked into the bathroom and opened the shower door.

"Even though, I like what I see, there is no way I am going to give up my hot coffee for that ice-cold water. You're nuts." She giggled.

After about ten minutes, I got out of the shower and toweled myself dry. I felt great and was happy that the weekend was a total success. I put shorts, a tee-shirt, and my Converse shoes on.

"Do you have room for me on that sofa?" I teased. It was a huge sofa. Ten of me could've sat there.

"For you, of course my dear." Renata echoed my sarcasm. "Come, have a seat next to me. Not sure if your coffee is still hot."

I sat down and inhaled deeply.

"Now, it's just fun for the rest of the day." I announced.

"Seba, how do you manage to live your life so intensely and so passionately?" Renata asked.

"I live with the motto of no regrets. I don't know when my time comes to an end; so, I live every day as if there is no tomorrow. "I replied seriously.

"I wish I could live like that, but I am too busy focusing on all the problems in my life. It's a hectic world and sometimes, I can't slow it down. I know that this weekend getaway is incredible, but tomorrow, I have to go back to work and to reality." Renata sighted with sadness.

I felt her. I knew exactly what she was talking about.

"Maybe tomorrow might be different." I tried encouraging her.

Renata smiled, and continued, "how can things be different?"

"We don't know the future. It can only be predicted based on the past, but if you create your own future and not be an observer than you can have fun and play on this earth as if you had the joy and happiness of a young child." I replied.

"Oh, Sebastian, you are too much of a dreamer." Renata exhaled.

"Dreaming is fun. It teaches you what's possible." I laughed.

"So, listen, it's almost 10 AM, and we have some time before the tennis match. The event opens at 11. It's a beautiful day, so perhaps we can take a taxi to the arena and walk around, get some sun, and have lunch?" I suggested. "The match is the best of three sets, so I figure it should last at least for 2 to 3 hours. We won't have to rush because I have reserved an evening flight. That should give us enough time to enjoy ourselves and feel no pressure about leaving early."

"Sounds like a plan." Renata nodded in agreement. "I just want to enjoy this Sunday with you, Seba. I don't really care about the tennis."

"Trust me, you will care about the tennis match when you see the two titans go at it." I assured her. "Agassi is one of the best American tennis players of all time. He is always exciting since he thrives off the energy of the crowd. Nadal is very young, only 19 years old, but he has just won the French Open for the very first time. Tennis has never seen anyone who plays with the intensity of Nadal. He only focuses on one point at a time, but with the grit of no other player. If he does not get injured, he might become one of the greatest players of all time." I summarized.

"Sounds exciting. I can't wait to see them play." Renata said without much enthusiasm.

I turned the TV on and watched it, while Renata was getting ready. She would wear the third and final dress I had purchased for her. She locked herself in the bathroom for about an hour. When she finally came out, my jaw dropped. The piece looked great on a mannequin, but her wearing it made me lose my breath. The contrast between the white fabric and her brown honey colored skin was stunning. Her skin was glowing. The dress was tight around her midsection as well as her bust. The skirt was short and flowy. Renata wore white high heeled shoes which matched the dress perfectly and completed her sexy but elegant look.

"I'm ready. How do I look, Seba?"

"You look stunning. Irresistible. I think this dress is my favorite of the three." I stated with admiration.

We packed our bags and went down to the lobby. I asked the front desk to take care of our luggage and was assured they would take care of everything and hold our bags, until we are ready to reclaim them on our way to the airport. The concierge ordered a taxi for us, and it arrived promptly. I told the driver where we were going, and he informed us that the place where the Rodgers Cup was held was only 15 minutes away.

As we left the premises, Renata and I discussed our great experience at the hotel and how wonderful were the employees.

While I was not into taking pictures, Renata, on the other hand, took pictures of everything. She was obsessed with the pictures. I was teasing her all the time about that. But as we drove, she showed me all the pictures of our weekend together. Only then, I appreciated her little hobby.

"I will never forget this weekend, Seba." She said tearfully. "These memories will last a lifetime, and I thank you for our time spent together and all the gifts. Truly unforgettable."

We arrived at the arena in no time. It was around noon, and as we got in line to enter it, we realized how hungry we were. The food court was in the middle of the public grounds.

"Hold my hand." I told Renata. "It's packed here, and I don't want to lose you."

Renata nodded and took my hand. We zig zagged our way through the crowd and started approaching each food stall to check out what was offered.

"So, my dear, what are you in the mood for?" I inquired. "There's grilled steak, sushi, crepes, and sandwiches. What does your belly desire?"

"Well, we already had sushi at the hotel in Toronto. I also ate the crepes at the mall here, so let's try something different. Let's look at the sandwiches?" She suggested.

We walked over to the stall that offered French sandwiches. We stared at the menu board for a couple of minutes.

"I know what I want." Said Renata.

"And what is that, my dear?" I asked.

"I want the croque-monsieur."

"Well done! I will have the same. Simple but tasty." I agreed.

We ordered, picked up our sandwiches up and sat down at the nearby table.

"You know, this venue reminds me of Lincoln Road in Miami Beach. I love sitting there and people-watch." Renata noted as we chewed our food and looked at the crowds passing by.

"It's cool to just sit back and look at the different people and see how they are dressed. Trying to figure out if they are happy or sad." Renata continued.

"How can you tell if they are sad?" I asked.

"Well, they typically have glazed appearance in their eyes. They are not really focusing on anything, just on auto pilot. Life is passing by them. They are almost like zombies." She noted sadly. "To me, it's sad, because I always like to be happy. Happiness attracts good things and good people. It's all in the vibe."

"I would have to agree with you. Let's get your happy butt into the stadium, so we can reserve our seats." I smiled.

"You're so funny, Seba." Renata giggled.

We walked into the large open arena. It was a beautiful day. Fortunately, the rain was not in the forecast. We approached the lower level box section and were escorted to our seats. Once again, my secretary did a wonderful job in picking our seats. We were placed in the shade, away from the sun. We still had about half an hour until the players were going to come out, so I decided to get us some champagne.

"There you go, madame." I stated ceremoniously while extending a flute to Renata. "Bubbly for the princess."

"Why thank you, Seba. That is very nice of you."

"A toast to living every day as if it was your last." I suggested raising my glass.

"I would like to correct your toast, to forever." Renata smiled timidly.

"Forever?" I asked.

"Yes, may this moment last forever." Renata nodded.

"Perfect."

Our glasses clinked, and we kissed. Then, Renata held my arm close to her chest as we watched the crowd slowly come into the stadium. We were startled by the loud rock music that filled up the stadium. And I knew, the players were about to be introduced.

The first one to come out was Rafael Nadal. He was a young phenomenon from Spain. He was very individualistic and different. One could see that in his manner of dressing and presenting himself. Instead of the white polo, he wore a red sleeveless shirt highlighting his sculpted muscles. He looked more like a boxer than a tennis player. He was already drenched in sweat. He approached his chair and dropped off his bag on the floor and started his usual pre-game rituals. The next player to be introduced was the great American tennis star Andre Agassi. He walked out appearing confident and comfortable. He participated in that event in Montreal many times in the past and was a veteran of the tour. Over the years, he's lost most of his long hair and was now proudly showing his baldness. Agassi and Nadal had many common features, among those, top physical shape and methodical approach to the game.

As the players started their warmup, we noted with pleasure, we had the best seats. We were so close; we could see everything that was happening on the court in detail. It was amazing to observe the two people who by their sheer appearance had the power to quiet thousands of people in mere seconds.

"The game is about to begin." I told Renata as I kissed the tips of her fingers. "Whom are you going for?" I inquired.

Renata hesitated to answer, but after a pause and consideration, she said that she was supporting Agassi. She honestly admitted that she didn't know anything about Nadal while Agassi was a legend.

"I also think it's cool he was married to Brooke Shields." I added.

"Yes, but now he is married to Steffi Graf. One of the best female tennis players of all time. Can you image the tennis genes of their kids?" She exclaimed in admiration. "What about you, Seba? Who are you going for?"

"Growing up, my idol was Agassi. Can you believe I even purchased the same denim outfit he wore in the 90s? But I have to say that at only 19 years of age, Nadal is already ranked number 2 in the world, and he's just won his first Major at the French Open. I also love Spain. I was studying Spanish in Madrid for a few months, so I have to go with the young gun." I replied thoughtfully.

When the match started, the players went hard at it from the very beginning. The ball was flying back and forth with incredible power and velocity. Nadal was able to break serve and won the first set 6-4. I explained to Renata that tennis was pretty simple. One had to hold serve and execute great returns. Agassi was very well known for exactly that talent. His return of serves was unparalleled. He would usually get inside the baseline and then hammer back the returns.

"I thought tennis was much more complex." Renata noted.

"In reality it is, but if you break it down into those two main points, you typically have a winner." I replied.

The second set was the opposite. Agassi, with his great return of serve, broke Nadal's service game and won the set 6-4. They were tied at 1-1. As we entered the 3rd set, the players have been on the court for almost two hours. The third and final set was a battle, just the way Nadal liked it. It seemed the tougher the fight was, the more interested in the challenge he was.

Some tennis players approached their game like an artists, but Nadal was a pure fighter. He managed beating Agassi in the 3rd set by 6-2, and thus, winning the championship. In his unique and customary way of celebrating the win, Nadal shook hands with Agassi and then walked over to the middle of the court and just opened his arms in triumph and leaned his head back with his eyes closed. It was as if he was absorbing all the positive energy of the crowd to refuel his tank.

"This kid is going to make history." I stated with exuberant satisfaction. "If he can remain healthy and avoid serious injuries, he has the chance to be the greatest player of all time."

Once the match finished, we walked out of the arena and looked for a taxi. It took us more than 30 minutes to get one, but I wasn't worried. It was only 5 PM; we had three hours to spare before our flight at eight. During our ride we discussed how great the match was. We also agreed we had to go to another tennis match, perhaps in March, during the Miami Open. I was sad to think that our incredible weekend was coming to an end. Renata was happy and in love with me. We were in a strange position because we could not talk about our future. We were scared because we had separate distinct lives; we lived in different countries and were driven by our professional ambitions. We agreed to speak about the present moment only.

When our flight took off, Renata slept on my shoulder. Once the plane landed, we went our seperate ways in two taxis since it was Sunday night, and we both needed rest before work on Monday.

Chapter 14

I was awakened by the loud sound of the alarm clock. I reached for my phone. It was 5 AM. I haven't spent a day in Toronto and once again, I was heading to the airport. That time, I was going to Chicago.

I had to return to work and shift my focus on developing the level 3 process maps, so that I could give it to my team lead Shanti, to develop the desktop standard operating procedure, which would be used for the general users in Chennai, India.

At that point in my career, I could do business trips in my sleep. I would literally be half awakened. Just enough to know where I was going, and what I was doing. Such as getting in the security line, placing my laptop in a bin, and taking my shoes off. I would then board the plane and place my head in the opening between my seat and the one next to me. In less than 30 seconds, I would be asleep. That sleep would be relaxing and comfortable like I was at the hotel room, in my bed. Most of the time, I was still asleep when the plane was about to land, and the stewardess would tap me on my shoulder asking to raise my seat back for the arrival. Besides being accustomed to constant travel routines, I also knew Toronto's O'Hare Internation Airport with my eyes closed.

By 9 AM, I started waking up. I was ready to face the day. In addition, I always traveled light, my PC bag and carryon only. Thus, it was very easy to move around. I exited the plane with the crowd, and since I didn't need to claim any luggage, I left the airport. Once out, I flagged the taxi and headed to the Hudd's service delivery center.

During my ride to Hudd's center, I recalled the good times when I started working as a senior consultant at Arthur Andersen. Those were the good times when the company hired stretch limousines to pick us up at the airport and drive us for an hour to the Arthur Andersen University in St. Charles. Not only did we acquire new skills but had a lot of fun. We even had a social center with free-flowing draft beer for all new hires. Back then, the company really knew how to impress the young talent and make them feel as a part of a great business family. Unfortunately, due to the Enron scandal, the US government pretty much tore the company that was almost 100 years old with over 100,000 employees down. It was sad. I, however, didn't lose my job like most of the other employees, but was actually acquired by KPMG Consulting, which later changed its name to BearingPoint Consulting.

"Sir, we have arrived. The building is on your left." I heard the driver's voice amid my recollections. I thanked the man and paid the fare using my corporate card.

After I entered the building, I looked through my notebook to find out the information regarding my contact person, and where I was going. I was meeting with Hudd's Mid-West and West Coast Regional Finance Director. Her name was Claire McDermot. As soon as I arrived at the 39th floor, I walked over to the receptionist.

"Good morning, my name is Sebastian Kosta, and I'm here to meet with Claire McDermot." I said with a smile.

"Good morning." She replied. "Let me check her calendar. Yes, we do have your meeting with Claire at 10 AM. Why don't you take a seat, and Ms. McDermot will be out in a few minutes?"

I thanked the receptionist and sat down. Since I had a little free time, I decided to check on Renata.

"Good morning, my princess. I hope you slept well?" I texted her.

"Oh my God, Seba. I miss you already." She replied in seconds.

"I am in Chicago." I wrote.

"What? But it's only 10 AM!"

"Yes, I took the first flight out. Did you get enough sleep?" I asked Renata.

"I got to work a little late. I think, I am still tired and overwhelmed from our amazing weekend." She replied.

"Glad you liked it!"

In that instance, I heard the sound of the clicking heels, and when I looked up from my phone, I saw a red-haired woman entering the reception area and walking towards me.

"Got to go. Bye!" I quickly texted to Renata and got up from my seat.

"Good morning." She greeted me. "I assume, you are Sebastian?"

"Yes. Are you Claire?" I smiled.

"That's me."

"It's a pleasure to meet you." We shook hands.

"Likewise. How was your flight?" Claire inquired.

"To be honest, I slept right through it. It felt more like a cab ride than a three- and half-hours flight."

"That's great! Why don't you follow me to my office?"

We walked for a bit and then entered a large area. The executive offices were located around the perimeter of the area, and the center was occupied by cubicles. We crossed the area, passing by the cubicles, and Claire opened the door into her private office. The office was large and filled with light from the floor to ceiling windows. The first thing I did was to scan the books on her shelves and looked for other pertinent details that would give me an inside look into her personality. My father taught me that. The practice worked best to break the ice. I made a mental note that Claire was a mother of a boy and girl, and her husband was a pilot. And that was my way into establishing our business relationship.

"So, I see your husband is a pilot?" I asked nonchalantly.

"Oh, you noticed. Yes, he works for American Airlines."

"So, I imagine he travels more than I do." I joked, for it was obvious.

"Yes, it's very tough for us. During the week I am a single mom and have to manage work and my kids' school." Claire responded.

"I see how that might be very challenging." I agreed. I had no clue, actually.

"Flying planes was always his biggest passion. He started as a Marine and flew helicopters in Afghanistan at first. Now, that he is a civilian pilot, flying 737s across the US and the Caribbean, it's less stressful for us." She noted.

"Well, at least you must get really nice travel perks."

"That is true. We always have two major vacations a year. One in the winter and the other one in the summer."

"So, Claire, per our phone conversation, I am here to take a deep dive in your account receivables, credit and collection processes. Remember, my focus is not on changing anything or making any improvements right now. Perhaps, once the operation moves to India, we will focus on continuous improvements over the years. But now, I am only looking at documenting the current state. Like I previously mentioned, I would need to spend a couple of days taking notes of the process in order to create the operation manuals for our new general users in Chennai." I moved our small talk into the needed direction.

"Yes, I do remember our conversation." Claire affirmed. "And I have three clerks for you to sit down with this week and to shadow their work. The first person you will meet today is Simon Freely. He is our account receivables clerk for the Midwest region. As a note, we have standard processes and procedures, therefore the west region will be the same for the all three processes."

"That's great." I replied. "That will reduce my time for completion."

"We had a very strong internal consulting team which helped us develop best practices. Our CEO was previously a partner at Ernst and Young, so he recruited a very gifted team." Claire mentioned. "Tomorrow, you will meet with Eddie Houser who is the supervisor for credit. On Thursday, you will meet with Nathan Daniels who handles our collections. When are you going back to Toronto?"

"I've scheduled my flight for Thursday afternoon. At 4 PM."

"Then you can use Thursday morning to follow up with any additional questions for all three people interviewed and me, of course."

"Thank you so much. I really appreciate you meeting with me today and for setting up my meetings with your team." I told Claire.

"Let me take you to Simon. You can meet with him and start documenting the process." She suggested.

We walked over to the other side of the office near the cafeteria, to Simon's cube.

"Good morning, Simon." Claire greeted him.

"Hello, Claire." Simon got up from his chair.

"Last week, I mentioned about the consultant coming from Toronto. Simon, meet Sebastian."

"Hi, nice to meet you, Simon." I offered my hand for a handshake.

"The pleasure is mine." Simon replied.

"He will work with you today. He will shadow you and learn what you do on a daily basis." Claire added. "Please help him with whatever he needs since outsourcing is the number one initiative for Hudd right now, and we need to execute well, or we will suffer later."

"Don't worry. I have all my work documented, so it should be rather simple for Sebastian to modify it into whichever format he chooses." Simon assured us.

"Thank you, Simon." Claire nodded and turned to me. "Sebastian, I will leave you two alone. If you need anything, please come by my office."

"Thank you, Claire." I smiled.

From 11 AM to 5 PM, I was with Simon, and we literally documented every click of the mouse in order to correctly capture the desktop procedure. After only a small break for lunch, I was heads down learning the account receivables process. That was rather easy for me since most companies handled the AR processes similarly. The only difference was, Hudd dealt with millions of customers, and their office could not handle making calls to "past due" customers. Therefore, the demand letters were sent multiple times, and the collection center in Montreal handled the phone calls.

In Chicago, they basically monitored the accounts for the payments and then sent the standard letters to the customers. Since Hudd was basically treated as a utility company, their receivables were very low. Simon was a "go-getter" and kept close track of his accounts. I took really good notes and made copies of his documented procedures. At night, when I was back at the hotel, I used all that information to develop the detailed design of level 3 process maps for account receivables. Before heading back to Toronto, I got a sign off on my process flows from each of the three supervisors I was meeting.

The next two days were identical to my first one. I took detailed notes and collected all the documented standard processes. The whole thing became very repetitive and lost its appeal, but I had to get it done. I would get to the office by 9 AM, briefly meet with Claire, and then she would introduce me to the credit and collection supervisors.

At night, I would stay up late making sure my Visio diagrams were created exactly how I documented them. Whenever I would get a chance, I would call Renata, to catch up and see how she was doing. Our conversations were brief. I just wanted to let her know I was thinking of her. I was actually worried that our memories of the great weekend and the incredible connection between us was going to fade out.

Before I knew it, it was already Thursday morning. My goal for the day was to get a sign off from Claire and the three supervisors. At around 1PM, I was planning on leaving the office and going to the O'Hare airport. I intended to get there early enough to connect my laptop and send the finalized level 3 process maps to Shanti. I needed for her to review those and update the standard operating procedure deliverables. Those would be sent for Scott's approval along with the weekly status report.

On Wednesday, Renata asked if we could see each other upon my return on Thursday evening. I told her I would've loved to, but I had our T minus 30 meeting with all the top partners and the client sponsors. I had to pull an all-nighter on Thursday in preparation for the upcoming meeting.

I always preferred to be over prepared in any situation. One night, without sleep, would not kill me. I was planning on hanging out in my hotel room and listen to Jack Johnson while I prepared the template for the presentation. The presentation itself was provided to me, and I had to complete about 15 pages of the high-level materials which summarized every area of my responsibilities regarding the project. The strategy was to transition the US operations to India on July 11th and repeat the same with the Canadian side on July 18th.

Aside from reviewing the main points, the overall message was, my AR tower was in the green for the "go-live", but I did have one area of concern which was customer service. The current plan of action was for the transactional staff to also handle the incoming calls automatically from the US and Canada centers of excellence, or they would have to transfer over manually.

In my professional opinion, handling the transactional accounting work, answering the phone calls and responding to the billing inquires constituted two different skill sets. I highlighted that point as a red flag for our upcoming discussion with the Senior Leadership. At 4 AM, I was exhausted but satisfied with the completed work. I had only three hours of sleep left before heading to the office.

Chapter 15

At around 8 AM, I arrived at the office. By then, all the transition managers were there, along with Scott, the project management's office Senior Manager. The T-30 meeting was our first major milestone, and everyone was on edge to successfully deliver their areas of service.

"Good morning, Sebastian. Thanks for sending in the deliverables from your trip to Chicago." Scott greeted me. He seemed to be in a good mood. "I know you have a tight timeframe over the next two weeks. Do you still think you can do it?"

"Absolutely!" I exclaimed. "My team and I will work hard to get the rework done and delivered in the next two weeks. I have already communicated with the Finance Directors for the both offices in Connecticut and New York, and they have already planned my trip. Now it's just a matter of showing up."

"I've already mentioned to our Senior Leadership about your unfortunate rework and they understood, so don't worry about that during today's meeting. You just want to highlight the need for the different timelines." Scott reassured me.

"Thanks, Scott. I will keep you posted."

The T-30 meeting was about to start, and I was scheduled two go second in the group. I was supposed to start at 10:30 AM, and I had 30 minutes. While I was waiting, I rehearsed the presentation about three times from start to finish. By then, I had full confidence in my subject matter and the areas I wanted to highlight. Amy, our receptionist, came over to my team desk and said, "Sebastian, the team is ready for you."

I thanked her, picked up my laptop and the notepad and followed Amy into the board room. As soon as the door opened before me, I was greeted by our top regional partner for the Finance Transformation team, Gary Duncan.

"Hi, Sebastian. How the heck, are you?" He thundered.

He was a tall white man with a full head of gray hair. We met on my first day at the delivery center in Toronto.

"Hi Gary, it's nice to see you once again." I replied cheerfully.

"So, Sebastian, I know you've been traveling quite a bit but, as I mentioned in our last meeting, I want to get to know you better. I am leaving tomorrow morning but would like to meet you tonight for a drink." Gary suggested.

Even though, I barely slept and felt very groggy, I knew such an opportunity would not come again any time soon. I wanted to do everything in my power to get promoted to partner, and I knew the control was in Duncan's hands.

"Yes, Gary. I'd love to meet you tonight." I tried to sound as enthusiastic as possible.

"Great." He tapped me on my back. "I'll meet you at the hotel at 8 PM?"

"That works for me." I agreed.

"Ok, why don't you have a seat at the table? Scott will join us as well. The rest of the group will be here remotely via the telephone." Duncan said.

As soon as my presentation appeared on the big screen, I felt a bit weird about being in a huge board room with only Gary and Scott in attendance. It would be nice to meet everyone face to face, but since everyone was located all across the US and Canada, the remote conference calls were the only means to stay connected.

"Good morning, ladies and gentlemen." Scott started. "The accounts payable tower has just completed their T-30 review. Now, we will review the AR tower with Sebastian Kosta. As an FYI, Sebastian is also handling the credit and collection transition to India. He has a full plate as you might understand. Why don't we start by briefly introducing ourselves, so that Sebastian is aware of who is on call? First, the Accent team, then the Hudd members."

One by one, everyone introduced themselves. They also gave brief descriptions of their areas of responsibilities. In total, we had five Senior Executives from Accent and six from Hudd. One name in particular got my attention. He was the number one partner for Accent in India, and the leader for all the delivery centers in that country. His name was Manesh Vivek and oddly enough, I've never heard of or seen his name in any of my onboarding documents. I didn't want to be too intrusive in my inquiries about him, at the same time I knew, Manesh Vivek was the key person to know once I was in Chennai, India.

As soon as the introductions were completed, I began discussing each PowerPoint slide. I pretty much gave them a highlight overview of the main points. I explained that all the level 2 process maps and standard desktop procedures were completed as well as the knowledge transfer in Toronto. In addition, the level 3 documents for Hudd's Midwest and West Coast operations were going to be completed that week. As to the level 3 documents for Canada and the US's East Coast, those were going to be ready in the next two weeks. I proceeded to discuss the timeline that showed the 'go-live' dates of July 11th for the US and July 18th for Canada.

Once I finished speaking, Gary asked me about the areas of concern if there were any. "Tell me about the red flags?" He asked.

"At this time, Gary, we have only one red flag which is the customer service or the lack of it." I replied without hesitation.

"Can you please articulate your concerns for all of us?" Gary asked.

"Yes. The current plan is to move all back-office operations to Chennai and have the superusers and general users handle both the transactional work and taking the phone calls. In my opinion, even though they are all highly skilled, they don't have the right skill set to handle the billing questions. To be quite honest, their verbal English skills are not of the quality a call center would expect especially in relations to the home security business." I explained.

"Why wasn't that discussed before?" Gary roared.

"It never came up before. We didn't see it as a major issue since the call volumes were low." Scott interjected. "Remember, all the emergency calls will be still handled in the US and Canada. The customer billing questions are being outsourced. We figured, the supervisor who handles those transactions would be best equipped to deal with those issues."

"Thanks, Scott, but I think Sebastian has a point, we did not go deep enough before. At a minimum, your team in Chennai will need to go through an English immersion program and an accent neutralization course before 'go-live'." Duncan noted.

"Gary, I am going to assign Sebastian as the point person for the customer service track. Since I know he already has his plate full, I will have Amanda from accounts payable helping Sebastian. She has the bandwidth which you just saw in her earlier presentation. Does that work for you, Sebastian?" Scott turned to me.

"Of course, sir. I was the one who brought up the red flag, so I'll do everything in my power to resolve the issue. You can count on me." I assured Gary and Scott.

My presentation lasted for exactly 30 minutes. That was just enough time for an overview and discussion of my points of concern. Overall, I felt it went well. Usually, the more responsibility one took, the higher were the rewards. In that case, I was a step closer to being considered for partner.

When I got back to the hotel, I was very happy about the meeting going well. My condensed project plan was reviewed and approved by the Senior Leadership. I did not have much time; it was already a bit past 7 PM. I decided to take a shower and wear something business casual for my meeting with Gary. I figured a dress shirt; slacks and a blazer would work. I didn't need to wear a tie, it was a personal, "getting to know each other better" type of a meeting. I headed down to the club lounge where all the consultants liked to socialize. There, the wine and beer were free, and they always had some delicious appetizers.

As soon as I walked into the large room, I looked around. It was an L-shaped modern space. It had two formal living rooms complete with a few flat screen TVs, all displaying CNN. I noticed Gary was already there, talking to the waiter. I figured he was ordering a drink.

"Hello, Gary. How are you? Have you been waiting for a long time?" I asked shaking Gary's hand.

"Oh, hi, Sebastian. It's nice to see you and no, I just sat down and ordered a Scotch." He replied with a wide smile.

I took a seat on a small couch to the right of Gary who was comfortably occupying a large armchair.

"Would you like to order something?" He asked me.

"You've mentioned you have Scotch. What type?"

"Black label, of course!" Gary laughed. "You know how we partners roll, right?"

"I'll have the same." I replied.

The waiter came by and took my order. He also brought us some salted nuts to snack on.

"So, tell me Sebastian, how do you think you did today?" Gary asked after taking his time to enjoy a sip of his drink.

"I can confidently say that the presentation was delivered on point as planned, and the questions asked were the ones I expected and was ready for."

"You know that the preparation is 50% and the execution is the remaining 50%?" Gary continued. "The next two weeks will be difficult for you, especially since now, you have to worry about the customer service track. Are you sure you can execute the project?"

"I have no doubts in my abilities. I will do whatever it takes to get the job done." I replied firmly.

"I do believe in you, Sebastian. You have the pedigree, and now I'm observing true grit that is necessary for success in any type of business. I am just concerned about your well-being. Do you workout to relieve the stress?" He inquired.

"I workout just about every day during the week, Monday through Friday, even when I am on the road. I try to do that first thing in the morning to line up my day for success." I explained.

"Are you at the average level or an athlete?" Duncan inquired. He seemed genuinely interested.

"I run a half a marathon once a month. In January, I am planning to complete my first marathon in Miami."

"Oh wow! So, you must be in top shape." Gary exclaimed. "That's great. In this business, you need to workout to activate the natural dopamine and serotonin levels in your brain. That will keep your mood up and consequently, your productivity will be up as well. When you get to the partner level, you will no longer worry about yourself but your team and their families. It's a huge responsibility." He warned me as if he was reading my mind about dreaming of becoming a partner in the firm.

"What about your relationship status? Are you married?" He continued.

"Not at this time. I am currently single." I replied with a smile.

"The reason I asked was because good relationships, especially good marriages, are helpful in building the foundation for success. Now, I am not saying go out and get married tomorrow."

"Thanks for clarifying that point." I started laughing, and Gary joined it.

"You need to have a team at home that gives you the love and support that you need when you are stressed and overwhelmed away from home." He pointed out after the laughing pause passed.

"I see your point! However, living in Miami makes it very hard to find a woman that loves you for who you are. It seems like a vicious cycle where the men have to obtain all the toys and gadgets, and the women have to have the surgeries and buy fancy clothes to look attractive to the men. It's a very materialistic city." I noted.

"Do you consider yourself materialistic, Sebastian?" Duncan inquired seriously.

"Not really." I shrugged.

"What car do you drive?"

"A Porsche."

"What other toys do you have, Sebastian?" He proceeded.

"I also have two motorcycles."

"And you say you are not materialistic?" Gary grinned.

"I don't like to flash my cash. I have my toys because they bring me joy and happiness. To me, they are the pieces of art that I collect. And I like to collect things that go fast. I love the surge of adrenaline because it makes me feel alive and in the moment." I tried to explain my desire for the luxuriously fast vehicles.

"You know, people like you need to be careful, because it seems you'll do anything for a rush." Gary suggested. "By the way…" He continued. "You talk about joy and happiness. Are you religious?" That was the second time Gary mentioned religion.

"No, I am not religious." I replied simply.

"Do you believe in God, or do you think we are just like the animals grazing this planet?" He insisted.

"I respect all views, but I believe religion has been used throughout human history to manipulate the people and to serve certain groups in positions of power and privilege. Maybe not so much in modern times but definitely in the past. Religion was power. Those who controlled religion, controlled the people, the entire nations, in fact. The problem was and still is that many people tend to stick to their religious views and practices while rejecting other viewpoints. Even though, most religions promise enlightenment, most adherents never achieve it because they lack the necessary education or open mind. Many people lack faith. They follow the institution instead of the actual rules and commandments. In my humble opinion, and it's very unfortunate, religion itself is the cause of many wars and conflicts in the world." I stated passionately.

"You are a philosopher, Sebastian." Gary laughed.

I was suddenly grateful to Gary for his laughter. It was nice icebreaker to light up the discussion that was getting too serious and maybe even controversial.

"It's getting a bit too serious for a light evening talk." Gary said after he finished laughing. "But I want to tell you something, to end that discussion, you have to forget about materialism and passion for luxury. I know you believe yourself to be non-materialistic, but for God's sakes, your watch is more expensive than mine. You scream materialism. You need to dig deeper within yourself. What you are searching for is not in the outside world. If you look inside yourself, you will get all the answers, and that is where you will find the truth and unlock all of your opportunities."

I was so confused. But I nodded to Gary. I didn't really understand his statement, but I hoped if I agreed and didn't ask any questions, we would end that uncomfortable topic. It seemed he was telling me to search for another career.

"To close up, Sebastian, life is all about the decisions we make. You have a free will to make any decision you choose, but you'll have to live with the consequences of those decisions. If you really want to be a partner, you will have the ability to afford all the luxuries you desire. But there will be sacrifices. Real sacrifices. Just keep that in mind. Good luck in New York and much success in India. I am sure it will be an adventure you will never forget." Gary winked at me and grinned.

"Thank you, Gary. It was great to have a drink with you. Will you be at the T-5 meeting?"

"No, I have to get back to the States and focus on a couple of new big clients. Hopefully, the next time we sit face to face, we will be discussing your promotion to partner." Gary noted sincerely. I liked him very much.

"I really hope so. That's what I am shooting for." I admitted feeling at ease again.

When I returned to my hotel room, I opened a bottle of Cabernet. Even though, I thought Gary and I had a good conversation, I still felt something was missing. As I was mechanically sipping my wine, I realized that what I was really missing was a strong support system. I didn't have a wife or a girlfriend. Renata was special to me, but I believed our relationship was more of a summer fling than anything with a serious future potential. She did not want to move back to Miami. My family was there for me but in the moment of a crisis, I wasn't sure I could share my darkest secrets or worst fears with them. I believed Gary was correct in telling me that a future partner required a strong support system. I was a bit unsure what he meant by going deep and knowing my true self. I loved myself, and I knew who I was. I was very confused about the meaning of that comment.

I started sensing the effect of the Cabernet; I was feeling drowsy and lightheaded. I called it a night. I had the entire weekend of work ahead of me. I needed to get all the rest I could. Plus, I was scheduled for an early flight to New York on Monday morning.

As soon as I got in bed, the phone on the nightstand beeped. I had a text message. I was instantly irritated, but I reached for the phone to check who the message was from. It was from Renata. She remembered I had a busy week and wanted to check up on me and find out how the meeting went.

"So, did you do well today?" She asked.

"Yes, I even had a drink with the number one partner on our team." I replied.

"I am so happy for you, Seba. You are good at what you do. You deserve it." She encouraged me.

"Thanks, babes."

"So, am I going to see you this weekend?" She wrote.

"I was planning on working the entire weekend, babes."

"Seba, this is my last weekend in Toronto. My sister and I are going to Miami for a month for our summer vacation." She sounded desperate and upset.

"Ok, I can see you but only for a little bit. Why don't you stop by tomorrow night?" I gave up. "I will be working the entire day, but I will take a break and we'll hang out."

"Sounds like a plan! I will be there. Good night, Sebastian."

"Good night." I didn't know whether Renata was happy or irate. But I was so sleepy that I couldn't care less.

Chapter 16

After I woke up early next morning, I went for an hour-long run. Then, I came back to the room, sat down in the armchair and breathed deeply until my heart was beating at its normal resting pace. Shortly after, I picked up John Grisham's *The Partner* in Spanish and read a few chapters. Not only did I like to read, but I used the time to polish my Spanish vocabulary.

For the next 10 hours afterwards, I was locked up in my hotel room preparing deliverables for my project. I was in a zone. I lost track of time and did not think of anything but what I had directly in front of me. I only took a few breaks. The rest of the time was dedicated to work. I made a significant progress, and my productivity was cruising at high speed. I had to make the necessary sacrifices in order to deliver on time, to be on pace at the T-5 meeting. My team needed the green light for the July 11th "go-live" in India. I felt so committed to getting the work done that I went ahead and purchased my plane tickets; I was ahead of the deadline.

My flight was leaving Toronto on Friday, July 8th. Then it was connecting through Frankfurt, Germany and arriving in Chennai, India on Saturday, July 9th. The total flight time would be 22 hours. I've never in my life flown that far or for that long. Since I had difficulty sleeping on long flights on planes, I knew that I would have to get a new prescription for Xanax. I recalled that I had a liposuction surgery scheduled for the last weekend of June in Miami. Thus, I would ask the doctor for Xanax along with the other pain killers. When I met with Dr. Lerner for my first consultation, he gained my full confidence. He was a well renowned artist at his craft. He showed me a few images of his previous patients who underwent the same procedure. I loved what I saw.

He underscored that no one in Miami was more aggressive with the fat removal than him. He promised to remove all the fat I had even in-between the area where the abdominal muscles connected. He guaranteed that in few weeks after the surgery, once swelling would go down, the six pack I so much dreamt of having, would be evident. I was a bit worried about the procedure, but I pushed that aside and refocused on my work.

Before I knew it, I heard a knock on the door. It was Renata. That time, there was no surprise. She was casual. She was wearing black jeans and a red shirt. She was also wearing a simple ponytail exposing her long neck.

"There is my girl." I exclaimed excitedly before walking out the door, lifting Renata up and giving her a kiss. "So how long has it been since Montreal?" I asked playfully.

"One week." Renata giggled. "Too long."

I spun her around, kissed her again, and we entered the room.

"See, I've been a good boy. My laptop with all the paperwork." I motioned with my hand towards my work stuff.

"You've been very busy. I know this project is very important for you." Renata smiled and brushed my cheek. She proceeded to get on the bed and started jumping up and down.

"So how about some fun now?" She asked with a sly expression on her face.

"What did you have in mind?" I pretended to be at loss for ideas.

"Did you have dinner?" She inquired seriously.

"Nope."

"I have an idea!" She beamed. "Why don't I drive you to my apartment and cook for you?"

"Really?" I was in shock.

"We went to so many restaurants by now. This time, I was thinking of doing something special just for you. Something that shows how much I appreciate you. You will also get to know me a little better by seeing my home and tasting my cooking." Renata suggested.

"What about my work?" I was all in but tried to tease her.

"Just come for a few hours. I promise dinner and dessert, that's it."

"Dessert." I repeated slowly. "I like dessert. I wonder what that would be?"

"You will be home before your bedtime." Renata continued ignoring my previous question.

"Ok, I'm excited. Let's do it. Remember though, I won't be sleeping over." I warned.

"Done deal." Renata pulled my hand. "Let's head down. I left the car outside with the valet."

Once outside, I performed my customary jump into Renata's convertible, and we were off to her place.

"Hey, I even got some Coldplay on for you since I know how much you love them." Renata was eager to please.

"Thanks. The concert was amazing. I still can't believe I got to share that moment with you. I'll never forget that." I responded with a wide smile.

"And I won't forget that crazy motorcycle ride to Niagra Falls. Talk about the rush." She laughed.

"It's definitely been an adventure."

"Sebastian, you drive me nuts. I don't want to lose you." She suddenly became solemn and very serious.

"I feel the same, but remember, lets focus on the present moment." I said gently.

"You are right, focusing on the future only makes me anxious." Renata agreed. I knew she wanted to focus on the future. But I couldn't let that happen at that moment.

Before I knew it, we were by her condo.

"So, how did you find this place?" I asked as we walked to her apartment.

"Well, I was looking for something that would not be too much of a commute and close to the city. I am not the type to stay home on the weekends. I like to get out there and go dancing. Before my sister met her husband, we use to go dancing every weekend. But now, I lost my partner in crime. Since she was the more outgoing one, I pretty much followed her wherever she went." Renata admitted.

"What about now? Do you still go out much?" I inquired trying to sound casual.

"Not really. I work a lot. I am trying to save money, so I can bring my mom to Toronto."

"Are you planning to move her here?"

"Yes, my father died of a heart attack last year, and she is all by herself." Renata's voice turned heartbreakingly sad.

"I am really sorry to hear about your father." I hugged her. "I am fortunate and very grateful that my parents are alive and well."

"Sebastian, take advantage of every moment with them. Trust me, I wish I had more time with my dad. Just one last time to tell him how much I love him. He sacrificed everything for his family. Now, I want to reunite my mom with us. I want her to be here."

"That sounds like an amazing plan. Your mom sounds special. I would love to meet her." I whispered to Renata as she stepped away from me and extracted the keys from her purse. She looked at me and smiled before opening the door into her condo.

"Welcome to my humble abode. It's not big, but it has everything I need." She announced.

I took one glance and noted how cozy and inviting her apartment was. She had warm color hues throughout the place, and it was nicely furnished. She lived by herself, so there was a good-sized cute living room that also served as a dining room. I figured that by seeing a dining table set by the opposite wall.

"Wow. I really like your place. It feels like home. You are doing well for yourself." I complimented her.

"Wait until you try my delicious cooking. I use a special mojo sauce to spice things up." She giggled.

"So, what's on the menu tonight?" I wondered playfully.

"I am cooking a very traditional dish from Brazil. Since you are always on the road, I wanted to make something that reminded you of home. Do you like rice, beans, and piccadillo?" Renata asked heading towards the kitchen.

"Oh my God, that is my favorite." I followed her. "My mom used to make it for me when I was a kid. She used the brown pinto beans." I continued.

"That's what I am using." She said and extended her hand trying to stop me. "You stay here. I will be back soon. Relax, Sebastian." She gave me a wink and turned around.

I went over to her couch while she got busy in the kitchen.

"So, what type of music are you interested in tonight?" I yelled out to Renata.

"Why don't we start with Cafe del Mar? I loved the last time you played it."

I nodded without responding and connected my phone to her Bose speaker, which had a docking station. The music was relaxing. It felt like a mental massage.

"Am I smelling the beans already?" I asked feeling relaxed and happy on Renata's plush sofa with my nose picking up the aroma of my first home-cooked meal in a long while.

"Yes, I pre-cooked them overnight." Renata responded from the kitchen. "Now, I am just frying them with garlic and my special mojo sauce."

The smell of the garlic and frying beans was so good, I was experiencing some kind of food high. It really reminded of when I lived at home with my parents.

"I can't believe you are cooking for me. Few girls know how to cook these days." I uttered dreamily with my eyes half-closed and my stomach growling.

"My grandma always told me the quickest way to a man's heart was through his stomach. She taught me a bunch of recipes." Renata replied sounding very busy.

"Is she still alive?"

"No, God rest her soul. She was the matriarch of the family and lived to a month short of her 94th birthday."

"So, she lived a full life." I noted.

"Yes, I am happy to say that she was blessed."

After spending a while on the couch, I decided to check on Renata at the kitchen.

"Is there anything I can help you with?" I asked when I entered.

"I usually prefer cooking by myself, but perhaps, you can help me with the rice? That should be relatively easy. Do you know how to do it?" Renata looked at me with a smile. I think she already knew my reply.

"Not really." I admitted.

Her smile widened as she approached me and picked a large garlic and an onion.

"Use the chopping board to cut the onion into small squares. Then the garlic needs to be minced in tiny pieces. When you're done, cook the garlic until it's brown and then throw in the onion." She explained.

"That sounds pretty simple. Let me get to work." I pronounced enthusiastically reaching for the knife. I started cutting the onion. To my surprise, I wasn't tearing.

"Why am I not crying? I wanted for you to see me cry." I joked.

"Those are Vidalia onions. They are very sweet and don't make you cry when you slice them." Renata noted.

"Don't worry, Renata. You will never see me cry. I feel joyous and happy with you. Always." Renata was pleased. She looked straight into my eyes, approached me and gave me a long sensual kiss on the lips.

"Always." She whispered.

After about 30 minutes, the food was ready. Renata set the table, and I attended to opening a bottle of Merlot.

"It's all done. I really hope you like my home cooking." She invited me to take a seat at the table.

"It smells delicious. I can't wait to try it."

Once we took our respective seats, I poured wine into two glasses and proposed a toast.

"To celebrating the little things in life and showing gratitude for everything we have. Cheers to us." Renata nodded and we clinked our glasses.

Since Renata cooked a traditional Brazilian meal, I wanted to eat it in our customary way. I filled my plate with rice and added the picadillo on top. I completed the traditional way by pouring a spoonful of the sauce over my dish. Afterwards, I got to work with my fork smashing the entire thing. Renata appeared befuddled.

"What are you doing with your food?"

"I am using my fork to mash up the beans and then mix everything together. That is exactly how my father does it." I laughed.

"So, tell me a little about your father?" Renata inquired as we were sharing the most delicious meal I had in a while.

"You know, he was a typical dad who had three jobs and studied at night to get his law degree. After over a decade of struggling in Brazil, he got the opportunity to become an expatriate banker." I replied thoughtfully.

"How did that go?"

"We traveled a lot, which I loved. I was really young, so I could make new friends wherever the bank sent our family."

"Did you grow up with your dad being your best friend?" She continued.

"Not really." I shrugged. "He was too busy. He worked all day and once he got home, he just wanted to watch the news."

"So, you're a momma's boy?" She teased.

"Yeah, I think my Mom and I have an unbreakable bond. While my father was the ultimate financial provider, my Mom made our home and gave me all the love in the world and more."

"Was that enough that your Dad was mostly the money-maker?" Renata looked intently at me.

"My Dad grew up with very little, so he wanted for his kids to have everything. As long as we did well in school, he showered us with presents. He always used gifts as the incentives for doing well in school. He was a very tough disciplinarian. Perhaps, that is why I am very meticulous in everything I do." I explained.

"Yeah I think you might have a little OCD." Renata rolled her eyes.

"Why do you say that???" I laughed.

"I saw your closet. Everything was color coded and in place."

"Ohhh! I only do that, so I don't waste time looking for things." I tried justifying my anal obsession with order.

"Sure, you do." Renata didn't buy my explanation.

We spent the rest of the evening talking about our families and the past. It was nice to get to know each other even better. We were done with the Merlot, and it was getting late. As much as I wanted to spend more time with Renata, I had to get back to work.

"Let's have some dessert, at least." She asked. "Before I take you back?"

I nodded in agreement. Renata got up from the table and returned with a plateful of the medjool dates. They were very large and plump.

"You know, back in the days, in the Middle East, whenever someone was going on a journey through the dessert, they ate dates. To be exact, they would eat 7 dates and wash them down with a glass of milk. That meal would keep them nourished for more than a day. Imagine that?" I told her.

"You have a journey to India ahead of you, and I pray for your safe passage. Every time I have a date, I will pray for your safe return." Renata pronounced with the tears in her eyes.

It was time for me to leave. We got up and embraced each other. We remained that way for a long time. Our hug turned into kisses and our kisses led to her bedroom. As we were sprawled across her bed, I turned and whispered into Renata's ear, "I can't spend the night. I'm sorry."

"I know, but I won't see you for a few weeks. I already miss you." She breathed out with exasperation.

I covered her lips with mine and as we kissed, we started undressing each other. Renata was not in a hurry. She knew I had to leave, but she wanted to keep me near for as long as possible. We took our time. By now, I knew what she liked, and she knew how to turn me on. That night, we had passionate sex. We could feel the heat and tenderness of our bodies, and we lusted to be with each other again and again. Somehow, that night reminded me of our first date. Making love to her was like dancing together in harmony; bodies and souls united as one. My hands were all over her, and the imprints of her lips were all over my body. We indulged in pleasure, stealing a little piece of heaven that night. I could tell by her movement that she was fully invested in me. But then, it was time to leave.

"Why are you getting up?" Renata moaned.

"I have to get back. I need to finish my work. Remember, I am leaving first thing Monday morning. I will be on the road for weeks." I explained in a serious tone. "As much as I love spending time with you, I have to dedicate myself to my work. I need to make it to partner this year."

"Ok, don't worry, Seba. There is no need to get flustered. I will take you back to your hotel." Renata got up and started getting dressed.

We drove in silence. The energy between us with filled with confusion, frustration, even awkwardness. It felt like we went from everything to finished in seconds. Even though, we had a very good time together, neither one of us knew where we were heading. Something inside of me suspected we were nearing the end of our beautiful short romance. My priorities were set, and love and relationships weren't at the top of the list. It was all about my career.

"Seba!" Renata's voice interrupted my thoughts. "I feel like we are going in circles. It so hard for me to think of not being with you. I have fallen for you and don't want to lose you."

"I know Renata. I feel the same. But we live two separate lives. You have plans with your family here. I have my family in Miami. My career is about to take off." I replied decisively.

"Do you believe in long distance relationships? Asked Renata.

"No. I don't." I was firm.

"Why?"

"Because they are too difficult to maintain. One or the other will eventually find someone else and cheat." I was getting frustrated with that useless conversation.

"You don't think our love is strong enough?" Renata inquired naively.

"I've never been in a relationship lasting longer than six months. I've always been fascinated by women, and that made it very hard for me to be faithful to one. Especially, if she lived in a different city, state or even worse, a different country." I hoped if I sounded cold, it would be less painful for her.

We arrived at the hotel, but instead of coming out, I just sat in the car. The air was filled with tension and sadness. Silence lasted for a while.

"Seba. I love you and would do anything to stay with you." Renata finally spoke out.

"What about moving to Miami?" I asked.

"I don't know." She shrugged and looked down. "We are not officially dating. We haven't been together for long. Based on your stories, you have a long list of conquests in Miami. And you are asking me to uproot my life, to leave my sister?"

"And you did mention about your mom coming to live with you." I added.

"Yes, that's the plan."

"Listen, let's sleep on it. Tomorrow is another day. Who knows what the future brings?" I tried encouraging Renata…and myself. "If we are meant to be, then it will happen."

"I am in love with you." Renata looked up at me, and I saw tears running down her cheeks.

"I love you too." I answered honestly before covering her lips with mine.

"I will be in touch." I said leaving the car. It was too hard to peel myself off Renata.

She wiped the tears off and looked at me with a smile.

"Sweet dreams, Sebastian."

Chapter 17

I was awakened by the alarm clock on my phone. It was 5 AM, the time to be a road warrior. I quickly performed the 300 sit-ups and push-ups, took a shower and got dressed. I was in a mood for a good run. But that was impossible. I had an early flight to New York. I was so accustomed to traveling that I could perform the routines in my sleep. But I was wide awake, granted, short on time. I picked up my carryon, left the room and jumped into the taxi that was already waiting for me by the entrance. With that, I was off to the airport. While I was in the taxi, I thought that I always had blackouts when I was traveling. Some parts of my trip I remembered very well. Others I didn't. It seemed I was half-asleep while on the move.

I landed in La Guardia and went straight to the car rental section. I liked using National Car Rental, because it was the quickest way to get a car. The cars were parked in the huge lot, and the keys were inside. That saved me valuable time, which was everything for my job.

It took me about an hour to get to Stamford, Connecticut where the Hudd office was located. That was the company's shared service center. In the past, Hudd had centralized its operations from North America to that particular office. Now, after making huge savings with the transaction processing, the only way to further reduce the costs was to outsource and condense the payroll costs.

I arrived at the office and took the elevator to the 19th floor where I found the receptionist. The remainder of my visit was similar to the one in Chicago. I met the person in charge of the finance department and then, for the rest of the week, I met with the clerks or the supervisors of the account receivables, credit and collections individually. My nights were consumed by documents and an abundance of data. I needed to make certain the processes in Connecticut and Chicago were identical. Since the center was shared, the processes in place were standard. That was the best practice. Consequently, I created my Visio maps and sent them to Shanti, my team lead. With those, she could focus on developing the standard operating procedures for training the users.

On Thursday, I was ready to fly back. Even though, Toronto was not home, I got so accustomed to my environment, subconsciously, I started calling it home. I drove back to the airport, dropped off the car and took my 4 PM flight. Mission accomplished!!! The interviews were held, my team was working on the final deliverables for Scott's review. Everything was ready for Friday's status meeting.

I laid back and put my Bose headphones on. I didn't feel like listening to music, so I just turned the noise cancelling function on, closed my eyes and relaxed. I knew it was just the beginning of the project. The biggest challenge was the forthcoming work with Amanda. I took advantage of the time on the plane and slept to recharge my batteries.

The weekend flew by fast. I managed to steal some time to get my laundry done, that was it. On Monday, I was back on the plane to New York City. I had one week only to get all the level 3 process flows documented for the eastern region. Since that was my third time visiting the Hudd office regarding the same topic, I was pretty much on cruise control. I met the people I needed and got the right information required for our training of the general users. The week went by quickly. Most of the time, I was sitting in front of my laptop playing with Visio diagrams. I had very little personal free time, but I would spend it alone at some local restaurants. That definitely wasn't the most exciting part of my job but at least, it wasn't boring.

My next flight was to Miami, where I was going to stay for that weekend. I had a surgery with Dr. Lerner scheduled for Friday and then, I was going to spend Saturday and Sunday recovering from the procedure. I was looking forward to my surgery. Actually, excited about it. After working out for years and not being able to get rid of the fat around my lower abdominals, I knew that liposuction was the only way I could achieve the results I wanted. I was also looking forward to the weekend of rest and relaxation. I didn't tell anyone I was coming home. The doctor told me if the surgery was performed on Friday morning, I would be able to return to work on Monday. I knew there was a chance I would be in severe pain, but I figured, the results would be worth it. Since no one knew I was coming home, and I didn't tell anyone about the surgery, I needed someone to drive me home after the procedure. Thus, Dr. Lerner has arranged for the services of a nurse. She was going to pick me up on Friday morning and drive me to the clinic. Once the surgery was done, she would drive me back to my house and stay with me overnight.

Chapter 18

On Friday morning, I woke up feeling exhilarated. It was amazing to sleep in my own bed, my actual own bed. As much as I loved my accommodations in Toronto, nothing was as comfortable as my bed in Miami. Every time I slept in it, I understood that it was well worth paying all that money for that mattress. I took a shower and put a comfortable sweat suit on. I then received a call from the front desk announcing that my guest has arrived. Perfect, my nurse was downstairs. I had to move quickly. It was already 8:30 AM, and my surgery was scheduled for 9.

As I descended into the lobby, I noticed a woman dressed as a nurse. She smiled warmly as we made eye contact.

"Good morning, I am Sebastian Kosta. You must be my nurse?" I asked cheerfully.

"Good morning, Mr. Kosta. Yes, I am. My name is Nancy."

We shook hands.

"Hi Nancy, it's a pleasure to meet you."

"Mr. Kosta, if you don't mind, we will take my car. It's parked in the front." She announced.

"Sure, whatever is easier."

"It's very roomy in the back and will let you stretch out after the surgery. Plus, I am used to driving it." Nancy explained.

As we drove to Miami Beach, I started contemplating the risks involved. I was from Brazil, the country where plastic surgeries were performed all the time. Many foreigners came to Brazil for the surgeries that were much cheaper there than in the US or Europe. I also heard many stories about the women, who had liposuction surgeries, then suffered complications and died. I understood that was something, the average person would not do. If my parents knew, they would have a fit. But I wanted that perfect six pack. That was very shallow of me, I knew that, but I just couldn't help it. I understood the risks, but I was always a risk taker. I believed in the doctor, professionally, and I had no doubts, the surgery would be a success.

We arrived at the clinic that was conveniently located next to Lincoln road; one of the most famous streets in Miami Beach. The reason I chose Dr. Lerner was because of his reputation and appearance. He was in his 50's and in unbelievable shape. You could tell, he had a tremendous appreciation for the human body. He loved what he did and was a true artist.

As I walked into Dr. Lerner's office, I checked-in at the reception, and I sat down with Nancy.

"To be honest, Nancy, I think your job will be very easy with me. I am very independent. I just didn't want to tell my family about this surgery since I knew they would object. I pretty much need for you to drive me back home. Once there, I think a little supervision will be more than enough."

Before Nancy could reply, the receptionist approached me, "Mr. Kosta, we will now take you inside to prepare for the surgery. You did not eat or drink anything since last night, correct?"

"No, I did not." I affirmed.

"Perfect." She said. "Follow me, please."

I was led into the pre-op room, where I changed into the hospital gown. My heart was beating fast, and my hands were sweaty. I was obviously nervous. I experienced the same sensation I had before jumping off the plane in Panama, my first-time sky diving. Even though I was scared, I had to take the leap of faith and face my fears. As I continued waiting, I looked at the doctor's portfolio showing the before and after pictures of many of his best surgeries. For the most part, the differences were profound. The abdominal sections of the men shown were significantly better after the procedure. The doctor added, however, that most of the men started working out after the surgery. Since, I was already very athletic, I expected for my results to be even better.

By that time, the fear passed, and I was excited to see the outcome in a couple of weeks.

Within moments of my calming myself down, the door opened, and Dr. Lerner came in accompanied by the nurse practitioner.

"Good morning, young man. How are you doing? Are you ready to do this?" Dr. Lerner beamed at me.

"Hey doc, I was a bit nervous, but now I am ready."

"Good! Don't be nervous." Dr. stated and came up closer. "So, what I am going to do now is have you lay down, and I will use this blue pen to trace exactly where I can aggressively remove the fat around your abs. We will do our best to get as much fat out as possible."

He began quickly drawing lines around my stomach. He handled the pen as the artist he was. He's done that thousands of times, and his pen stroke was flawless. As he talked to the nurse regarding the surgery, his attention to detail was incredible.

"Sebastian, I am now going to administer several shots. They should not hurt much. That is to start the melting process of the fat molecules around your belly region. In 15 minutes, you will be ready for the anesthesia."

"Will I be completely knocked out?" I inquired.

"Oh, most definitely. Like I've mentioned before, the surgery would be very aggressive, and I will be performing at a high level. Trust me, that is one hell of a workout for me. Any questions?" Dr. Lerner looked at me.

"How long is the recovery period?" I asked.

"Today, definitely complete post-op rest. Furthermore, I recommend you rest throughout the weekend. The less you move and strain your abs, the better and faster you will heal. When are you planning on getting back to work?"

"I have to fly back to Toronto on Monday morning."

"That's fine. As long as you get as much bed rest as possible, you should be ok. I am going to give you a corset-like belt for your abdominals. We will put it on you as soon as the surgery is finished. Try to keep it on at all times. Especially during your flight. Pressure change. You know."

"Even when I sleep?" I asked without enthusiasm. I hated wearing anything when sleeping.

"Yes, for two weeks. Afterwards, you can decide whether you need to wear it for longer."

"Thanks, doc. Now please perform your magic and let's get it over with." I exclaimed.

"You bet. Nurse, please take him to surgery. We will begin in 15 minutes."

I was wheeled into a large surgical room with one bed and large lamps in the middle. It was very cold there. Once I was situated, the nurse pulled my arms above my head and strapped them to the bed. She did the same to my ankles.

"This is so you don't move during the surgery." She noted.

Besides Dr. Lerner and the nurse practitioner, there was an anesthesiologist. He would administer general anesthesia and monitor my breathing and vitals throughout the surgery.

"Sebastian, can you hear me? Asked the anesthesiologist.

"Yes, I can." I replied. I wanted to be asleep already. I was getting anxious again.

"I am going to insert the IV into the top of your right hand. It should only burn for a few seconds." He stated while doing exactly that.

"Ohh!" I flinched.

"Sorry to pinch you, buddy. Now relax. That's where the fun starts, so enjoy it."

All of a sudden, I felt my mouth getting dry, my thoughts in disarray, the sounds moved to a faraway distance, and I quickly passed out.

It seemed that only a few seconds passed. But when I opened my eyes and the initial blur receded, I was in a small, dark room. There was a nice relaxing music playing in the background. I felt that my midsection was completely bandaged, and I was covered with a heavy blanket. On the side of the bed, there was a remote. I could call the nurse with it. I did just that.

"How are you doing, Mr. Kosta?" I heard her voice.

"Just to let you guys know, I am awake." I blabbed.

"Thank you. We will be there shortly."

Minutes later, the nurse entered the recovery room and turned the lights on.

"How are you feeling, Mr. Kosta?" She asked.

"To be honest, I can't feel a thing."

"That's the anesthesia. Still working. With every hour passing, you will start feeling your body more and more."

Before the nurse was even able to finish the sentence, Dr. Lerner walked in.

"Wonderful, you are already awake. I want to tell you the surgery went awesome. We were able to remove all the fat around your abs and even in-between, as you wanted. Now, right below the belly button, we removed as much as we could, but it's a very tricky area since you have many nerve endings there. I didn't want to get too aggressive and cause you permanent numbness around that area. There still might be some interstitial fat beneath. With a good diet and exercise, you should be able to get rid of the remaining fat in that zone. I want you here in a week, so I can remove the stitches and check you out. Do you have any other questions?" The doc asked.

"When can I start working out again?

"The sooner the better, but I recommend no exercise for the next two weeks."

"Thank you, Dr. Lerner." I mumbled weakly.

"No, thank you for being an excellent patient. See you next Friday."

"Nancy, what time is it?" I asked my nurse when already in the car on the way home.

"It's 1 PM. Your surgery lasted for two hours, and then you spent about an hour in recovery. How are you doing? Are you feeling ok?" She asked gently.

"I feel fine, but my mouth is a little dry."

"Here is your water bottle."

"Thank you, Nancy."

As we continued, I was looking through the window, enjoying the beauty of Miami. It was so nice to see the cruise ships, the palm trees, the water and the blue sky. I even rolled down the window to smell the fresh air and the scent of the ocean. I was very happy to finally have the surgery behind me. I knew the hardest part was over. Dealing with the pain of recovery would be easy for me. Just like any other physical challenge, I could overcome the pain.

When we arrived at the Four Seasons, Nancy helped me get out of the car. She also wanted to assist me to the elevator, but I did not let her. I had my sweats and sunglasses on; I did not want for anyone to notice anything was wrong with me. As soon as we entered my apartment, I asked for her help to go to the bathroom. I then laid down in bed with a glass of water next to me and the remote control.

"Nancy, I am going to sleep now. Can you make me a ham and cheese sandwich for lunch and a glass of milk, please?"

"Of course, Sebastian. I will be outside if you need anything."

"Thank you."

When I woke up, I turned over to see the time, it was 9 PM. I slept a lot. I guess it was due to the lingering effect of the anesthesia. I was very hungry and tried to get up on my own. But as I moved, I felt like my midsection was going to explode. I felt the unbearable pain and soreness. I needed pain killers immediately.

"Nancy!" I yelled out. "Could you please come in here."

Nancy ran in before I even finished calling her.

"Are you ok?" She asked.

"No, I am hungry and in a lot of pain." I moaned.

"I will give you the pain killers now." She reassured me.

"What type of the medication is it?" I asked.

"Oxycontin." She replied and left. Nancy returned shortly with my sandwich and a glass of milk. I thanked her and immediately took the pain killer. After I ate my dinner, I decided to watch some TV, but I fell asleep within minutes.

The next time I woke up, it was 5 AM. I called Nancy again and asked her to give me pain killers since I felt like fire ants were crawling on my stomach. By then, the effects of the anesthesia were completely gone, and I had to rely solely on the oxycontin and bed rest. I've taken pain killers in the past, but that one was different. It did not only eliminate the pain but made me feel very good. I knew, I could only take the administered dose and only until I was in pain. Oxycontin was highly addictive and not a joking matter. After I started feeling better, Nancy brought some scrambled eggs with cream cheese on a bagel. I ate it and went back to sleep.

I woke up because someone was gently patting me on the shoulder. It was Nancy.

"Sebastian, it's noon. You hired me to stay with you for 24 hours. How are you doing?" She asked.

"The pain is uncomfortable, but I can manage. Let me see if I can get up and go to the bathroom on my own." I suggested.

Even though, it was very painful, and my abdominal area was stiff, I somehow managed to walk alone to the bathroom. At that point, I didn't feel it was necessary for Nancy to remain with me any longer. Thus, I paid her fee, and she left my apartment. I took another pain killer and decide to remain in bed. Over the next 24 hours, I slept as much as I could. I only got up to go to the bathroom or eat.

When Sunday finally arrived, I was able to get around. That evening, I started preparing for my next day flight back to Toronto. I packed my bags, had dinner, and opened my laptop. I wanted to review the plan for next week. It was going to be the beginning of the superuser knowledge training on the standard operating procedures. I had an important week ahead. Also, I inherited a customer service and would have to work with Amanda from accounts payable to develop a plan and execute it. By then, I've completely recovered over the 48- hour period, and even though, my body was not there yet, my mind felt sharp. It had to be, since no one could even suspect I had a surgery and was recovering from it. I decided to wear my waist belt below my shirts, so no one could see anything. Anyway, as per the doc's recommendations, I had to wear it for two weeks. It was coming to India with me.

The next morning, I woke up struggling with every move I made after getting out of bed. I still could not take a shower, so I simply got a wet cloth and cleaned my face and around my body the best I could.

I gingerly strolled my carryon with my laptop case on top. As always, I said good morning to the concierge and left my condominium. My usual routine of going to the airport was not as automatic as I was accustomed to. I was wide awake and in a lot of pain. Not even the strongest pain killers could help with all that movement. I could barely mask my suffering. I grinded my teeth and had tears in my eyes as I boarded the plane and asked someone if they could help me place my carryon into the above compartment.

I took a deep breath and sat down. Even though, I preferred the isle, that time I selected a window seat to make it easier to lean on and sleep. Once I felt more comfortable and relaxed, I fell asleep as I usually did on my early morning flights. I, however, had a very disturbing and unpleasant delirium. The discomfort I felt in my abdominal region was unbearable. I knew that I would have to become accustomed to the pain over the next two weeks.

When I arrived at the war room, I felt like I traveled through hell.

"Good morning, Sebastian. I see you've just arrived." Lee Choppard greeted me with a smile. She looked at me and noticed that I had little to no reaction to her greeting. By then, she knew me.

"Are you ok? You don't seem to be all there?" She asked worriedly.

"I am fine. I just overdid it working out this weekend, and I am very sore. Thank you for asking, Lee." I grimaced.

"You need to take it easy on the weights, big guy. We need you here in top shape; especially mentally." She laughed.

"Don't worry, Lee, my brain is razor sharp, and I should get better as the week progresses." I assured her.

"Don't forget, we have our final T-5 meeting next Monday before "go-live"."

"Yes, yes. I have it on my calendar, and my team will be ready." I nodded.

I sat down at my desk and greeted my team. They were still wearing the ski jackets. I found it comical.

"Good morning, team. Is it freezing outside, or did I forget we are in the middle of the summer?" I teased them.

"Good morning, Mr. Kosta. It's just very difficult for us to adjust to the weather here." Said Vihaan, the system engineer. "In India, it is hot all year long. Perhaps, when you visit the delivery center there, you will have to go in your speedos."

"Thank you for the nice comeback, Vihaan." I tried to laugh. It was excruciating. "So, how are we doing? Shanti, you are the team lead. Please report on our current status?" I became instantly serious.

"Yes, sir. Our status is currently green, and we are in line for our T-5 meeting."

"Did we build the new system architecture for our operations in Chennai?" I continued.

"Yes, we have." Vihaan took the initiative. "I have already modeled the new architecture and will start beta testing in a few days."

"Did you run this new model by Lee?" I was curious and impressed by my team's readiness.

"Yes." He nodded with a smile. "She is onboard and gave us the green light to proceed."

"That's wonderful news. Great job, everyone!" I tried applauding. Damn abdominals!

"Shanti, where are we on recruiting local talent?"

"There are many good universities in Chennai, and we have a local recruiting company used by the delivery center. The requisitions have been delivered and a pool of candidates have been identified. Currently, we are in the first round of interviews and should have offer letters being sent in the next two weeks."

"Also, wonderful news." I was thrilled. "I have to say, you, snow birds, have done a great job during my absence."

My team started laughing. I was pleased, and they seemed happy. It felt great!

"Let's start the week strong and please, keep me updated on any news. Remember, I don't like surprises, so keep me in the loop." I finished our team meeting on a high note, even though, internally, I was dying from pain and discomfort.

For the rest of the week, I remained in pain, but I had a mission to accomplish and nothing would stop me in achieving my goal. One afternoon, when I was completely saturated by my work on the deliverables, I was rudely interrupted by Amanda Perkins.

"Where are we on the customer service track?" She asked without 'hello' or 'how are you?' "Are you even working on that part of the project, or do you want for me to do it?"

"You know, it would be nice if you greeted me first with a 'hello' before your started probing me for answers?" I asked feeling irate.

"Sebastian, we have our final meeting in a week, and you haven't once approached me." She retorted.

"Yes, I am sorry about that, but as you know, I've been on the road for two weeks and working nonstop. And to make you happy, I did spend some time already working out the solution, and I don't think it would be complicated to execute." I assured Amanda.

"For you, everything is easy. You are too laid back. I don't like your style." She wouldn't stop attacking me.

"Fair enough." I said calmly. "I will handle that. You don't have to worry about it. It will be my responsibility and not yours."

She shrugged her shoulders, grunted loudly and walked back to her desk. I was not happy with our conversation, to say the least. Her tone was irritating. She had no respect for me as a manager, and that didn't look good around my team. I resorted to speak with her privately and forcefully, if the incident happened again.

Most of my time, for the reminder of the week, was spent in the war room. I finished all my trips and the interviews with our client Hudd. Then, the time came to prepare for the T-5 meeting. It would be similar to the one we had for the T-30. The difference was in details. Every area of the outsourcing effort would be examined. The meeting was being held locally, next Monday, July 4th. I was going to spend the rest of Tuesday and the entire Wednesday on finalizing the reports with my team. On Thursday, I only had half a day at the office. Then, I was off to the airport right after lunch. As was the norm, I would continue working on my laptop on the plane.

At that point, it's been almost a week since the surgery. I was still bandaged up around my waist. For the first week after the surgery, I could not take a full shower, because I still had the stitches and the dressing to protect the wound. I was excited I was going to see Dr. Lerner on Friday. It was our first post-op visit where he was going to remove the stitches and the dressing. I was on my way to full recovery. Also, that visit would be the first time I was going to see my abdominal region after the surgery. By now, the pain was manageable, but I still felt some discomfort. I guessed that was normal.

Chapter 19

I arrived in Miami in early evening. Since I was only away for one week, I left my Porsche parked at the airport. I found my car immediately, because I always parked in the same spot. I opened the front hatch and placed the carryon inside.

"Oh, it's so nice to be home." I said to myself.

I turned the car on and drove to Brickell Avenue. Home was only 15 minutes away. Since it was the middle of the summer, it was very hot and humid. I did not lower the top but just turned up the air conditioner. Most of the ride was on the I-95 Interstate highway. I enjoyed being back in my car. The sound from the upgraded exhaust filled the cabin; I was excited to be home. I was planning on spending the weekend alone. It was a very busy and hectic week, and all I looked for was the weekend of relaxation and tranquility. I also did not want for anyone to see me with the waist band on. As a man, I didn't feel comfortable telling people I had a cosmetic surgery. Even though, in Miami, it was accepted and considered a norm, I didn't want anyone asking questions.

As soon as I entered my building, I parked the car, grabbed my luggage and headed up to my apartment. It was so nice to just walk in and be at home. It was a week of masking a lot of pain and now, I could get comfortable and relax on the sofa. I turned the TV on and resorted to laying down and relaxing, maybe even taking a nap, but my peaceful plans were interrupted by the loud ringing of my phone.

"Hey, babes! How are you?" It was Renata.

"I am great now that I am hearing your voice." I smiled.

"We didn't get to talk this week." She mentioned.

"No, I was swamped with work. I spent every day at the office, from early morning until late evening. By the time I got back to the hotel, I was so tired that I would just pass out in bed. I really wanted to talk to you, but I had no time. By the way, where are you?" I asked.

"Seba, I am here in Miami."

"No way! That's awesome."

"You should meet us." Renata suggested.

"Who are us?" I laughed.

"My sister and I, and a few of our friends." She explained. "We are heading to South Beach, to a few clubs."

"I would love to, but as you know, I am leaving to India soon, and I have to spend this weekend locked up in my apartment, working. I am really sorry. I would have loved to see you." I replied sadly. "How much longer are you going to be in Miami?"

"I think for a month." Renata answered. She sounded very disappointed.

"Then I am sure we will have time to see each other." I tried cheering her up.

"I miss you, Seba. I really want to see you." She sighed.

"I feel the same way, Renata, but I have to focus, or my team will not be ready for the "go-live" in 2 weeks." I stated. "I promise, I will make it up to you. When this project is over, we will go away somewhere, and I will be all yours. I promise."

"Ok, good night, sweetheart." Renata whispered cheerfully. I loved how understanding she was.

"Good night, Renatinha."

The next morning, I woke up at 9 AM. Within an hour, I had an appointment with Dr. Lerner. I freshened up, got dressed, had some breakfast and was out the door. I felt so good, and the weather was so nice that I decided to lower the top of my convertible. It was a beautiful drive over the MacArthur Causeway heading to Lincoln road. The beautiful birds were flying through the sky, and I was enveloped by the smell of the ocean. There were cyclists riding over the bridge and the early morning joggers and runners performing their daily sprints. People in Miami loved their outdoor activities, nearly everyone was in great shape. People surrounding me, in everyday life, always looked hot. That was one of the reasons, I went for the surgery, to be in top shape. I also planned to partake in the ING Marathon scheduled for January. Thus, I had plenty of time to recover and get ready.

When I arrived at the clinic, I didn't have to wait. I was taken in right away. The front desk girl recognized me right away.

"Hello, Mr. Kosta. You look great. How are you feeling?"

"I feel much better. Thank you. But I still have a burning pain in some areas." I replied.

"That's normal. It's only been a week. The doctor will see you shortly."

About 5 minutes later, the nurse called me inside the waiting room. As I sat there, on the patients' bed, my abdomen region started burning. Something did not feel right.

About 15 minutes later, Dr. Lerner walked in with the nurse. "Hello Sebastian. How are you?"

"I'm doing okay, but I have this burning pain in the area near my lower abdominal region." At that point, it was difficult for me to speak.

"Ok, Sebastian. Why don't you take off your shirt, and I will remove your waist band? Let's see what's going on underneath."

When the doctor took off the waist band, and I saw my abdomen, I was horrified. It looked terrible with the black and blues everywhere. Furthermore, my skin appeared inflamed and lumpy.

"Sebastian, don't worry about how it looks right now." Dr. Lerner hurried to calm me. "Remember, my surgeries are very aggressive. But you do look swollen. Did you get a lot of rest this week?" He questioned me.

"No, I had to take a flight to Toronto, for work." I admitted.

"You need to get rest, Sebastian." The doctor was displeased.

"I am not going anywhere this weekend."

"If you really rest, without too much action and commotion, you will heal better. All the swelling will go down in the next two to three weeks. The bruising will work its way down your body. Don't freak out if you notice it around your legs. Now, where was the burning feeling coming from?"

"Right around my pelvic region on both sides."

"Oh yes, I see what is hurting you. You have two cysts filled with blood. This is normal. It doesn't happen with all the patients, but since you have been up on your feet a lot, that is not so unusual. We just have to drain the blood." The doctor suggested. I felt relieved.

The nurse brought a large needle and Dr. Lerner got to work. He first pierced the cysts.

"Once we drain it, you will be good as new." He explained.

He removed the blood in both cysts. Even though it did not hurt, it was strange to have those two blisters filled with blood. I was very worried initially, but doctor's calm professionalism put me at ease.

"Ok, Sebastian, now I am going to remove the stitches. You will feel a pinch, but it should not hurt."

He removed the stitches right above my pubic region, inside my belly button, and then on both of my lumbar sides.

"Ok, you are all done. Now you can take a shower." He smiled and removed the gloves.

"Finally!" I exclaimed. "That will be the first thing I am doing when I get back home."

"Aside from the cysts, I think your recovery is going well. Like I've mentioned, the swelling would take another 3 weeks to go down completely. Try to wear your waist band for as long as you can. The more you wear it, the better the results. In a month, you can slowly get back to working out. Your next visit should be around one month from now."

"Actually doctor, I will be in India at that time." I noted.

"Ok, not a problem! Just go ahead and book it with the receptionist when you are back in Miami. Remember to call me if you need anything."

"Thank you, doctor." I could finally take a deep breath and stop stressing imagining that there was something wrong with me.

The rest of the weekend was very relaxing. I was able to take a shower which was amazing. It was still a challenge to move around easily, thus, I resorted to staying in, resting and watching as much TV as I wanted. I never really let myself do that. I was always busy, always on the run, working out or working, partying or hanging out. But at that time, I had a good excuse. Besides that, I smoked a lot of shisha that weekend. I would wake up, eat something, and then after the meal smoke the double apple flavored shisha. It was a good time to reflect on how much I had accomplished in my life.

I started out as a successful private banker. After 2 years, I got bored with the job and decided to get my Series 7 broker's license. I immediately landed a job at Morgan Stanley. It was much more challenging than banking. Luckily, most of my bank clients followed me into that new venture, and my portfolio was healthy for someone with little experience.

We traded stocks daily; taking advantage of the markets' fluctuations and various political and economic changes affecting the markets. It was a risky strategy. I learned that over time. We made money with the movement of the stock. We would find a blue-chip stock with high volatility and purchase on bad news. Once recovered, we would repeatedly buy and sell the stock in high volumes to make thousands of dollars each day. Unfortunately, when the correction of the market happened, I would have to hold the stock, thus, my commission would be flat. In the year 2000, there was a major correction in the market, and I got out. I chose to get my MBA instead of looking for another job. Soon after graduation, I became a management consultant. I've been climbing up ever since. During the past eight years, I bought two properties: the condo in Miami, at the Four Seasons and my vacation condo, in Panama. I was looking forward to getting back in shape after my full recovery, so I could get back to surfing. Surfing was the main reason I bought my place in Punta Pacifica, Panama.

The next day, on Sunday, around 2 PM I got a text from Renata.

"Hey, stranger. Have you forgotten about me?" She asked.

"No, princess, I got home on Thursday evening and just wanted to relax this weekend. I've been away from home for quite some time, I needed to take a break." I admitted.

"I agree with you, but just because you wanted to chill out and relax, doesn't mean I can't be with you." She insisted.

"No, of course not."

"Seba, I miss you. I really want to see you before you head back to Toronto."

"I have to warn you, I am little under the weather." I lied.

"That's fine. I don't mind getting what you have." As always, Renata was a good sport.

About 30 minutes later, the front desk called me to announce I had a visitor.

"Please let her up." I left the door open and returned to the couch with my hookah burning non-stop.

A few minutes later, Renata came running in. I placed the shisha handle down on the coffee table, and she literally jumped on me.

"Here I am!" She yelled out happily. "I missed you so much, Seba. It's been a couple of weeks since I last saw you and ever since our weekend in Montreal, I couldn't stop thinking about you. You are all I care about!" She seemed too impatient to tell me everything in one breath.

As I grimaced to hide my pain, she mounted over me. "I love your apartment. The views from up here are amazing. I feel like an eagle soaring in the air." She got up, and I breathed a sigh of relief. It looked like she didn't care if I spoke or replied. She just needed to say what she had to. She then approached the window facing the south east.

"Is that Key Biscayne?"

"Yes, that's the bridge I run up and over on the weekends." I finally spoke.

"Did you run this weekend?" Renata turned around and looked at me.

"No, like I told you, I didn't feel well."

"Yes, your face is a little red." She squinted and nodded.

If she only knew how much pain I was holding inside. I didn't want to tell her the truth. I didn't want for her to know about any insecurities.

"Can we go to your bedroom? I can usually learn a lot from

someone's house especially their bedroom." That was a weird statement, but I let it go.

"Sure, let me get up." I struggled to get off the sofa.

"Are you ok?" Renata sounded worried.

"Yes, I'm just in pain." I admitted honestly.

We walked into the bedroom.

"Did you hire a designer, or did you do it yourself?" Renata was impressed.

"I did everything by myself." I replied proudly. "I don't believe in paying high fees for the interior designers who know nothing about me. How could they design my living space if they were complete strangers?"

"That's true. You've done an amazing job." She complimented me and walked over to the bed.

"Can we have some fun time together?" Renata whispered seductively.

"I'd rather not today." I hated myself for letting Renata come over. I knew it was a huge mistake from the get-go.

"Come on, Seba." She begged. "I missed feeling you inside of me. I came here to be with you. Let me take that shirt off." She came close and reached for the buttons on my shirt. After she opened them one by one, staring in my eyes lustily, she proceeded to take it off. I wasn't in the mood for sex. The pain was too intense. But, at the same time, I loved having sex with her.

"Listen, you're going to have to ride me today." I gave in.

"That sounds fun. I love riding you."

She undressed, and we ended up naked on my bed. She instantly got on top guiding me inside of her. It felt so good, until she started moving.

As she rocked me forcefully, up and down, the area where the stitches were removed started to hurt badly. Pain beat the pleasure, and my entire face contorted in suffering.

"Seba, what's wrong?" She stopped and got off me in seconds. Before I could even open my mouth, she looked at me attentively.

"Oh my God!!!" She yelled out. "You had a surgery. I can tell you had surgery. That's why you are in so much pain." She seemed to talk to herself. "What was it? Why did you have a surgery? Did you have lipo?" She showered me with questions.

"No, it was not lipo." I tried making something up. I should've been better prepared for a possible discovery of my condition. "I got very sick last week and went to the hospital. They had to remove my appendix. That's why I am in so much pain."

"Seba, in Brazil liposuction is very common. I know what those scars look like. Look, you even have the scars in several places. If it was your appendix, it would only be one scar." Renata was too smart and observant for my bullshit story.

"They performed an arthroscopic surgery, and that's why I have multiple incisions. It wasn't lipo." I tried sticking to my story.

"It was lipo. I know it. But it doesn't matter, I still love you." Renata was one of a kind. I couldn't deny that any longer.

Something inside of me felt different. I didn't want for anyone to find out, I had any insecurities, especially about my body. I always knew, only God was perfect, but I really wanted that ideal six pack. I was ready to do anything for that. And I did. I said nothing, just looked at Renata and walked out of the bedroom. She joined me minutes later. She was dressed and very calm. She sat right by me and reached for the hookah pipe.

"You know that stuff is bad for you?" She said after exhaling. I looked at her and laughed.

"It's not that bad. Just a vapor with a hint of apple. The smoke is filtered by the water." I explained after having a good laugh about Renata taking a puff and then saying how bad that stuff was for me.

"I'm sure, it still has some nicotine, and it might get you addicted." She continued unfazed.

"I just do it to relax. You know how hectic my job is, plus all the traveling. When I get home, I sit back and just admire the view and smoke some shisha to chill out. Actually, I call it chillaxing."

"Just don't overdo it. Nothing in excess is good for you."

"Not even sex?" I teased.

"Sex is different." Renata winked at me.

We both laughed.

"I think the only addiction I can't resist is sex." I stated honestly. "I can cut out smoking shisha, eating bad food, and even drinking, but I can't stop having sex."

"With me!" Renata added. "Only with me!"

"What are you saying? Are we exclusive now?" I took a doubletake.

"I am. I hope you are too. I only want you, Sebastian. Nobody else. I love you." She said looking trustingly into my eyes.

Renata spent a few more hours with me, and then had to return home. Her family was also in Miami, and they were having dinner that night. After Renata left, I ate and prepared my bags for the next day. I was returning to my final week in Toronto. Then, I would be traveling across the Atlantic and Indian Oceans to my final destination, in the south east tip of India. Even though, I was excited, part of me was already missing Renata. I initially wanted for her to come with me, but I later learned, it wasn't the best place for tourists. While I would be working, my poor Renata would have to be confined to the hotel. It wasn't fair for her. To make matters worse, I was going to be working the night shifts, so our waking hours would not coincide. It would be impossible for her to come. The plan was to continue communicating, using my international calling cards provided by the company. Then, upon my return, we would see where we were. As we initially agreed, we would keep our relationship in the present moment.

Chapter 20

The next day, after many hours of travel, I arrived at our offices in Toronto, right into the war room. It was almost lunch time, and our T-5 was scheduled to begin promptly at 1PM. As it happened before, each one of us had only 30 minutes to give a detailed account of the tracks we managed. That time around, I was the 3rd in line because Lee Choppard was presenting before me, since top management wanted to hear everything about the System's Integration track before turning to accounting.

When Lee was about to go into the board room, I came up to her. She appeared calm and assured. She carried her laptop and a thick folder with documents. I wasn't worried about Lee. She was always prepared.

"Good luck, Lee. Knock it out of the park." I told her.

"Thanks, I really hope it goes well." Lee smiled at me. I was a hundred percent sure she would do great.

"It will. Be confident." I whispered to her as she pushed the door and walked in.

While I was waiting for my turn, I decided to catch up with Premal.

"Hey Premal, how are you? Did you get here this morning or last night?" I asked.

"What's going on, Sebastian. I actually came in last night. I had a few things I needed to finish for my presentation today, and my kids would not let me focus on my work. So, I left early and worked at the hotel the entire Sunday night." He explained.

"How old are your kids?"

"I have a girl who is 4, and a boy who is 3- years- old."

"Wow, back to back!" I couldn't imagine how he managed. "You must have your hands full on the weekends."

"I think, that's an understatement." He laughed. "You see, my wife is an attorney, and she works during the week and leaves the kids at the preschool. At night, she takes care of them. When the weekend arrives, it's my turn, and I become a full-blown Mr. Mom. I actually get more rest during the week."

"It seems like you spoke Chinese to me right now." I echoed his laughter. "It's hard for a single guy to comprehend what you've just said."

"You will understand one day. When you get married and have kids. You can't be a bachelor forever." Premal noted.

"You're right, one day, when I can no longer party with my friends, I will have to retire. I have too much fun in Miami." I hoped that day wasn't coming anytime soon.

"So, when are you leaving for India?" I asked Premal.

"I'm leaving next week. I should be there on Thursday, July 14th. That way, I can enjoy the weekend and fight the jet lag before going to work on Monday."

"Your family is originally from India, right?"

"Yes, I came to the US as a kid."

"Do you speak the local language?" I asked.

"I do. In India, there are many languages, over 20, if I'm not mistaken. I speak Hindi, which is widely known. I'm sure with Hindi and English, I will be able to communicate with the locals just fine." Premal explained.

"Great! I will need your help then." I smiled to Premal.

"Don't worry, Sebastian. You will be fine. Indian people are nice, and you will get to experience and learn the new culture. That is always exciting."

I looked at the time; I was next. Amanda was finishing up her presentation, and Amy showed up to tell me I was next at the board room.

I came up to my team desk and got my computer bag. Everything was there, my PC, important files, and the handouts of my presentation.

"Ok, Sebastian. They are ready for you." Amy announced. "Please, follow me."

I followed Amy into the room and noticed it was filled with people. Scott, the Senior Manager in charge of the project, stood up and shook my hand.

"Welcome, Sebastian. Why don't you hook your laptop up to the overhead projector and we will get started?" I greeted Scott and everyone and got to work. Once I was ready, I took my seat beside Scott, next to the projector. Scott was nice enough to assist me by handing out the copies of the presentation for those in the room. Half of the audience consisted of Hudd's senior leadership, the rest of the people were our senior leadership, headed by Manesh, Accent's Global Senior Partner from India. He was attending on behalf of Gary who had another engagement in conflict with our meeting.

"Good afternoon, Sebastian. This is Manesh, calling in from India. You have 30 minutes, starting right now. Please walk us through the key slides. Our panel of guests, is divided equally between Accent and Hudd and will be overviewing your presentation. To save time, I would ask everyone present to refrain from asking questions until Sebastian completes his presentation. Thank you. Sebastian, the floor is yours." Manesh invited me to start, and I got up before the projector.

I began my presentation by highlighting the areas of main focus. Therefore, my first slide displayed all the areas we had to cover, five of them were in the green and three in yellow. I decided to focus on the yellow areas. The first one in yellow was the Organizational Design of the delivery center. We were about a week away from "go-live", and the shared services manager for the entire delivery center has not been hired yet. That was outside of my control, and I didn't think it would affect the execution of our work on a daily basis. I was sure, the other people in the reporting positions would be able to handle any issues that needed attention. The next yellow area was the Sarbanes Oxley review of the documentation. I assured the audience there was no need for concern since those documents were currently under review and would be ready for "go-live". The third and final yellow area of concern was marked as Transformation Integration. Not all of my superusers have been adequately trained in the transaction processing.

"We believe, we will be able to catch up, gain ground and finish all the knowledge transfer." I finalized my presentation. Scott looked up at me and gave a positive affirmation.

"The only other issue here, is with our bank reconciliation process. Citibank needs to send our monthly bank statements to Xerox, which in turn will scan and index them. I am concerned that either the bank or Xerox might drop the ball." I explained. Larry Eiselt, our Accent Partner noted, "this is a normal concern on any outsourcing project. Just keep track of your reconciliation process and reach out to both, Citibank and Xerox, when you identify the root cause of the problem. I would not be too concerned about that."

The next slide showed the table I developed for capturing the status of each one of my business unit visits in Canada and throughout the US. It displayed the number of documents, the types of documents, and if they were reviewed by the subject matter expert, transition managers, and by the finance director of Hudd. In my case, all the documentation was completed and reviewed by all parties. We moved on to the next slide, which discussed the Sarbanes Oxley documentation and the completion dates. The fourth slide showed our knowledge transfer and training progress with my team of superusers. There was not much to discuss since everything was marked green. The fifth slide exhibited a monthly calendar highlighting the timeframe from 'go-live' date to 30 days after the event and the subsequent months of support needed by the Hudd transition team back in the US and Canada.

The final slide was the most important. It discussed the stabilization scenarios. Everyone, present at the board room, watched carefully and as on cue, started taking notes. The first scenario was in the red, dealing with the possibility of not receiving the bank lockbox documents (checks and remittances) at Xerox, where they would be scanned and indexed.

"Don't worry, Sebastian. This is a vendor relationship which we have to manage using predefined service level agreements. I believe it's important to capture but should not hold us back at all for the 'go-live'." Larry assured me and the audience.

The next scenario was the accounts receivable having a backlog since the usage of a lockbox was a new concept for all the business units in US and Canada. John Nagy, our Finance Director for Hudd Canada, explained, "All the business units were extensively trained on the new procedure. It is documented, and the standard operating procedure is located in each business unit. I will make sure there is no delay in the process. The 'go-live' date will not be affected, we will be here after, for support."

"The final scenario, which I marked yellow, is the possibility of the increasing volume of customer calls by the AR/Billing team which might take away from the transaction processing. My original idea is to handle customer calls separately through an existing call center." I proposed.

"Sebastian, this is Manesh." I heard the voice. I turned to where it was coming from. "Unfortunately, we do not have the time or budget to recruit and hire the staff necessary to support Hudd. Having a dedicated call center was never negotiated by Hudd and would be an additional service which we can provide in the future if it is warranted."

"Yes, Sebastian." Scott joined in. "I believe Manesh is correct. Hudd never signed up for a call center. We have several in India and China and would be ready at the moment's notice, if Hudd requested the additional service."

"Very well. At that, my presentation is over. Any further questions?" I looked around the board room.

No one spoke up. It seemed everyone was clear on everything I presented. I thanked the audience for their time and started disconnecting my laptop.

"Good job, Sebastian." Scott was pleased. "You were under a lot of pressure to get this done. I still can't believe you did all the rework in only 3 weeks. I am definitely going to give you a great review on your performance feedback for this project. Your next month in India should feel like a vacation compared to what you've just went through. Keep up the good work."

"Thank you, Scott." I nodded and after wishing everyone a good day, I left the room.

As soon as I walked over to my desk, I was approached by Premal.

"So, are you all done?"

"Yes, it went better than I expected." I replied, feeling a sense of relief.

"You know, you must have been well prepared. I heard Amanda went in and was grilled by our client counterparts. She walked out with a blank look on her face." Premal whispered.

"I'm sorry to hear that." I lied. I wasn't sorry at all.

"So, are you ready for India? Are you leaving directly from Toronto?" He changed the topic.

"No, I still need to finish up with my team here, and then go back to Miami to get my larger bags. Since I will be there for about a month, I need to take more stuff. A carryon would be insufficient."

"I hear you, man. I am doing the same. I will see you in Chennai, next week. Stay out of trouble. At least until I get there."

We both laughed.

The next two days were spent heads down with my team. All the data capturing has been performed and validated. To finish up, we had to complete the superuser knowledge transfer. It was most likely the least interesting part of the project since we had to sit for hours review-ing the materials and polishing up the standard operating procedures. From time to time, I got the questions from my team usually regarding the procedures, and I would verify if the documentation was correct. We also went through the plan on how to take that new information and transfer it to the general users in Chennai. My six team members would be the supervisors for the processes, but the general users would ultimately become the clerks handling the day-to-day transaction- pro-cessing activities. Therefore, it would be crucial for the general user training.

On Thursday, the time came for me to visit the war room one last time before my trip to India. I spent the day with my closest team-mates, Amy, the receptionist, Lee, our system integration specialist, and Premal. Even though Premal was married with kids and had his hands full, he was still an easy-going cool guy, the one to go out with and share a beer or few. He was very down to earth and had many stories from his single days. It was fun to hang out with him and relive those moments. It was basically what we had in common. He even gave me a few advices for if and when I got married.

"Marriage is not easy." He said. "A woman tends to change when kids are born. You just have to learn how to fall in love with her again. And every 5 years or so, you both grow and again, you need to fall in love with each other. You just need a lot of patience when you get married." I thought it was very deep and brilliant.

I left the office right after lunch, at around 1PM. By 8, I was already walking into my apartment in Miami. It was good to be home. The first thing I did, was to take off the waist band. I took a deep breath and relaxed on the sofa. By then, it'd been two weeks since the surgery, and I still felt very uncomfortable. The pain lessened, but the bruising had moved from my abdominal region all the way down to the upper part of my calves. That worried me, but I did recall Dr. Lerner saying that would happen.

I went into the bathroom and turned on the music. Of course, it had to be Coldplay. I took a long hot shower and cleaned up the scars from the surgery. I still could not believe I had actually gone through it. At least now it was over, and in a few weeks, I could throw away the waist band.

After I got out of the shower, I put on a t-shirt and boxers and sat down on the sofa again. I decided to call Renata one last time before flying out the next morning. I dialed her number and waited for her to answer.

"How funny. I was just thinking about you, Seba. Our minds must be in synch." She stated as she answered the phone.

"I wanted to call and say goodbye. I am leaving to India tomorrow." I noted quietly.

"I figured it was this weekend. Is it a direct flight?"

"I don't think they have any planes with that fuel capacity. I have to switch planes in Frankfurt, Germany."

"Have you ever been to that airport?" Renata continued.

"No, but it's an international airport, so don't worry, I shouldn't get lost."

"I am going to miss you, Seba. It's going to be hard." I heard tears in her voice.

"Yes, it will be hard for me too. I can't believe I am saying that, but I am falling in love with you. It's a very strange statement for me, because I have never loved another woman. You are the first." My heart was way ahead of my brain. I wasn't sure if I'd be saying that having thought it through. But I meant every word. "I, however, look forward to my journey to India. I think it will be an adventure. I love to learn new cultures and have always been fascinated with the history of India." I instantly changed the topic to lighten things up.

"Well my dear, please be careful over there. Did you do all your vaccinations?" Renata inquired. It was cute how worried and methodical she was.

"Oh yes, a couple of weeks ago. Don't worry. I am probably the most prepared person you know, and, in a few weeks, I will be back. It should go by very quickly." I assured her.

"So how will we be able to talk to each other?"

"I have to work the night shifts, therefore during the day I will be sleeping. Our only window of opportunity will be on the weekends. I still don't know how I am going to get used to working from 6 PM to 3 AM." I was concerned about that.

"Just try to keep yourself busy, so that when it's time to sleep you are very tired, and you pass out. You need to get your sleep every night." Renata advised.

"Ok, my dear. I will be thinking about you." I promised. "I'll call you the first chance I get."

"I love you, Seba." Renata whispered.

"I love you too." I echoed her.

Chapter 21

The next day, I made it to the airport, exactly two hours before my 9 PM eight-hour flight on Lufthansa Airlines. As I waited for boarding, I read John Grisham. I loved reading, it helped me get immersed in the adventures of the story, visiting different time periods and locations.

About an hour later, the boarding started. The plane was a two-leveled Boeing 747. I was sitting at the lower level, but close to the stairs. That way, I could see all the people going up to the upper level. I loved people-watching. I could not tell if they were successful or rich just by their appearances, but I figured the seats had to be more expensive. I always heard there was a bar up there, and one could stretch their legs during long flights. Since it was an eight-hour flight, I figured I would just take a Xanax and put on some relaxing music to listen on my headphones. I asked the flight attendant not to wake me up for meals, since I already ate at the airport. About 30 minutes later, I was completely out.

When I woke up, I slightly opened the window shade. It was light outside. I must have slept the whole night. It was almost 6 in the morning, and I enjoyed watching the sun rising from the East. For me, seeing the sunrise was always special.

"Good morning, ladies and gentlemen. This is your captain speaking. We are about to make our decent into Frankfurt International Airport. Please raise your seats back to the upright position and fasten your seatbelts." I heard the voice coming from the loudspeakers.

I couldn't believe how fast the time passed. The miracle of Xanax! In about 30 minutes, the plane landed. I felt good since I was well-rested. I had a four-hour layover in Frankfurt before my second flight directly to Chennai.

As soon as I got off the plane, I followed the stream of passengers. That gave me a good orientation around the unfamiliar airport. It was my first time at that particular airport, and I marveled at its beauty and cleanliness. The floors were very similar to Miami's airport and were covered in carpet. Pretty much the whole airport was designed to give people a lot of space and keep them relaxed. I even saw a few dogs that were used for people to pet and smile. Then, I walked by a restaurant in the middle of the concourse. It was shaped like an old pirate ship. I looked closely and noticed, no one was smoking. At times like that, especially at the airports, my awareness was heightened, and I tended to notice every detail, every movement, and every sound around me. Admittedly, that could get quite exhausting.

I started looking for a comfortable corner where I could relax for a few hours, but shockingly, I couldn't find any available seat anywhere. Thus, I decided to go up to the second floor. There, the situation was the same. Nothing available. Then, I noticed a McDonalds. For some weird reason, people were allowed to smoke there. It seemed as if it was the only place where people could smoke in the concourse. I hated the smell of cigarette smoke, so I quickly went in, purchased a Big Mac with fries and took a seat outside the restaurant where luckily, I found a table with some seats available. I ate my lunch and then tried to relax. The next flight was going to be a tougher one, it was a day flight. It was also going to be longer, approximately 12 hours. I would be arriving in Chennai around midnight. I hoped my driver would still be waiting for me.

PART 3
India

Chapter 1

After twelve hours onboard, I finally arrived in Chennai, India. I walked off the plane and followed all the passengers through the immigration and customs control. I knew, all of us had to go to the same area, so I did not bother reading the signs. Once there, I joined the line for international travelers. When it was my turn to speak with the customs' officer, I tried to be as friendly and polite as possible. I definitely did not want to cause any problems by answering anything in the wrong way.

"Good evening, Mr. Kosta." The officer greeted politely. "What is the purpose of your visit?"

"Good evening. I'm here on a business trip." I replied courteously.

"Who do you work for?" He asked.

"I work for Accent. I am here for a business outsourcing project for one of our clients."

"How long will you be staying in Chennai?"

"I will be here for one month." I continued answering the standard questions.

"What will be your primary residence while you are here?"

"I will be staying the Park Sheraton Hotel."

"Thank you very much, Mr. Kosta. Enjoy your stay. You may proceed."

Since all of the people in the immigration line were either going to baggage claim or exiting the terminal; I continued to follow them. In my case, I needed to pick up one large luggage from baggage claim. I was tired and hurting at that point. I traveled for over 20 hours, and my last leg to India felt unbearably long since I was unable to sleep. The pain from the surgery was very intense, and I knew that I needed a hot bath to relax.

I left on Friday night, and it was Saturday, almost midnight. I wanted to get my bag and quickly make it to the Park Sheraton. It was regarded as the best hotel in Chennai and the center location for foreign visitors.

After waiting for about 30 minutes, I finally got my bag from the carousel. I then placed my computer bag on top of the carryon and exited the airport. As soon as I stepped out of the sliding doors, I felt a massive wave of heat and humidity hitting me with an incredible force. Mind you, it was nighttime in Chennai. I immediately started sweating and was desperate to find my driver. As I looked ahead, I could see a swarm of people, mostly men, Indian natives, and they were all screaming and waving signs. I had no idea what they were saying, but I ignored the noise and focused on the signs they held. Surely enough, I found a middle-aged man, wearing a white customary garb, holding my name tag. I quickly approached the man.

"Are you, Mr. Kosta?" He inquired looking me up and down like I was an alien.

"Yes!" I exclaimed.

"Please follow me." He said with a smile.

We walked into the parking lot that was filled to capacity. Most of the cars looked so outdated, they could easily pass as vintage. I was definitely not in the US anymore. He opened the door to the back seat of his car, and then went around to place my luggage into the trunk. As I sat down, the old smell of the interior hit me in the nose. The seats were worn out. The dashboard was scratched and dusty. The driver got inside the car.

"Sir, may I offer you some cold water or a coke?" He asked politely.

He had a small cooler in the passenger seat. I asked for water and thanked him. The car did not have A/C, so all the windows were open. I took my first sip and sat back for the ride.

"How was your trip, sir?" The driver asked. To be honest, I was so tired, I didn't want to speak. Plus, the heat was unbearable.

"Very long. Glad that it's over."

"You are staying at the Park Sheraton. Correct?"

"Yes. That's where I will be staying." I nodded.

"Sit back and relax, sir. We should be there in 30 minutes." I smiled and slumped into the seat.

As we continued on route to the hotel, I could not believe that heat. I knew that it would be summer there, but Miami summer seemed arctic in comparison. As we drove, I looked at the streets and buildings. To my surprise, all the streets were small, and the roads were single lane. There were no highways too. There were cows and horses wondering around. No tall buildings. I did not see any high-rise or mid-rise developments. There were many shops; all closed because it was nighttime. One thing, that did make a very good first impression, was the outdoor aroma. As we drove with the windows opened, I picked up a beautiful strong scent of jasmine. I could not believe that for as long as we drove, I could still smell it. It seemed the entire city was enveloped in the scent.

As the driver promised, we arrived at the hotel in exactly 30 minutes. Since it was very late, there was no one at the front desk, and I had to ring the bell for someone to help me. Shortly after, the overnight supervisor approached.

"Good evening, sir. Do you have reservations with us?" A pretty middle-aged woman asked me.

"Yes, it should be under Sebastian Kosta." I smiled at her.

"Oh yes, here it is." She looked up from the computer. "Welcome to the Park Sheraton, Mr. Kosta. It appears that you will be staying with us for one month?"

"Yes, this will be my new home away from home."

"Excellent, Mr. Kosta. Your two keys for your room are in this envelope. If you proceed to the right, your room is all the way down the hall on the second floor. Just take the elevator over there."

She pointed to where I was supposed to go. I thanked her, got my luggage and was finally on my way to rest.

As soon as I walked in, I noted how beautiful and clean my room was. It was probably one of the nicest rooms I've stayed in, and that counted for something since I always stayed at top-notch hotels. The floors were covered in polished marble, and the room was furnished in high-end traditional style. There was a separate living room with sofas and armchairs and a huge flat screen TV. The living room was divided by two sliding French wooden doors which led to the bedroom. The bedroom was very nice, but what took the cake was the bathroom. It was almost the same size as the bedroom, covered in a darker brown marble with a jacuzzi to the left and a shower stall to the right. In between the two, was a huge double-vanity set. I definitely did not need all that opulence, but it was nice since I would live there for the entire month.

Since it was already past 1AM, I decided to take a hot bath, relax and get to bed. Next morning, I planned to walk around and get acclimated and familiarize myself with the surroundings. But all I needed then was rest. Everything else was left for tomorrow.

Chapter 2

The next morning, it was Sunday, July 10th, and I woke up later than usual. I wasn't sure what I would have for breakfast. I haven't seen the entire hotel and knew nothing about the amenities and the services. I decided to look at the room service menu. It was quite extensive; half of it was created for the Indian natives, and the other for the Westerners. I ordered a three-egg omelet with breakfast potatoes and a toast with butter and strawberry jam.

After about 30 minutes, I heard the sound of the doorbell. I walked over to the entrance and opened the door.

"Good morning, sir." A young staff member showed up with a huge smile. He waved his head from side to side and was very friendly. I was impressed about how nice everyone I'd encountered so far was.

"Please allow me to set your breakfast table." I smiled and stepped aside. The guy wheeled the cart into the living room and placed the tray on the round glass table.

Once everything was ready, he pulled back the seat from the table. "Please have a seat, sir."

"Thank you for your kindness." I pronounced gratefully. "Do I leave the tray outside when I am done?"

"Oh no, sir. We are all about technology here, at the Park Sheraton. Next to your bed is what we call the command center. You can control everything from there. The lights, the TV, your air conditioner, and the music system. All the lights are coded by the location. Room service button is also located on that panel. You simply press the button, and someone will come to assist you."

"Wow, you guys are very high-tech." I was impressed.

"Yes, India is proud to be at the forefront of technology, and we value your comfort and security in the room. If you don't need anything else, I will go, Sir?"

"That would be it. Thank you very much." I was starving and couldn't wait to eat.

"It is my pleasure, Sir. Enjoy your meal."

After I finished my breakfast, I decided to play around with that high-tech command center. It was interesting because all the switches for all the lights in the entire room were located there. I could control the music in three rooms: the bedroom, the living room and the bathroom. There were two TV's, and both could be controlled by the command center. In fact, the entire hotel was just a touch away. It was so high tech, I could preprogram the lights, music and the TV to turn on and off at a predetermined time. That sophistication was more than what I had at home. I started thinking about an upgrade upon my return back to Miami.

Next, I wanted to get familiar with the hotel and the surrounding area. I put on the workout clothes, my waist band and headed down to the lobby. I stayed at the Sheraton hotels a couple of times in the past, but never one so glamorous. From what I was told, that was the best hotel in Chennai. I walked over to the concierge.

"Good morning. I would like to know where the gym is located."

"Good morning, sir. It would be my pleasure to show you. The gym is located one floor below, in the basement of the building. As soon as you walk out of the elevator, the gym is to your right. You can use your room key to gain access 24 hours a day."

"Great. Thank you!" I turned around towards the elevator.

"If I can be of further service, please allow me Sir."

"Thanks again." I yelled out before walking into the elevator.

I thought, commencing my tour with the gym, would be the best idea since I usually started my day there. I entered the elevator, and there was a bellhop working the elevator.

"To which level, sir?"

"To the basement, please. I am going to the gym."

"Oh yes, sir. Right away." He pressed the button. "Our gym has everything you need. Cardio equipment, weights, and a stretching area. I believe you will be quite content, sir."

"I hope so. I tend to use the gym a lot." I replied to the man.

The elevator doors opened, and I walked over to the right and saw the double doors. Once inside, I noticed the bellhop was correct in his description. For the cardio workouts, I could use the elliptical or the treadmill. There was a padded area for stretching and calisthenics. Overall, I was satisfied. It would be sufficient for a daily use. I could start the rehabilitation process from my recent surgery. The gym had everything I needed.

I went back upstairs to the lobby and revisited with the concierge.

"I'm back." I announced with a smile.

"Yes, sir. Did you like the gym?" He asked.

"Yes, and it will be perfect for my stay here. Thank you."

"Wonderful news, sir. Is there anything else I may have the pleasure to assist you with?"

"If you don't mind, I would like to get a tour of the amenities of the hotel."

"It would be my pleasure, sir. Let's start with the restaurant. When you exit the elevator, it will be to the left. We have one called The Residency, which has a view to the pool. It has a phenomenal international cuisine. Most of our guests use it for breakfast. Then, if you are looking for a bar and a night club, we have The Westminster. There is happy hour and live entertainment until midnight. Many people from the outside come here on the weekends to dance." He pointed out.

"Well, that sure is good to know. After a busy week, a few cocktails will come handy."

"Yes sir, and we also have the pool bar and the barbecue areas working on the weekends."

"That will make me feel right at home. Can I see the pool?" I inquired.

"Of course, sir. Let me accompany you."

We walked towards the back of the hotel and out to a fully enclosed terrace with a pool. The building around the pool area was L-shaped.

We walked along the edge of the pool where some guests were enjoying the sun. I immediately noticed, everyone there was a foreigner.

"Thanks for showing me the pool. With this heat and humidity, the pool is the paradise. By the way, what is your name?" It occurred to me that I was speaking to the gentleman for quite some time and didn't know his name.

"My name is Muhammad Sreenivasan. Most of our foreign guests simply call me Srini." He responded with a smile.

"It's a pleasure to meet you, Srini. I want to thank you for giving me this tour."

He shook his head from side to side. "Any time, sir. Please do remember that we have two concierges. On the weekends, we are both on duty. During the week, we alternate shifts. The second concierge is Muhammad Sharma, but most people call him Michael."

"Perfect, Srini and Michael." I repeated out loud.

"Sir, if you follow me to the other side of the pool, I can show you our spa?" Srini suggested.

"Oh yes, it's very important for me to get familiar with the spa. I love getting massages." I stated enthusiastically.

"Sir, please be aware that we are only permitted to perform lotion rub downs."

"Really? No massages?" I was so disappointed.

"No." Srini looked like he alone was guilty of instituting that rule.

"Okay, I will have to live with that."

We entered the facility and walked by the main entrance where the spa employee was seated.

"You can make all your reservations with the spa attendant either from your room or in person." Srini continued.

"I'd like to set up one for tomorrow, right before work"

"What time would that be, sir?" Asked the spa host.

"Well, I have to be at work by 6 PM, so why don't we plan for 4? I would like a woman."

"A woman, sir?" The host appeared taken aback.

"Yes, a woman for the massage or a rub down." I noted.

"Women are not allowed to give massages in India." The host explained.

"What? Is that a joke???" I was stunned.

"No sir, but we can provide you with a boy."

"I don't want a boy giving me massage."

"We can provide you with two boys if you wish, sir?"

"I don't want any boy touching me." I was flabbergasted.

"I'm sorry, sir, but women are not permitted." The host continued in the same calm voice.

"Okay, what else do you have to offer in the spa?" I gave up.

Srini walked me inside and showed me a roman tub. He approached the wall and turned a lever. Immediately, the water rushed into the tub in a fast-spiral fashion, and in about 2 minutes, the tub was completely filled up.

"You can either use it hot or cold. Once you are done, you just notify the spa attendant, and he will drain the water."

I've been to many spas and used different facilities. I've never seen a tub that was for one person at a time, and the water would be removed after each usage.

"I like this, Srini." Finally, something I did like about that spa. "After a hard workout, I think a cold-water bath, would do wonders for my body."

We walked back to the lobby.

"So that is pretty much all the amenities at the property." Srini smiled.

"That was a great tour. Thank you!" I shook Srini's hand and passed a twenty-dollar bill to him.

Once again, he thanked me and shook his head from side to side.

"By the way sir, how do you like your room?"

"I must tell you, it's one of the best rooms I have ever stayed in. I am also very impressed with all the technology in the room."

"Yes, your side of the hotel is the new modern section. We do have the other side which is more Indian traditional in its style." Srini explained.

"Interesting. I didn't know that. I thought all the rooms were the same."

"No, sir. Would you like to switch rooms?"

"No, no. I am very happy with mine." I laughed.

"Fantastic, sir. If you need further assistance, Michael or I will be here."

"One last question. I want to get out of the hotel and get familiar with the city and the location." I uttered trying to gauge Srini's reaction.

"Well sir, since I know you like to workout, there is a spinning cycle gym located two blocks from the hotel. In addition, if you walk towards the east, you will come across the 2nd largest beach in the world. It takes a very long time to reach the ocean. There aren't many stores located within walking distance from the hotel. You would have to take a taxi to get to the mall."

"Thanks, Srini. I am still a bit tired from my long trip to India, so perhaps, I will stay local around the hotel and visit the beach."

"Of course, sir, and when you are ready, I can help you with an excursion to the famous places or to the mall, if you would like to do some shopping."

"Sounds great. Thanks for all the help." I smiled to Srini before walking away.

The rest of my Sunday, I spent alone at and around the hotel. I didn't want to walk too far since it was brutally hot, and I was still wearing my waist band. It would not be possible to lay out in the sun during my trip since I had a few scars from the surgery and did not want them to get worse. I did venture out to the spinning gym, and it was at a small three-story building. The first two floors were for gym equipment while the top floor was reserved for spinning. For some reason, I did not feel comfortable in such a small environment. I thanked the employees for the tour, and I was off to the beach.

As Srini noted, the ocean was truly far away. The interesting thing about the beach, it was populated exclusively by the natives. There were no white people on the beach. The beachgoers were dressed in their customary clothing, and they either walked around the beach or were hanging out in small groups, mostly families. No one was laying out, getting tanned in the usual beach outfits. I couldn't understand how they could bear the heat. Just like at the spinning center, I did not feel comfortable walking towards the water. I simply observed the scenery and then turned back to the hotel. The feeling of being a stranger was overwhelming.

The remainder of the afternoon, I laid on my bed reading *The Partner* by John Grisham. Reading relaxed me, and I enjoyed letting my mind drift into the plot of the book. Every time, I found myself alone, I would take the time to recharge my mind, body, and soul. Books helped me do just that. Plus, the local TV did not really have anything I wanted to watch. There were a few international channels, but most were from India. Trust me, I spent no time watching TV.

From time to time, I got up and looked through the window. The view was to die for. The glass window was from the ceiling to the floor, and it spanned the entire side of the room; both the living room and the master bedroom. I observed the foreigners in the pool. Most of them couldn't bear the heat. That was obvious by how quickly they ran when their feet touched the dark grey slate tiles covering the entire area around the pool. Some people sunbathed, others swam, and yet others had lunch. My initial impression of the hotel and city was that foreigners, such as myself, stayed at the hotel for breakfast, lunch, and dinner. Their activities were also confined to the hotel. That was a sad idea. I wasn't used to any limitations. But most likely, that was going to be my new normal for the next 30 days.

That night, I tried to stay up as late as possible to adjust to my new working time. The next day, Monday, July 11th, was my first day of work. Let me rephrase that, my first night. I would start my shift at 6 PM and then finish around 2 AM. I needed to stay awake until at least 1 AM, since for the next month, I would be going to sleep around 3 AM.

I needed to order room service for dinner but had no idea what I wanted. I decided to choose something simple which would not give me food poisoning. I ordered a tuna sandwich on toasted rye bread and some fresh bananas for dessert.

After eating dinner, I felt so lonely that I urgently needed to call someone. That someone was Renata, of course. Chennai was nine hours ahead, and it was almost midnight. The phone rang a few times, and then she answered.

"Hello?"

"Babes, it's me, Sebastian." I tried sounding upbeat.

"Oh my God, how was your flight?" Renata was happy to hear me.

"You can't believe how long it felt. It's not easy to travel alone for 22 hours. The time went by so slowly." I complained.

"Did you sleep?"

"Yes, but only from Miami to Frankfurt. The second leg of my trip, to Chennai was during the day. It was impossible for me to sleep with all the lights in the cabin."

"I understand, baby." Renata was thoughtful. "How is your first impression of India?"

"Well, I have not seen too much in one day, but it's definitely a third world nation. There are no highways, no skyscrapers, and not much tourism. I think it was a good choice for you to stay there. Where are you by the way? Still in Miami?"

"Yes, I think I will be here for another 2 weeks, before I have to get back to work in Toronto."

"Well enjoy your time there with the family, and I miss you." I whispered feeling desire for Renata clouding my mind.

"I miss you too, Seba. I am not used to being without you anymore." She moaned.

"The time will go by fast. I'll be back in a few weeks." I tried cheering both of us up.

"Promise me you'll visit me soon in Toronto?" Renata asked.

"I'll definitely make some time for you. Maybe we can do something fun in August before the summer ends."

"That would be perfect."

"Take care, babes." I sent her a kiss.

"Bye, my love."

Chapter 3

The next morning, I woke up feeling well rested. I looked at my watch, it was 10 AM. That was an unusual time for me to wake up. I was always an early bird, but in Chennai, my biological and natural clocks were flipped upside down. I knew it would take me some time to adjust. Thankfully, the curtains were thick and dark, they created a complete blackout in my room. I decided, I needed to set a daily routine for myself to follow. I had to plan out my day until my shift started at 6 PM. The plan was, I would start my day with a light meal, like tuna sandwich and bananas with a bottle of water. After that, I would rest for a bit in the room until I was ready for the gym. After I finalized my plan, I ate and then got ready for my light workout. I decided to start my routine from the first day to set myself up on the right path.

As soon as I arrived, I was happy to see my project team there. Scott was on the treadmill. Lee was on the elliptical and Amanda was doing crunches in the stretching area.

"Hey, team!" I was thrilled. "Look at you, guys. Talking about our firm hiring type A personalities."

"What's up, Sebastian?" Scott waved.

"Hi, Seba. Good morning, I mean, good afternoon." Lee smiled.

Amanda had her headphones on and simply nodded with no smile as usual.

Scott gestured for me to come next to him on the treadmill.

"So, did you make it here alright?" He asked without slowing down.

"Yes, aside from the craziness outside the airport and trying to find my driver; everything else went fine." I responded while turning my machine on.

"Pretty tough to sit on the plane for that long." Scott uttered.

"You don't say. I thought I was going to lose my mind. Thank God, for the music and the alcoholic beverages." Scott laughed. "Since today is your first day at the delivery center, come one hour earlier to get your security clearance and set up your virtual private network." He advised.

"Will do, Scott."

"I will be at the pool if you need me." He stepped off the treadmill, and I nodded in reply.

I decided to start slow, by walking. It's been only two weeks since my surgery. Lee was next to me, on the elliptical, so I decided to pick her brain a little.

"Hey, Lee. How long have you been in India?" I started.

"I got here last week with Amanda. We were the first ones."

"How is it to work the night shift?"

"It takes 3 to 4 nights to get used to it. I try waking up around noon, so my days are not too long." Lee suggested.

"That's good advice. What about during the day? Do you go anywhere, or do you stay at the hotel?" I continued.

"For the first couple of days, I ventured out and got to know the city, but now I use my free time to work out and make sure my project is going well. Once in a while, I go by the pool, but the tile there is way too damn hot." She explained.

"I will ask the concierge about places to visit."

"Yes, Srini is amazing. He will definitely recommend the best places for whatever your needs are."

I walked for about 30 minutes, and then did a few stretches laying on the floor mat. By the time I finished stretching, the project team had already left the gym. I took a shower and put on my t-shirt and boxers and picked up the book. I think in total, I read for almost 3 hours. By then, it was time to go to work. I dressed up in business casual attire and went down to the lobby.

As I got out of the elevator, I ran into Srini. He held the door open for me.

"After you, sir." He smiled. What a nice man!

"Srini, I was coming to look for you. I need advice on where to go tomorrow afternoon?"

"Follow me to my counter, and I will give you the best options." He pointed to the front desk.

"Thank you." I followed him there.

"If you are looking for something to do in the afternoon, then I recommend you go to Spencer shopping mall. The best retail stores are located there. It's where the rich and the Westerners shop. All the fine brands are there, and they also have good restaurants, both Indian and International." Srini explained.

"Great, I will start my journey from there."

"Tomorrow Michael will be here, but he can assist you in getting a taxi. Most of the local people do not speak English, so he will explain to the driver where to take you and when to pick you up." He continued.

"That's wonderful. I don't know what I would do without you, Srini. Thank you!"

"Not a problem, sir. It is always my pleasure to serve you."

He moved his head from side to side again. I wasn't really sure what that meant, but if I were to guess, it had to mean he agreed with me. It must've been the same as us, Americans, nodding our heads up and down. I laughed to myself; I knew I would have to learn that new gesture if I hoped communicating correctly with the locals.

Srini helped me get a taxi, and I was off to the Accent delivery center. When I climbed into the car and just said 'Accent delivery center', the driver nodded his head from side to side. He did it exactly like Srini. So, I started nodding my head from side to side and laughing.

As we drove through the streets of Chennai, I decided to try and chat with the driver. Taxi drivers were usually the most knowledgeable people about everything happening in the city.

"Sir, do you speak English?" I asked.

"Yes, a little bit." He looked at me through his rearview mirror.

"Are we going to downtown?"

"We are going to the city, sir."

I was a bit confused but didn't ask any more questions. I sat back in my seat. All the windows were open, and the hot wind was blowing hard in my face. As we drove, I looked around and just saw people in rural landscapes. The streets were one way and there were no concrete sidewalks, just sand. As we continued our drive, I noticed many cows on the streets. A little further down, I saw a man urinating on the side of the street. It was sad. Everything looked sad. The only consolation was the ever-present scent of jasmine. The aroma was intoxicating. I've never experienced something so amazing and strong in the natural open air. I was on the lookout for a jasmine tree. I finally saw one. It was very tall, and the white flowers were in full bloom. I made a mental note to try that fragrance in my apartment back at home. Apparently, jasmine heightened my senses and gave me intense pleasure.

Once we arrived, I asked the driver how much the fare was. The Indian currency was the Rupee, but US dollars were readily accepted. He told me it was $20 for the ride. I thought he was full of it; it was too expensive for only a 20-minute drive. He saw an American and wanted to take advantage of me. I did not complain and simply gave him the money. Forty dollars a day for the rides to and from work was crazy. It was a fortune to pay that over the month. But I was in a foreign country and did not want to anger anyone. I recalled when I was in Mexico for business, the taxi driver took me to a faraway location, and when I refused to pay, he pulled out a gun. Let's just say that I learned my lesson.

I arrived on time. One hour earlier, as Scott suggested. I had to get settled and go through the initial orientation. My shift was starting soon. As I climbed out of the taxi, I noticed the armed guards at the entrance of the delivery center. I was unsure if Chennai was a dangerous city, but I assumed it was a very poor one. You couldn't even call it a city. It was comprised of the old, low level buildings and abandoned commercial properties. Aside from that, there were mostly run-down houses. It was not a beautiful place, but I, nevertheless, was ready to dive into the new culture.

From the outside, the delivery center appeared a bit weathered down. It was vastly different from the fancy glass-enclosed building in Toronto, occupied by Hudd. It looked like a bunker, wrapped by the heavy concrete wall and serious security. There were two stories. When I approached the entrance, I saw a reception area with the Accent logo. At least that looked familiar, and I was at the right location.

"Hello, my name is Sebastian Kosta. I work for Accent in Miami. Today is my first day here." I announced.

"Hello, Mr. Kosta. How are you today?"

"After a very long flight and some rest, I am doing well which is surprising. A few pains here and there, but I feel good overall."

"That is excellent, Mr. Kosta." She nodded her head from side to side. I assumed she was a local hire.

"Which client will you be representing here at the delivery center?"

"I am the transition manager for the accounts receivable for our client Hudd."

"Very well, sir." She smiled. "I will contact your project team, so that they may show you your work area."

"Thank you very much." I moved my head from side to side with a grin. I enjoyed that new thing.

"My pleasure, sir. I hope you enjoy your stay in Chennai."

I wasn't so sure about that, but once again, I awkwardly nodded my head from side to side. She did the same back to me. It was amusing being in a foreign country, and imitating their customary ways, but I knew that was the only way to communicate effectively.

About 5 minutes later, a friendly face appeared. It was Shanti my team lead.

"Hello, Sebastian. Welcome to my country." She was happy to see me.

"Hey, where is the ski jacket?" I teased her.

"This is the weather we are accustomed to. It was freezing in Toronto." She laughed.

"But it was summer there!" I objected with a smile.

"Yes, but you can see how much warmer and more humid the environment it is here, in Chennai."

"Yes, I feel like I was placed inside the stove. I'm constantly sweating. It will be good for losing some weight."

Shanti started laughing. She was wearing a white linen dress and open sandals.

"The delivery center is business casual. If you wish, you can wear pants with a polo shirt. That will make you more comfortable." She suggested.

"I brought long sleeve shirts and suits. I guess I will have to go shopping."

"Please follow me, Sebastian. I will take you to get your security clearance badge first. You will need it to navigate through the delivery center. Pretty much every door requires the badge." Shanti noted.

"Wow, you guys are top security here." I pronounced with fascination and some concern.

"Yes, it's because we have a lot of information from our clients stored in the servers and laptops. There are many classified documents here as well."

"I assumed there would be." I nodded. "But armed guards! Why?"

"Remember, Sebastian, this is not a very civilized city. The client has to be assured there is high security." Shanti explained.

"I understand."

"This is our security office, and the gentlemen here will get you the badge. That way, you can go to the bathroom without me. Obviously." Shanti giggled.

"You have a wonderful sense of humor." I teased her.

"Do you have your Accent letter which you presented to immigration and a picture ID?" She asked. I opened the folder I brought with me and extracted what she asked for.

Shanti handed my paperwork along with the passport to the officer on hand. There was another officer watching the monitors. It appeared there were cameras in just about every room. All that security made me feel a little uncomfortable.

"Sir?" The officer nodded his head from side to side.

"Yes?" I echoed him.

"Please stand by the wall. You may not smile, and your hair needs to not cover your face."

It appeared the officer had a prior military service. He was very methodical and serious. I initially wanted to joke about my hair, but I decided against that, so I just conformed and stood there while they took a picture.

"The next step, sir, is to take fingerprints of both hands."

"Is this really necessary?" I thought the whole thing was an overkill.

"It's the protocol at the delivery center for all foreign visitors." He remained completely unfazed.

"But I'm not a visitor, I work for Accent." I tried objecting, even though I knew it was useless.

"Your fingerprints, Sir."

He proceeded to take the digital prints of my fingers on both hands. The entire procedure was uploaded into the computer, and afterwards, the officer handed me the security ID badge with my picture.

"This badge will let you enter the facility." He explained. "There are some areas that are off limits to you, the high security areas."

"Great." I said mockingly.

"Sebastian, we are all done. Let me take you to your workstation." Shanti was just in time before I would lose it on that pompous security officer with his high security areas.

I followed her down the corridor. We had to use our badges individually at many entrances, until we finally arrived.

"Okay, Sebastian. This is your workstation." Shanti pointed to an empty desk.

It was a simple cubicle. There were other desks all around me. No privacy!

"Here is a list of extensions for our project team. After you set up, I will take you to our team."

"Sounds good, Shanti." I couldn't explain why, but I was on edge.

"Now, Sebastian, there is a very important policy at all workstations."

"More fingerprints?" I joked irritably.

"Once your shift ends, you cannot leave anything on your desk. If they find something, that could serve as grounds for termination." Shanti stated ignoring my previous remark.

"Are you serious?" I thought the whole thing was ridiculous.

"Yes. You see, when you leave, another shift comes in to use your workstation for another client. You don't want to leave anything on your desk, even if it's not confidential." Shanti explained patiently.

"Okay, I got it. I will make sure to leave it in tip top shape." I gave up on sarcasm.

I took a seat and pulled out my computer. They provided me with the login instructions for the delivery center. I made sure my VPN was working and connected to the local printer. I then looked up Shanti's extension and tested the phone call.

"Hi, Shanti. I am all set up. Where do I find, you guys?" I inquired.

"Just walk out the room you are in. Don't forget to use your badge. We are straight down the hall, to your left. You will see the whole team of superusers in our individual cubicles."

"Great. I'll be right over."

As soon as I walked in, I saw my entire team. Everyone was there. They were happy to be home. No one was wearing ski jackets anymore. One by one, they greeted me with the typical swinging of their heads. They all laughed when I mimicked the gesture.

"See, I am learning." My initial funky mood was gone, I felt at ease.

I decided to check on our progress. I knew Shanti, my team lead, would give me a full report.

"Shanti, please tell me where we are at?" I asked her.

"We went live about an hour ago. All our systems are connected and running perfectly as if we were still in North America."

"What about the phone calls? Are we receiving them?" I continued.

"Yes, we had a few calls from our internal customers at Hudd."

"Meaning all our 1-800 numbers are working correctly?"

"Yes. We will do everything to process the transaction work while handling the internal calls and customer inquiries." Shanti assured me.

"So, we are officially live." I was excited.

"Yes, we are!" She echoed my sentiment.

"Great. I want a status report at the end of each day, from every superuser, so that I know where they are at. If they are encountering any difficulties, I want to know sooner rather than later."

"Will do, Sebastian." Shanti nodded.

"Thanks, if you need me, you know where to find me."

I walked back to my desk and decided to kill the silence with some music. I took out my Bose headphones and covered my ears. It was very nice to listen to music while I was working. It energized me. Even though, no one else used headphones, I figured it would not be a problem. For the next few hours, I focused on my project plan. I wanted to make sure the major milestones were clear and evident. At that point, I was there mostly in supervising capacity. I needed to verify that the accent neutralization class was underway, and we were making progress on the phone calls. Our clients at Hudd would also be attending those classes; ultimately, they were the ones signing off on course completion. Part of the 'go-live' support was to monitor transactions for any backlogs or delays. I also needed to make sure all the systems were up and running every day. Compared to the work in North America, the one in Chennai would be a vacation.

At around 10 PM, Shanti came by my workstation and informed me the dinner was ready. As I followed her and the rest of my team, we entered a very large cafeteria.

"This is the place for meals. Breakfast, lunch and dinner. It's a 24-hour operation. We typically eat between the 10 PM and midnight." Shanti explained as I was checking out the place.

"Thanks, Shanti."

"There is the Indian section for the locals, and a separate one for the international food. The typical food you find in America." Shanti continued.

I decided to be adventurous on the first night and stayed behind my team. "Remember, Indian food is typically spicy." Shanti warned me.

"I am ok with the spices. I eat hot wings all the time. I am sure my stomach can handle it." I assured Shanti who smiled in return.

When it was my turn to try the local cuisine, it turned out that the only dish for that day was made from chicken, potatoes, and red peppers with curry sauce. That mixture was served on a bed of the white basmati rice. It smelled delicious, and I couldn't wait to try it.

After I got my food and sat down, I looked around the room. There must have been at least 100 people in the cafeteria. Most of them were natives. There was a small group of foreigners, but I did not recognize anyone.

"Tell me how you like the chicken curry?" I heard Shanti's voice. She appeared to have some kind of a tease behind her innocent question. I couldn't understand why.

I said nothing and just sent a spoonful of the dish into my mouth. Moments later it hit me, my eyes tripled in size, and I couldn't breathe. That had to be the hottest spice that I have ever tasted. Shanti started laughing.

"Drink some water. I think you should get pizza." She continued chuckling.

I wanted to join her in laughter, but I couldn't. My eyes were blinded by the tears, and my nose was filled with mucus. I had to drink the whole bottle of water. The last thing I wanted was to get an upset stomach on my first night in Chennai. Once, I could see where I was going, I followed Shanti's advice and got in line for pizza.

After dinner, we all went back to work. I put my headphones on and continued keeping myself busy. In reality, I wasn't that busy, I was bored, the time was barely moving; within several hours, I was very sleepy. I wasn't used to that schedule yet. At 1 AM, I still had two hours to go. It was crazy.

At 2 AM, I got the status reports from my team members. For the next hour, I reviewed and concluded that our 'go-live' was a resounding success. I had no issues that needed upper management's special attention, but I still had the next day meeting with Scott. I was going to update him on the "go-live" from my perspective. At 3 AM, I turned off my laptop and made sure to clean up my desk. Like really clean up my desk! I think I got rid of all the tiny pieces of dust in every nook and cranny.

After having to use my security badge three times, through three different exits, I was finally out of what I called the dungeon in my mind. There was a line of taxis waiting to take the employees back to their homes or hotels. Most of us, the Accent people, stayed at the Park Sheraton, but the Hudd employees chose the Fisherman's Cove resort hotel as their home away from home. I decided against sharing a ride with anyone. Thus, I got in the next available car and named my destination. The driver didn't speak a word of English, furthermore, it was unbearably hot and humid, both inside and outside the car. I was instantly drenched in sweat.

As we drove back, I peered out the window. I was tired. It was a long day and night. I was horrified realizing how difficult it would be to get accustomed to the night shifts.

As soon as we arrived, and I saw the hotel, I started feeling better. I knew, comfort was just several steps away. I paid the $20 fare and dragged my feet into the room. Once there, I took a lukewarm shower. I was making sure I got clean without being awakened. I towel dried myself and immediately jumped in bed. Before I knew it, I was asleep.

Chapter 4

The next day, I woke up and had no idea what time it was. The good thing about my new schedule was, I could sleep in, every day. Thus, I woke up at noon feeling very well rested. I wanted to venture out a bit, so I decided I would go to the main shopping center in Chennai. Srini told me it was the place to go; it was called Spencer Shopping Mall. I got ready and headed down to the lobby. Srini wasn't working that afternoon, but his colleague, Michael was at the front desk.

"Hello there. You must be Michael. Sebastian Kosta. Srini told me about you." I greeted him.

"Yes, sir. Pleasure to meet you. How are you today?" Michael smiled at me.

"Very well. Adjusting to my new schedule. Does the hotel provide a 'to go' bag for lunch?" I inquired.

"Yes, sir. We have sandwiches, chips and fruit. I can have them ready for you, Sir." Michael offered.

"That would be perfect." I nodded gratefully. "Michael, Srini told me yesterday about the shopping center."

"Oh yes, sir. That would be Spencer mall."

"Can you please help me flag down a taxi, and let the driver know where I am going?"

"Not a problem, sir. I will try to book someone who speaks English. That way, you can arrange for him to pick you up and bring you back to the hotel." Michael offered.

"That would be wonderful. Thank you, Michael. I won't need more than two hours."

Michael nodded, and we walked out into the scorching hot street. There, he came up to the taxi and had a short conversation with the driver. I saw them both nodding their heads in agreement. He then waived me to the car and opened the door to the back seat. I thanked him again, gave him a tip, and off I went.

As we drove to the mall, I looked through the window. It was all the same. I was originally from Brazil, so I was accustomed to poverty. The buildings were all made out of concrete cylinder blocks and unpainted. The streets had many potholes, which I could feel throughout the ride. There were horses and cattle on the streets along with roosters. I saw only natives. In fact, I haven't seen one white person for the entirety of the ride. After about 20 minutes, the car stopped near a large complex. There was a huge sign in the center, which read "Spencer Mall". I checked my watch, it was 1PM. I asked the driver to pick me up at that very spot at 3PM. He did the customary nod. I paid the fare and thanked him.

"I hope he comes back." I mumbled under my nose.

The exterior of the mall was shabby. It was a huge building, mostly made out of brick. I saw some kids playing soccer outside. I stood for a little observing them play. That was their life. They probably didn't know or see anything else. Unlike me, they seemed content with their surroundings. After some time, I walked inside. I wanted to find the map to know where I was going and where all the brand stores were. That wasn't the mall I was used to. Definetely not the mall I visited with Renata in Montreal. Spencer Mall had a local flavor to it; it had small stores, mostly electronic and apparel. Then, I noticed the brand I knew, Lacoste. I was very excited to see at least some familiar name. I went there. As soon as I stepped inside, I was met by two smiling salesmen who spoke perfect British English.

"Good afternoon, sir. May we be of assistance?" One asked me.

"Yes, I am looking for a typical polo shirt."

"Oh yes, we have them in many colors. What color are you looking for?"

"Several. How much are the shirts?" I wanted to compare the prices.

"The polo shirt is $US 40." He answered politely.

"Really?" I was floored. I couldn't believe I heard that right. I grabbed one of the shirts and felt the fabric. It was very soft and appeared to be authentic. It was literally half the price it was in the US. I liked that place a bit more.

"Let me try one in medium and one in large to get a proper size?" I asked.

"Sir, I believe you are a large, but yes, try both to see which one fits better." The salesperson picked the two shirts in blue and led me to the fitting room.

I tried the large first, and the man was spot it. It fit perfectly and looked great.

"I will take the blue, white, pink, and orange, all in large." I announced feeling super excited over such a deal.

"Wonderful, sir. I will get you all the new ones with the original sealed wrapping." He exclaimed happily. "Is there anything else you would like to try before I go?"

"I will also take that cap." I pointed to the one right on the display.

"Very well, sir." He smiled and left.

The salesman returned sometime later with my shirts and the cap. I was very excited. I paid less than half from what I would pay in the US.

Right by the Lacoste store, was Adidas. I figured I would check it out since in a couple of weeks I could get back to my training. The prices were ridiculous. I couldn't believe that. By then, I figured that if nothing else, I would entertain myself by shopping in Chennai. I picked several athletic shorts and matching long sleeve workout shirts which were good for the outdoor training to protect me from the sun.

"Let me help you with those items, sir." The salesman swiftly took the attire from me and placed it on the table. He started folding them neatly.

"Is there anything else I can help you with, sir?"

"I would like some jogging shoes." I stated while looking around the store.

"What size are you, sir?"

"I am a size 10."

"I will bring you a selection of our best jogging shoes." He offered.

"Thank you."

While I continued exploring the store, the second salesman brought three boxes and invited me to try the sneakers on. I was the only one in the store. Then I remembered, it was a Tuesday afternoon. Most people were working at that time. I really didn't want to waste time trying all three pairs, so I asked for the best and the most expensive ones. I tried those on, they fit perfectly. I pictured myself running on the beach in those shoes in two weeks or less.

"I am all set." I announced happily.

After I paid for everything and added another three bags to the Lacoste one, I thought how much fun I was having, and how different was the mall in Miami from the one in Chennai.

Two hours of shopping made me tired. I went down to the first floor and sat at the table. I ate lunch prepared for me by the hotel in a "to-go" bag. I didn't have anything to drink, so I went to the food stand and asked for a Diet Coke. The sales guy nodded, took out a can of Coke, poured it in what looked like a Ziplock bag and stuck a straw into it. He gave me that while throwing the actual Coke can into a large container behind him. I've never seen anything like that!

As I drank, I was thinking about Renata. I missed her and wanted to reach out to her, but it was night in Miami. I decided to call her on my way to the delivery center. I knew she'd be happy. I thought of how difficult it was to speak with anyone back at home. The 12-hour difference was horrendous. My family or Renata would be able to talk when I worked, and when I was available, they were sleeping. I realized, it had been a few days since I heard Renata's voice. I wanted to talk to her, let her know I was fine, and was having fun shopping.

After I finished eating, I decided to watch the people walking around the mall. They all were Indian natives. Once again, I did not see any white people. The natives moved in large groups. I assumed family and friends. There were little children running and playing; just like in any other mall. The place was not busy, I thought of how it looked on the weekends, probably packed. What was mostly interesting, the clothing stores were empty, but all the locals were going to the electronic stores. I decided to visit one, just to see why everyone was going there.

"May I be of service, sir?" I was greeted by the salesman.

I smiled but didn't reply. I didn't even know what I wanted or needed there.

"Let me look around, and I will get back to you." I said politely.

I didn't need a phone or a laptop, but I always wanted a professional camera. It was always a dream of mine to learn photography. Perhaps, I could buy a camera.

"Do you have professional cameras?" I asked after a short time of thinking about photography.

"But, of course, sir! Which brand are you interested?"

"I've heard amazing things about Canon."

"Would you like the 5 or 6 series?" The salesman inquired.

"What's the difference?" I had no clue what he was talking about.

"The picture quality is perfect on the 6D. This is the type of camera that can last more than 20 years." He said and picked up one from the display. He handed it to me. It was very heavy. I wondered how anyone could carry it around. It was also loaded with buttons. I knew I would have to take a photography course just to learn how to use it.

"How much is this camera?" I decided to get it anyway.

"The original sales price for the 6D is $US3,000, but if you buy it today, I can sell it for you for $US2,000."

"Wow, it's not cheap!" I exclaimed.

"No, sir. But you want the professional one. They are not cheap at all."

"If you include this telephoto lens, I will take it." I suggested.

"That lens is $US400." The salesman was taken aback at first.

"I will buy it right now. You don't have to wait for another buyer." I was pressing, but I had nothing to lose. If that worked, ok, if not, fine as well.

"Okay, sir, you have a deal." He gave up rather quickly.

I asked for the carrying case for the camera and other accessories. After the sales person finished packing everything, I paid and was out.

After I left the store adding yet another shopping bag to my ridiculous stack, I realized it was time to meet the taxi driver and get back to the Sheraton. When I stepped outside, I was pleasantly surprised to see my driver already waiting for me. He got out of the car with a smile and helped me with the bags. I kept the camera case with me in the back of the taxi. I figured I had a lot of time in the afternoon, and I would learn professional photography. For the first time in days, I felt happy and upbeat. I understood why women called shopping, the retail therapy. Apparently, it worked.

As soon as we pulled up to the hotel, the bell boy immediately showed up with the cart. He extracted all the bags from the trunk.

"Mr. Kosta, I will bring your belongings up shortly."

I smiled and tipped the boy. I had to get back to the room and start getting ready for work. I wanted to check in with my team to make sure everything was fine. In the meantime, I couldn't wait to inspect my new camera. I had about 30 minutes for that.

As soon as I walked into the room, I opened the case and started taking pictures of the pool deck. Both in automatic and manual modes. I was excited about the camera. At that point, I couldn't wait to start exploring the surroundings.

As I was taking pictures and playing with my new camera, the bell boy showed up with my bags. I unpacked and folded all the clothes, and then looked at the time, it was almost 5 PM. I had to take a quick shower and get ready for the night shift.

About 30 minutes later, I was back at the lobby, showered and ready for my second night at work. It was very tough to get used to the new schedule. Something I've never had to do before. I took the same taxi ride to the delivery center and used my badge to let myself inside. It was strange, every section of the center was protected by the badge, and I still couldn't get used to the armed guards.

As soon as I got situated at my desk, I thought it would be great to start my shift with a status report of our 'go-live' date. I went looking for Scott. I found him at the conference room, in the middle of the office surrounded by glass. I approached the glass encasement and waved to him. After some time, Scott finally noticed me. He waved at me and raised his hand showing all five fingers. I figured Scott was telling me he would be free in 5 minutes. I responded by showing that I would be back. In the meantime, I decided to find my team. After walking through several sections, I saw Shanti. She in turn, took me to the section reserved specifically for the Hudd accounts receivable team. All five of my team members were there. As I looked around the room, I could see the flags of many other clients. That was a major operation for Accent, and now I understood the presence of heavy security.

I pulled out a chair and sat next to Shanti.

"So, how is everyone doing? No more ski jackets?" I teased them again.

Rikki, our accountant, responded first, "no, sir. We are home now. We are very comfortable in this weather. But how are you handling the heat?" The tease was on me.

"It's brutal here. Last night, when I was returning home from work, I was dripping in sweat from head to toe." I admitted.

"Here, we use our native dresses and attire. They are made from the finest local silk which keeps us cool amid the heat and humidity." Shanti noted.

"I guess I have to go shopping for similar silk shirts." I started laughing. Everyone echoed my laughter. I suddenly felt a nudge on my back. When I turned around, I saw Scott.

"How are you, my friend? I see you are still in one piece." He joked.

"Hi Scott. How are you?" I continued laughing. "I'm starting to like it here. Minus the schedule."

"It's tough. I know." Scott nodded sympathetically.

"Scott, please, join us. We are about to discuss how our 'go-live' day went yesterday." I invited him.

"Great. I am all ears." Scott pulled out a chair and sat down.

"Shanti, as the team lead, please give us an overview of our tracks, and if we are encountering any issues or red flags." I turned to Shanti.

"Yes, Sebastian. The day started well. We tested all our systems, and we were able to sign-in and obtain our user access. Our emails are up and running. We are receiving emails and phone calls from the internal and external customers. Our system-generated-canned reports are available, and we can see our receivables at any moment in time. So far so good."

"Any issues?" Asked Scott.

"Well, today we arrived at the center and were met by a backlog of receivables as well as customer messages." Shanti noted.

"Is this something system-related or process-driven?" Inquired Scott.

"I believe it's just a matter of manpower. We need to work the receivable list to reduce the amount of customers who are past due. I will work with my team to reach out to those customers and make sure the payments were sent."

"Remember, Shanti, we do have system generated demand letters that over time get progressively stronger in context. Leverage the technology." Scott got up from his chair. "Great job for the first day team. Let's keep up the good work." He showed thumbs up.

"Shanti, I am going to be at my workstation. Please, come and get me for dinner." I asked her after staying quiet through the entire update.

"Will do, Sebastian." Shanti nodded. "Scott, do you want to join us for dinner?"

"Sorry, I can't. We have the conference room reserved all night for us to review the performance of each of our tracks. It's the only conference room we are allowed to use." He stated apologetically.

"The security is really tight around here." I shared my observation.

"Yes, this is not one of our own delivery centers. I mean it is, but we've just purchased this third-party outsourcing company in India. We are using their facility while our state-of-the-art building is being developed." Scott explained.

"When will the Accent facility be ready for operation?" I was excited, even though, I wouldn't be here for longer than a month.

"In about 18 months. Get familiar with the staff here. It will be useful for you in the future, since you will be staying here for four weeks." Scott advised.

"Thanks, Scott." I replied. "I was actually planning on meeting the managing director of the delivery center."

"Great idea!" Scott gestured thumbs up. "His name is G. Reedy."

"Yes. I will look for him later on."

"Very well. You guys have a great workday. I'm out. And, Sebastian," Scott turned to me again. "Don't lose your badge. You need it everywhere, even to use the restroom."

I nodded in agreement and laughed.

I headed back to my workstation and once there, I unpacked all my working files and opened my laptop. It was very quiet around my area of the building, so once again, I took out my Bose headphones and started listening to music, a little bit of Coldplay, Jack Johnson, and India Arie. By then, I was fully settled in and no longer had jet lag. I felt very good.

My team was doing a very good job, and I started venturing out by myself in Chennai. I knew things would get even better once Premal arrived on Thursday. Even though, he was married with two kids, he still seemed like a guy who had a very successful previous single life. We got along very well back in Toronto, and I was hoping to get to know him even better in Chennai.

After a couple of hours, Shanti came by to tell me they were going to the cafeteria. I locked my laptop and followed her. Once there, I saw my team. They were very pleasant and welcoming. After my first night experience with the curry, I decided to go straight to the international cuisine line. The natives had their own line, and every night there was a different hot plate. It was interesting to observe them in conversation. They wore the traditional Indian garments and were very social among themselves. Everyone there was highly skilled. They all had their university degrees and some, like Shanti, had a master's degree.

Later, I learned, Chennai was a great location for outsourcing since many universities were located in or around the city. The culture was woven into education. That trend was spreading throughout the entire country of India, and the natives studied hard in hopes of joining the American technology companies of the future.

That day, the international meal of the day was a lasagna and garlic bread. I got my portion and took a seat next to my team members.

"No spicy food tonight, Sebastian?" Teased Arjun, our business analyst.

"No, thank you. The food here is so spicy, it doesn't burn only on the way in but on the way out as well." I laughed rolling my eyes.

"Too much information, Sebastian." Shanti laughed.

"So, what did you do today before work?" Asked Rikki, our accountant.

"I got out of the hotel and visited Spencer Mall."

"Oh, that is a wonderful shopping mall. We don't have anything international for foreigners except Spencer Mall. It's huge and has many good stores."

"Yeah, I didn't see many westerners there. I thought it would be filled with the international guests, but I only saw the natives." I pointed out.

"You have to remember, Sebastian, Chennai is becoming very popular for outsourcing, and not only Accent is here, but many other consulting companies. Each one of those companies needs to hire local talent. Therefore, there are many native Indians that come here looking for work. I believe most of the foreigners stay in or close to their hotels." Shanti explained.

"You are absolutely correct, Shanti. The day I visited the beach, next to the hotel, I did not notice any foreigners. It was filled with local people walking on the beach or just hanging out."

"Yes, we have the second largest beach in the world here. I believe the largest is where you are from, Miami Beach."

"Wow, I was not aware of those statistics." I was surprised.

I finished eating and thanked my team for being so nice and welcoming. I hoped, we would do such dinners every night.

The rest of my working shift was spent on planning the meetings for the accounts receivable team and the training for customer service. The team was getting proficient in the English accent neutralization course, but they still needed a couple of weeks to really nail it.

It's been a couple of days since I arrived, and I still haven't spoken with my family. In fact, it's been a while since I spoke with my parents. I decided to text my mom to let her know I was fine. She was happy to hear from me and wished me luck with the project. I had a courteous relation with my parents. But not a lovey-dovey one. We never got into the details of ever day life. They just wanted to know I was doing well at work, and my health was fine. Whom I really missed, was Renata. I knew that for the most part, I would be spending the days in India by myself. I could not call her from work, so I decided to text her.

"How is my special girl doing?" I wrote.

"Finally, I hear from you. Babes, you had me worried." She responded within minutes. I could feel her joy through the text message. She was happy to hear from me.

I, in turn, was very happy to be back in contact with her. I felt like I left a piece of my heart back at home. That piece was Renata.

"I am sorry, baby, but the time difference is almost 12 hours ahead, and I can't seem to find the right time to call or text you." I explained. "Are you still in Miami?"

"Yes, I am here for another two weeks and then back to Toronto."

"Partying hard?" I was hoping she responded no.

"We go out with my friends, but all I can do is think about you."

That reply made my eyes watery.

"Well, try having fun with your sister." I texted.

"I miss you and can't wait to see you, Seba." She continued.

"I will visit you in Toronto, before summer ends." I promised.

"Please. I want to see you."

"Take care, sweetheart." I wrote.

"Take care, my love."

I removed the headphones and looked at the time. It was just about 3 AM. The second day was over, I was going back to the hotel. I was happy to have communicated with my mom and Renata. I was so far from home, in the distant part of the world. Every day was a new beginning, and I had no idea what I was going to encounter the next day. But I was excited about the unknown.

Chapter 5

The next several days were pretty much the same as my second day in India. I didn't have too much time and didn't want to venture too far. There wasn't too much of sightseeing in Chennai for tourists. As I've mentioned before, there were only foreigners in the pool of the hotel. I wasn't too interested in lounging by the pool. It was too hot, and I didn't want to show up to work all tanned. Therefore, for the next two days, I invested in myself. I went back to Spencer Mall and purchased a second large travel bag. I bought all kinds of cool shirts from Diesel, shoes from Kenneth Cole, and driving shoes from Puma. It was fun to go around and just spend money without reservations. I didn't like trying the clothes at the stores. It was my thing. Instead, I measured the shirts on my chest and shoulders and purchased them based on their appearance and not the fit. Then, once at the hotel, I tried everything on, at my own pace. If anything needed to be returned, I would visit the mall the next day.

At one point, my investment banker from Morgan Stanley called me regarding my spending in India. Apparently, my checking account had run down to zero. I told him to sell some stock and add an additional $15,000 to the account. I was having fun shopping for myself, and there were some items I had to have because the prices were so much cheaper than in the US. Since I could include the dry cleaning in my expenses, I sent all my new items to get washed and folded at the hotel. That way, when the clothes were delivered, I could simply place them neatly in the drawers.

On Friday, before going to work, I decided I would test out my new camera by visiting the snake park. I wasn't a big fan of snakes, but I thought being outside in nature would be great for my mind, and

I would surely have some great photos after that excursion. I had to explore and discover the exciting parts of Indian nature. I looked at that as a great adventure. Since I was able to get up and have brunch earlier that day, I took a local bus. One of its destinations was the park with snakes and the crocodiles.

I waived hello to Srini and headed out the door with the camera in hand. The valet approached me outside of the hotel.

"Can I help you, sir?" He asked politely.

"Yes. I wanted to know where the local bus stops. The one that would take me to the snake park?"

"Oh yes, sir. It stops here. Are you going to the snake park today?"

"Yes, I have a few hours to kill, so I figured I would go there for a change."

"I believe you will enjoy it very much. It is a beautiful park with many species of snakes." The valet attendant was more excited than me. Snake-watching was not my most thrilling form of entertainment.

"Well, I just hope they are well contained. I don't want to get a snake bite."

"No, sir. Don't worry. You will be fine. Look, here comes the bus."

As I looked towards the entrance, I saw a very old bus with all the windows open and filled with the local people.

"Take care." I told the valet attendant and started walking towards the bus.

"Enjoy your day, sir."

I boarded the bus and tried to find the seat next to the window. I was lucky to get one. After I sat down, I got my camera ready on automatic mode to take pictures of the city and the people. As we slowly moved forward, I noted to myself, even though, India was high in technology, the landscape of the city was poor. The infrastructure was old and decaying. It wasn't like the modern cities I was used to during my travels across North America or Europe. The people appeared to be very poor. Their clothes were worn and dirty. Most worked in the streets. However, without much physical beauty, Chennai had a mesmerizing aroma. No matter where I went, there was always the lovely smell of

Jasmine. That fragrance overpowered the city's decay and lack of modern amenities.

Chennai was a developing city with many students. There were people from other cities in India. They moved to Chennai in search of economic opportunities. That was their Indian dream. The locals were young and hungry for the ways of the West. They wanted for their local economies to become the booming technological centers. That was their new path for the future. I felt that the locals were excited to see me. I was a young white businessman, well-dressed and successful. That made them assured in the future success of their city. Everyone was very nice to me.

As the bus was driving towards the park, I immediately started taking pictures of the entrance. I was very short on time, I had only two hours before I would return to the hotel and head to work after that. I was actually excited about the shift, because I knew Premal flew in last night. I was looking forward to seeing him. I was happy to have a friend there; it would be much more fun to visit places in his company. However, for that day, it was only me and the snakes. As I walked around the park, each venue had its own distinct scenery. I snapped several closeups showing the simple beauty of the snakes with their detailed ornate skins and colors. They were in all shapes and sizes, from a few inches to 17 feet long. I've never seen so many different species of snakes. I imagined the pictures would be amazing. My next venture in photography would be editing those pictures, but that was another chapter.

As I continued walking in the park, the heat started getting to me. My shirt was drenched in sweat. I walked over to a vendor who was selling water. I bought two bottles. One, I drank immediately, and the second, I kept in my bag. It was time to check out the crocodiles. The creatures had a man-made beach created especially for them. The crocs were sunbathing. One had its mouth open. The shutter in my camera was moving quickly, as I snapped many pictures of those prehistoric beasts. It was interesting to see the Indian species of the crocs, because I was more familiar with the Florida gators from the Everglades. The Indian crocodiles had long narrow noses. It was amazing to see how big they were. I definitely wouldn't want to get stuck alone on that beach.

It was getting unbearably hot, and I decided to find some shade. A few feet away, I spotted several benches under the trees. As I approached one, I saw a beautiful blonde woman sitting there. She appeared to be in deep thoughts. She didn't even notice me.

"Hi. My name is Sebastian." I whispered trying not to startle her.

"Oh, hi!" She was startled anyway. "Samantha." She replied after taking a few seconds to recover.

"Enjoying the weather?" I joked. It was too hot to breathe.

"It's not that bad." She smiled. "Are you enjoying the snake park? First time?"

"Yes. I have a few spare hours before work."

"I assume you are a management consultant?" She continued.

"Yes. And you?"

"Me too." She nodded. "I've been here for almost a month. I work for IBM."

"This is my first week here, so I am pretty lost. There isn't much to do." I stated in exasperation.

"You are right. Not the most exciting and fun place. That's why most foreigners stay at their hotels." Samantha agreed and looked at the crocodile pond.

"Incredible to see the crocodiles laying there, so close to us." I followed her gaze.

"Yes, they are beautiful. They are pretty much the oldest species alive since the dinosaurs walked the Earth."

"Amazing." I echoed her sentiment. "Hey, do you want some water? I have another bottle in my bag."

"Thanks, but I came prepared. This is not my first rodeo in Chennai."

We both laughed out loud.

"It's nice to talk to someone from home. Where are you from?" I inquired.

"I was born in Texas but live in the New York City." Samantha replied.

"That's cool. So, you're a city slicker like me."

"Where do you live, Sebastian?"

"I live in Miami."

"Awesome. I go there a lot. Miami is pretty nice." She beamed.

With those words, Samantha got up and walked towards the guard railing.

"Take a look at that big one sitting on the boulder. I am sure it could eat a whole pig." She invited me to join her in watching the crocs. Once I came closer, I reached for my camera and took a few pictures.

"Cool camera. Is that a Canon full frame?" She complimented.

"Yes, I just bought it. I was so bored that I became a shopaholic and an aspiring photographer." I explained.

"You know, if you are interested in site seeing, you have to visit the tomb of St. Thomas the Apostle. It's about an hour away by bus, but it's well worth the travel."

"I am not very religious." I started with my usual explanation when anything religious was mentioned.

"You don't have to be religious to appreciate the history there. Go. Make the trip. You will be impressed. It was the best tour I've ever had in Chennai since I'd arrived. Just check it out. It's pretty amazing." Samantha noted passionately.

"Okay, I will look into that." I promised. "Thank you for the recommendation."

"I have to get going. I also work the night shift. It was a pleasure meeting you, Sebastian. Good luck with your project." Samantha stated and walked away before I could even say goodbye or ask where she was staying.

After I recovered from what seemed like Samantha's unexplainable run, I boarded the bus back to the hotel and once I arrived, I laid on the bed for a little bit. I wanted to review the photographs of the day. It was truly amazing to see the snakes and the crocodiles up close. The camera's display showed vivid pictures, and I got excited about creating a photo album of the trip. I caught myself being excited and finally, at peace about being in Chennai.

When I finished with the photos, I showered and got dressed. I still had to wear the waistband which made it uncomfortable to sit for hours at the delivery center. I still had a week to go with the waistband. I was looking forward to not wearing it anymore. One more week would complete my month-long recovery from the surgery. I still had some discomfort in my abdominal area, but no more sharp pains. I was also looking forward to getting back to sports and my workouts.

I went downstairs to the lobby, and since it was Friday, both Michael and Srini were at the concierge counter.

"Hello, gentlemen." I greeted them "How are you doing?"

"Very well, sir." Srini replied with his kind smile.

"How are you, sir? How was the mall? Michael asked.

"I think I've bought too much stuff. One day, I even ran out of money." I admitted.

"Really, sir?" Michael was sincerely shocked.

"Yes, I had to call my bank and ask for more. I guess I need to find other activities that don't cost so much money."

"Please remember, sir, that tomorrow night, we are having a party to celebrate the Formula 1 race. We have an Indian driver that represents our country. We organized the watch party for all of our guests." Srini announced pridefully.

"That is a great idea!" I smiled. I was actually excited.

"Yes, sir." Michael nodded. It's for all the hotel's guests to enjoy the race and have a few drinks and appetizers."

"Sounds like a plan. I will be there." I promised.

As soon as I reached the delivery center, I ran into Premal. He arrived last night and was excited to see his teammates and me. I put my computer bag on the desk and approached Premal. We hugged and shook hands.

"Welcome to Chennai, my friend." I exclaimed.

"How the hell are you, Sebastian???" He laughed. "Surviving in my country?"

"Well, I'm alive, no snake bites for now." I also laughed.

"Oh yeah?" Premal grinned.

"Yeah, I went to the snake park today."

"Cool, I'm excited for you. Actually, I've never been to Chennai as well. I was born in Mumbai. So, it's new for me too." Premal noted.

"At least, you speak the language. Hope you can help me out here."

"Well, there are many dialects in India, but I am sure I, and we will manage."

"How was your flight by the way?" I asked.

"Too long. Twenty-two hours in economy class. Not fun." Premal sighted.

"Well, you are here now. I am going to my desk, but let's have dinner tomorrow. That way we can relax and catch up." I suggested.

"Are you staying at the Park Sheraton?" Premal inquired.

"Sure am. And you?" I asked.

"Yeah, man. It's a really nice hotel. The rooms are huge." He responded. "So, I will see you later, Sebastian?"

"For sure. I will come and get you around dinner time." I promised.

"Cool. See you then."

As I walked to my workstation, I thought how happy I was that Premal was finally here. I liked my entire project team, but Premal was a friend. I sensed we had a lot in common. He was a fun guy. I was sure we would be able to hang out and have a great time. Premal being there, would definitely make my Indian adventure even more fulfilling. I was optimistic about our friendship. I didn't like to party by myself, and I knew that he could be a real friend outside of work.

I sat down and turned my laptop on. At that moment, John Nagy approached me. He's just finished the accent neutralization session with our Indian natives.

"Hey, John. Are they getting better?" I asked.

"Yes, I think the learning curve is steep, but in a few weeks, they should get a better hang of the English accent. For many, English is their first language, but they have more of a British accent." He explained.

"Well, India was colonized by the British, so I understand." I agreed.

"I'll tell you, it's a lot easier than training Chinese people. That area was an option for Hudd, and we decided against it. But maybe in

China, the premises would be nicer than this facility." It was obvious, John hated the place as much as I did.

"Remember, John, this delivery center is only temporary. Accent is currently developing a new state-of-the-art building." I pointed out.

"But the people here are all Accent employees, right?" John asked.

"They should be." I assumed. "I have to find out. I have yet to meet with the delivery center's management."

"I hope they have a long history in Accent and were not recently acquired."

"That should not be the case. I will keep you posted." John seemed too concerned over everything. But I decided against getting into long discussions about his reservations.

"Thanks, Sebastian."

"You bet." I put my headphones on and returned back to work.

"Sebastian! Sebastian!" I heard my name through the music. I looked up and removed my headphones. It was Amanda.

"How is the account receivables' track going?" She was standing right next to my desk.

"Aside from having a backlog, we are running smoothly. I asked my team to focus on the demand letters and phone calls to reduce the outstanding AR balance." I replied calmly.

"Are they using scanned and indexed images from Xerox?" She continued.

"Of course, we tested that aspect at T-30 and then again at T-5. But why are you so concerned about my track?"

"I just don't want to see any problems with our team." She acted like she was the only one disturbed about everything. It was irritating.

"Listen, I am taking good care of my track, and I don't foresee any issues going forward. Trust me. I am on top of this." I continued speaking calmly, even though, I was on edge inside.

She did not seem very happy about my responses, but she was asking questions about my project and not her own. I guessed she had some free time and was going around and asking each project team manager for status updates. I knew she wanted to be promoted quickly, but what annoyed me the most, she was getting into things that were none of her concern or area of involvement. Scott was overseeing the entire project, and she was stepping over his authority. I showed Amanda the conversation was over by placing the headphones back on and turning to my laptop.

I was concentrating on work for about an hour. I saw nothing around me. When I finally took a break and looked up, I noticed I was all alone in my section. I figured it would be a good time to call Renata. It was Friday morning for her, so I guessed it would be easy to reach her. I dialed Renata's number. The phone rang a few times and then, she picked up.

"Hello?" I heard her sexy voice.

"It's me, babes. Can you hear me?"

"Yes, but the connection is not perfect."

"I just called… to say… I love you." I started singing the words from the famous song by Stevie Wonder.

"You are so funny, Sebastian. You're a great singer." Renata laughed, but I could tell how happy she was. "Aren't you working now?" She asked.

"Yes, but there is no one around, and I missed you." I whispered into the phone.

"I miss you too. I can't wait for you to come back. I'm so worried about you being all the way on the other side of the world." She noted.

"Don't worry, baby. I am ok. I am getting to know this place, and my buddy has just arrived. It should be much better now." I explained. "Did I wake you up?"

"No, I am having breakfast." Renata made a chewing sound.

"How funny. I am about to have dinner."

"So, you've been there for almost a week." She announced. Like I didn't know that. "What have you been doing?"

"Just shopping and sightseeing. I even bought this really cool camera. I can't wait to show you the pictures." I knew Renata would appreciate that.

"You know I'm crazy about pictures, Seba. We will go through them when you get back."

"Okay, sweetheart, I am going to have dinner with my team now." I told her.

"Well, you have a good night there, and I will pray for your safe return."

"Thanks, babe. Bye."

For the first time since I came to Chennai, I was really excited about the meal. Premal was here. That meant interesting conversation and good company.

I found Premal and tapped him on the shoulder. "It's time to eat. Get your team together, and we'll get a big table for everyone." I suggested.

"Where is the cafeteria?" He asked.

"Leave your stuff here, and I will show you." We gathered our teams and headed to the cafeteria.

"So, how was your 'go-live', Premal?" I asked as we were walking.

"It went well. I was not expecting any surprises since we had tested everything before. Remember, the general ledger team has only internal customers, and we don't have any customer-facing activities. Therefore, my stress level is lower than yours. I just have to make sure the superusers and the general users have access to Great Plains, our accounting system. Most of our work is at the end of the month when we are closing our books. I view this trip as a vacation since all the work has been done. My team handles the daily job, and I just get called for any issues." He explained.

"So, we are both on vacation." I high fived with Premal.

"Pretty much. Compared to all the traveling you had to do before, this phase should be rather simple."

We had our dinner and then decided, we would share a taxi back to the hotel once our shifts ended.

Before I knew it, it was almost 3 AM. The time flew by after dinner; I was so buried in Excel tables; I didn't notice its passage.

I met Premal by the exit, and we shared the ride. At first, we were silent. The driver was on his phone, and we were waiting for him to get going. It was so hot, we immediately started sweating. I couldn't take that.

"Could you please tell this guy to get moving?" I asked Premal.

In his own language, Premal told the driver to turn the A/C on. The driver wasn't happy, but he obliged. I was in shock! For the whole week, I thought those cars didn't have A/Cs, but I didn't even care to think, they refused to use them to save on fuel.

"Are you fucking kidding me!!!" I flipped out. "These taxis have air conditioning?"

"Yes, and I assume you were overcharged." Premal noted calmly.

"You think?" I continued fuming.

"How much were you paying each way?"

"20 bucks!!!"

"I am sure, I can get them to cut that fare in half." Premal grinned.

"This is fucking amazing!" I exclaimed excitedly. "I am really happy you are here, Premal. Even that freakin' head-shaking was driving me nuts." I laughed.

"Don't worry, I will handle it. It definitely helps to be able to speak Hindi."

In a few minutes, the inside of the taxi became cool and pleasant. When we arrived at the hotel, I was happy to find out that once again, Premal was right. The fare was only ten dollars. I knew things would be easier with someone who understood the culture and the language. But more than that, Premal was also a great friend.

Since it was Friday night …or morning, we decided to have a few drinks. Our biological clocks started to flip, and I noticed that I didn't feel sleepy at all. I went to my room first and changed into a t-shirt and shorts. I also made sure to pick up the scotch from my minibar, just in case Premal didn't have enough of it. His room was located in the older part of the hotel.

As I entered that side, I noticed a huge difference compared to the one where I was staying. There, the décor was Indian and very traditional. The door to Premal's room had an elaborate metal ring in the center for knocking, there was no doorbell like in my part of the hotel. I knocked on his door.

"Hey, buddy!" Premal opened immediately. "I see you raided your minibar."

"Yes, a little." I laughed. "I even brought a bucket of ice."

"Cool. Come on in." He invited.

As I walked into his room, I noticed it was as big as mine, maybe even bigger. It was covered in high quality mahogany wood and styled very classically and tastefully. It had traditional furnishings, and I didn't think it had all the technological features that I had. I wondered why Premal stayed in that part of the hotel. Maybe he was nostalgic about India and his native culture.

We took a seat in the living room and turned the TV on. It was very late, but we were wide awake. We were able to find Fashion TV. I loved that channel, but as far as I was aware in Miami, it was provided only to the people who lived in Miami Beach. I was very pleasantly surprised to find out that our hotel carried it as well. It was filled with the best music and beautiful models. It was a great backdrop for a chill evening with a few drinks.

"Here you go, man. Welcome to my homeland." Premal brought my drink.

"It was a mission getting here, but now we have to make the best of it." I replied as we clinked our glasses. "So, why didn't you get the modern room?"

"You know, I am more of a traditionalist. The modern room is for the international traveler. I am sure it has all the technology. Here, things are simple. Only a TV and an old- school phone." He answered with a smile.

"Yeah, my room is all digital. There is even a command center where all the lights, TV, and the electronics are connected."

"Too much for me. I actually visited both parts of the hotel and chose the traditional room since it reminds me of home."

"Remember though, we are here for a month." I objected. "Traditional is good, but maybe you need comfort more than nostalgia."

"Yes, perhaps, I might follow your lead and switch rooms." Premal responded after some consideration.

"Here's a toast to working the night shifts." I switched the topic.

"Not sure if I'm excited about that, but let's make it an adventure."

Premal laughed about my crazy toast. "So, tell me, Sebastian, how was your first week in Chennai?"

"Not bad. I thought I would enjoy the beach a bit more, but the foreigners don't venture out much."

"The beaches here are very sacred. They are used for spiritual fulfillment. You know India is a very religious country, and there is a lot of history here. The Europeans did everything to take over this beautiful country. They even tried to destroy our history and customs. But my people are strong-willed and relentless when it comes to their faith. Many people who come to India have a spiritual awakening since the relics are all around." Premal spoke thoughtfully.

"Yes, I am actually planning on visiting the tomb of St. Thomas the Apostle, on Sunday."

"I wish I could go with you, but I need to prepare for my 'go-live', on Monday." He noted.

"I understand." I nodded and took a sip of my drink.

"I am sure you will love it. I heard a lot about that site. They say it's the best place for tourists to visit in Chennai." Premal pointed out.

We finished our second mini bottle of scotch and decided to sit back and enjoy the music and the beautiful women on Fashion TV.

"Are you planning on marrying anytime soon?" Premal asked after we stayed silent for some time.

"No way, man. I live in Miami, and it's almost impossible to find a good girl there. Most just want a man with a big fat wallet."

We laughed out loud. "Maybe on one of your trips, outside of Miami, you will find the one?" He suggested hopefully.

"It's funny you mentioned that, because I met someone in Toronto." I smiled thinking of Renata.

"I knew it. You always came to work on Monday with a grin. Who is she?"

"She is originally from Brazil. She is stunning. Dark silky hair with a smile that is contagious. She is always so cheerful and happy. You know, I have never felt like that for any other girl." I had butterflies in my stomach just speaking about Renata.

"But how did you meet her? We worked so much in Toronto." Premal wondered.

"It's a funny story. Many years ago, I met her sister at a party. We hit it off and remained in touch. My plan was to see her when I got to Toronto. But when I did reach out to the sister, I found out she was married. I was very upset and disappointed. But then she introduced me to her younger sister, Renata."

"Dude, are you telling me you slept with both of them???" Premal appeared stunned.

"There were many years in between and our lives changed. When I met Renata, I was actually more attracted to her than the sister I already knew. She was gorgeous, and I would do anything to have her." I stated passionately.

"Which you did. Sebastian, you are too much. I love hearing your bachelor stories. I think those are the best times of our lives."

We looked up at the TV screen and saw the models walking up the runway.

"Cheers to being single!" I exclaimed.

At around 6 AM, I decide to call it a night. I started feeling tipsy and sleepy. The last thing I needed was to wake up with a hangover. We made plans for an outing on Saturday night. We were not sure exactly what to do but decided to play it by ear. But then, all I wanted was to get to bed. I had a very intense week, and as soon as I laid my head down on the pillow, I was out.

Chapter 6

The next morning, I woke up and immediately checked the clock. It was 2 PM. At any other time, I would be horrified, but I figured I needed that long and revitalizing rest. Thankfully, I had no hangover, probably, because before getting in bed, on my way from Premal's, I drank the entire bottle of water.

I didn't have any plans for that day. I figured I would order room service, skipping breakfast and going straight to the lunch menu. Since my arrival to Chennai, I was ordering only tuna sandwiches and bananas. I was not brave enough to order any Indian food. I believed my first experience would be my last. I felt that tuna sandwiches and bananas would be the safest and healthiest bet. I was a man of habits, and once I found something I liked, I would stick to that.

After about 20 minutes, my lunch arrived. I ate the sandwich and then decided to read the book until it was cool enough to go to the pool. I didn't want to burn my feet like I witnessed happening to so many people during the week. It was relaxing to eat and then lay in bed with a good book. It was calming, and it put my mind at ease. The book I was reading was about an attorney who came to Brazil. It was very interesting, the real page-turner. In a couple of hours, I read almost 70 pages. Immersing myself in reading would make me forget about everything else in the world. The time flew by.

At 5PM, I decided to go for a swim. I stood before the mirror as I removed my waist band. I checked my stomach and noted happily that the bruising and swelling was almost gone. However, there still was some discoloration around my knees and calves. But the doctor warned me about that. With time, it would disappear too.

I put on my swim shorts and checked myself out again. I loved that the bottom of my stomach was completely flat. All the fat was gone. What stood out the most, was the new shape of my belly button. Even though, I saw much improvement, I, nevertheless knew, there was still a lot of work to be done at the gym to get those perfect abs. I grabbed my stuff and headed down.

By the time I came out to the pool, the worst heat had subsided. I didn't have to jump like a mad man trying to avoid burning my feet. I took my shirt off and slowly walked into the warm water. I thought about Renata, but at the same time, I caught myself thinking that I enjoyed spending time alone. I felt tranquil and at peace, and that, considering that there was a lot of noise and commotion around the pool area. It was Saturday, thus, many kids were running around and jumping in the water. I assumed some of the foreign guests brought their families along with them. I thought it was crazy, but none of my business.

I just laid back and floated in the water, watching the sky and the clouds. In my head, I pretended to be listening to Coldplay. I was alone in this world. Thousands of miles away from my friends and family. I accepted my reality and knew, for the next three weeks, I would have to learn to enjoy living there. I would have to develop new habits, new routines, and make new friendships. In every consulting project, the situation was the same. The only difference with that particular project was the distance. I was really far away. I got out of the pool and decided to take a nap on a lounge chair. It felt very calming and relaxing to listen to the birds chirping, feeling the breeze on my body and face and overhear the conversations in different languages. Since I was alone, I became an observer instead of a participant. I watched the lives of others.

Later that evening, I decided to call Renata. The phone rang several times before she answered.

"Hello?" I could never get enough of her voice.

"Renata, it's me, Seba. Did I wake you up?" I greeted her.

"Yes, we went out to one of the clubs in South Beach last night. I got to bed very, very late." She explained sleepily.

"If you want, I can call you later."

"No, it's okay. I have to get up anyway. I need to take my friend's dog for a walk." She explained.

"Do you miss me?" I whispered.

"I miss you like crazy. I can't wait until you're back. Sometimes, I can't even fall asleep thinking about you being alone in India." Renata replied. She sounded sad.

"Don't worry about me." I tried calming her down. "Yes, I am alone most of the time, but I am getting to know myself much better than I ever had."

"What have you learned so far?" Her voice changed from sad to foxy.

"That it's okay not to be in control all the time. I have always worked hard to get the things that I have but, I now know it's fine to do your best and be patient and just let thing happen. I accept that I am alone here, and I am okay with that. I have you in my heart."

"Sebastian, I feel like this summer was a dream. I am scared that soon it will be over, and I have to wake up." Renata whispered tearfully.

"Listen, I don't know what the future holds, but I know that I am on the right path. We just have to stay true to our hearts. Let's not let our brains get in the way of things." I stated forcefully. Renata didn't reply.

"By the way, when are you leaving Miami?" I decided to lighten up our conversation.

"My sister and I are going back to Toronto in one week."

"That means, I won't see you in Miami, because I arrive the second week of August." I was disappointed.

"I would change my flight, but I can't miss any more work. I won't have any vacation days left." Renata explained.

"Don't worry, I still have vacation days, and I will come and see you in Toronto. I really don't want this to be a summer fling. I believe we have more than that." I assured her.

"Yes, Seba, I agree. I do think we have something special. Possibly, a future together."

"Like I said before, let's be patient, if it's meant to be then we will be together. With all this free time, I can't stop thinking about you, and

I can't wait to hold you in my arms. Good night, my queen." I said gently.

"Good night, my king." Renata replied lovingly.

I hung up the phone with a heavy heart. I felt empty. It was very hard to be so far away from the woman I loved. And staying in the room all night wasn't going to help me. I got dressed and decided to visit Premal. We made plans last night, and I hoped he didn't forget about them. I knocked on the door. He opened in seconds.

"Hey, man. What's up? Are you ready for tonight?" I asked as we shook hands.

"For sure, man. What are we doing?" Premal stepped aside letting me into his room.

"Well, I ran into the concierges. You know Michael and Srini?"

"Yes, they're good guys." He nodded.

"Well, they offered to take us out and show us around once they are finished with their shifts." I announced.

"Cool." Premal was excited. "I am looking forward to hanging out with the natives tonight."

"I really don't know what to expect, but I am also very excited." I echoed his sentiment. "In the meantime, let's go down to the main bar and have a drink or two before the guys finish their shifts?" Premal suggested. I nodded, and we left his room.

We headed to the upper lobby. From there, one could have a bird's eye view of the bar and the restaurant below. Apparently, that was the place to be on the weekends. All the foreigners from the surrounding hotels came there. That night was a special night. It was a pole position viewing party for the F1 event in India. One of the drivers was Indian, thus, putting his country on the map for Formula 1. Racing was a relatively new sport for India, but the people fell in love with it immediately and became very passionate about the whole thing. We walked down the stairs, approached the bar and found two empty seats.

"Gentlemen, how may I be of service tonight?" The bartender asked us.

I looked at Premal. "The same as last night?"

"Yes." He agreed.

"Let me have two Johnny Walker Black Labels on the rocks, please." I asked.

"Make it a double, please." Premal interjected.

"Yes, sir. Coming right up."

As we waited for our drinks, I looked up at the big screen and saw the coverage of the upcoming F1 event.

"You know, that was my dream as a young boy?" I shared with Premal.

"To be a race car driver?" He asked in disbelief.

"Yes, I believed, I had all the physical and mental capabilities to do that."

"And what happened?" Premal appeared fascinated with my revelation.

"I always blamed my parents for not allowing me to pursue my dream. I blamed it on them. In reality, I should have gone after it. You know, join a local go-cart team and work my way up. I know it's an expensive sport, but if you are really good, the money will find you." I noted thoughtfully. It was the first time, I admitted that it wasn't really my parents' fault of me not becoming a race car driver.

"It's not that easy, my friend. Those guys start racing at 5 years old. It consumes them from an early age, and it's their life. You also need a ton of sponsors to get you the seat." I was pleasantly surprised about Premal's knowledge of the sport.

"Yes, yes, I know that, but I believed I had the capability. Anyway, now, I just race my Porsche on the weekends whenever I get a track day available."

"That's pretty cool. It must be fun to race your car on a track."

"For me, it's the biggest rush."

"Are you one of those adrenaline junkies?" Premal grinned.

"I would have to admit, I am. I like to face fear head-on." I noted with pride. "Plus, I have so many things on my bucket list that I have already checked off."

The bartender placed our drinks before us.

"Cheers, to our bucket lists!" Premal raised his glass, and we cheered to our dreams. After taking a small sip of whiskey and enjoying its warm and woody flavor, Premal looked at me.

"Tell me about your bucket list, Sebastian. What have you done already and what is missing?"

"I've always wanted to hang glide, sky dive, and go bungee jumping." I admitted.

"Wow, man! That's intense!" Premal was in awe.

"Those, I've done." I added. "I would definitely do sky diving again but never bungee jumping. That felt like death, I literally thought, I would die. Let's just say, I did not like it."

"And what are you still missing?" It touched me how attentive and caring Premal was about my life's story.

"A family. A wife and kids." I said sincerely.

"Yes, it's pretty awesome having a family you can call your own. I have to be honest with you, the first 4 to 5 years of marriage are very tough, but if you can survive those, then it's a wonderful place to be at. And what else are you missing?"

"I want to be a partner in this firm." I stated and looked at Premal. I wanted to hear his opinion and see his reaction.

"Well, my friend, you still have a lot of work ahead of you. Finding a wife is not easy and making it to partner, is even harder, in my opinion. But I'm sure you can do both."

Our conversation was amazing. Premal and I were getting along great. Even though, he was married, he still had the spirit of a single person and wanted to venture out if not for the women then simply for the adventure. After an hour flew by, we went to check on Michael and Srini. We came right in time since their shifts had just ended. The four of us were ready to go out and party.

"Good evening, Mr. Kosta." Waved Srini.

"Listen, if we are going to get along, you have to simply call me Sebastian." I scolded him jokingly.

"Yes, sir." And he shook his head from side to side.

"No mister or sir. Just Sebastian." I continued.

"And you can call me Premal too." Premal chimed in.

After both men waved their heads in their customary fashion, I asked.

"So, Michael, what is the plan for tonight?"

"Well, nothing crazy. We just have a group of friends that like to light a bond fire on the beach." Michael replied with a wide smile.

"Is there any alcohol involved?" I inquired pretending to be very serious.

"Yes, Sebastian. We have a cooler filled with local goodies." Srini responded.

"That will be cool. I haven't tried anything local yet." I was instantly excited.

"Let's take a taxi since my friends are already there." Michael suggested.

"Sounds like a plan." I imitated their head-wave. "I pay on the way there. Premal, you got the fare on the way back."

"Deal." Premal tapped my shoulder and we left the hotel.

We jumped into the old Indian-manufactured minivan. It looked like a hippie van from the American 60's. It was custom painted inside and out. Even though, it was rusty, it still worked but didn't have an A/C. Some doors missed the glass. Like any other night, that one was hot and muggy, but for the first time since I arrived in Chennai, I wasn't bothered by the discomfort. Our spirits were high. We were looking for an adventure and it was fun to go out with Premal who knew the language and a pair of local guys. I knew we would get a different perspective on life in Chennai compared to what most foreigners saw or experienced.

As soon as we arrived, we noticed a long line of people entering the beach. Apparently, that was the place to be. I walked slowly behind everyone, carefully observing my surroundings. Most people around were young men, in their 20's. There were very few women. And even those few were with their boyfriends.

In spite of the constant heat and humidity, it was still a beautiful evening. Since Chennai did not have any tall buildings and lots of lights, we could clearly see the sky and every star. The view was truly magical. As I sat down, I inhaled deeply, and that same scent of jasmine filled my entire being. I was intoxicated by the aroma and felt truly happy. I've never smelled anything that intense, not even during the bloom seasons in the US. I knew, the scent of jasmine, would be one of the most vivid and unforgettable memories of my visit to Chennai.

Premal came up and handed me a bottle of the local beer.

"Enjoy, my friend." He grinned.

As I took a sip of it, I closed my eyes and let my taste buds do the job. Afterwards, I opened my eyes and looked into the bond fire before me. The locals were dancing and frolicking around the fire. They had a lot more energy than me. I was just happy to be outside of the hotel, experiencing something new. Once again, I found myself being the observer. It was great to immerse into the new culture and to realize that no matter how different we were in origins, still we were very similar as humans. Unlike us, the Westerners, those locals had a profound connection with nature. They enjoyed the little things and respected the fire, the ocean, and the sky above us.

Srini and Michael sat down next to us, and we toasted with our beers.

"Are you guys having fun?" Michael asked hopefully. "We just have a simple radio with local music. I know it's not what you listen to in the US, but it's great for dancing." He continued apologetically.

"We are having a great time, Michael." Premal said with a huge smile.

"Do you want to dance?" Srini inquired and got up.

I looked around and noticed very few women. None by themselves. I looked at Premal.

"You want to dance with these guys?" I asked hesitantly. Premal got up and laughed.

"Sure, why not!" He extended his hand. "Come on, Sebastian!"

I stood up and joined Premal, Srini, Michael and others in circle around the fire. The music was a typical Indian Bollywood style, and it was very fun to dance to it. While dancing, I finished my beer and got another one. Even though, the dancing felt strange, I enjoyed it very much. I tried imitating Michael and Srini's moves. It was more of a tribal dance than anything we had going in the West. It was pretty fast-paced and coordinated, so after 5 to 10 minutes, I was exhausted and sat down on the rocks. I was out of breath. Premal came over and handed me a joint.

"For real?" I started laughing.

"Hey, we are partying with the locals in India, my friend. Why not?" He was tipsy and happy.

"Exactly, why not?" I thought to myself.

"Okay, I will do a hit." I nodded and took the joint from Premal. I placed it between my lips and puffed really hard. There wasn't too much smoke coming out, so I borrowed the lighter, lit it once again, and took another hit. I inhaled deeply and held it inside my lungs. Then, after a few seconds, I exhaled the smoke. I didn't feel a thing. I did another hit, but I felt no high.

"What kind of weed is this crap? I don't feel a thing." I yelled out, not being sure whom I was talking to.

I wasn't big on weed. In reality, I've never had a good experience. Most of the times, it made me feel a bit paranoid. I gave up the joint on my last try and decided to just stick with the beer.

Around 3 AM, we called it a night. It was a fun time, and it was exciting to be with the local crowd, but I was looking forward to the next day's adventure. I was going to the tomb of St. Thomas the Apostle. I was very excited; more than one person had told me that the tomb was a very special site, a must for a visit. When I got back to the hotel, I drank the whole bottle of water before going to sleep. That was my remedy against any possible hangover.

Chapter 7

The next day, I woke up, and the first thing I did was to open the blackout shades. It was a beautiful sunny day, not a cloud in the sky. I felt very good considering, we were drinking until 3 AM. I assumed, sleeping until noon and drinking plenty of water is what saved me. I needed to hurry up because the excursion was starting at 1 PM. There were two trips available: one in the morning, another, in the afternoon. I needed my sleep; thus, I chose the afternoon trip.

As soon as I made it to the lobby, I saw Michael at the concierge booth.

"Good morning, Michael. Did you make it home alright last night?" I greeted him.

"Good morning! Yes, but I am a bit tired from the lack of sleep." He sighted. Unlike me, Michael couldn't sleep until late.

"What time did you start your shift?"

"I had to be here at 9 AM, sir."

"Wow, you are definitely running on a deficit of sleep. Make sure you get some rest tonight." I advised.

"Most definitely, sir." He nodded.

I looked through the double revolving doors at the entrance, and I could see people getting on the bus. I hoped that bus had air conditioning. I was only taking a backpack and a large bottle of water. And, of course, my new camera! I boarded and took a seat in the middle right hand side of the bus. The engine was on, and to my satisfaction, it was nice and cool inside. It was time to go, and since I did not know anyone on board, I just put my headphones with Coldplay on.

The tour consisted of visiting two locations. The first one was a fifty-minute drive to see the boulder, where St. Thomas the Apostle was killed. The second location was the church where he was buried. The ride was nice and comfortable. We drove through some beautiful places with lush nature. It was obvious, the ground was very fertile and there were farms all over the place. Once we got close to our first site, the tour guide stood up and turned the microphone on.

"Hello, ladies and gentlemen. We have arrived at one of the most sacred sites in India. Today, you will be visiting the Mount of St. Thomas the Apostle. He sailed to the south western part of India in 43 A.D., from the present-day Italy, formerly, the Roman Empire. He was one of Jesus's twelve original apostles. He was and still is widely known for being the Apostle who doubted the resurrection of Jesus. In fact, he stated that he would have to see the wounds on Jesus's hands and feet with his own very eyes to believe the resurrection was real. Then, St. Thomas had a vision, in which Jesus appeared and showed his wounds to him. He told St. Thomas that after seeing that, he was a believer.

In order to spread the faith and convert people to Christianity, Thomas the Apostle went to India and introduced the new Christian faith to the native people of the land. He was also a skilled carpenter and built seven churches in the area. The architectural techniques used by St. Thomas were inspired by and learned from the Greeks. With time, St. Thomas fell under continuous suspicions and prosecutions by the locals. That made him flee to the east. Let's now go and visit the place where St. Thomas was killed in 72 AD."

After we exited the bus, I got my camera ready. As we walked towards the sacred place, I noticed it was packed with locals and tourists from all over the world. I started snapping pictures of everything right away, from the signs announcing the historic significance of the site to the natural surroundings. I was truly in awe of the moment I was experiencing. I was born in a Catholic faith, but I wasn't very religious. Like Thomas, I also had my doubts in regard to Jesus Christ. I always knew he existed. There was way too much scientific evidence of his existence and history on Earth. By God, we even changed the calendar to reflect the magnitude of His significance. Even though, I went to Catholic school, and my family was religious, I had a hard time believing that God placed his own son on Earth to be sacrificed in his name. I had a personal belief that all of us were God's children, but only a few obtained the highest level of enlightenment, like the prophets. I believed Jesus was one of those blessed souls, and that made him one with God. The problem was that most people would think you were crazy if you walked around saying you were the son of God. I couldn't really blame those who didn't believe him. I thought Jesus felt that his oneness with God had to be shared in order to save people from themselves.

It was really an incredible experience to think deeply about the divinity of God. I've never thought so much about the topic until I came to the Mount of St. Thomas. I figured that might be the reason why people from all over the world went to that site. I continued following the tour guide and taking pictures throughout that beautiful excursion. We walked up the hill, perhaps 100 yards, and reached the top where we saw a gigantic granite boulder. The guide started speaking again.

"Here we are, ladies and gentlemen. We have reached the Mount of St. Thomas the Apostle. He tried to survive the persecutions by escaping to the south east region of India. Even though, he was very popular, he still had many enemies. They did not believe in his preaching and did not believe in Jesus. He fled to this boulder, and that's where he was wounded by someone's lance and left behind, bleeding to death. After St. Thomas died, he was pronounced a martyr."

I took many pictures of the boulder. I was in awe over the whole story. It was real physical evidence of the Apostle's life. And if Thomas lived, then Jesus did as well. It was approximately 2000 years ago. Crazy to even think of that much time passing. To me, it sounded like a long time, but in reality, 2000 years in history was nothing. I took a few more pictures and then sat down leaning on the boulder. I could see beauty all around me, the nature, the sky, the sun. That was exactly what Thomas saw as he was slowly dying. The history had it that Jesus invited Thomas to follow him. But Thomas refused, because he wasn't sure where Jesus was going. It was fascinating. I felt some kind of awakening, a religious epiphany. That place made me completely assured that it was all true. Jesus existed; the Apostles existed. They were meant to spread God's light and save the world and humanity.

After about an hour of walking around the site and documenting my experiences, I boarded the bus. I did not feel like listening to any music. It was a bit challenging to be in the moment, because my thoughts kept racing though my head. That visit has impacted me. I wanted to become a better person, to give back to the world. I just didn't know how to do that. India was indeed a magical place.

We drove back to the city of Chennai and went to the Basilica of St. Thomas the Apostle. Apparently, in the 16th century, his remains were transferred to that place, to the church that was built in his honor. Because of St. Thomas' legacy, the name Thomas was very popular in India.

We got off the bus and entered the church. It wasn't large. Not like the ones in Spain or Italy. In fact, it was very modest and rather bare. But it had a powerful aura. Inside, many local people were praying, it was filled with the flickering candle lights. Out of respect for the praying people, I decided to stand aside and just admire the place. For some reason, I got very emotional as I observed everything, the worshipers, the history and the church. I felt blessed to learn about that place and being able to visit it. I had no idea India had such Christian sites. I also thought about St. Thomas' journey. If it took me 22 hours on the plane, how long was his trip on those pre-historic vessels. It was mindboggling.

After I spent considerable time taking everything in and thinking about the significance of St. Thomas' life, I approached the tomb. It was open, and underneath, there was a statue of the Apostle. I saw many worshipers crying over the tomb. It was a touching moment. Thanks to St. Thomas, there was a large Christian community in India. I took a few more pictures and then sat down. I wanted to be in the moment. I read a prayer and promised to change many of my ways upon my return home. I wanted to get closer to God.

After another incredible hour, the tour was over. We were heading back to the hotel. I knew that personal spiritual awakening, would be something I would never forget. To see evidence of the existence of Jesus Christ and St. Thomas the Apostle was very profound and impactful. It made my job at the delivery center seem miniscule, even meaningless. I knew I had to go back to work the next morning, thus I had to get my mindset back in the right direction. I had three more weeks in Chennai, to provide post 'go-live' support. But I was looking forward to finishing up that project and coming back home. I suddenly understood how much I missed my family, especially my mom, who was always there for me and was my real best friend. In her eyes, I would always be her baby boy. Even at 32 years old, she still called me her baby. I was getting home sick; I could feel that.

Chapter 8

The next day, I woke up and immediately jumped out of bed. I was fully charged. I guessed it was due to me going to bed earlier than usual and not drinking any alcohol the night before. I decided to workout before breakfast. It's been three weeks since my surgery, and I was feeling much better. There still was a bit of swelling, but I figured wearing the waist band for one more week should eliminate all the inflammation. Instead of walking on the treadmill, I decided to use the elliptical for ten minutes and afterwards, work on the stretching of my abdominal muscles. A few minutes into my training, Scott walked into the gym.

"How's it going, Sebastian. Did you have a good weekend?" He asked.

"Hi, Scott. Yes, believe it or not I managed to venture out with the locals and do some Bollywood dancing."

"Are you serious?" Scott couldn't imagine me doing that.

"I wanted to get a feel for the culture in India, and even though, it was simple; it was quite magical. The people are very spiritual here. I even visited the Tomb of St. Thomas the Apostle." I said with pride.

"Wow, I heard it was a really cool place to visit."

"Yes, I highly recommend it."

"On a different note, how is our project track going?" Scott was instantly all-business.

"Well, we went live with all the tracks except for the General Ledger. That would be happening today. How was your weekend, Scott?"

"I didn't have as much fun as you." Scott smirked. "I was heads down with Lee making sure all the Great Plain instances were working correctly, and we had full functionality in all the Hudd business units in North America. But on your front, everything is going according to plan, right?"

"We have had a few bumps here and there, but for the most part, everything is in the green." I replied confidently.

"Well, that is great news." Scott smiled.

"I have no doubt, this project is going to be a success." I noted without hesitation.

"I really hope so. I am rooting for you, Sebastian. Plus, Gary wants you to be promoted soon, pending the outcome of this project, of course. But I promise, I will work with you and support you if you decide to be considered for partner." Scott assured me.

"I very much appreciate it, Scott." I nodded gratefully.

"Well, keep it up, rock star. Now, I have to burn some calories before all that jasmine rice gets me huge." Scott laughed and walked away heading towards the treadmill.

I finished the elliptical and decided to lay on the stretching mat. I was beaming with excitement. The opportunity was real. After 8 long years, I would have my shot at becoming partner, and my career would be set. The typical partner made so much money, they could generally retire at the age of 50. The average American worked until 65 years of age having a 401k of approximately $100,000. My retirement funds would be in the millions. Fifty was very young. It would give me enough time and financial stability for my future family. Everything was falling into place, I felt like the stars were aligning for me. I just had to finish the project strong, and the rest would happen naturally.

I went upstairs and took a shower. For the next few hours, it was time to just sit back and enjoy my book. It felt so good to feed my mind with interesting stories from John Grisham, at the time, my favorite author. His books would literally take the reader away to far destinations. He painted each scenery perfectly, and the characters were very relatable.

After reading, I started thinking about my future partnership and the path to Accent. When I finished my undergraduate, I attempted taking the LSAT for law school. My father was a lawyer, and I never met a broke lawyer. I took the test three times, but somehow, I did not fare well in standardized testing. I did much better on the GMAT and decided to get my MBA. It was a good choice; it opened the doors to Accent. Accent has been around for almost 100 years and had its offices in all major countries around the world. The company's employees were highly skilled and talented. It was stimulating to be in that environment. The work was very challenging, but at the same time, it was never boring. I was placed on a new project every three to four months. It was always in a new city or country, new people and new challenges. I really felt that was the right company for me and wanted to continue building my career there, until retiring young and ready for life. That was the dream.

After much reflection and dreaming of the future, I noticed that I forgot what I read. I resolved to re-read the chapters. I was enjoying my time alone, and it felt great to invest in myself. I dressed up in my business casual attire. It was time to go to work, which was rather light at the moment. I planned on touching base with my team and then just hang out at my workstation.

When I arrived at the delivery center, I found my workstation messy. I was surprised that it was covered with a stack of papers, documents, and handouts. I was very shocked to see that, because it was a serious violation of the rules. The workstations had to be cleaned after each shift, failure to do so, could result in termination. I quickly gathered all the documents and took them to the room we were usually forbidden to use. My security badge worked, and I was able to gain access. I wanted to leave the papers where they would be easily discovered by management. I wanted them to know the papers weren't mine. I wondered who left the papers on my desk and why they chose me. Perhaps, there was something for me to see there. Finally, I decided to look through them.

In early childhood, I was very good with puzzles. I would spend hours trying to figure out the correct pattern for all the pieces to fit properly. As I looked at each paper, I started to create piles of relevance. The first pile was about money. I saw many payroll files of the general users, the wages appeared to be very low. I also found many documents with the discussions of Accents' 401K plans. There were even a few documents on pay awards through stock payments. I knew about those types of benefits for executive partners, but not for employees in Chennai. I assumed that whoever left those documents for me to see was promised something that wasn't realistic to fulfill. I knew the main purpose of business process outsourcing was labor arbitrage; a reduced payroll expense due to the weaker labor laws in developing economies, such as India. I've never even contemplated that people would be so unhappy with what they earned.

The next pile I grouped together was made of status reports for the different tracks, including those of my team and others. As I probed deeper into the reports, I noticed many of the peripheral projects were in the red. The timelines extended before my project started and went further than when I was supposed to complete it. Those status reports were from the Project Management Office, created by Scott. I found it alarming that the overall project was at risk, and Accent was losing millions of dollars in service level agreements. At the same time, Scott seemed calm and upbeat when I saw him at the gym. I was confused and very concerned. Perhaps, that was the reason he worked through the whole weekend.

The room had a conference phone, and all of a sudden, the lights turned on and a voice came through.

"Mr. Kosta. What are you doing in this room? You have no authority to be there."

It was the delivery center's security, I figured.

"I just needed the room to finish up some work." I responded calmly.

I quickly gathered all the papers and documents and placed them into my computer bag. I knew that was highly classified information, and someone wanted for me to have it. Perhaps, they hoped I would do something about that.

"I need you to report to Mr. Reedy's office immediately, sir." The voice announced. "We need to discuss this security breach."

Within a few minutes, two armed guards appeared at the office and escorted me to the second floor to meet G. Reedy.

"Good evening, Mr. Kosta. Our systems have identified that you entered a secured room. That room is reserved for partners only." Mr. Reedy announced as soon as I walked into his office.

"It's funny that you mention that, because I've been here for a week and haven't seen even one partner." I stated calmly. "Not in the hotel and not at the delivery center. Thus, the highest-ranking employee is the senior project manager. Is there something about India that keeps the partners away?" I continued in the same unfazed manner.

"No, that is not the case. Let's get back to why you were in the room." Mr. Reedy insisted.

"I felt like breaking the barriers. I don't appreciate being forbidden something without explanations, especially considering my position."

"Mr. Kosta. You need to respect the rules of the delivery center. You should know better being an employee of Accent."

"What are you talking about?" I raised my voice. "This center is not even an Accent center. It's a third-party outsourcing provider in India. We purchased you guys. You have no idea how Accent operates on a daily basis. How long have you been an Accent employee?" I pressed on. The best defense was an offense. I knew that.

To my surprise G. Reedy replied that he was with Accent for three months only.

"See, there is no way you understand our culture and the ways of doing business. I mean really, guys. Armed security. Is that really necessary?" I inquired sarcastically. "I think this meeting has gone on for long enough. I am going to talk to my people back in the US, because this delivery center is being run very poorly." I concluded forcefully.

I noticed the delivery center director and his team flustered, but I was very distraught and just wanted to get out from that office. I did not feel comfortable with the way I was questioned and treated.

I left Mr. Reedy's office with the guards following me all the way to my workstation. I sat down and took a deep breath. I decided I needed to listen to some music to chill out and relax. That whole experience made me very nervous, and I needed to redirect my attention. As much as I tried to immerse myself into my work, I could not help wondering who left those documents on my desk. I wasn't sure what to do with them, but I believed there had to be some significance. Both I and the person who left the documents could lose our jobs. I was going to do everything to take the papers back to the US. I resolved to safeguarding the documents and keep them close until I got back to the hotel.

At around 10 PM, I went to see Shanti. She told me the backlog was fully under control and it was a matter of a few days before the team was back on track. The team shut down their workstations, and we went to dinner. When Shanti and I approached the waiting line, I noticed that many people, whom I'd never seen before were greeting me. I wasn't sure if I met them at the beach that past weekend, but they were overly nice and respectful. Part of me wandered if they knew the person who placed those documents on my desk. Perhaps, my visit to G. Reedy's office became public knowledge. Perhaps, they thought I was going to fight for their rights. All I knew was that whole experience made me feel very uneasy. I couldn't wait to get back to the hotel.

After eating a sandwich, I quickly returned to my workstation. Even though, I still felt uncomfortable, at least there, I was alone and could relax with my music. Unfortunately, my time alone did not last too long. I was interrupted by Amanda. She wanted to talk to me.

"I can't believe you knew about the backlog and haven't done any-thing thing about that." She stated angrily.

"Hey, calm down. There is no reason to raise your voice." I had to exercise self-control. "Let's go into a private office to discuss this."

I decided to take her back into the forbidden office. I really wanted to be a disrupter and show that I wouldn't be bossed around by some newbie.

"Sebastian, we are not allowed to go there." She noted still sound-ing angry.

"I don't care. I don't want you making a scene in public just like you did in Toronto."

"What the fuck are you talking about?" She turned red. "You are never on top of your shit. I always have to clean up your mess."

"Listen to me, you little bitch, I rank hire then you, you have to respect that." I said in the same calm manner.

"I don't give a fuck about the hierarchy." She yelled out. "I am going to say it how I see it. I don't think you are doing your job."

"If you want to fucking know, I knew about the backlog, and it had been addressed. In a few fucking days, it will cease to be an issue." I pointed out staring straight into her angry eyes.

"How do you know that?"

"Because I know my team, and I trust them to get their jobs done. Remember, this is not your track. Focus on your shit not mine." With those words I walked out of the office.

I've had enough of her and the whole day. It was almost three in the morning, and I was exhausted. Aside from feeling uneasy, I was also tense. My head was going to explode. I decided to return to my workstation, get my bag and leave. But when I approached the door to my desk, I discovered it was locked and security badge didn't work. I had to call another employee and use their badge to gain access to my workstation and pack up my computer. I was fed up and had enough of that shit. Between G. Reedy and Amanda, I just wanted to get out of there.

I grabbed all my belongings and made sure the important files were in my bag. As soon as I walked out of the office, I saw the same armed guards at the other end of the hallway. I had to move quickly; they were coming for me. I approached the nearest hallway exit door, and it did not work. My heart started beating fast. I had no clue about the security protocol in the center. I didn't know what rights I had. I just knew, those people were after me for some reason. I saw another employee in the hallway and asked them to open the door for me. They did with a smile. From there, it was a race to the outside. The two guards were following me closely. It seemed as if they wanted to appear calm and not cause panic. As I raced out the front entrance, holding my bag, I jumped into a waiting taxi.

"Go! Go! Go!" I screamed.

"Go where, sir?" The driver appeared confused and startled.

"To the Park Sheraton!" I continued yelling.

"You got it." He said calmly.

"Please go fast." I hurried him.

As we started to move, I saw the two guards run out of the door and discovered I was able to escape. I've never had people with guns chasing me, my adrenaline was kicking, and my heart was pumping. I was panicked, alarmed, and scared for my life. I had no idea what could happen to me in India. I knew something like that would never happen in the US. But I wasn't in the US. I had no doubt, there was something very important in those files, and I decided, I was not going back to the delivery center, because I did not feel safe.

Once I arrived at the hotel, I felt better. I started having reservations about my decision of not returning to work at the center. But then I thought that my team was in full control of the situation, there was no necessity for my physical presence there. I would just work from the hotel, and that would be it. I was so stressed that I took a Xanax and passed out in seconds.

Chapter 9

The next day was Tuesday, July 19th. I woke up and tried to follow my regular routine. I went to the gym, had brunch and then began working. I didn't see anyone from work at the gym. I, however, paid no attention to that fact. Once I started working at my room, I was stunned to find out that my virtual private network was turned off. I had no access to my work emails. I also could not access the shared drive. I tried using my calling card to reach out to Shanti. Shockingly, my calling card was no longer active as well.

"Well, I guess I am officially on vacation." I told myself.

I tried to remain calm at that point. The idea of looking for Scott or my other colleagues who stayed at the hotel flashed in my mind, but for some reason, I pushed it away.

The Wi-Fi in the room was working, so I could check my personal emails and surf the internet. I had two weeks until my return to Miami. I wasn't sure what to do. I was still a bit scared over last night's incident with the papers and irritated over Amanda's disrespectful demeanor.

I was very concerned about not having access to the work network, but I decided to go down to the lobby and check the status of my company's credit card on file. I went to the front desk and asked them to do just that.

"Sorry sir, but your company's American Express card is not going through. It worked initially to book your reservation, but I've just tried processing your incidentals, and it did not work."

After that, I was upset and shocked. I had only $300 in cash and my own personal credit card.

"Did they fire me? Am I no longer part of Accent? Why hasn't anyone contacted me?" I was very confused. I gave the front desk my personal card and kept the cash for emergency purposes.

I returned to my room feeling very pissed off. How could they lock me out of the delivery center, cancel my credit card, and leave me unable to make any calls??? Who did they think they were? I was at loss for words and ideas. I decided against getting on the first flight and coming back to the US. I didn't want to act out on impulse. I had the hotel covered, and I could wait for a few days to see what was going on. Since I was finishing my book, I decided to buy another one. That would keep me occupied. I went down to the hotel's store. As I wondered over the different titles, I came across an interesting one, *"The Monk Who Sold His Ferrari."* It was written by Robin Sharma who was of Indian descent, but his family moved to Canada, where he grew up.

I quickly picked up the book and read the summary on the back. It was about a famous attorney who became very rich over the years but sacrificed his health in doing so. He was unhappy and depressed, until he traveled across the world to live with monks in Tibet. There, he went through a spiritual awakening and found himself again. I felt related to that attorney. I was on the other side of the world going through a spiritual awakening of my own. I decided to buy the book and read it.

I went back to my room and started pacing around. Maybe I was overthinking, but I sensed like I was being watched. I was scared again, thus, I decided I wanted to leave the room. I looked outside the window, at the pool area. The Indian kids were playing around and seemed completely immune to the heat. Their feet weren't burning from the blistering granite tiles. I decided to go downstairs and figure out why their feet weren't affected. All the other tourists weren't able to walk barefoot, but the Indian kids could stand on the tiles for a while.

I got dressed for the pool and left my room. I found a lounge chair in the shade. As I sat there, I simply observed the children. They ran around the pool but in the same pattern. I was really curious. I stood up from my chair and came closer to the water. Then I figured it out!!! The entire pool area was covered in granite, but there was a little pathway made with porcelain tile. It was heat resistant and remained cool throughout the day. It was amazing how those children figured that out considering everything was made in the same color and size.

I decided to go for a swim. I took off my shirt and sandals and walked along the porcelain tile. For a moment, I just stood there. My feet were not burning. I dove into the pool and listened to the silence beneath the water. That tranquility relaxed me. I told myself, "fuck it. I wasn't going back to the delivery center. I mean, I had armed security chasing me off the premises." I no longer cared about the project. In my mind, 'go-live' happened, and it was a success. The backlog was taken care of, and the customer service training was nearly completed. My services were no longer needed. Even though, they cut me off financially from the company's resources, I still had plenty of my own money. I am sure I would find the way out. I didn't want to panic, so I simply enjoyed my swim.

I did a few laps and then relaxed and looked over the hotel's building. It was a U-shaped structure wrapped around the pool. Since it was still early, and the night shift hasn't started yet, I figured all my team leads were in their rooms. I tried to guess where Premal's room was. I starred at each window as if I knew he was watching me by the pool. I hoped everyone was watching me, because I wanted for them to know that I was calm and relaxed. I've done nothing wrong not to be. In fact, I was going to enjoy the upcoming days by investing in myself. I felt good. I felt empowered. I was going to survive that experience and make it back home. But I had to play it cool and stay confident that nothing bad would happen to me. I got out of the pool and dried myself off. As I used the towel around my face, I once again looked up to the rooms. I felt as if someone was looking at me. It was just my instinct telling me that. I walked on the path of the porcelain tiles, and something made me turn around. When I did, I noticed a tall white man delicately walking over the granite. His feet were burning. I knew, if I could figure out the pool puzzle, I could find my way out of that shitstorm.

I returned to the room feeling instantly tired. Maybe it was because I had only a few hours of sleep. What bothered me was the fact that only a few minutes ago, at the pool, I felt great and invigorated, but then, my disposition changed drastically. I couldn't understand or explain that. I decided to watch some TV. I was excited to find ESPN, I loved sports. There was a soccer match on, Real Madrid, my favorite team, vs. Manchester United. As I watched the game, I started dozing off but then I was suddenly terrified of falling asleep. I knew I wasn't myself, but I tried making the best of it. Every hour or so, I was trying to text Renata. The texts weren't going through. Then I tried calling my parents. No luck. The calling card wasn't working. The phone line in the room worked, but without my international calling card, I could not make any calls. I couldn't even call Lufthansa to reschedule my flight. I was trapped in that hotel.

As the days went by, my condition worsened. I wasn't sleeping. I didn't want to keep taking Xanax, because my body was getting used to it, and it was not as effective anymore. Plus, I didn't want to get addicted to it. I stopped going to the pool and pretty much stayed in my room. My thoughts were constantly racing, and I kept going back to why everything happened. Why were the documents placed on my desk? Who placed them there? What did they want for me to do with those papers? Why was Amanda on my case? Those questions were constantly racing through my mind.

I believed it was a puzzle that I needed to figure out. With the lack of sleep, I also started to get a bit paranoid. I would walk around the perimeter of the room; next to the glass window facing the pool. Then, suddenly, without any reason, I got obsessed with the air conditioning vents. Those were the horizontal vents that ran across the side of the bedroom and the living room. As I peered inside the vents, it appeared there was a camera there. Then I found one in my bedroom and another one, in the living room. Could that be true? I believed it was a terrible invasion of privacy for the hotel to have the cameras in the rooms. Or was it just my room?

Periodically, I would get in bed trying to relax. I needed to sleep to recover and get my mind thinking straight. As the hours went by, I was in total darkness. My agitation periods would switch with the calm ones. When I was no longer nervous or agitated, I felt as the observer. I observed everything. I stared at the light passing through the shades. I watched it move across the floor. It was the light of the moon. As a child, I was scared of the dark.

Chapter 10

I opened my eyes; it was bright out. I survived another day. It was a Friday morning. The sun made me more peaceful and calmer. Just seeing the sun made me feel better. There was something about the daylight. It made me more optimistic. I suddenly felt the need to pray. With my newfound faith, I prayed to St. Thomas for his guidance. I asked for him to make things clear for me and help me go back home.

All of a sudden, I was surprised to hear the phone ring. I've been alone for four days, without any human contact.

"Hello?" I answered timidly.

"Sebastian, it's your mother. Something happened to your father." I heard her tearful voice on the other end.

"What? Mom, what happened to him?" I started yelling.

"We are at the hospital. He had a heart attack. We don't know if he is going to make it. We really need for you to come home. Sebastian, please come home now." She begged.

I hung up the phone, again feeling completely disoriented and broken. I couldn't, in fact, I didn't even try controlling the tears running down my face. Perhaps, they found out about the situation with my company, and that gave him a heart attack. My brother and sister would kill me if they learned I was the cause of his ailment.

I urgently needed to get out from that room, that hotel and Chennai. I wasn't sure what to do, but I got a jolt of adrenaline and anger consumed me. I was in rage. All the workouts and training made my muscles strong. I've become tense and felt like a trapped lion that needed to escape from his cage. I ran up to the glass window and forcefully hit it with both fists. I wanted to break the glass and jump out. Then my mind started racing, and I focused on my father's possible death. Would I be the cause? I could not live with myself. My life would cease to exist. Then, something inside of me forced me into the bathroom. I opened my bag and took out a bottle of Xanax. I decided that I could not live with that pain. I put all the pills in my mouth, filled up a glass of water, and then I paused. I literally froze.

As I stood there, the day turned to night. The veins in my arms started protruding. I looked in the mirror, and my face was getting discolored. I was about to commit suicide. But then, a thought appeared in my head. Maybe, I could make it back in time to see my Dad? Maybe the heart attack was not as severe as originally appeared? There was a chance I could see my father. I threw all the pills out in the toilet and returned to the room.

I had to regain my composure. I needed to use my brain power to get me out of there. I began looking around the room for anything that could help me. I was lost and alone. I didn't know what to do. I started to cry. I needed to see my father one more time. He was my hero. He was a strong man. He could survive. As the tears poured out, I started talking.

"Dad, I am getting out of here. I will find the way! Please don't die. I love you." I looked around the room for anything that could help me. Something that could get me out. I focused on the coffee table. It had over fifty match boxes spread all over it. There was something there I could use. As I looked at the images and descriptions on the covers of the matches, I began to play another puzzle. I mixed and matched the colors, sizes, objects until I found what I was looking for. I had no idea what it meant in Hindu, but I found two identical matches with the inscription of "i kno".

Somehow, that had meaning to me. It resonated with my inner spirit. I recalled my experience of visiting the two sites at the Tomb of St. Thomas the Apostle, and the lessons I learned. That trip made me rediscover Jesus and faith. I believed he existed, and I had no doubt, there was a piece of God in every human. I was assured, he was the most enlightened person to ever walk the Earth. I knew he was with me at that moment. He would get me out of that room and take me back home.

I then developed the plan. First, I needed to get a traditional room without any technology. I needed to get somewhere I felt safe, and where I could relax. Second, I had to change my flights. I still had Wi-Fi and my personal email. I decided to send a mass communication to the partners at Accent and to some of my friends and family. I needed to tell my story. I needed to tell them what happened to me. So, I crafted a detailed email describing how a stack of random documents were placed on my desk, and how I was chased out of the delivery center by the armed guards. I also informed them that my credit and calling cards were disconnected. I told them, my father had a heart attack and was in the hospital. I threatened to sue, if I wasn't placed on the next flight out of Chennai. I needed to send out that email urgently, because who knew how long I would have until eventually even my Wi-Fi would be shut down as well. Everything else was disconnected. That was my last chance to contact the world. I pressed 'send'. I then checked in my "Sent" folder to make sure the email left the outbox successfully.

About an hour later, I heard the phone ringing. I answered it. To my surprise, it was my old friend from high school, Mike McGrath.

"Seba, my friend. What is going on? I just received your email and got worried about you, man. What is wrong?" He asked.

"Hey, man. It's really crazy but to make a long story short, I think I found some stuff that might be incriminating to my employer, and they know I have it. Now, I am stuck in my hotel in India without my company's credit or calling cards. I am so freaked out; I am scared to leave my room." Mike listened to what I told him and paused for a few seconds. He was a helicopter pilot in the Marines.

"You just take it easy there, lion. Everything is going to be alright. You need to calm down." He tried to encourage me.

"I even feel like I am being monitored in my room." I continued.

"Then pack your shit and get the fuck out of there. I am just like you, Seba, I don't trust those big corporate companies. They work their people to death and give them nothing in return. All the profit stays with the ownership and the top executives. You have to consider you are now on a mission to get home." He stated passionately.

"Yes, Mike. I need to get out of here."

"Reach out to the people you know. There has to be someone you feel comfortable with." He advised me.

"I've made a few friends here." I tried reasoning out loud. "Few coworkers and the people at the hotel."

"That's your answer." Mike yelled out. "The hotel people can get you out. They can help you with your flight. Do whatever is necessary to make it back to the US. You need to see you Dad, Seba. You need to see him alive." He stimulated me.

"Why didn't I think of that myself." I wondered silently.

I hung up the phone and wiped away the tears. It was time for me to be strong and tough. I needed to be the fighter I once was. The adrenaline started to pump throughout my body, and I picked up the two sets of matches and placed one in each hand. I then turned them around so that the words "I Kno" could be read by whomever was facing me. I thought what I was about to do would make me look like I'd lost my mind. However, to me, it was the only way out. I walked over to the side of the bed and pressed the concierge button on the command center. All of a sudden, Srini answered.

"Good afternoon, Mr. Kosta. How may I be of service today?" He wouldn't call me Sebastian while he was at work.

"Is Michael with you?" I asked without the usual greeting and a small talk.

"Yes, sir."

"Then I need for both of you to come up to my room right away." I uttered.

"Certainly, sir. We will be there shortly." Srini assured me.

I quickly packed my bags and went to the bathroom to wash my face to appear normal and presentable. I took off my shirt and stared at the mirror. Over the past two weeks, I lived off of only tuna sandwiches and bananas. I lost a lot of weight. If I were to guess, I would've assumed, at least ten pounds. I took off the waist band, and my six pack was clearly evident. I no longer needed the band, so I dumped it into the garbage bin. I felt and looked thin and worn out. I haven't slept in four days, but I needed to push myself further to get on that plane and return back to the States.

In less than five minutes, the doorbell rang. I knew the time had come. The plan that I have developed was my only way out. I knew that both Srini and Michael were extremely religious. I went ahead and tucked in my shirt, combed my hair and grabbed the matches. As I did before, I placed one in both hands. Making sure they were facing in the right direction. I then opened the door and walked out into the hallway. I spread my arms out and revealed the matches by opening my hands. They immediately looked down into my hands and read "I Kno". From that moment, I lost my sense of the present. I was conscious but only as the observer. The words that came out of my mouth were not my own. They were from my inner being, my soul.

"Dear God, he is an enlightened one." Srini exclaimed and took a step back.

"He has seen God." Michael echoed.

"Yes, I have." I pronounced solemnly. They appeared in complete shock. Their expressions displayed simultaneously worry and excitement.

"Are you okay, sir?" Michael asked gently.

"Yes, I am fine." I replied calmly. "I need to switch rooms. I no longer like this room. I would like to be placed in one of the more traditional rooms."

"Yes, sir." They answered in unison. They seemed scared but still did everything I asked. We were walking to the elevator. Both Srini and Michael helped me with the luggage.

"Please come with us, sir. We will speak with the manager to switch your room."

"Thank you." I whispered.

As we walked into the elevator, I felt like my subconscious and conscious minds merged into one. I did not have any thoughts anymore, my brain blacked out. I observed and reacted with zero thinking. I was not sure how I was going to pull everything off, but somehow, I was okay. Some other form of intelligence was guiding me. The elevator opened at the lobby and the guys took me to the hotel lounge.

"Sir, please sit down and relax. Stay here with Srini, and I will speak with the manager." Michael told me and walked away.

As I was sitting down, I mechanically observed my surroundings. There were a few people at the bar. A couple walking by with a dog. I observed the brass ornaments on the bar and even the reflections from those ornaments. Srini talked to me, and I listened, but at the same time, I was staring at the TV. There was a tennis match. It was Championship Sunday at Wimbledon, and Federer was playing the American Andy Roddick. I could not believe I could watch the match and speak to Srini at the same time. I was calm and relaxed. I felt like I just had a deep tissue massage. I was no longer tired. Srini was finally at ease, because I appeared normal and in total control.

Michael returned and announced that the arrangement about the room change was made.

"That's great." I nodded without much emotion. "Could you please find Premal? He is also staying in one of the traditional rooms. Please tell him I need his help with switching my flights. I need to leave Chennai as soon as possible. My father is in the hospital back at home, and I need to see him."

"Absolutely, sir. I will make sure to contact him right away." Srini touched my shoulder.

"Srini, I need for you do it now. Now. Please."

"Yes, sir." Srini stood up and hustled away to the front desk.

"How is living in the US, sir?" Michael asked trying to distract me while we waited for Srini. "I've always wanted to visit America."

"You know, Michael. You've been so helpful that perhaps, I can help you visit or even move there." I suggested thoughtfully. "If that is something you desire?"

"Of course, sir!!!" Michael exclaimed excitedly.

"I live in the Four Seasons in Miami. With your background in hospitality, I am sure we can work on a transfer for you. I'm friendly with the president of the board of directors of the residential condo association. They would hire you in an instant with my recommendation. You just need to get your papers straight."

Michael nodded readily. Still unable to believe his luck. He quickly extracted his business card and extended it to me.

"Excellent. I'll make sure to reach out to you once I am back in the US." I promised.

When Srini came back, he informed me that the message was sent to Premal.

"Sir, we have your key to the new room. Please follow me."

I got up mechanically and followed both guys down the corridor to the elevator.

"Sir, Mr. Premal mentioned he would be speaking with a gentleman named Scott and would be contacting you directly after."

"Excellent, Srini. You both are doing a great job. Thank you."

We used the elevator to get to the ninth floor.

"Room 925, sir." Srini informed me.

"Thank you, Srini."

Srini and Michael brought my bags in, I tipped them and locked the door. I was finally alone. I felt much better. I wasn't paranoid anymore because my new room had none of the crazy technology I had in the previous room. I was coming back to normal, not feeling like a caged animal anymore. Now, I had to be patient and wait for Premal, who was my main point of contact at Accent. I trusted him.

After I spent some time walking around the room and breathing steadily, I unpacked a few necessities. For the first time in days, I decided to check the date and time. It was Sunday, July 23th, approximately 8 PM. I was a bit hungry, so I called room service and ordered the usual, a tuna sandwich and a banana. I didn't want to know about the outside world; I did not turn on the TV. I did not need to overwhelm my mind with any commercials or news stories.

It was crazy how powerful the media had become in modern times. They could use the internet and the TV to influence billions of people instantly. They dictated every trend, from politics and religion, to fashion and things which we didn't need or care about. The media and the advertising giants worked together to brainwash humanity. It was all about the materialistic possessions and desires. I no longer wanted that life. I was influenced by St. Thomas and the book, *"The Monk Who Sold His Ferrari."* I was a changed man.

I decided to get some sleep. I knew that my state of mind was not entirely back to normal, and I needed to get better before a long flight back to Miami. As much as I tried to relax and sleep, I still felt agitated. The fight or flight adrenaline was still in my system, and I could not shut that off. If only I knew how to press a button, like a computer, and force myself into a sleep mode.

As I laid flat on my back, staring at the ceiling, I tried easing my mind through meditation. Even though, I could not sleep, I could still try to relax my body and my mind. I willed myself to think about the good moments in my life. I remembered Renata and our beautiful journey to Niagara Falls in Canada. I recalled us riding on the motorcycle and feeling the breeze on our faces. All of a sudden, the room phone rang.

"Hello?" I answered frantically.

"Sebastian?"

"Premal." I breathed his name out with relief.

"I got your message about your father being in the hospital." He told me.

"Yes, Premal. I need to see my father as soon as possible." I had tears in my eyes.

"Don't worry, man. I already spoke to Scott; you are leaving tomorrow."

"Really?" I got choked up, because I could not believe I was finally leaving India.

"What time?" I asked without caring that Premal heard me cry.

"Your flight is at 10 AM. Therefore, we need to be out of here at the latest by 7:30 AM. Don't worry, I will arrange for the transportation. Meet me in the lobby at 7 AM, okay, Seba?"

"Yes, I will be ready." I stated resolutely.

"Get some rest, my friend. It's a long flight."

"Thanks for helping me, Premal."

"You bet, Seba."

I got back in bed feeling exhilarated. I knew that I would not sleep. My brain was wired like I drank several cups of Sumatra coffee. Just like the night before, I closed my eyes and let my mind wonder and do its thing. I thought what happened to me was very strange, at the same time, I was absolutely sure that Accent knew about those documents, and they also knew I had them. Perhaps, they were worried I might share them with the press. Maybe, I would need to hire an attorney to represent me? Even though, I felt better in the new room, I was still a bit paranoid about my situation. From fighting with Amanda, finding the mysterious documents to being chased out of the delivery center by the armed guards, I was scared, really scared.

Chapter 11

I awoke at the first sight of the sunlight creeping through the edges of the drapes. I jumped out of the bed and went straight to the restroom. I looked like a mess. I needed to shower and shave. I also needed to get my mindset ready for the long travel ahead. Before showering, I decided to do a hundred push-ups. I needed to get my focus on. I needed to be on top of my game. After I was done with the push-ups, I was sweaty and happy, even though, I could only do 50. I decided to shave first because I'd grown a beard over the past few days of me not taking any care of myself. After I was ready, I stopped and closed my eyes. Since I had very little sleep in the past five days, I wasn't myself. I was worried to be in public. Did I look normal or off?

I still felt like my subconscious and conscious minds were fused together. I still could not think but just acted upon and reacted to my environment. The words would just come out from my mouth. I did not have to think at all.

I was at the lobby at 6:45 AM, Premal showed up at exactly 7 AM. He had no luggage. I would be flying alone.

"Good morning, champ. How are you?" I greeted him.

"Not bad. Ready to head back home?" Premal asked.

"I am really worried about my Dad." I uttered sadly.

"Yeah, man. When I heard the news last night, I knew we had to get you back."

"Was Scott okay with everything?" I inquired.

"Yes. Apparently, someone from your family contacted him. He immediately switched your flights."

"I'm glad he did."

"So, let me help you with your bags." Premal took one of my suitcases, and I took the other one placing my computer bag on top.

"Thank you, Premal." I whispered as we rolled the suitcases towards the exit. As we walked through the lobby, I saw the employees who worked there. As I passed each one, I bowed my head and thanked them.

When we came outside, I saw the black Mercedes waiting for us.

"Wow, a Benz in India for me." I exclaimed with a surprise.

"Yes, man, you are getting the royal treatment here."

I thanked the two valets and we got into the car.

While we were heading to the airport, I was looking through the window. It was the last time I saw that city. I had no doubts about that. The city had a rural charm, and the scent of jasmine was intoxicating. I knew, every time I smelled jasmine; I would remember India.

As we arrived at the airport, I noticed how busy it was. Hundreds of people were running around, catching flights, landing in Chennai. The usual business of airports. It felt chaotic after the tranquility of the taxi. Once I stepped out of the car, I was lost and confused. I could not read the signs since they were all in Hindi or other Indian languages. There were no English signs anywhere. Premal tapped my shoulder and guided me to the curbside check in. Once again, I tried not to focus on all the people around me. I was still not thinking but simply reacting. People pushed me accidentally, and I just moved with the motion.

"You are all set." I heard Premal's voice. "I have checked you in to your flight. You have two hours to hang out. Your gate is G5."

"Thank you, Premal." I mumbled.

The only thing I comprehended was my gate number. I would have to figure out how to get there. Apparently, Premal had to head back to the hotel.

"One more thing, Sebastian. Just remember to keep moving. You got it?"

"Yes." I nodded. "Thank you again, my friend."

"Take care of yourself and good luck."

I took my passport and the required travel documents, placed them in my shirt pocket and grabbed my luggage. It was a bit challenging to wheel the two suitcases, but I'd done that before. As I walked up the ramp to the inside of the airport, I started noticing the armed guards with the dogs. Their assault rifles were openly displayed, and they were dressed in full military gear. I knew I had to hold my composure. That was a high security area, full of cameras. I didn't want the cameras to have any effect on me. I was still uneasy after the hotel room experience with the cameras.

As I roamed through the airport, I felt overwhelmed. I could not find concourse G. Then all of a sudden, I saw a man that looked European. He was dressed in a business suit and was talking to one of the local people. He must be familiar with the airport. I walked up to him,

"Sir, do you speak English?"

"Yes, of course. I am from Germany."

"Are you on the flight to Frankfurt?"

"Yes. Do you need help?" He asked with a smile.

"Yes, I am lost. I can't read the signs, and I need to go to concourse G." I explained.

"Don't worry, my friend. We are on the same flight. Follow me, and I will take you there."

I was so relieved! I had a guide. Without him, I would have never made it to my gate. Once there, I thanked the man and took a seat.

I was so tired from the lack of sleep, my mind started playing tricks on me. Even if I wanted to think, I wouldn't have been able to. My brain wasn't working correctly. I lost the sense of time. I needed help. I did not know when to board the flight because they were not speaking English. I sat frozen in my seat and watched my bags. As people started boarding, I watched them but couldn't move.

Then, all of a sudden, Premal jumped in front of me.

"Let's go, man! You got to go, if not, you are going to miss your flight."

He grabbed me by the color and lifted me up. Until then, I thought I was hallucinating.

"Come on, let's go!" I followed him without even asking how he was there. He left me before the security check and said he was returning back to the hotel. I was lost.

We approached the Lufthansa crew, and they checked my boarding pass.

"I am coming with you, Sebastian." I heard Premal's voice.

"What?" I was confused. "Why would Accent pay for Premal to fly with me all the way to Frankfurt, Germany? I could not figure that out, but I held on tightly to my computer bag.

Perhaps, I was right about having sensitive documents, and Accent being concerned about my intentions.

As we approached the airplane, I noticed it was the same 747, but this time, we had seats in first class; on the upper deck.

"Man, could you fucking believe that? First class tickets. We are getting the fuck out of here." Premal was excited.

"What did he mean by that? I thought. "Would he also be going home to his family?" I was already confused before, but after Premal joined me on that flight, I was completely lost.

Once I approached my seat, I placed all my bags in the space above. I took out my headphones and my new book and sat down. I knew that would be a long trip and since it was a day flight, there was little to no chance of me sleeping. I would have to occupy myself with music and reading. Premal sat next to me. He seemed excited and full of energy.

"Are you also going back home?" I asked suspiciously.

"No, I talked to Scott, and he was concerned about you, and he advised me to try and book a seat on the same flight. It all happened so fast. I was walking out of the airport, back to the car when he called. He told me to go with you. I rushed back to the counter and purchased a ticket for this flight." He explained.

"Wow, I can't believe Accent would go out of their way, to make sure I get home ok." I didn't buy Premal's explanation. "Premal, you know this is a 12-hour flight, right?"

"Yeah, man. I don't give a shit. Just to be able to miss a day in the delivery center works fine for me." He smiled.

"Ladies and gentlemen, this is Erick Grossmann, the chief flight attendant. On behalf of Captain Schmidt and the entire crew, we would like to welcome you onboard Lufthansa flight 1841, nonstop service from Chennai, India to Frankfurt, Germany. Our flight time will be 11 hours and 32 minutes. We will be flying at an altitude of 36,000 feet at a ground speed of 525 miles per hour. At this time, make sure your seat backs and tray tables are in their full upright positions, and your seat belts are properly fastened. In addition, all portable electronic devices must be set to the 'airplane mode' until further notice. Thank you and enjoy your flight." We heard the voice from the loudspeaker.

I was not in the mood to talk. I just wanted to meditate and relax because the sleep deprivation was definitely getting to me. I just sat there watching the monitor, showing our current location and the north western trajectory all the way up to Germany. I knew it would be a difficult flight because my body was not holding up too well. My brain was fried, but Premal's words were tattooed in my mind. He told me to keep moving. Therefore, as the flight took off, I slowly moved my legs and arms. I tried to be in constant motion. At that point, I didn't trust anyone. I couldn't comprehend why he was on the flight. There was no way Accent would spend funds on two first class tickets for no reason. There had to be something behind Premal's sitting next to me. Were we meeting someone in Frankfurt? Did Accent have something planned out for me? Was this some sort of a weird stamina test to check if I could handle the stress of the job?

I kept overthinking and whipping myself into frenzy while Premal sat upright and was calmly reading the newspaper. If Accent was so concerned about my health, then why didn't Premal mention anything about my reactions or actions? He just proceeded like everything was normal, and we were on a mini vacation. For some reason, I started freaking out about why every Indian I met in Chennai had an English name. A nickname. I started to wonder if Premal was his real name. For some reason, he has been by my side since the beginning. Going back to Toronto, he was the only one I trusted. He was the only one I befriended. We bonded in India; both at work and on the weekends. Was he tasked with shadowing me throughout the project? Once again, the adrenaline started pumping. I was extremely focused on the present moment. Every time he crossed his legs, I crossed my legs to keep the practice of moving.

About halfway through the flight, I noticed Premal fell asleep. It's been over 5 days since I last slept, and my eyes were burning. I felt like my body was going to collapse, and I was going to lose consciousness. I got scared. For some odd reason, I thought that maybe if I let myself fall asleep, I would never wake up. Even though this was a farfetched idea, I believed it could happen. And once you truly believe in something the result is usually true. I made it a mission not to fall asleep and keep moving. I would cross and uncross my legs, move my arms, and lift my torso up occasionally. Since my backrest was lower than Premal's, I kept my left arm behind his seat. Every time I started falling asleep, I would slap the back of his seat.

"What the fuck, man? Why do you keep on hitting the back of my seat?" He yelled out.

"I'm sorry, Premal, but I can't fall asleep. I keep trying to wake myself up." I replied honestly.

"What is wrong with you?" He was annoyed.

"I haven't slept in many days, and I'm worried if I fall asleep, I will lose consciousness."

"That is ridiculous, Sebastian. You need to sleep. Take advantage of the flight and sleep." Premal said in a calmer tone.

I took his advice, at least I made it appear that I fell asleep. I closed my eyes but continued wiggling my feet. He quickly fell back asleep as most people around us have. At that point, the humming noise of the aircraft was getting on my nerves. I grabbed my Bose headphones and turned on the noise cancellation feature. In a matter of seconds, all the noise vanished. For the next two hours, I meditated and felt like my body and mind were recovering from exhaustion.

Then, all of a sudden, I had an involuntary reaction, and my arm smacked the back of Premal's seat again. He woke up very upset.

"What the fuck is going on??? You keep hitting my seat while I am sleeping. Do you not want me for to sleep on this flight? Just because you can't sleep, don't fuck up my flight."

We've been in the air for 8 hours, and we still had another 4 to go. Premal was irritated about not getting his rest while I was getting used to being constantly awake. At that point, I could handle the handicap of not being fully rested. I did not need my whole brain to function. I felt as if another intelligence has taken control over me and was guiding me from the inside.

Premal raised his seat back and looked very unhappy.

"What are you thinking, Sebastian?" He uttered angrily. "You know, we seemed to get along very well, but I have questions about your intentions. I am here to get you to Frankfurt and to your connecting flight to Miami."

"Wow, you're also going to take the leg to Miami?" I asked sarcastically. "What are you some type of a hero?"

"No, Sebastian. We all got very concerned about you?" He replied calmly.

"Is Premal your real name? I mean everyone in India changes their names to something that is easier to pronounce."

"Sebastian, you know my name. Let's not play this game."

"Actually, I would love to continue this 'so-called game' with you. What made you all so concerned about me?" I asked.

"For once, those headphones." He grabbed and lifted them up as evidence of my madness. "You used them every night at the delivery center." Premal noted.

"And what is wrong with listening to my favorite playlists?" I couldn't understand his point.

"It just didn't look right. It seemed as if you wanted to isolate yourself."

"Not at all. I just liked relaxing and listening to my music. I socialized plenty with my team during the work hours and also during dinner. But when I was alone at my desk, I would turn them on."

"Oh really, then what can you tell me about this?" He stood up and opened the overhead cabin space and took something out of his bag. What the fuck is this, Sebastian?"

To my astonishment, he was holding my waist belt which I used after the surgery. I remembered throwing it away into the bathroom garbage can of my original room. How the hell did he get it? And what was so shocking about it? He acted like he found an explosive in my hotel room. Perhaps, I was right about the surveillance? He had to go into my old room to find the belt. Premal couldn't be trusted.

"How did you get that?" I was pissed off.

"It doesn't matter how I got it." He replied.

"What is your real name? Who are you?" He paused and did not answer. I started thinking quickly, and the name Manesh appeared in my mind. He was the so-called Indian partner that was on our T-30 and T-5 calls, but even then, I didn't see him, I only heard his voice. I've never seen Manesh at the delivery center. In fact, I didn't see any partners at the center. Perhaps, they felt it was too dangerous to be there, since it was a third world country. Just the amount of the required vaccinations alone, would make anyone concerned, even scared. I had a feeling that Premal was Manesh. I was going to find out the truth.

"I don't believe your name is Premal." I stated after we stayed silent for a while.

"Oh really. That's what you think, Seba?" He grinned and turned his head to me. I nodded without replying. That was exactly what I believed.

"Well, you are right. My name is not Premal. My name is Manesh. I've been tasked to watch you since the project started. What you did in a matter of weeks; couldn't been done in months. You took over the project that was in shambles, and you fixed it in no time and apparently, without too much effort as well. The partnership was impressed and wanted to keep a close eye on you. We wanted to see how you would react to finding those documents at your workstation." He explained quietly.

"That was a test." I said that to myself rather than to Premal... Manesh.

"Yes, we needed to see how you would handle those reports. Did you bring them?"

"Of course, I did. It was one of the reasons I left."

"Sit back, Sebastian. We will be landing in Frankfurt soon. Everything you need to know will be explained when we arrive there."

I lowered my seat and closed my eyes. I felt uneasy sitting next to him. I wasn't sure if I believed his story. I just could not figure out many things that were happening over the last week. Perhaps, I was not losing my mind. Maybe that all was just a part of some fucked up test by Accent.

Chapter 12

My scenario analysis was interrupted by the voice of the captain, "Good evening, ladies and gentlemen. We are about to start our decent into Frankfurt, Germany. The local time is 9 PM. Please, straighten up your seats and fasten your seatbelts. I would ask our cabin crew to prepare for landing."

I was excited about landing in Germany. It was a familiar environment with the airport signs in English. I didn't need anyone's help anymore. I was no longer lost.

Once we landed, I stood up and grabbed my belongings from the overhead cabin. Premal/Manesh did the same and we exited the plane. As soon as I took a few steps into the concourse, I had vivid memories of my first visit to that very same airport two weeks ago. Apparently, Manesh did not connect in Frankfurt. He was a bit lost.

"Manesh, are you okay?" I inquired.

"Yes, but since I barely slept on the plane, I am extremely exhausted."

"Try being awake for 5 days." I laughed.

"Let's find a place to sit down. I want to make a phone call. I think I have a reception now." Manesh said.

As we walked through the main passage of the concourse, I saw a familiar café.

"Let's take a seat here. I need a cigarette." He suggested to my utter shock. Premal never smoked around me.

"Manesh, you can't smoke here." I objected.

"Sure, I can. This is Europe. Everyone smokes here."

I recalled that the only place where I saw people smoking was the McDonalds upstairs. One of the waiters came by and told Manesh the café was a non-smoking area. He was pissed off and agitated. He needed to get his fix and was in terrible shape after the flight. I've grown accustomed to the lack of sleep. It was amazing how far the human body could be pushed.

Since Manesh couldn't smoke at the café, he was very agitated.

"Where the fuck can I smoke?" He growled.

"I told you, upstairs, at the McDonalds." I replied patiently.

"Let's go there then." He said impatiently.

Manesh appeared to be on the brink of a breakdown. As soon as we made it to the second floor; we noticed all the people smoking there. He immediately took out his cigarette and the lighter.

"Oh man, I really needed this cigarette. This trip has been a nightmare." He stated exhaling with satisfaction.

"And you thought you were having a vacation." I said sarcastically.

"Didn't turn out that way." He replied and took out his phone.

"Who are you calling?" I asked suspiciously.

"I am calling your mother."

"What? Why would you be calling my mother?" I was stunned.

"To tell her we landed in Frankfurt."

"You are full of shit. I bet you are calling Scott. This is all a part of your fucked-up test. You can tell Scott that I am just fine. I passed."

He looked at me and put away his phone.

"Don't worry, Sebastian. Everything has been taken care of. Shortly, they will be here."

"Who will be here???" I yelled out startling some people around us.

At that very second, I saw two airport security guards approaching us.

"Please go with them, Seba. They will tell you everything you need to know. Like I said before, everything has been taken care." The agents surrounded me without saying a word. I was completely lost. I couldn't understand what was happening.

They accompanied me downstairs to what appeared to be a security office. Then they opened the door to a back room. There was a hospital bed there. The woman came literally out of nowhere and addressed me in perfect English with a German accent.

"Please have a seat or lay down. Make yourself comfortable." She said. After I did just that, she extended her hand and gave me two pills with a glass of water.

"They will help you sleep." She explained.

I knew I wouldn't be able to sleep because I'd convinced myself that if I fell asleep, I might not wake up. But, nevertheless, I took the pills.

"Relax, sir. If you don't, the medication might not work." She whispered.

"Who do you work for? Do you work for Accent? Is this all part of the test? Did I make it to partner?" I asked every question crossing my mind. But the woman ignored me and walked away.

About 45 minutes later, she reappeared and checked on my status. I was still wide awake. Those pills did nothing for me. I would need a tranquilizer to knock me out.

"Okay, sir. Please get back in bed." She ordered.

At that moment, a man in uniform joined her in the room. Together, they lifted the top of the bed, and as on cue, the back door opened, and I saw the ambulance waiting outside. The two paramedics from the ambulance came out and helped put me inside the vehicle. I had no clue what was happening. They closed the doors, with one of the paramedics remaining by my side. Then, for a long while, there was no action. I just laid there while the paramedic ignored me.

"Excuse me, but what is going on? Why am I being held here?" I asked the paramedic. He looked at me and said nothing.

All of a sudden, I heard the sirens turning on, and the ambulance started moving. I did not know where I was going but I assumed the hospital. They probably did not have a tranquilizer at the airport to knock me out. So, off we went. I could not see much except through the two small windows. It was an overcast and rainy day. I've never been to Frankfurt. Everything appeared new to me. What bothered me the most, was the thought that I was going to miss my connecting flight. I also had no idea where Manesh went. I was still very confused about the whole story, and that made me very angry. If that was some kind of a test, at that point, I was literally sick of it.

When the ambulance finally slowed down and then stopped, I knew we'd arrived somewhere. The doors opened, my paramedic got up and the other one joined him in wheeling me out of the vehicle. I kept asking them were they were taking me, but they just ignored me. As I was wheeled through a long hallway, I felt exasperated. I was afraid to scream. I knew they would lock me up at the mental ward. The adrenaline was racing through my veins, so I was no longer tired. I was alert and ready for anything. They helped me out of the bed and sat me into the wheelchair. Then, the paramedics turned the lights on in one of the rooms and told me to wait for the doctor. With that, they left.

As I sat waiting, I scanned the room. It was small and clean, and smelled of bleach, like most hospitals. There were no windows. There was just a round table with two chairs. Perhaps, the security agents brought me there for an interview. Maybe they wanted to verify my mental stability. I was just hoping the doctor would come soon and give me something for me to pass out. I was worn out.

I didn't know how much time passed, but finally, I heard the steps behind the door. Then it opened, and a tall man and a woman walked into the room. The woman was in her mid to late thirties. She had short brown hair. The man was in his fifties, gray-haired and heavy set.

"Good evening. My name is Dr. Shmitz and this is Dr. Zimmerman." The man introduced himself and his female colleague. "We understand you had a long flight from India and some problems falling asleep."

"Yes doctor. I have been under severe stress from my job and from being in an uncomfortable environment." I replied absent-mindedly.

"What do you mean by the uncomfortable environment?" The female doctor asked.

"Well, my hotel room was filled with technology. There was a command center next to my bed which controlled the lights, the TV, and the telephone. This might sound crazy, but I noticed two cameras inside the air conditioning vents." I explained.

"How did you know those were cameras?" He asked.

"I could see the mechanics and the shiny lenses. They reflected the light."

"Are you sure?" The doctors exchanged concerned glances.

"I did my best to analyze them. I'm telling you I am not crazy. I saw the lenses." I stated.

"Do you know what day it is?" The female doctor asked.

"I think it's either Sunday night or Monday night. I just remember seeing the Wimbledon finals on the TV. It was yesterday. So, it's Monday."

She wrote something down in her notepad.

"And what month and year is it?" She continued.

"We are in July, and it's 2005." I replied.

"Okay, Mr. Kosta. Now, I need to test your memory. Can you please listen to the sequence of numbers and repeat them back to me?"

I had no idea why she was asking those questions.

"9-2-7-5-1, please repeat that."

"9-2-7-5-1." I repeated.

"Very well. Now, 3-7-2-6-9-4-1."

"Okay, 3-7-2-6... I can't remember the rest." I was annoyed. "I haven't slept in days. I'm exhausted. I really need to sleep. Can you please give me something to knock me out?" I begged.

"Sir, we have to conduct this interview and then proceed with a few exams." The doctor said.

Their interview was picking at my brain, and I wasn't up to speed. All I needed was some sleep. My body has lost its ability to shut itself down. I needed heavy medication to pass out and relax. I was at the hospital, so I knew it was only a matter of time before I was given what I needed. Then I could rest and take my flight back home.

Dr. Shmitz interrupted my racing thoughts. "You've mentioned you were under a lot of stress at work."

"Yes." I nodded.

"What happened?" He inquired.

"To make a long story short, I had an argument with a coworker and then, I found some corporate documents that showed really poor performance from not only my team but the entire project itself. The status report was in red. We were at risk of defaulting on the terms of our service levels agreement. To top that off, we were running behind schedule."

"Did you keep those reports?" The female doctor asked.

"Of course! If not, people would think I was crazy." I explicated.

"And what happened after?"

I told the doctors my entire story of running from the security guards, being locked up in my hotel room, and the rest.

"But why didn't you sleep for so many nights?" The female doctor asked after listening attentively.

"I got scared. I was in a foreign country where I did not know anyone that I could trust. I didn't speak the language, so it made it even harder. It might sound odd but, I believed if I let myself fall asleep, I would not wake up. I know this all sounds strange, but it really did happen. Anyone who's been sleep deprived for so many days, would most likely react in the same way. Don't you agree?" I asked with desperation.

"This is not a therapy session. We are here to examine your physical and mental states. Shortly, the nurse will come to take you for more exams." Doctor Zimmerman noted.

"But can't you just give me something to knock me out?" I felt I would start crying at any moment. "That's all I need. I will be much better after I get rest. I know myself. Please help me."

They didn't respond to me, just exchanged glances, turned around and left the room. I had no idea where my belongings were, and I did not have my phone. I wanted to reach out and call someone for help, but I couldn't. The adrenaline kept pumping through my veins, and all the talk was getting me even more upset. I needed to sleep, and after that, fly back home.

After about 10 minutes, a nurse came by and took me to an examination room. It was late and the hospital was very quiet. I did not see other patients or visitors. I had no idea what section of the hospital I was in. I got up from the wheelchair and sat in a long upright chair with the computer equipment all around me. What types of exams were they planning on giving me?

"Mr. Kosta, we are going to scan your brain. I need to place these electronic leads all over your head. Don't worry, you will not feel the current." The nurse announced softly.

"Are you going to electrify me??? This could not be happening!" I was instantly agitated.

"Please relax, sir, or I will need to call the staff to restrain you even further." She tried to calm me down.

I was already restrained; both my arms and legs were strapped. But I needed to resist. I had to protect myself. I didn't even know the name of the hospital or where in Frankfurt I was. She pressed the call button and called for the security. In a moment, two men appeared, and one held my feet and the other, my arms. The nurse opened my mouth and placed some sort of a device in it. She then turned to the computer and told me to relax. She promised the exam would be over soon.

Indeed, five minutes later, the exam was over. I did not feel any pain. She removed the leads from my head and mentioned I would be heading to my room to relax.

"There is one more thing I need to do. Gentlemen, please hold him." Again, I tensed my body and tried to escape. She pulled out a very large needle. They held my right arm in place while she administered the shot. Immediately, my mouth went dry, and my yelling was subdued. Next, I just collapsed on the chair.

When I opened my eyes, I was in bed. The other bed, next to me, was vacant. I inhaled and exhaled. I felt very well rested. I wanted to sit up, but my body wouldn't listen to me. They must have given me the tranquilizer. I needed to speak to someone. I needed to get out of there. I slept through the whole night, and I was ready to go home. All of a sudden, a nurse showed up in my room.

"Oh, you are awake. I was wondering when you were going to wake up. You slept for over two days." She told me.

I was in shock! How the heck did I sleep for that long??? I tried to say something, but I could only make mumbling sounds.

"Mr.Kosta, you are now under our care. You have been heavily sedated. It might be difficult to talk right now, but it will get better." She promised.

All I could do was talk to myself. "What the fuck did they give me?" I was thinking. "Where am I?"

After I felt better and stronger, I walked out of my room and looked down the hallway. The nurse noticed me.

"Hi. Oh, you want to look around, Mr. Kosta? Please, follow me. I will give you the tour."

The first room to the right had a group of men and women. They were all adults, from their late twenties and into the seventies. They did not look normal. They were playing like a group of children.

"You will get to play here, just like the rest of them." The nurse told me. "We have many interesting things to do. We have classes to color, draw, build puzzles and even music. They love music."

Even though, I could not speak, I finally understood where I was. For some fucked up reason, they decided to put me in a mental ward. How could they? I mean, I was a top executive at the top management consulting firm. I made deep into the six figures. I was worth a few millions of dollars. That could not be happening to me. As was the case in India, I would have to figure out the plan to get off those meds and get on the flight back to Miami. I could not panic; I needed to understand my surroundings and the people there. She took me back to my room and told me to rest.

"Whenever you feel stronger, take a walk down the hallway. It's good to get out. And don't worry, your speech will get better with time." She assured me.

As I got back in bed, I noticed the windows were covered shut. I couldn't see the outside. I felt like a caged dog with a muzzle on. I could not speak, but I could think. And since I slept for over 2 days, my mind was feeling much better.

A few hours later, it was lunch time. I was helped out of the bed and accompanied to the dining room. I didn't understand what they were saying since the people there were locals from Frankfurt. I wasn't sure if anyone spoke English. I saw an old man playing with a tennis ball. He chased it around the room like a dog. Then, there was a middle-aged woman, who appeared overly happy. She must have been on really good medications. She sang and laughed non-stop. Then I noticed a woman in her twenties. She was the only one that looked normal. She was pretty. She was slim and had short brown hair. She watched the people in the room just like I did. I got in line behind her and muffled "hello". She understood me and said "hi". I placed my hand on my heart and slurred "Seba". She again understood and told me her name was Minna. I was happy I met someone who seemed normal. Perhaps, she could help me.

We were given some mac and cheese with vegetables. They also gave us carbonated water. As soon as they poured the water, Minna covered my water with her hand.

"Don't drink that. It will make the medication stronger. You have to put the bottles next to your window, so that the warmth can take out the bubbles." She whispered.

I nodded looking gratefully into her eyes.

"The first day is the worst, tomorrow you will be better and able to speak." She encouraged me.

At the end of our lunch, the nurse called each one of our names. It was time to take our medication. As much as I did not want to take any more meds, the nurse would make us open our mouths and then show our tongues once we had swallowed the pills. I knew if I resisted, security would get called, and it would get worse for me. I tried to follow all the rules.

Up next was a group activity. We were given coloring books and crayons. It was very relaxing. Made me focus and gather my thoughts. I did not use my brain to complete that exercise. Then, the nurse came by my desk, "Very good, Mr. Kosta. I think you're ready for something more challenging."

She handed me a crossword puzzle. That required thinking and concentration. I couldn't do that easily. I thought it was because of the medication. Next, she gave me block puzzles which were used in Montessori schools. They required a higher level of thought process. As much as I tried, I could not accomplish the task.

"Relax, it's your first day. Don't try to do too much. The drugs won't allow you to do it. As you get better, they will lower the dosage of your medications." Minna told me gently.

I put the blocks down and just placed my head on the table. Minna put her hand on top of my head. I couldn't believe that even in that crazy place, I found compassion.

I got up and went back to my room. I was no longer wired or agitated. I was at peace. I knew with time I would get out. For the rest of the day, I took cat naps. I couldn't believe I got a good sleep. Just that alone made me very happy. Periodically, I was awakened to take the medication. I would take the pills and go back to bed.

Chapter 13

The next morning, I woke up feeling even better than on the first day. My thinking was still slow, but it was better. The nurse came into my room and told me I had visitors. I was eager to see who was there. All of a sudden, I saw my mom walk into the room. I jumped up and gave her a bear hug. While still hugging her, I looked up. I couldn't believe my eyes. But my Dad stood right behind her.

"Oh my God! Dad! I thought you were at the hospital?" I exclaimed through tears.

"He wasn't, baby. I am sorry we had to make up that story. It was the only way to get you out of India, away from your job and get you real help." My Mom explained apologetically.

My speech was much better, but the words were still slurred.

"So, you are telling me that you made it all up?" I couldn't believe my ears.

"Unfortunately, yes, my son. We had too. It was the only way you would have left."

"Wow!" That was all I could say.

"You are safe now, son. You are with your family. We are going to get you out of here." Dad said and hugged me.

The nurse walked in again. That time, she was accompanied by Dr. Schmitz.

"Hello, Mr. and Mrs. Kosta. I am Sebastian's doctor. I know you came here to take him back to the US. But before we discharge him, we will need the name of the psychiatrist in Miami to sign the release documentations and the transfer form." He pointed out.

"But doctor, what does he have? We were never informed about his condition. They just told us where he was." My Dad sounded very concerned.

"I understand. Well, after careful investigation and examination, we have determined that your son suffers from bipolar disorder. This is a mental health illness which he will have to deal with for the rest of his life." The doctor pronounced the horrific diagnosis.

"You must be wrong." My Dad objected passionately. "He has an incredible mind. He graduated with an MBA, on top of his class. He's been working as a senior executive for almost ten years. He has no history of mental illness. This can't be true."

"I'm sorry, sir, but from my professional opinion, Sebastian has experienced psychosis. He's been under our care and observation for the past 4 days. You can get a second opinion, but I recommend he remains on the medications until he meets with a psychiatrist in Miami. We also recommend that he stays in our care for the next two days. We are worried about his flight back to Miami."

"So, I can't leave today?" I was horrified.

"It's okay, son. Only two more days. We will visit you every day, until we get you out." My Mom comforted me. The doctor and the nurse left the room.

"Mom, Dad, they are wrong. They have no clue. There is no way I am bipolar. Bipolar people are crazy, and I am not crazy." I stated passionately. Even my speech sounded nearly perfect.

"Don't worry, son. We will call our friends in Miami. We will get you the best doctors. We will get a second opinion." Mom assured me.

I looked at the blacked-out window, "It drives me insane that I have been here for 4 days, and I can't see the sun or the sky. I want to breathe the air, see the trees, and feel the wind on my face. I am locked up here. I can't even drink water." I stated with exasperation.

"Why can't you drink water?" My Mom came up to the window ledge and looked at the bottles I kept there. "Aren't they going to get hot there." She asked. Even though, the window was shut, the glass and the seal were still heating up from the outside.

"I met this woman and she told me the sparkling water was bad for the medications. And if I put it on the ledge, the heat would remove the bubbles."

"And who is this woman, Seba?" Dad inquired. My parents were very confused.

"She is a friend. She helped me here. I will introduce you to her." I promised.

I stood up and we all walked out of the room. Suddenly, I saw a big, tall, muscular man. He looked angry and disturbed. He kept grabbing his head and punching his chest. He looked like a military veteran. Perhaps, he suffered from PTSD. As we tried walking quietly by him, he groaned and grabbed me by the shoulder. He then pushed me against the wall.

"We have to kill them. We have to kill them all. Do you understand that, soldier?" He was shaking me violently.

I nodded and said, "Yes, I understand."

"Good. Now follow me like a good soldier."

My poor parents appeared speechless and unable to help, but thankfully, Minna came running out of nowhere and separated the soldier from me.

"Don't worry, Akbar means no harm. He's seen a lot on the battlefield as a soldier." She explained.

"Hello, my name is Minna." She smiled at my still-stunned parents and extended her hand for the handshakes.

"Mom, Dad, this is the woman I told you about." I chimed in.

"It's a pleasure to meet you, Minna. Thank you for helping our son." My Dad smiled at the young woman.

"He doesn't belong here with us. You need to take him home." She stated categorically.

"Yes, we are trying to get him out, but we are waiting for some paperwork."

"Well, it was a pleasure meeting you both. Seba, I will see you at lunch." Minna nodded and walked away.

"Okay, Minna. I will see you then." I smiled.

"Sweet girl." My Dad noted.

"She seems really nice. I wonder why she is in here." Mom wondered.

"I don't know, Mom." I sighted.

We went back to the room. My parents stayed for a while. It was great to finally see them, most importantly, seeing my Dad in good health. I was glad they found me.

"By the way, who told you I was here?" I was curious.

"Oh honey, it was your coworker. What was his name. I believe he said it was Premal." Mom informed me.

"Dad, do you think you can ask the ward if we can go outside?" I asked hopefully.

"Yes, son. I will ask. I will be right back."

A few minutes later, he came back with the nurse. She let us come out for a little bit. I was thrilled. She recommended to stay out of the direct sunlight. My Dad took off his baseball cap and placed it on my head.

"Let's go, son. Let's walk outside." He said.

As soon as I saw the sky above, I started shaking, and my throat got tight.

"Son don't worry. We are here with you. Let those tears come out." Dad hugged me tightly, and I cried like a little kid.

I've gone through hell that week. I've almost lost my mind. But as I was walking slowly in the garden, accompanied by my parents, I felt much better. I looked up trying to find my window, then I looked around. There was a narrow stream across the lawn. I came up to it, to touch the water. If felt very cold on my fingertips, but that sensation made me feel alive. I was so happy that there was a future ahead of me. I wasn't quite sure if I would remain with Accent or management consulting in general. I liked the money, but I wasn't very passionate about the job. What I really wanted to do was to live and be happy and at peace with myself.

As we continued our walk, we saw a family of ducks. They were beautiful, and they all followed the mother duck in a single line. It was incredible to observe the nature around us and those wonderful ducks. It felt great to be free. I held my mother's hand, and that gave me a warm feeling inside. I was safe. I just needed to live through two more days at the ward. Then, I would have my freedom. Freedom to go home.

When we returned to my room, I told my parents I wanted to rest. They kissed me and said they would be back the next day. We could do our walk again. I hugged them, and they left. It was time for lunch. After lunch, I took a nice relaxing nap. As the day progressed, my speech got much better. I could communicate now. I sat down next to Minna, and she placed her hand over mine.

"I am happy for you. You parents are here. Soon, you will be going back home." She said tenderly.

"And what about you, Minna? You seem fine. When are you leaving?" I asked in the same tender voice.

"Not for a long time." She replied sadly.

"How long have you been here?"

"I have been here for 9 months."

"Why so long?" I was stunned. I couldn't imagine being there for almost a year.

"I am scared to go back to my husband." She answered fearfully.

"Did he do something to you?"

"No, I love my husband, and I'm grateful to him for taking care of our two daughters."

"Then why, Minna? Why did you say you were scared to return to him?" I wasn't following. But at that very moment, she started crying.

"Why are you crying?" I took her hand in mine.

"Because I feel guilty." She replied through tears.

"Guilty of what?"

"Of not loving my baby girl." I was so lost. I just stared at her. "You see, when I gave birth to Valentina, I felt no love for her. I did not have the maternal connection with my baby. I didn't even want to take care of her." She explained.

"And how do you feel now?"

"I feel better. They come to visit me on the weekends. I think, I'm falling in love with her."

"It must be hard to see them go."

"Yes, I just feel guilty all the time. Guilty before my husband. Guilty before my children. For not being there for them." She continued.

"You need to get out of here, Minna." I told her resolutely. "They need you. I will leave shortly, and you need to leave too. This is not the place for us."

We finished our lunch, and as usual, they called our names to give out the medications. Afterwards, I returned to my room and took more cat naps. Even though, I was still at the ward, I had hope for the future. I didn't know what would happen, but I was only 32 years old, and I had my whole life ahead of me. I still planned on getting married and having kids of my own. I always wanted to be that cool Dad my child could come with any issue or question. To be there to pick them up from school. To go to their plays. To see them playing sports. Life would make a full circle, and from a millionaire ambitious playboy, I wanted to become a great parent who would guide his son or daughter in discovering their purpose and help them achieve their goals. Wasn't that the calling of any good parent?

Chapter 14

The next day, I woke up and was pleasantly surprised by seeing my parents in the room.

"We missed you so much that we decided to meet you here for breakfast." Mom beamed and kissed me.

"It's great to see you both first thing in the morning." I smiled back.

"We've taken care of everything already." My Dad was always all-business. "We've got you a great doctor in Miami. His name is Dr. Valderama. He is highly respected and regarded as one of the top psychiatrists in the country. One of our friends is his patient and says, he is fantastic. We also, have other great news!"

"What Dad?"

"I spoke to our attorney, and he informed us, the hospital cannot hold you here if we sign a release form. I already spoke with Dr. Shmitz, and you are coming home today!"

"I don't believe it. That is truly great news. I can't wait to get back home." I was ready to cry.

"Well, let's pack your bags and get out of here. Where is your luggage?" Mom asked.

"I have no idea." I admitted. "It was on the plane, but I never made it to baggage claim."

"Let me check with the nurse." Dad got up and walked out of the room.

While I was waiting with my mom, someone knocked on the door. It was Minna.

"Hi." She greeted us. "I've just run into your Dad. You are leaving today! How amazing!"

"Yes, apparently I can leave without spending an extra day here." I replied happily.

"That's great to hear, Sebastian. I am really happy for you. Go home and find yourself. Dig deep and find out why you were put on this Earth. We all have a purpose here. Obviously, whatever you were doing before, was not the right thing." My Mom smiled at Minna and then looked at me.

"Thank you for your sweet wishes." I told Minna. "I also hope you see your family soon. They need you. And thank you for being my friend."

"Bye, Sebastian." Minna came up and kissed me on the cheek. She then said goodbye to my Mom and left the room.

"Great news! They have your bags." My Dad thundered happily five seconds after Minna left.

"Oh, thank God." I breathed out. And as on cue, two orderlies walked in wheeling my luggage. I immediately grabbed my computer bag. It was untouched.

"What do you have there, son?" My father saw how quickly I jumped to check my computer bag.

"Dad, here is the proof, I wasn't going crazy. These are all the documents someone left on my desk. They show the unfair pay structures and how the delivery center was in the red for the most of their status reports." I explained.

Chapter 15

By the rules of the hospital, I had to leave in a wheelchair. So, my Dad pushed me all the way to the entrance. There was a minivan waiting to take us to the airport.

"Let's go home now!" My Dad exclaimed and we started driving out of the hospital grounds.

We didn't talk much during our ride. I was still under the influence of yesterday's medications. My Mom had the list of everything I was given during my stay at the ward. Apparently, I was on two medications: Lithium, 600 mg once a day, and Risperdal, 4 mg, four times a day. I thought Lithium was a form of salt, and the other crap made me stop thinking. I couldn't analyze anything with that Risperdal.

Once we arrived at the airport, we returned the minivan and checked in. Our flight was scheduled for 8 PM. But it was only 11 AM. My Dad wanted to check if we could get on the earlier flight. The Lufthansa representative was very accommodating and switched us to the 2 PM flight. We were thrilled. It was obvious, we were anxious to leave Frankfurt. It was not a good experience for any of us. We walked to the gate and sat down. My mother went to get some sandwiches for lunch. It was also the time for my medication. She brought me a bottle water, and I took my pills. It felt great to eat a ham and cheese sandwich. I was on tuna and bananas for far too long. I didn't think, I'd ever eat a tuna sandwich again.

At approximately 1:30 PM, the first-class passengers started boarding. My Dad wanted for me to be very comfortable, thus, he purchased first-class tickets for our flight to the US. We boarded, and I sat in the middle between my parents. I finally felt safe. I was going home. I was with my family. I could breathe normally again. The storm passed; I've survived it. I felt drowsy and wanted to sleep, but before that, I wanted to listen to one song by Coldplay. It was called Fix You. I put my headphones on and pressed play. The music enveloped me, and the words started entering my mind:

When you try your best and you don't succeed,
When you get what you want, but not what you need
When you feel so tired, but you can't sleep,
Stuck in reverse.
When the tears come streaming down your face,
'Cause you lose something you can't replace,
When you love someone, but it goes to waste
Could it be worse?
Lights will guide you home
And ignite your bones
And I will try to fix you.

About the Author

"I've always strived to be successful in everything I did or planned on doing. In spite of achieving considerable success in my primary career, I felt incomplete. Writing filled that void. It became one of my truest passions, and I was going to pursue it with as much energy and dedication as I'd applied to everything else throughout my life."

Ricardo de Leão, the author of *Euphoria*.

Ricardo de Leão was born in 1973, in São Paulo, Brazil. When he was 3 years old, his family moved to the United States. At the early age, Ricardo became an avid sports enthusiast. He loved to participate in sports as much as he loved watching and following them. Whether it was ice hockey, judo, swimming, tennis or wrestling, de Leão always strived to be the best. His nature of a fearless leader propelled him to work hard and excel in everything he took on. In fact, his first memory from an early childhood in Brazil involved the very prediction about Ricardo being a natural leader. That happened when his mother took her young son to a spirituality center where Ricardo went through a ritual of cleansing from all the negative energy surrounding the society at that period of time. That's where the prediction about Ricardo's inborn leadership was made. Among all the sports he participated in, surfing was his truest passion, the love of his life. It was through surfing and his incredible connection with the ocean and nature that Ricardo started developing his awareness of spirituality and deep connection with nature and people. Ricardo de Leão attributes his ambitious nature and commitment to never quitting or giving up to sports in general and surfing in particular.

After graduating with an undergraduate degree in Finance, Ricardo pursued further and went on to obtain an MBA in International Business. After forming a considerable educational portfolio, one of Ricardo's professors urged him to become a management consultant. The career that guaranteed extensive traveling and a great salary. At first, de Leão enjoyed the high life and the travels, but at the same time, he felt something was missing, something he couldn't figure out at the time. After ten years in consulting, a personal and shocking crisis forced Ricardo to change his entire life. He couldn't travel any more, thus, he had to look for a new career path.

After meeting the love of his life and marrying her, Ricardo de Leão settled down and turned to property management in South Florida. While working at the ultra-luxury resort in Bal Harbour, under the Ritz-Carlton umbrella, he started thinking about writing. He was initially stunned by the urge because he never thought of writing or dreamt of becoming a writer. At the same time, he felt God himself was whispering to him the importance of this first book. He had to start writing or he was destined to lose his mind. After Ricardo figured out his true passion, everything became clear. His purpose was set. His goal was real. His writing would not only fix himself, but he truly believed through his writing he could help the people of the world find everlasting peace and true love for oneself and others.

De Leão conceptually envisioned his novel for over a decade. He had a title and the idea, but the actual writing happened at the hospital bedside, on the night when his daughter Victoria was born. Ever since he started writing, he had never looked back.

Today, Ricardo de Leão is a happily married father of two. He enjoys nature, sports and the simplicity of universal constants such as love, truth, joy and spiritual enrichment through kindness and writing. *Euphoria* is his first novel. It has an auto-biographical nature and through it, Ricardo wants to reveal his life, its ups and downs, and teach the readers some valuable life lessons in acceptance, spirituality and self-awareness. His ultimate vision is to bring the world together through education and understanding and acceptance of our difference or lack thereof. We are one world, one humanity, one global citizen on this beautiful small planet called Earth.